The Invasion of 1910

The Invasion of 1910

William Le Queux

MINT EDITIONS

The Invasion of 1910 was first published in 1906.

This edition published by Mint Editions 2021.

ISBN 9781513281001 | E-ISBN 9781513286020

Published by Mint Editions®

 MINT
EDITIONS

minteditionbooks.com

Publishing Director: Jennifer Newens
Design & Production: Rachel Lopez Metzger
Project Manager: Micaela Clark
Typesetting: Westchester Publishing Services

Contents

BOOK I
THE ATTACK

I

The Surprise

Two of the myriad of London's night-workers were walking down Fleet Street together soon after dawn on Sunday morning, 2nd September.

The sun had not yet risen. That main artery of London traffic, with its irregular rows of closed shops and newspaper offices, was quiet and pleasant in the calm, mystic light before the falling of the smoke-pall.

Only at early morning does the dear old City look its best; in that one quiet, sweet hour when the night's toil has ended and the day's has not yet begun. Only in that brief interval at the birth of day, when the rose tints of the sky glow slowly into gold, does the giant metropolis repose—at least, as far as its business streets are concerned—for at five o'clock the toiling millions begin to again pour in from all points of the compass, and the stress and storm of London life at once recommences.

And in that hour of silent charm the two grey-bearded sub-editors, though engaged in offices of rival newspapers, were making their way homeward to Dulwich to spend Sunday in a well-earned rest, and were chatting "shop" as Press men do.

"I suppose you had the same trouble to get that Yarmouth story through?" asked Fergusson, the news-editor of the *Weekly Dispatch*, as they crossed Whitefriars Street. "We got about half a column, and then the wire shut down."

"Telegraph or telephone?" inquired Baines, who was four or five years younger than his friend.

"We were using both—to make sure."

"So were we. It was a rattling good story—the robbery was mysterious, to say the least—but we didn't get more than half of it. Something's wrong with the line, evidently," Baines said. "If it were not such a perfect autumn morning, I should be inclined to think there'd been a storm somewhere."

"Yes—funny, wasn't it?" remarked the other. "A shame we haven't the whole story, for it was a first-class one, and we wanted something. Did you put it on the contents-bill?"

"No, because we couldn't get the finish. I tried in every way—rang up the Central News, P.A., Exchange Telegraph Company, tried to get through to Yarmouth on the trunk, and spent half an hour or so pottering about, but the reply from all the agencies, from everywhere in fact, was the same—the line was interrupted."

"Just our case. I telephoned to the Post Office, but the reply came back that the lines were evidently down."

"Well, it certainly looks as though there'd been a storm, but—" and Baines glanced at the bright, clear sky overhead, just flushed by the bursting sun—"there are certainly no traces of it."

"There's often a storm on the coast when it's quite still in London, my dear fellow," remarked his friend wisely.

"That's all very well. But when all communication with a big place like Yarmouth is suddenly cut off, as it has been, I can't help suspecting that something has happened which we ought to know."

"You're perhaps right after all," Fergusson said. "I wonder if anything *has* happened. We don't want to be called back to the office, either of us. My assistant, Henderson, whom I've left in charge, rings me up over any mare's nest. The trunk telephones all come into the Post Office exchange up in Carter Lane. Why not look in there before we go home? It won't take us a quarter of an hour, and we have several trains home from Ludgate Hill."

Baines looked at his watch. Like his companion, he had no desire to be called back to his office after getting out to Dulwich, and yet he was in no mood to go making reporter's inquiries.

"I don't think I'll go. It's sure to be nothing, my dear fellow," he said. "Besides, I have a beastly headache. I had a heavy night's work. One of my men is away ill."

"Well, at any rate, I think I'll go," Fergusson said. "Don't blame me if you get called back for a special edition with a terrible storm, great loss of life, and all that sort of thing. So long." And, smiling, he waved his hand and parted from his friend in the booking-office of Ludgate Hill Station.

Quickening his pace, he hurried through the office and, passing out by the back, ascended the steep, narrow street until he reached the Post Office telephone exchange in Carter Lane, where, presenting his card, he asked to see the superintendent-in-charge.

Without much delay he was shown upstairs into a small private office, into which came a short, dapper, fair-moustached man with the bustle of a person in a great hurry.

WILLIAM LE QUEUX

"I've called," the sub-editor explained, "to know whether you can tell me anything regarding the cause of the interruption of the line to Yarmouth a short time ago. We had some important news coming through, but were cut off just in the midst of it, and then we received information that all the telephone and telegraph lines to Yarmouth were interrupted."

"Well, that's just the very point which is puzzling us at this moment," was the night-superintendent's reply. "It is quite unaccountable. Our trunk going to Yarmouth seems to be down, as well as the telegraphs. Yarmouth, Lowestoft, and beyond Beccles seem all to have been suddenly cut off. About eighteen minutes to four the operators noticed something wrong, switched the trunks through to the testers, and the latter reported to me in due course."

"That's strange! Did they all break down together?"

"No. The first that failed was the one that runs through Chelmsford, Colchester, and Ipswich up to Lowestoft and Yarmouth. The operator found that he could get through to Ipswich and Beccles. Ipswich knew nothing, except that something was wrong. They could still ring up Beccles, but not beyond."

As they were speaking, there was a tap at the door, and the assistant night-superintendent entered, saying—

"The Norwich line through Scole and Long Stratton has now failed, sir. About half-past four Norwich reported a fault somewhere north, between there and Cromer. But the operator now says that the line is apparently broken, and so are all the telegraphs from there to Cromer, Sheringham, and Holt."

"Another line has gone, then!" exclaimed the superintendent-in-charge, utterly astounded. "Have you tried to get on to Cromer by the other routes—through Nottingham and King's Lynn, or through Cambridge?"

"The testers have tried every route, but there's no response."

"You could get through to some of the places—Yarmouth, for instance—by telegraphing to the Continent, I suppose?" asked Fergusson.

"We are already trying," responded the assistant superintendent.

"What cables run out from the east coast in that neighbourhood?" inquired the sub-editor quickly.

"There are five between Southwold and Cromer—three run to Germany, and two to Holland," replied the assistant. "There's the cable from Yarmouth to Barkum, in the Frisian Islands; from Happisburg, near Mundesley, to Barkum; from Yarmouth to Emden; from Lowestoft to Haarlem, and from Kessingland, near Southwold, to Zandyport."

"And you are trying all the routes?" asked his superior.

"I spoke to Paris myself an hour ago and asked them to cable by all five routes to Yarmouth, Lowestoft, Kessingland, and Happisburg," was the assistant's reply. "I also asked Liverpool Street Station and King's Cross to wire down to some of their stations on the coast, but the reply was that they were in the same predicament as ourselves—their lines were down north of Beccles, Wymondham, East Dereham, and also south of Lynn. I'll just run along and see if there's any reply from Paris. They ought to be through by this time, as it's Sunday morning, and no traffic." And he went out hurriedly.

"There's certainly something very peculiar," remarked the superintendent-in-charge to the sub-editor. "If there's been an earthquake or an electrical disturbance, then it is a most extraordinary one. Every single line reaching to the coast seems interrupted."

"Yes. It's uncommonly funny," Fergusson remarked. "I wonder what could have happened. You've never had a complete breakdown like this before?"

"Never. But I think—"

The sentence remained unfinished, for his assistant returned with a slip of paper in his hand, saying—

"This message has just come in from Paris. I'll read it. 'Superintendent Telephones, Paris, to Superintendent Telephones, London.—Have obtained direct telegraphic communication with operators of all five cables to England. Haarlem, Zandyport, Barkum, and Emden all report that cables are interrupted. They can get no reply from England, and tests show that cables are damaged somewhere near English shore.'"

"Is that all?" asked Fergusson.

"That's all. Paris knows no more than we do," was the assistant's response.

"Then the Norfolk and Suffolk coasts are completely isolated—cut off from post office, railways, telephones, and cables!" exclaimed the superintendent. "It's mysterious—most mysterious!" And, taking up the instrument upon his table, he placed a plug in one of the holes down the front of the table itself, and a moment later was in conversation with the official in charge of the traffic at Liverpool Street, repeating the report from Paris, and urging him to send light engines north from Wymondham or Beccles into the zone of mystery.

The reply came back that he had already done so, but a telegram had reached him from Wymondham to the effect that the road-bridges between Kimberley and Hardingham had apparently fallen in, and the line was blocked by débris. Interruption was also reported beyond Swaffham, at a place called Little Dunham.

"Then even the railways themselves are broken!" cried Fergusson. "Is it possible that there's been a great earthquake?"

"An earthquake couldn't very well destroy all five cables from the Continent," remarked the superintendent gravely.

The latter had scarcely placed the receiver upon the hook when a third man entered—an operator who, addressing him, said—

"Will you please come to the switchboard, sir? There's a man in the Ipswich call office who has just told me a most extraordinary story. He says that he started in his motor-car alone from Lowestoft to London at half-past three this morning, and just as it was getting light he was passing along the edge of Henham Park, between Wangford village and Blythburgh, when he saw three men apparently repairing the telegraph wires. One was up the pole, and the other two were standing below. As he passed he saw a flash, for, to his surprise, one of the men fired point-blank at him with a revolver. Fortunately, the shot went wide, and he at once put on a move and got down into Blythburgh village, even though one of his tyres went down. It had probably been pierced by the bullet fired at him, as the puncture was unlike any he had ever had before. At Blythburgh he informed the police of the outrage, and the constable, in turn, woke up the postmaster, who tried to telegraph back to the police at Wrentham, but found that the line was interrupted. Was it possible that the men were cutting the wires, instead of repairing them? He says that after repairing the puncture he took the village constable and three other men on his car and went back to the spot, where, although the trio had escaped, they saw that wholesale havoc had been wrought with the telegraphs. The lines had been severed in four or five places, and whole lengths tangled up into great masses. A number of poles had been sawn down, and were lying about the roadside. Seeing that nothing could be done, the gentleman remounted his car, came on to Ipswich, and reported the damage at our call office."

"And is he still there?" exclaimed the superintendent quickly, amazed at the motorist's statement.

"Yes. I asked him to wait for a few moments in order to speak to you, sir."

"Good. I'll go at once. Perhaps you'd like to come also, Mr. Fergusson?"

And all four ran up to the gallery, where the huge switchboards were ranged around, and where the night operators, with the receivers attached to one ear, were still at work.

In a moment the superintendent had taken the operator's seat, adjusted the ear-piece, and was in conversation with Ipswich. A second later he was speaking with the man who had actually witnessed the cutting of the trunk line.

While he was thus engaged an operator at the farther end of the switchboard suddenly gave vent to a cry of surprise and disbelief.

"What do you say, Beccles? Repeat it," he asked excitedly.

Then a moment later he shouted aloud—

"Beccles says that German soldiers—hundreds of them—are pouring into the place! The Germans have landed at Lowestoft, they think."

All who heard those ominous words sprang up dumbfounded, staring at each other.

The assistant-superintendent dashed to the operator's side and seized his apparatus.

"Halloa—halloa, Beccles! Halloa—halloa—halloa!"

The response was some gruff words in German, and the sound of scuffling could distinctly be heard. Then all was silent.

Time after time he rang up the small Suffolk town, but in vain. Then he switched through to the testers, and quickly the truth was plain.

The second trunk line to Norwich, running from Ipswich by Harleston and Beccles, had been cut farther towards London.

But what held everyone breathless in the trunk telephone headquarters was that the Germans had actually effected the surprise landing that had so often in recent years been predicted by military critics; that England on that quiet September Sunday morning had been attacked. England was actually invaded. It was incredible!

Yet London's millions in their Sunday morning lethargy were in utter ignorance of the grim disaster that had suddenly fallen upon the land.

Fergusson was for rushing at once back to the *Weekly Dispatch* office to get out an extraordinary edition, but the superintendent, who was still in conversation with the motorist, urged judicious forethought.

"For the present, let us wait. Don't let us alarm the public unnecessarily. We want corroboration. Let us have the motorist up here," he suggested.

"Yes," cried the sub-editor. "Let me speak to him."

Over the wire Fergusson begged the stranger to come at once to London and give his story, declaring that the military authorities would require it. Then, just as the man who had been shot at by German advance spies—for such they had undoubtedly been—in order to prevent the truth leaking out, gave his promise to come to town at once, there came over the line from the coastguard at Southwold a vague, incoherent telephone message regarding strange ships having been seen to the northward, and asking for connection with Harwich; while King's Cross and Liverpool Street Stations both rang up almost simultaneously, reporting the receipt of extraordinary messages from King's Lynn, Diss, Harleston, Halesworth, and other places. All declared that German soldiers were swarming over the north, that Lowestoft and Beccles had been seized, and that Yarmouth and Cromer were isolated.

Various stationmasters reported that the enemy had blown up bridges, taken up rails, and effectually blocked all communication with the coast. Certain important junctions were already held by the enemy's outposts.

Such was the amazing news received in that high-up room in Carter Lane, City, on that sweet, sunny morning when all the great world of London was at peace, either still slumbering or week-ending.

Fergusson remained for a full hour and a half at the Telephone Exchange, anxiously awaiting any further corroboration. Many wild stories came over the wires telling how panic-stricken people were fleeing inland away from the enemy's outposts. Then he took a hansom to the *Weekly Dispatch* office, and proceeded to prepare a special edition of his paper—an edition containing surely the most amazing news that had ever startled London.

Fearing to create undue panic, he decided not to go to press until the arrival of the motorist from Ipswich. He wanted the story of the man who had actually seen the cutting of the wires. He paced his room excitedly, wondering what effect the news would have upon the world. In the rival newspaper offices the report was, as yet, unknown. With journalistic forethought he had arranged that at present the bewildering truth should not leak out to his rivals, either from the railway termini or from the telephone exchange. His only fear was that some local correspondent might telegraph from some village or town nearer the metropolis which was still in communication with the central office.

Time passed very slowly. Each moment increased his anxiety. He had sent out the one reporter who remained on duty to the house of

Colonel Sir James Taylor, the Permanent Under-Secretary for War. Halting before the open window, he looked up and down the street for the arriving motor-car. But all was quiet.

Eight o'clock had just boomed from Big Ben, and London still remained in her Sunday morning peace. The street, bright in the warm sunshine, was quite empty, save for a couple of motor-omnibuses and a sprinkling of gaily dressed holiday-makers on their way to the day excursion trains.

In that centre of London—the hub of the world—all was comparatively silent, the welcome rest after the busy turmoil that through six days in the week is unceasing, that fevered throbbing of the heart of the world's great capital.

Of a sudden, however, came the whirr-r of an approaching car, as a thin-faced, travel-stained man tore along from the direction of the Strand and pulled up before the office. The fine car, a six-cylinder "Napier," was grey with the mud of country roads, while the motorist himself was smothered until his goggles had been almost entirely covered.

Fergusson rushed out to him, and a few moments later the pair were in the upstairs room, the sub-editor swiftly taking down the motorist's story, which differed very little from what he had already spoken over the telephone.

Then, just as Big Ben chimed the half-hour, the echoes of the half-deserted Strand were suddenly awakened by the loud, strident voices of the newsboys shouting—

"*Weekly Dispatch*, spe-shall! Invasion of England this morning! Germans in Suffolk! Terrible panic! Spe-shall! *Weekly Dispatch*, Spe-shall!"

As soon as the paper had gone to press Fergusson urged the motorist—whose name was Horton, and who lived at Richmond—to go with him to the War Office and report. Therefore, both men entered the car, and in a few moments drew up before the new War Office in Whitehall.

"I want to see somebody in authority at once!" cried Fergusson excitedly to the sentry as he sprang out.

"You'll find the caretaker, if you ring at the side entrance—on the right, there," responded the man, who then marched on.

"The caretaker!" echoed the excited sub-editor bitterly. "And England invaded by the Germans!"

He, however, dashed towards the door indicated and rang the bell. At first there was no response. But presently there were sounds of a slow unbolting of the door, which opened at last, revealing a tall, elderly man in slippers, a retired soldier.

"I must see somebody at once!" exclaimed the journalist. "Not a moment must be lost. What permanent officials are here?"

"There's nobody 'ere, sir," responded the man in some surprise at the request. "It's Sunday morning, you know."

"Sunday! I know that, but I must see someone. Whom can I see?"

"Nobody, until to-morrow morning. Come then." And the old soldier was about to close the door when the journalist prevented him, asking—

"Where's the clerk-in-residence?"

"How should I know? Gone up the river, perhaps. It's a nice mornin'."

"Well, where does he live?"

"Sometimes 'ere—sometimes in 'is chambers in Ebury Street," and the man mentioned the number.

"Better come to-morrow, sir, about eleven. Somebody'll be sure to see you then."

"To-morrow!" cried the other. "To-morrow! You don't know what you're saying, man! To-morrow will be too late. Perhaps it's too late now. The Germans have landed in England!"

"Oh, 'ave they?" exclaimed the caretaker, regarding both men with considerable suspicion. "Our people will be glad to know that, I'm sure—to-morrow."

"But haven't you got telephones, private telegraphs, or something here, so that I can communicate with the authorities? Can't you ring up the Secretary of State, the Permanent Secretary, or somebody?"

The caretaker hesitated a moment, his incredulous gaze fixed upon the pale, agitated faces of the two men.

"Well, just wait a minute, and I'll see," he said, disappearing into a long cavernous passage.

In a few moments he reappeared with a constable whose duty it was to patrol the building.

The officer looked the strangers up and down, and then asked—

"What's this extraordinary story? Germans landed in England—eh? That's fresh, certainly!"

"Yes. Can't you hear what the newsboys are crying? Listen!" exclaimed the motorist.

"H'm. Well, you're not the first gentleman who's been here with a scare, you know. If I were you I'd wait till to-morrow," and he glanced significantly at the caretaker.

"I won't wait till to-morrow!" cried Fergusson. "The country is in peril, and you refuse to assist me on your own responsibility—you understand?"

"All right, my dear sir," replied the officer, leisurely hooking his thumbs in his belt. "You'd better drive home, and call again in the morning."

"So this is the way the safety of the country is neglected!" cried the motorist bitterly, turning away. "Everyone away, and this great place, built merely to gull the public, I suppose, empty and its machinery useless. What will England say when she learns the truth?"

As they were walking in disgust out from the portico towards the car, a man jumped from a hansom in breathless haste. He was the reporter whom Fergusson had sent out to Sir James Taylor's house in Cleveland Square, Hyde Park.

"They thought Sir James spent the night with his brother up at Hampstead," he exclaimed. "I've been there, but find that he's away for the week-end at Chilham Hall, near Buckden."

"Buckden! That's on the Great North Road!" cried Horton. "We'll go at once and find him. Sixty miles from London. We can be there under two hours!"

And a few minutes later the pair were tearing due north in the direction of Finchley, disregarding the signs from police constables to stop, Horton wiping the dried mud from his goggles and pulling them over his half-closed eyes.

They had given the alarm in London, and the *Weekly Dispatch* was spreading the amazing news everywhere. People read it eagerly, gasped for a moment, and then smiled in utter disbelief. But the two men were on their way to reveal the appalling truth to the man who was one of the heads of that complicated machinery of inefficient defence which we so proudly term our Army.

Bursting with the astounding information, they bent their heads to the wind as the car shot onward through Barnet and Hatfield, then, entering Hitchin, they were compelled to slow down in the narrow street as they passed the old Sun Inn, and afterwards out again upon the broad highway with its many telegraph lines, through Biggleswade, Tempsford, and Eaton Socon, until, in Buckden, Horton pulled up to inquire of a farm labourer for Chilham Hall.

"Oop yon road to the left, sir. 'Bout a mile Huntingdon way," was the man's reply.

Then away they sped, turning a few minutes later into the handsome lodge-gates of Chilham Park, and running up the great elm avenue, drew up before the main door of the ancient hall, a quaint many-gabled old place of grey stone.

"Is Sir James Taylor in?" Fergusson shouted to the liveried man who opened the door.

"He's gone across the home farm with his lordship and the keepers," was the reply.

"Then take me to him at once. I haven't a second to lose. I must see him this instant."

Thus urged, the servant conducted the pair across the park and through several fields to the edge of a small wood, where two elderly men were walking with a couple of keepers and several dogs about them.

"The tall gentleman is Sir James. The other is his lordship," the servant explained to Fergusson; and a few moments later the breathless journalist, hurrying up, faced the Permanent Under-Secretary with the news that England was invaded—that the Germans had actually effected a surprise landing on the east coast.

Sir James and his host stood speechless. Like others, they at first believed the pale-faced, bearded sub-editor to be a lunatic, but a few moments later, when Horton briefly repeated the story, they saw that whatever might have occurred, the two men were at least in deadly earnest.

"Impossible!" cried Sir James. "We should surely have heard something of it if such were actually the case! The coastguard would have telephoned the news instantly. Besides, where is our fleet?"

"The Germans evidently laid their plans with great cleverness. Their spies, already in England, cut the wires at a pre-arranged hour last night," declared Fergusson. "They sought to prevent this gentleman from giving the alarm by shooting him. All the railways to London are already either cut, or held by the enemy. One thing, however, is clear—fleet or no fleet, the east coast is entirely at their mercy."

Host and guest exchanged dark glances.

"Well, if what you say is the actual truth," exclaimed Sir James, "to-day is surely the blackest day that England has ever known."

"Yes, thanks to the pro-German policy of the Government and the false assurances of the Blue Water School. They should have listened to Lord Roberts," snapped his lordship. "I suppose you'll go at once, Taylor, and make inquiries?"

"Of course," responded the Permanent Secretary. And a quarter of an hour later, accepting Horton's offer, he was sitting in the car as it headed back towards London.

Could the journalist's story be true? As he sat there, with his head bent against the wind and the mud splashing into his face, Sir James recollected too well the repeated warnings of the past five years, serious warnings by men who knew our shortcomings, but to which no attention had been paid. Both the Government and the public had remained apathetic, the idea of peril had been laughed to scorn, and the country had, ostrich-like, buried its head in the sand, and allowed Continental nations to supersede us in business, in armaments, in everything.

The danger of invasion had always been ridiculed as a mere alarmist's fiction; those responsible for the defence of the country had smiled, the Navy had been reduced, and the Army had remained in contented inefficiency.

If the blow had really been struck by Germany? If she had risked three or four, out of her twenty-three, army corps, and had aimed at the heart of the British Empire? What then? Ay! what then?

As the car swept down Regent Street into Pall Mall and towards Whitehall, Sir James saw on every side crowds discussing the vague but astounding reports now published in special editions of all the Sunday papers, and shouted wildly everywhere.

Boys bearing sheets fresh from the Fleet Street presses were seized, and bundles torn from them by excited Londoners eager to learn the latest intelligence.

Around both War Office and Admiralty great surging crowds were clamouring loudly for the truth. Was it the truth, or was it only a hoax? Half London disbelieved it. Yet from every quarter, from the north and from across the bridges, thousands were pouring in to ascertain what had really occurred, and the police had the greatest difficulty in keeping order.

In Trafalgar Square, where the fountains were plashing so calmly in the autumn sunlight, a shock-headed man mounted the back of one of the lions and harangued the crowd with much gesticulation, denouncing the Government in the most violent terms; but the orator was ruthlessly pulled down by the police in the midst of his fierce attack.

It was half-past two o'clock in the afternoon. The Germans had already been on English soil ten hours, yet London was in ignorance of where they had actually landed, and utterly helpless.

All sorts of wild rumours were afloat, rumours that spread everywhere throughout the metropolis, from Hampstead to Tooting, from Barking to Hounslow, from Willesden to Woolwich. The Germans were in England!

But in those first moments of the astounding revelation the excitement centred in Trafalgar Square and its vicinity. Men shouted and threatened, women shrieked and wrung their hands, while wild-haired orators addressed groups at the street corners.

Where was our Navy? they asked. Where was our "command of the sea" of which the papers had always talked so much? If we possessed that, then surely no invader could ever have landed? Where was our Army—that brave British Army that had fought triumphantly a hundred campaigns, and which we had been assured by the Government was always ready for any emergency? When would it face the invader and drive him back into the sea?

When?

And the wild, shouting crowds looked up at the many windows of the Admiralty and the War Office, ignorant that both those huge buildings only held terrified caretakers and a double watch of police constables.

Was England invaded? Were foreign legions actually overrunning Norfolk and Suffolk, and were we really helpless beneath the iron heel of the enemy?

It was impossible—incredible! England was on the most friendly terms with Germany. Yet the blow had fallen, and London—or that portion of her that was not enjoying its Sunday afternoon nap in the smug respectability of the suburbs—stood amazed and breathless, in incredulous wonder.

II

Effect in the City

Monday, 3rd September 1910, was indeed Black Monday for London.

By midnight on Sunday the appalling news had spread everywhere. Though the full details of the terrible naval disasters were not yet to hand, yet it was vaguely known that our ships had been defeated in the North Sea, and many of them sunk.

Before 7 A.M. on Monday, however, telegrams reaching London by the subterranean lines from the north gave thrilling stories of frightful disasters we had, while all unconscious, suffered at the hands of the German fleet.

With London, the great cities of the north, Liverpool, Manchester, Sheffield, and Birmingham, awoke utterly dazed. It seemed incredible. And yet the enemy had, by his sudden and stealthy blow, secured command of the sea and actually landed.

The public wondered why a formal declaration of war had not previously been made, ignorant of the fact that the declaration preceding the Franco-German War was the first made by any civilised nation prior to the commencement of hostilities for one hundred and seventy years. The peril of the nation was now recognised on every hand.

Eager millions poured into the City by every train from the suburbs and towns in the vicinity of the metropolis, anxious to ascertain the truth for themselves, pale with terror, wild with excitement, indignant that our land forces were not already mobilised and ready to move eastward to meet the invader.

As soon as the banks were opened there was a run on them, but by noon the Bank of England had suspended all specie payments. The other banks, being thus unable to meet their engagements, simply closed the doors, bringing business to an abrupt standstill. Consols stood at 90 on Saturday, but by noon on Monday were down to 42—lower even than they were in 1798, when they stood at 47¼. Numbers of foreigners tried to speculate heavily, but were unable to do so, for banking being suspended they could not obtain transfers.

On the Stock Exchange the panic in the afternoon was indescribable. Securities of every sort went entirely to pieces, and there were no buyers.

Financiers were surprised that no warning in London had betrayed the position of affairs, London being the money centre of the world. Prior to 1870 Paris shared with London the honour of being the pivot of the money market, but on the suspension of cash payments by the Bank of France during the Franco-German War, Paris lost that position. Had it not been that the milliards comprising the French War indemnity were intact in golden louis in the fortress of Spandau, Germany could never have hoped to wage sudden war with Great Britain before she had made Berlin independent of London in a money sense, or, at any rate, to accumulate sufficient gold to carry on the war for at least twelve months. The only way in which she could have done this was to raise her rate so as to offer better terms than London. Yet directly the Bank of England discovered the rate of exchange going against her, and her stock of gold diminishing, she would have responded by raising the English bank-rate in order to check the flow. Thus competition would have gone on until the rates became so high that all business would be checked, and people would have realised their securities to obtain the necessary money to carry on their affairs. Thus, no doubt, the coming war would have been forecasted had it not been for Germany's already prepared war-chest, which the majority of persons have nowadays overlooked. Its possession had enabled Germany to strike her sudden blow, and now the Bank of England, which is the final reserve of gold in the United Kingdom, found that as notes were cashed so the stock of gold diminished until it was in a few hours compelled to obtain from the Government suspension of the Bank Charter. This enabled the Bank to suspend cash payment, and issue notes without a corresponding deposit of the equivalent in gold.

The suspension, contrary to increasing the panic, had, curiously enough, the immediate effect of somewhat allaying it. Plenty of people in the City were confident that the blow aimed could not prove an effective one, and that the Germans, however many might have landed, would quickly be sent back again. Thus many level-headed business men regarded the position calmly, believing that when our command of the sea was again re-established, as it must be in a day or two, the enemy would soon be non-existent.

Business outside the money market was, of course, utterly demoralised. The buying of necessities was now uppermost in everyone's mind. Excited crowds in the streets caused most of the shops in the City and West End to close, while around the Admiralty were great crowds of eager men and women of all classes, tearful wives of bluejackets jostling with officers' ladies from Mayfair and Belgravia, demanding news of their loved ones—inquiries which, alas! the casualty office were unable to satisfy. The scene of grief, terror, and suspense was heartrending. Certain ships were known to have been sunk with all on board after making a gallant fight, and those who had husbands, brothers, lovers, or fathers on board wept loudly, calling upon the Government to avenge the ruthless murder of their loved ones.

In Manchester, in Liverpool, indeed all through the great manufacturing centres of the north, the excitement of London was reflected.

In Manchester there was a panic "on 'Change," and the crowd in Deansgate coming into collision with a force of mounted police, some rioting occurred, and a number of shop windows broken, while several agitators who attempted to speak in front of the Infirmary were at once arrested.

Liverpool was the scene of intense anxiety and excitement, when a report was spread that German cruisers were about the estuary of the Mersey. It was known that the coal staithes, cranes, and petroleum tanks at Penarth, Cardiff, Barry, and Llanelly had been destroyed; that Aberdeen had been bombarded; and there were rumours that notwithstanding the mines and defences of the Mersey, the city of Liverpool, with all its crowd of valuable shipping, was to share the same fate.

The whole place was in a ferment. By eleven o'clock the stations were crowded by women and children sent by the men away into the country—anywhere from the doomed and defenceless city. The Lord Mayor vainly endeavoured to inspire confidence, but telegrams from London announcing the complete financial collapse, only increased the panic. In the Old Hay Market and up Dale Street to the landing-stages, around the Exchange, the Town Hall, and the Custom House, the excited throng surged, talking eagerly, terrified at the awful blow that was prophesied. At any moment the grey hulls of those death-dealing cruisers might appear in the river; at any moment the first shell might fall and burst in their midst.

Some—the wiseacres—declared that the Germans would never shell a city without first demanding an indemnity, but the majority argued that as they had already disregarded the law of nations in attacking our fleet without provocation, they would bombard Liverpool, destroy the shipping, and show no quarter.

Thus during the whole of the day Liverpool existed in hourly terror of destruction.

London remained breathless, wondering what was about to happen. Every hour the morning newspapers continued to issue special editions, containing all the latest facts procurable regarding the great naval disaster. The telegraphs and telephones to the north were constantly at work, and survivors of a destroyer who had landed at St. Abb's, north of Berwick, gave thrilling and terrible narratives.

A shilling a copy was no unusual price to be paid in Cornhill, Moorgate Street, Lombard Street, or Ludgate Hill for a halfpenny paper, and the newsboys reaped rich harvests, except when, as so often happened, they were set upon by the excited crowd, and their papers torn from them.

Fleet Street was entirely blocked, and the traffic stopped by crowds standing before the newspaper offices waiting for the summary of each telegram to be posted up upon the windows. And as each despatch was read, sighs, groans, and curses were heard on every hand.

The Government—the sleek-mannered, soft-spoken, self-confident Blue Water School—were responsible for it all, was declared on every hand. They should have placed the Army upon a firm and proper footing; they should have encouraged the establishment of rifle clubs to teach every young man how to defend his home; they should have pondered over the thousand and one warnings uttered during the past ten years by eminent men, statesmen, soldiers, and writers: they should have listened to those forcible and eloquent appeals of Earl Roberts, England's military hero, who, having left the service, had no axe to grind. He spoke the truth in the House of Lords in 1906 fearlessly, from patriotic motives, because he loved his country and foresaw its doom. And yet the Government and the public had disregarded his ominous words.

And now the blow he prophesied had fallen. It was too late—too late! The Germans were upon English soil.

What would the Government now do? What, indeed, could it do?

There were some who shouted in bravado that when mobilised the British troops would drive the invader into the sea; but such men were unaware of the length of time necessary to mobilise our Army for home defence—or of the many ridiculous regulations which appear to be laid down for the purpose of hindering rather than accelerating the concentration of forces.

All through the morning, amid the chaos of business in the City, the excitement had been steadily growing, until shortly after three o'clock the *Daily Mail* issued a special edition containing a copy of a German proclamation which, it was said, was now posted everywhere in East Norfolk, East Suffolk, and in Maldon in Essex, already occupied by the enemy.

The original proclamation had been found pasted by some unknown hand upon a barn door near the town of Billericay, and had been detached and brought to London in a motor-car by the *Mail's* correspondent.

It showed plainly the German intention was to deal a hard and crushing blow, and it struck terror into the heart of London, for it read as will be seen on next page.

Upon the walls of the Mansion House, the Guildhall, outside the Bank of England, the Royal Exchange, and upon the various public buildings within the City wards a proclamation by the Lord Mayor quickly appeared. Even upon the smoke-blackened walls of St. Paul's Cathedral, where, at that moment, a special service was being held, big posters were being posted and read by the assembled thousands.

There was a sullen gloom everywhere as the hours went slowly by, and the sun sank into the smoke haze, shedding over the giant city a blood-red afterglow—a light that was ominous in those breathless moments of suspense and terror.

Westward beyond Temple Bar proclamations were being posted. Indeed, upon all the hoardings in Greater London appeared various broadsheets side by side. One by the Chief Commissioner of Police, regulating the traffic in the streets, and appealing to the public to assist in the preservation of order; another by the Mayor of Westminster, couched in similar terms to that of the Lord Mayor; and a Royal Proclamation, brief but noble, urging every Briton to do his duty, to take his part in the defence of King and country, and to unfurl the banner of the British Empire that had hitherto carried peace and civilisation in every quarter of the world. Germany, whose independence had been respected, had attacked us without provocation; therefore hostilities were, alas, inevitable.

When the great poster printed in big capitals and headed by the Royal Arms made its appearance it was greeted with wild cheering.

It was a message of love from King to people—a message to the highest and to the lowest. Posted in Whitechapel at the same hour as

PROCLAMATION

WE, GENERAL COMMANDING THE 3RD GERMAN ARMY,

HAVING SEEN the proclamation of His Imperial Majesty the Emperor William, King of Prussia, Chief of the Army, which authorises the generals commanding the different German Army Corps to establish special measures against all municipalities and persons acting in contradiction to the usages of war, and to take what steps they consider necessary for the well-being of the troops,

HEREBY GIVE PUBLIC NOTICE:

(1) THE MILITARY JURISDICTION is hereby established. It applies to all territory of Great Britain occupied by the German Army, and to every action endangering the security of the troops by rendering assistance to the enemy. The Military Jurisdiction will be announced and placed vigorously in force in every parish by the issue of this present proclamation.

(2) ANY PERSON OR PERSONS NOT BEING BRITISH SOLDIERS, or not showing by their dress that they are soldiers:

(*a*) SERVING THE ENEMY as spies;

(*b*) MISLEADING THE GERMAN TROOPS when charged to serve as guides;

(*c*) SHOOTING, INJURING, OR ROBBING any person belonging to the German Army, or forming part of its personnel;

(*d*) DESTROYING BRIDGES OR CANALS, damaging telegraphs, telephones, electric light wires, gasometers, or railways, interfering with roads, setting fire to munitions of war, provisions, or quarters established by German troops;

(*e*) TAKING ARMS against the German troops,

Will Be Punished By Death.

In Each Case the officer presiding at the Council of War will be charged with the trial, and pronounce judgment. Councils of War may not pronounce Any Other Condemnation Save That Of Death.

The Judgment Will Be Immediately Executed.

(3) Towns Or Villages in the territory in which the contravention takes place will be compelled to pay indemnity equal to one year's revenue.

(4) The Inhabitants Must Furnish necessaries for the German troops daily as follows:—

1 lb. 10 oz. bread.	1 oz. tea.	1½ pints beer, or 1
13 oz. meat.	1½ oz. tobacco or	wine-glassful of
3 lb. potatoes.	5 cigars.	brandy or whisky.
	½ pint wine.	

The ration for each horse:—

13 lb. oats.	3 lb. 6 oz. hay.	3 lb. 6 oz. straw.

(All Persons Who Prefer to pay an indemnity in money may do so at the rate of 2s. per day per man.)

(5) Commanders Of Detached corps have the right to requisition all that they consider necessary for the well-being of their men, and will deliver to the inhabitants official receipts for goods so supplied.

We Hope In Consequence that the inhabitants of Great Britain will make no difficulty in furnishing all that may be considered necessary.

(6) As REGARDS the individual transactions between the troops and the inhabitants, we give notice that one German mark shall be considered the equivalent to one English shilling.

The General Commanding the Ninth German Army Corps,
VON KRONHELM.

BECCLES, *September the Third, 1910*.

in Whitehall, the throngs crowded eagerly about it and sang "God Save our Gracious King," for if they had but little confidence in the War Office and Admiralty, they placed their trust in their Sovereign, the first diplomat in Europe. Therefore the loyalty was spontaneous, as it always is. They read the royal message, and cheered and cheered again.

As evening closed in yet another poster made its appearance in every city, town, and village in the country, a poster issued by military and police officers and naval officers in charge of dockyards—the order for mobilisation.

The public, however, little dreamed of the hopeless confusion in the War Office, in the various regimental dépôts throughout the country, at headquarters everywhere, and in every barracks in the kingdom. The armed forces of England were passing from a peace to a war footing; but the mobilisation of the various units—namely, its completion in men, horses, and material—was utterly impossible in the face of the extraordinary regulations which, kept a strict secret by the Council of Defence until this moment, revealed a hopeless state of things.

The disorder was frightful. Not a regiment was found fully equipped and ready to march. There was a dearth of officers, equipment, horses, provisions, of, indeed, everything. Some regiments simply existed in the pages of the Army List, but when they came to appear on parade they were mere paper phantoms. Since the Boer War the Government had, with culpable negligence, disregarded the needs of the Army, even though they had the object-lesson of the struggle between Russia and Japan before their eyes.

In many cases the well-meaning efforts on the part of volunteers proved merely a ludicrous farce. Volunteers from Glasgow found themselves due to proceed to Dorking, in Surrey; those from Aberdeen were expected at Caterham, while those from Carlisle made a start for Reading, and found themselves in the quiet old city of Durham. And in a hundred cases it was the same. Muddle, confusion, and a chain of useless regulations at Aldershot, Colchester, and York all tended to hinder the movement of troops to their points of concentration, bringing home to the authorities at last the ominous warnings of the unheeded critics of the past.

In that hour of England's deadly peril, when not a moment should have been lost in facing the invader, nothing was ready. Men had guns without ammunition; cavalry and artillery were without horses; engineers only half-equipped; volunteers with no transport whatever; balloon sections without balloons, and searchlight units vainly trying to obtain the necessary instruments.

Horses were being requisitioned everywhere. The few horses that, in the age of motor-cars, now remained on the roads in London were quickly taken for draught, and all horses fit to ride were commandeered for the cavalry.

During the turmoil daring German spies were actively at work south of London. The Southampton line of the London and South-Western Railway was destroyed—with explosives placed by unknown hands—by the bridge over the Wey, near Weybridge, being blown up, and again that over the Mole, between Walton and Esher, while the Reading line was cut by the great bridge over the Thames at Staines being destroyed. The line, too, between Guildford and Waterloo was also rendered impassable by the wreck of the midnight train, which was blown up half-way between Wansborough and Guildford, while in several other places nearer London bridges were rendered unstable by dynamite, the favourite method apparently being to blow the crown out of an arch.

The well-laid plans of the enemy were thus quickly revealed. Among the thousands of Germans working in London, the hundred or so spies, all trusted soldiers, had passed unnoticed, but, working in unison, each little group of two or three had been allotted its task, and had previously thoroughly reconnoitred the position and studied the most rapid or effective means.

The railways to the east and north-east coasts all reported wholesale damage done on Sunday night by the advance agents of the enemy, and now this was continued on the night of Monday in the south, the objective being to hinder troops from moving north from Aldershot.

This was, indeed, effectual, for only by a long *détour* could the troops be moved to the northern defences of London, and while many were on Tuesday entrained, others were conveyed to London by the motor-omnibuses sent down for that purpose.

Everywhere through London and its vicinity, as well as in Manchester, Birmingham, Sheffield, Coventry, Leeds, and Liverpool, motor-cars and motor-omnibuses from dealers and private owners were being requisitioned by the military authorities, for they would, it was believed, replace cavalry to a very large extent.

Wild and extraordinary reports were circulated regarding the disasters in the north. Hull, Newcastle, Gateshead, and Tynemouth had, it was believed, been bombarded and sacked. The shipping in the Tyne was burning, and the Elswick works were held by the enemy. Details were, however, very vague, as the Germans were taking every precaution to prevent information reaching London.

III

News of the Enemy

Terror and excitement reigned everywhere. The wildest rumours were hourly afloat. London was a seething stream of breathless multitudes of every class.

On Monday morning the newspapers throughout the kingdom had devoted greater part of their space to the extraordinary intelligence from Norfolk and Suffolk and Essex and other places.

That we were actually invaded was plain, but most of the newspapers happily preserved a calm, dignified tone, and made no attempt at sensationalism. The situation was far too serious.

Like the public, however, the Press had been taken entirely by surprise. The blow had been so sudden and so staggering that half the alarming reports were discredited.

In addition to the details of the enemy's operations, as far as could as yet be ascertained, the *Morning Post* on Monday contained an account of a mysterious occurrence at Chatham, which read as follows:—

> Chatham, *Sept. 1* (11.30 P.M.)
>
> "An extraordinary accident took place on the Medway about eight o'clock this evening. The steamer *Pole Star*, 1200 tons register, with a cargo of cement from Frindsbury, was leaving for Hamburg and came into collision with the *Frauenlob*, of Bremen, a somewhat larger boat, which was inward bound, in a narrow part of the channel about half-way between Chatham and Sheerness. Various accounts of the mishap are current, but whichever of the vessels was responsible for the bad steering or neglect of the ordinary rules of the road, it is certain that the *Frauenlob* was cut into by the stem of the *Pole Star* on her port bow, and sank almost across the channel. The *Pole Star* swung alongside her after the collision, and very soon afterwards sank in an almost parallel position. Tugs and steamboats carrying a number of naval officers and the port authorities are about to proceed to the scene of the accident, and if, as seems probable, there is no chance of raising the vessels, steps will be at once

taken to blow them up. In the present state of our foreign relations such an obstruction directly across the entrance to one of our principal warports is a national danger, and will not be allowed to remain a moment longer than can be helped."

Sept. 2

"An extraordinary *dénoûement* has followed the collision in the Medway reported in my telegram of last night, which renders it impossible to draw any other conclusion than that the affair is anything but an accident. Everything now goes to prove that the whole business was premeditated and was the result of an organised plot with the object of 'bottling up' the numerous men-of-war that are now being hurriedly equipped for service in Chatham Dockyard. In the words of Scripture, 'An enemy hath done this,' and there can be very little doubt as to the quarter from which the outrage was engineered. It is nothing less than an outrage to perpetrate what is in reality an overt act of hostility in a time of profound peace, however much the political horizon may be darkened by lowering warclouds. We are living under a Government whose leader lost no time in announcing that no fear of being sneered at as a 'Little Englander' would deter him from seeking peace and ensuring it by a reduction of our naval and military armaments, even at that time known to be inadequate to the demands likely to be made upon them if our Empire is to be maintained. We trust, however, that even this parochially minded statesman will lose no time in probing the conspiracy to its depths, and in seeking instant satisfaction from those personages, however highly placed and powerful, who have committed this outrage on the laws of civilisation.

"As soon as the news of the collision reached the dockyard the senior officer at Kethole Reach was ordered by wire to take steps to prevent any vessel from going up the river, and he at once despatched several picket-boats to the entrance to warn in-coming ships of the blocking of the channel, while a couple of other boats were sent up to within a short distance of the obstruction to make assurance doubly sure. The harbour signals ordering 'suspension of all movings,' were also hoisted at Garrison Point.

"Among other ships which were stopped in consequence of these measures was the *Van Gysen*, a big steamer hailing from Rotterdam, laden, it was stated, with steel rails for the London, Chatham, and Dover Railway, which were to be landed at Port Victoria. She was accordingly allowed to proceed, and anchored, or appeared to anchor, just off the railway pier at that place. Ten minutes later the officer of the watch on board H.M.S. *Medici* reported that he thought she was getting under way again. It was then pretty dark. An electric searchlight being switched on, the *Van Gysen* was discovered steaming up the river at a considerable speed. The *Medici* flashed the news to the flagship, which at once fired a gun, hoisted the recall, and the *Van Gysen's* number in the international code, and despatched her steam pinnace, with orders to overhaul the Dutchman and stop him at whatever cost. A number of the marines on guard were sent in her with their rifles.

"The *Van Gysen* seemed well acquainted with the channel, and continually increased her speed as she went up the river, so that she was within half a mile of the scene of the accident before the steamboat came up with her. The officer in charge called to the skipper through his megaphone to stop his engines and to throw him a rope, as he wanted to come on board. After pretending for some time not to understand him, the skipper slowed his engines and said, 'Ver vel, come 'longside gangway.' As the pinnace hooked on at the gangway, a heavy iron cylinder cover was dropped into her from the height of the *Van Gysen's* deck. It knocked the bowman overboard and crashed into the fore part of the boat, knocking a big hole in the port side forward. She swung off at an angle and stopped to pick up the man overboard. Her crew succeeded in rescuing him, but she was making water fast, and there was nothing for it but to run her into the bank. The lieutenant in charge ordered a rifle to be fired at the *Van Gysen* to bring her to, but she paid not the smallest attention, as might have been expected, and went on her way with gathering speed.

"The report, however, served to attract the attention of the two picket-boats which were patrolling up the river. As she turned a bend in the stream they both shot up alongside out of the darkness, and ordered her peremptorily to stop. But the only answer they received was the sudden extinction of all lights in the steamer. They kept alongside, or rather one of them did, but they were quite helpless to stay the progress of the big wall-sided steamer. The faster of the picket-boats shot ahead with the object of warning those who were busy examining the wrecks. But the *Van Gysen*, going all she knew, was close behind, an indistinguishable black blur in the darkness, and hardly had the officer in the picket-boat delivered his warning before she was heard close at hand. Within a couple of hundred yards of the two wrecks she slowed down, for fear of running right over them. On she came, inevitable as Fate. There was a crash as she came into collision with the central deck-houses of the *Frauenlob* and as her bows scraped past the funnel of the *Pole Star*. Then followed no fewer than half a dozen muffled reports. Her engines went astern for a moment, and down she settled athwart the other two steamers, heeling over to port as she did so. All was turmoil and confusion. None of the dockyard and naval craft present were equipped with searchlights. The harbourmaster, the captain of the yard, even the admiral superintendent, who had just come down in his steam launch, all bawled out orders.

"Lights were flashed and lanterns swung up and down in the vain endeavour to see more of what had happened. Two simultaneous shouts of 'Man overboard!' came from tugs and boats at opposite sides of the river. When a certain amount of order was restored it was discovered that a big dockyard tug was settling down by the head. It seems she had been grazed by the *Van Gysen* as she came over the obstruction, and forced against some portion of one of the foundered vessels, which had pierced a hole in her below the water-line.

"In the general excitement the damage had not been discovered, and now she was sinking fast. Hawsers were made fast to her with the utmost expedition possible in order to tow her clear of the piled-up wreckage, but it was too late. There was only just time to rescue her crew before she, too, added herself to the under-water barricade. As for the crew of the *Van Gysen*, it is thought that all must have gone down in her, as no trace of them has as yet been discovered, despite a most diligent search, for it was considered that, in an affair which had been so carefully planned as this certainly must have been, some provision must surely have been made for the escape of the crew. Those who have been down at the scene of the disaster report that it will be impossible to clear the channel in less than a week or ten days, using every resource of the dockyard.

"A little later I thought I would go down to the dockyard on the off-chance of picking up any further information. The Metropolitan policemen at the gate would on no account allow me to pass at that hour, and I was just turning away when by a great piece of good fortune I ran up against Commander Shelley.

"I was on board his ship as correspondent during the manœuvres of the year before last. 'And what are you doing down here?' was his very natural inquiry after we had shaken hands. I told him that I had been down in Chatham for a week past as special correspondent, reporting on the half-hearted preparations being made for the possible mobilisation, and took the opportunity of asking him if he could give me any further information about the collision between the three steamers in the Medway. 'Well,' said he, 'the best thing you can do is to come right along with me. I have just been hawked out of bed to superintend the diving operations which will begin the moment there is a gleam of daylight.' Needless to say, this just suited me, and I hastened to thank him and to accept his kind offer. 'All right,' he said, 'but I shall have to make one small condition.'

"'And that is?' I queried.

"'Merely to let me "censor" your telegrams before you send them,' he returned. 'You see, the Admiralty might not like to have too much said about this business, and I don't want to find myself in the dirt-tub.'

"The stipulation was a most reasonable one, and however I disliked the notion of having probably my best paragraphs eliminated, I could not but assent to my friend's proposition. So away we marched down the echoing spaces of the almost deserted dockyard till we arrived at the *Thunderbolt* pontoon. Here lay a pinnace with steam up, and, lighted down the sloping side of the old ironclad by the lantern of the policeman on duty, we stepped on board and shot out into the centre of the stream. We blew our whistles and the coxswain waved a lantern, whereupon a small tug that had a couple of dockyard lighters attached gave a hoarse 'toot' in response, and followed us down the river. We sped along in the darkness against a strong tide that was making up-stream, past Upnor Castle, that quaint old Tudor fortress with its long line of modern powder magazines, and along under the deeper shadows beneath Hoo Woods till we came abreast of the medley of mud flats and grass-grown islets just beyond them. Here, above the thud of the engines and the plash of the water, a thin, long-drawn-out cry wavered through the night. 'Someone hailing the boat, sir,' reported the lookout forward. We had all heard it. 'Ease down,' ordered Shelley, and hardly moving against the rushing tideway we listened for its repetition. Again the voice was raised in quavering supplication. 'What the dickens does he say?' queried the commander. 'It's German,' I answered. 'I know that language well. I think he's asking for help. May I answer him?'

"'By all means. Perhaps he belongs to one of those steamers.' The same thought was in my own mind. I hailed in return, asking where he was and what he wanted. The answer came back that he was a shipwrecked seaman, who was cold, wet, and miserable, and implored to be taken off from the islet where he found himself, cut off from everywhere by water and darkness. We ran the boat's nose into the bank, and presently succeeded in hauling on board a miserable object, wet through, and plastered from head to foot with black Medway mud. The broken remains of a cork life-belt hung from his shoulders. A dram of whisky somewhat revived him. 'And now,' said Shelley, 'you'd better cross-examine him. We may get something out of the fellow.' The foreigner, crouched down shivering in the stern-sheets half covered with a yellow oilskin that some charitable bluejacket had thrown over him, appeared to me in the light of the lantern that stood on the deck before him to be not only suffering from cold, but from terror. A few moments' conversation with him confirmed my suspicions. I turned to Shelley and exclaimed, 'He says he'll tell us everything if we spare his life,' I explained. 'I'm sure I don't want to shoot the chap,' replied the commander. 'I suppose he's implicated in this "bottling up" affair. If he is, he jolly well deserves it, but I don't suppose anything will be done to him. Anyway, his information may be valuable, and so you may tell him that he is all right as far as I'm concerned, and I will do my best for him with the Admiral. I daresay that will satisfy him. If not, you might threaten him a bit. Tell him anything you like if you think it will make him speak.' To cut a long story short, I found the damp Dutchman amenable to reason, and the following is the substance of what I elicited from him.

"He had been a deck hand on board the *Van Gysen*. When she left Rotterdam he did not know that the trip was anything out of the way. There was a new skipper whom he had not seen before, and there were also two new mates with a new chief engineer. Another steamer followed them all the way till they arrived at the Nore. On the way over he and several other seamen were sent for by the captain and asked if they would volunteer for a dangerous job, promising them £50 a-piece if it came off all right. He and five others agreed, as did two or three stokers, and were then ordered to remain aft and not communicate with any others of the crew. Off the Nore all the remainder were transferred to the following steamer, which steamed off to the eastward. After they were gone the selected men were told that the officers all belonged to the Imperial German Navy, and by orders of the Kaiser were about to attempt to block up the Medway.

"A collision between two other ships had been arranged for, one of which was loaded with a mass of old steel rails into which liquid cement had been run, so that her hold contained a solid impenetrable block. The *Van Gysen* carried a similar cargo, and was provided with an arrangement for blowing holes in her bottom. The crew were provided with life-belts and the half of the money promised, and all except the captain, the engineer, and the two mates dropped overboard just before arriving at the sunken vessels. They were advised to make their way to Gravesend, and then to shift for themselves as best they could. He had found himself on a small island, and could not muster up courage to plunge into the cold water again in the darkness.

"'By Jove! This means war with Germany, man!—War!' was Shelley's comment. At two o'clock this afternoon we knew that it did, for the news of the enemy's landing in Norfolk was signalled down from the dockyard. We also knew from the divers that the cargo of the sunken steamers was what the rescued seaman had stated it to be. Our bottle has been fairly well corked."

This amazing revelation showed how cleverly contrived was the German plan of hostilities. All our splendid ships at Chatham had, in that brief half-hour, been bottled up and rendered utterly useless. Yet the authorities were not blameless in the matter, for in November 1905 a foreign warship actually came up the Medway in broad daylight, and was not noticed until she began to bang away her salutes, much to the utter consternation of everyone!

This incident, however, was but one of the many illustrations of Germany's craft and cunning. The whole scheme had been years in careful preparation.

She intended to invade us, and regarded every stratagem as allowable in her sudden dash upon England, an expedition which promised to result in the most desperate war of modern times.

At that moment the *Globe* reproduced those plain, prophetic words of Lord Overstone, written some years before to the Royal Defence Commission: "Negligence alone can bring about the calamity under discussion. Unless we suffer ourselves to be surprised we cannot be invaded with success. It is useless to discuss what will occur or what can be done after London has fallen into the hands of an invading foe. The apathy which may render the occurrence of such a catastrophe possible will not afterwards enable the country, enfeebled, dispirited, and disorganised by the loss of its capital, to redeem the fatal error."

Was that prophecy to be fulfilled?

Some highly interesting information was given by Lieutenant Charles Hammerton, 1st Volunteer Battalion Suffolk Regiment, of Ipswich, who with his company of Volunteer cyclists reconnoitred the enemy's position in East Suffolk during Monday night. Interviewed by the Ipswich correspondent of the Central News, he said:

"We left Ipswich at eight o'clock in order to reconnoitre all the roads and by-roads in the direction of Lowestoft. For the first twelve miles, as far as Wickham Market, we knew that the country was clear of the enemy, but on cautiously entering Saxmundham—it now being quite dark—we pulled up before Gobbett's shop in the High Street, and there learnt from a group of terrified men and women that a German reconnoitring patrol consisting of a group of about ten Uhlans under a sergeant, and supported by other groups all across the country to Framlingham and Tannington, had been in the town all day, holding the main road to Lowestoft, and watching in the direction of Ipswich. For hours they had patrolled the south end opposite Waller's, upon whose wall they posted a copy of Von Kronhelm's proclamation.

"They threatened to shoot any person attempting to move southward out of the town. Three other Germans were on the old church tower all day making signals northward at intervals. Then, as night closed in, the Uhlans refreshed themselves at the Bell, and with their black and white pennants fluttering from their lances, clattered backward in the direction of Yoxford.

"I had sent scouts off the main road from Woodbridge, through Framlingham, Tannington, and Wilby, with orders to push on if possible to Hoxne, to join the main road to Harleston, which I judged must be on the enemy's flank. Each man knew those difficult crossroads well, which was necessary, we having to travel noiselessly without lights.

"In the bar-parlour of the Bell at Saxmundham we held consultation with a sergeant of police and a couple of constables, from whom we gathered some further information, and then decided to push cautiously north and ascertain into what positions the Uhlans had retired for the night, and, if possible, the whereabouts of the enemy's march outposts. I had with me twelve men. Nine of us were in uniform, including myself, but the other four preferred to go in mufti, though warned of the risk that they might be treated as spies.

"Carefully, and in silence, we got past the crossroad, to Kelsale, on past the Red House, and down into Yoxford village, without meeting a soul. We were told in Yoxford by the excited villagers that there were foreign soldiers and motor-cyclists constantly passing and repassing all day, but that soon after seven o'clock they had all suddenly retired by the road leading back to Haw Wood. Whether they had gone to the right to Blythburgh, or to the left to Halesworth, was, however, unknown.

PROCLAMATION.

CITIZENS OF LONDON.

THE NEWS OF THE BOMBARDMENT of the City of Newcastle and the landing of the German Army at Hull, Weybourne, Yarmouth, and other places along the East Coast is unfortunately confirmed.

THE ENEMY'S INTENTION is to march upon the City of London, which must be resolutely defended.

THE BRITISH NATION and the Citizens of London, in face of these great events, must be energetic in order to vanquish the invader.

The ADVANCE must be CHALLENGED FOOT BY FOOT. The people must fight for King and Country.

Great Britain is not yet dead, for indeed, the more serious her danger, the stronger will be her unanimous patriotism.

GOD SAVE THE KING.

HARRISON, *Lord Mayor*.

Mansion House,
London, September 3rd, 1910.

THE LORD MAYOR'S APPEAL TO LONDON.

Our expedition was a most risky one. We knew that we carried our lives in our hands, and yet the War Office and the whole country were anxiously waiting for the information which we hoped to gain. Should we push on? I put it to my companions—brave fellows every one of them, even though the Volunteers have so often been sneered at—and the decision was unanimous that we should reconnoitre at all costs.

"Therefore, again in silence, we went forward, determining to take the Lowestoft high road. Where the enemy's outposts were, we had no idea. Quietly we skirted Thorington Park, and were just ascending the bridge over the Blyth, before entering Blythburgh, when of a sudden we saw silhouetted on the slope against the star-lit sky a small group of heavily-accoutred German infantry, who had their arms piled beside the road, while two were acting as sentries close at hand.

"At once we were challenged in German. In an instant we flung ourselves from our machines, and took shelter in a hedge opposite. Several times was the gruff challenge repeated, and as I saw no possibility of crossing the bridge, we stealthily turned our cycles round and prepared to mount. Of a sudden we were evidently perceived, and next second shots whistled about us, and poor Maitland, a private, fell forward upon his face in the road—dead. We heard loud shouting in German, which we could not understand, and in a moment the place seemed alive with the foreigners, while we only just had time to mount and tear away in the direction we had come. At Haw Wood I decided to pass the river by a by-road I knew at Wissett, avoiding Halesworth on the right. As far as Chediston Green all was quiet, but on turning northward to Wissett at the cross-roads outside the inn we perceived three men lurking in the shadow beneath the wall.

"With one of my men I abandoned my machine, and crept softly in their direction, not knowing whether they were farm labourers or the enemy's outposts. Slowly, and with great caution, we moved forward until, on listening intently, I heard them in conversation. They were speaking in German! On my return to my section, Plunkett, one of the privates in mufti, volunteered to creep past without his machine, get to Aldous Corner, and so reconnoitre the country towards the enemy's headquarters, which, from Von Kronhelm's proclamation, we knew to be at Beccles.

"Under our breath we wished him God-speed, and a moment later he disappeared in the darkness. What afterwards happened we can only surmise. All we know is that he probably stumbled over a length of barbed wire stretched across the road, for of a sudden the three lurking Germans ran across in his direction. There was a sound of muffled oaths and curses, a quick shuffling of struggling feet, and the triumphant shout in German as a prisoner was secured.

"The truth held us breathless. Poor Plunkett was captured as a spy!

"We could do nothing to save him, for to reveal ourselves meant capture or death. Therefore we were compelled to again retire. We then slipped along the by-roads until we reached Rumburgh, narrowly avoiding detection by sentries stationed at the fork leading to Redisham. Rumburgh was the native place of one of my men named Wheeler, and fortunately he knew every hedge, wall, ditch, and field in the vicinity. Acting as our guide, he left the main road, and by a series of footpaths took us to the main Bungay Road at St. Lawrence. Continuing again by circuitous footpaths, he took us to the edge of Redisham Park, where we discovered a considerable number of German infantry encamped, evidently forming supports to the advance line of outposts. It then became difficult how to act, but this dilemma was quickly solved by Wheeler suggesting that he being in mufti should take the other two plain-clothes men and push on to Beccles, we having now safely passed the outposts and being actually within the enemy's lines. No doubt we had penetrated the advance line of outposts when we struck off from Rumburgh, therefore there only remained for us to turn back and make good our escape, which we did by crossroads in the direction of Bungay. Wheeler and his two brave companions had hidden their cycles and rifles in the ditch outside the park, and had gone forward with whispered good-byes.

"Presently we found ourselves at Methingham Castle, where we again saw groups of Germans waiting for the dawn, while squadrons of cavalry and motor-cyclists were apparently preparing to move out along Stone Street to scour all the country to the south-west. These we at once gave a wide berth, and succeeded at last in getting down to the Waveney and crossing it, little the worse, save for a wetting. Near Harleston, four miles to the south-west, we came across two of our men whom we had left at Woodbridge, and from them learnt that we were at last free of the enemy. Therefore, by three o'clock we were back again in Ipswich, and immediately made report to the adjutant of our regiment, who was anxiously awaiting our return to headquarters. The scene during the night in Ipswich was one of terror and disorder, the worst fears being increased by our report.

"Would Wheeler return? That was the crucial question. If he got to Beccles he might learn the German movements and the disposition of their troops. Yet it was a terribly risky proceeding, death being the only penalty for spies.

"Hour after hour we remained in eager suspense for news of the three gallant fellows who had risked their lives for their country, until shortly after eight I heard shouts outside in the street, and, covered with mud and perspiration, and bleeding from a nasty cut on his forehead, the result of a spill, Wheeler burst triumphantly in.

"Of the others he had seen nothing since leaving them in the market-place at Beccles, but when afterwards he secured his own cycle, the two other cycles were still hidden in the ditch. Travelling by paths across the fields, however, he joined the road south of Wissett, and there in the grey morning was horrified to see the body of poor Plunkett suspended from a telegraph pole. The unfortunate fellow had, no doubt, been tried at a drum-head court-martial and sentenced to be hanged as a warning to others!

"During the two and a half hours Wheeler was in Beccles, he made good use of eyes and ears, and his report—based upon information given him by a carter whom the enemy had compelled to haul supplies from Lowestoft—was full of deepest interest and most valuable.

"From my own observations, combined with Wheeler's information, I was enabled to draw up a pretty comprehensive report, and point out on the map the exact position of the German Army Corps which had landed at Lowestoft.

"Repeated briefly, it is as follows:—

"Shortly before three o'clock on Sunday morning the coastguard at Lowestoft, Corton, and Beach End discovered that their telephonic communication was interrupted, and half an hour later, to the surprise of everyone, a miscellaneous collection of mysterious craft were seen approaching the harbour; and within an hour many of them were high and dry on the beach, while others were lashed alongside the old dock, the new fish-docks of the Great Eastern Railway, and the wharves, disembarking a huge force of German infantry, cavalry, motor-infantry, and artillery. The town, awakened from its slumbers, was utterly paralysed, the more so when it was discovered that the railway to London was already interrupted, and the telegraph lines all cut. On landing, the enemy commandeered all provisions, including the stock at Kent's, Sennett's, and Lipton's, in the London Road, all motor-cars they could discover, horses and forage, while the banks were seized, and the infantry falling in, marched up Old Nelson Street into High Street and out upon the Beccles Road. The first care of the invaders was to prevent the people of Lowestoft damaging the Swing Bridge, a strong guard being instantly mounted upon it, and so quietly and orderly was the landing effected that it was plain the German plans of invasion were absolutely perfect in every detail.

"Few hitches seemed to occur. The mayor was summoned at six o'clock by General von Kronhelm, the generalissimo of the German Army, and briefly informed that the town of Lowestoft was occupied, and that all armed resistance would be punished by death. Then, ten minutes later, when the German war-flag was flying from several flagstaffs in various parts of the town, the people realised their utter helplessness.

"The Germans, of course, knew that irrespective of the weather, a landing could be effected at Lowestoft, where the fish docks and wharves, with their many cranes, were capable of dealing with a large amount of stores. The Denes, that flat, sandy plain between the upper town and the sea, they turned into a camping-ground, and large numbers were billeted in various quarters of the town itself, in the better-class houses along Marine Parade, in the Royal, the Empire, and Harbour hotels, and especially in those long rows of private houses in London Road South.

"The people were terror-stricken. To appeal to London for help was impossible, as the place had been cut entirely off, and around it a strong chain of outposts had already been thrown, preventing anyone from escaping. The town had, in a moment, as it seemed, fallen at the mercy of the foreigners. Even the important-looking police constables of Lowestoft, with their little canes, were crestfallen, sullen, and inactive.

"While the landing was continuing during all Sunday the advance guard moved rapidly over Mutford Bridge, along the Beccles Road, occupying a strong position on the west side of the high ground east of Lowestoft. Beccles, where Von Kronhelm established his headquarters, resting as it does on the River Waveney, is strongly held. The enemy's main position appears to run from Windle Hill, one mile north-east of Gillingham, thence north-west through Bull's Green, Herringfleet Hill, over to Grove Farm and Hill House to Ravingham, whence it turns easterly to Haddiscoe, which is at present its northern limit. The total front from Beccles Bridge north is about five miles, and commands the whole of the flat plain west towards Norwich. It has its south flank resting on the River Waveney, and to the north on Thorpe Marshes. The chief artillery position is at Toft Monks—the highest point. Upon the high tower of Beccles Church is established a signal station, communication being made constantly with Lowestoft by helio by day, and acetylene lamps by night.

"The enemy's position has been most carefully chosen, for it is naturally strong, and, being well held to protect Lowestoft from any attack from the west, the landing can continue uninterruptedly, for Lowestoft beach and docks are now entirely out of the line of any British fire.

"March outposts are at Blythburgh, Wenhaston, Holton, Halesworth, Wissett, Rumburgh, Homersfield, and Bungay, and then north to Haddiscoe, while cavalry patrols watch by day, the line roughly being from Leiston through Saxmundham, Framlingham, and Tannington, to Hoxne.

"The estimate, gleaned from various sources in Lowestoft and Beccles, is that up to Monday at midday nearly a whole Army Corps, with stores, guns, ammunition, etc., had already landed, while there are also reports of a further landing at Yarmouth, and at a spot still farther north, but at present there are no details.

"The enemy," he concluded, "are at present in a position of absolute security."

IV

A Prophecy Fulfilled

This authentic news of the position of the enemy, combined with the vague rumours of other landings at Yarmouth, along the coast at some unknown point north of Cromer, at King's Lynn, and other places, produced an enormous sensation in London, while the Central News interview, circulated to all the papers in the Midlands and Lancashire, increased the panic in the manufacturing districts.

The special edition of the *Evening News*, issued about six o'clock on Tuesday evening, contained another remarkable story which threw some further light upon the German movements. It was, of course, known that practically the whole of the Norfolk and Suffolk coast was already held by the enemy, but with the exception of the fact that the enemy's cavalry vedettes and reconnoitring patrols were out everywhere at a distance about twenty miles from the shore, England was entirely in the dark as to what had occurred anywhere else but at Lowestoft. Attempts similar to that of the Ipswich cyclist volunteers had been made to penetrate the cavalry screen at various points, but in vain. What was in progress was carefully kept a secret by the enemy. The veil was, however, now lifted. The story which the *Evening News* had obtained exclusively, and which was eagerly read everywhere, had been related by a man named Scotney, a lobster-fisherman, of Sheringham, in Norfolk, who had made the following statement to the chief officer of coastguard at Wainfleet, in Lincolnshire:—

"Just before dawn on Sunday morning I was in the boat with my son Ted off the Robin Friend taking up the lobster pots, when we suddenly saw about three miles offshore a mixed lot of curious-looking craft strung out right across the horizon, and heading apparently for Cromer. There were steamers big and little, many of them towing queer flat-bottomed kind of boats, lighters, and barges, which, on approaching nearer, we could distinctly see were filled to their utmost capacity with men and horses.

"Both Ted and I stood staring at the unusual sight, wondering whatever it meant. They came on very quickly, however—so quickly, indeed, that we thought it best to move on. The biggest ships went along to Weybourne Gap, where they moored in the twenty-five feet of water that runs in close to the shore, while some smaller steamers and the flats were run up high and dry on the hard shingle. Before this I noticed that there were quite a number of foreign warships in the offing, with several destroyers far away in the distance, both to east and west.

"From the larger steamships all sorts of boats were lowered, including apparently many collapsible whale-boats, and into these in a most orderly manner, from every gangway and accommodation-ladder, troops—Germans we afterwards discovered them to be to our utter astonishment—began to descend.

"These boats were at once taken charge of by steam pinnaces and cutters and towed to the beach. When we saw this we were utterly dumbfounded. Indeed, at first I believed it to be a dream, for ever since I was a lad I had heard the ancient rhyme my old father was so fond of repeating:

> "*He who would old England win,*
> *Must at Weybourne Hoop begin.*'

"As everybody knows, nature has provided at that lonely spot every advantage for the landing of hostile forces, and when the Spanish Armada was expected, and again when Napoleon threatened an invasion, the place was constantly watched. Yet nowadays, except for the coastguard, it has been utterly unprotected and neglected.

"The very first soldiers who landed formed up quickly, and under the charge of an officer ran up the low hill to the coastguard station, I suppose in order to prevent them signalling a warning. The funny thing was, however, that the coastguards had already been held up by several well-dressed men—spies of the Germans, I suppose. I could distinctly see one man holding one of the guards with his back to the wall, and threatening him with a revolver.

"Ted and I had somehow been surrounded by the crowd of odd craft which dodged about everywhere, and the foreigners now and then shouted to me words that unfortunately I could not understand.

"Meanwhile, from all the boats strung out along the beach, from Sheringham right across to the Rocket House at Salthouse, swarms of drab-coated soldiers were disembarking, the boats immediately returning to the steamers for more. They must have been packed as tightly as herrings in a barrel; but they all seemed to know where to go to, because all along at various places little flags were held by men, and each regiment appeared to march across and assemble at its own flag.

"Ted and I sat there as if we were watching a play. Suddenly we saw from some of the ships and bigger barges, horses being lowered into the water and allowed to swim ashore. Hundreds seemed to gain the beach even as we were looking at them. Then, after the first lot of horses had gone, boats full of saddles followed them. It seemed as though the foreigners were too busy to notice us, and we—not wanting to share the fate of Mr. Gunter, the coastguard, and his mates—just sat tight and watched.

"From the steamers there continued to pour hundreds upon hundreds of soldiers who were towed to land, and then formed up in solid squares, which got bigger and bigger. Horses innumerable— quite a thousand I should reckon—were slung overboard from some of the smaller steamers which had been run high and dry on the beach, and as the tide had now begun to run down they landed only knee-deep in water. Those steamers, it seemed to me, had big bilge keels, for as the tide ebbed they did not heel over. They had, no doubt, been specially fitted for the purpose. Out of some they began to hoist all sorts of things, wagons, guns, motor-cars, large bales of fodder, clothing, ambulances with big red crosses on them, flat-looking boats—pontoons I think they call them—and great piles of cooking pots and pans, square boxes of stores, or perhaps ammunition, and as soon as anything was landed it was hauled up above high-water mark.

"In the meantime lots of men had mounted on horseback and ridden off up the lane which leads into Weybourne village. At first half a dozen started at a time; then, as far as I could judge, about fifty more started. Then larger bodies went forward, but more and more horses kept going ashore, as though their number was never-ending. They must have been stowed mighty close, and many of the ships must have been specially fitted up for them.

"Very soon I saw cavalry swarming up over Muckleburgh, Warborough, and Telegraph Hills, while a good many trotted away in the direction of Runton and Sheringham. Then, soon after they had gone—that is, in about an hour and a half from their first arrival—the infantry began to move off, and as far as I could see, they marched inland by every road, some in the direction of Kelling Street and Holt, others over Weybourne Heath towards Bodham, and still others skirting the woods over to Upper Sheringham. Large masses of infantry marched along the Sheringham Road, and seemed to have a lot of officers on horseback with them, while up on Muckleburgh Hill I saw frantic signalling in progress.

"By this time they had a quantity of carts and wagons landed, and a large number of motor-cars. The latter were soon started, and, manned by infantry, moved swiftly in procession after the troops. The great idea of the Germans was apparently to get the beach clear of everything as soon as landed, for all stores, equipment, and other tackle were pushed inland as soon as disembarked.

"The enemy kept on landing. Thousands of soldiers got ashore without any check, and all proceeding orderly and without the slightest confusion, as though the plans were absolutely perfect. Everybody seemed to know exactly what to do. From where we were we could see the coastguards held prisoners in their station, with German sentries mounted around; and as the tide was now setting strong to the westward, Ted and I first let our anchor off the ground and allowed ourselves to drift. It occurred to me that perhaps I might be able to give the alarm at some other coastguard station if I could only drift away unnoticed in the busy scene now in progress.

"That the Germans had actually landed in England was now apparent; yet we wondered what our own fleet could be doing, and pictured to ourselves the jolly good drubbing that our cruisers would give the audacious foreigner when they did haul in sight. It was for us, at all costs, to give the alarm, so gradually we drifted off to the nor'-westward, in fear every moment lest we should be noticed and fired at. At last we got around Blakeney Point successfully, and breathed more freely; then hoisting our sail, we headed for Hunstanton, but seeing numbers of ships entering the Wash, and believing them to be also Germans, we put our helm down and ran across into Wainfleet Swatchway to Gibraltar Point, where I saw the chief officer of coastguard, and told him all the extraordinary events of that memorable morning."

The report added that the officer of coastguard in question had, three hours before, noticed strange vessels coming up the Wash, and had already tried to report by telegraph to his divisional inspecting officer at Harwich, but could obtain no communication. An hour later, however, it had become apparent that a still further landing was being effected on the south side of the Wash, in all probability at King's Lynn.

The fisherman Scotney's statement had been sent by special messenger from Wainfleet on Sunday evening, but owing to the dislocation of the railway traffic north of London, the messenger was unable to reach the offices of the coastguard in Victoria Street, Westminster, until Monday. The report received by the Admiralty had been treated as confidential until corroborated, lest undue public alarm should be caused.

It had then been given to the Press as revealing the truth of what had actually happened.

The enemy had entered by the back door of England, and the sensation it caused everywhere was little short of panic.

Some further very valuable information was also received by the Intelligence Department of the War Office, revealing the military position of the invaders who had landed at Weybourne Hoop.

It appears that Colonel Charles Macdonald, a retired officer of the Black Watch, who lived in the "Boulevard" at Sheringham, making up his mind to take the risk, had carefully noted all that was in progress during the landing, had drawn up a clear description of it, and had, after some narrow escapes, succeeded in getting through the German lines to Melton Constable, and thence to London. He had, before his retirement, served as military attaché at Berlin, and, being thoroughly acquainted with the appearance of German uniforms, was able to include in his report even the names of the regiments, and in some cases their commanders.

From his observations it was plain that the whole of the IVth German Army Corps, about 38,000 men, had been landed at Weybourne, Sheringham, and Cromer. It consisted of the 7th and 8th Divisions complete, commanded respectively by Major-General Dickmann and Lieutenant-General von Mirbach. The 7th Division comprised the 13th and 14th Infantry Brigades, consisting of Prince Leopold of

Anhalt-Dessau's 1st Magdeburg Regiment, the 3rd Magdeburg Infantry Regiment, Prince Louis Ferdinand von Preussen's 2nd Magdeburg Regiment, and the 5th Hanover Infantry Regiment. Attached to this division were the Magdeburg Hussars No. 10, and the Uhlan Regiment of Altmärk No. 16.

In the 8th Division were the 15th and 16th Brigades, comprising a Magdeburg Fusilier Regiment, an Anhalt Infantry Regiment, the 4th and 8th Thuringen Infantry, with the Magdeburg Cuirassiers, and a regiment of Thuringen Hussars. The cavalry were commanded by Colonel Frölich, while General von Kleppen was in supreme command of the whole corps.

Careful reconnaissance of the occupied area showed that immediately on landing, the German position extended from the little town of Holt, on the west, eastward, along the main Cromer Road, as far as Gibbet Lane, slightly south of Cromer, a distance of about five miles. This constituted a naturally strong position; indeed, nature seemed to have provided it specially to suit the necessities of a foreign invader. The ground for miles to the south sloped gently away down to the plain, while the rear was completely protected, so that the landing could proceed until every detail had been completed.

Artillery were massed on both flanks, namely, at Holt and on the high ground near Felbrigg, immediately south of Cromer. This last-named artillery was adequately supported by the detached infantry close at hand. The whole force was covered by a strong line of outposts. Their advanced sentries were to be found along a line starting from Thornage village, through Hunworth, Edgefield, Barningham Green, Squallham, Aldborough, Hanworth, to Roughton. In rear of them lay their picquets, which were disposed in advantageous situations. The general line of these latter were at North Street, Pondhills to Plumstead, thence over to Matlash Hall, Aldborough Hall, and the rising ground north of Hanworth. These, in their turn, were adequately supplemented by the supports, which were near Hempstead Green, Baconsthorpe, North Narningham, Bessingham, Sustead, and Melton.

In case of sudden attack, reserves were at Bodham, West Beckham, East Beckham, and Aylmerton, but orders had been issued by Von Kleppen, who had established his headquarters at Upper Sheringham, that the line of resistance was to be as already indicated—namely, that having the Holt-Cromer Road for its crest. Cuirassiers, hussars, and some motorists—commanded by Colonel von Dorndorf—were acting independently some fifteen miles to the south, scouring the whole country, terrifying the villagers, commandeering all supplies, and posting Von Kronhelm's proclamation, which has already been reproduced.

From Colonel Macdonald's inquiries it was shown that on the night of the invasion six men, now known to have been advance agents of the enemy, arrived at the Ship Inn, at Weybourne. Three of them took accommodation for the night, while their companions slept elsewhere. At two o'clock the trio let themselves out quietly, were joined by six other men, and just as the enemy's ships hove in sight nine of them seized the coastguards and cut the wires, while the other three broke into the Weybourne Stores, and, drawing revolvers, obtained possession of the telegraph instrument to Sheringham and Cromer until they could hand it over to the Germans.

The panic in both Sheringham and Cromer when the astounded populace found the enemy billeted on them was intense. There were still many holiday-makers in the Grand and Burlington Hotels in Sheringham, as also in the Metropole, Grand, and Paris at Cromer, and these, on that memorable Sunday morning, experienced a rude awakening from their slumbers.

At Cromer the enemy, as soon as they landed, took possession of the post office, commandeered all the stores at shops, including the West-End Supply Stores and Rust's; occupied the railway station on the hill, with all its coal and rolling stock, and made prisoners of the coastguards, the four wires, as at Weybourne, having already been cut by advance agents, who had likewise seized the post office wires. A German naval party occupied the coastguard station, and hoisting the German flag at the peak of the staff in place of the white ensign, began to make rapid signals with the semaphore and their own coloured bunting instead of our coastguard flags.

In the clean, red-brick little town of Sheringham all the grocers and provision-dealers were given notice not to sell food to anyone, as it was now in possession of the invaders, while a number of motor-cars belonging to private persons were seized. Every lodging-house, every hotel, and every boarding-house was quickly crowded by the German officers, who remained to superintend the landing. Many machine guns were landed on the pier at Cromer, while the heavier ordnance were brought ashore at the gap and hauled up the fishermen's slope.

Colonel Macdonald, who had carefully marked a cycling road-map of the district with his observations driving in his own dog-cart from one point to the other, met with a number of exciting adventures.

While in Holt on Monday evening—after a long day of constant observation—he suddenly came face to face with Colonel Frölich, commanding the enemy's cavalry brigade, and was recognised. Frölich had been aide-de-camp to the Emperor at the time when Macdonald was attaché at the British Embassy, and both men were intimate friends.

They stopped and spoke, Frölich expressing surprise and also regret that they should meet as enemies after their long friendship. Macdonald, annoyed at being thus recognised, took the matter philosophically as the fortunes of war, and learnt from his whilom friend a number of valuable details regarding the German position.

The retired attaché, however, pushed his inquiries rather too far, and unfortunately aroused the suspicions of the German cavalry commander, with the result that the Englishman's movements were afterwards very closely watched. He then found himself unable to make any further reconnaisance, and was compelled to hide his map under a heap of stones near the Thornage Road, and there leave it for some hours, fearing lest he should be searched and the incriminating plan found upon him.

At night, however, he returned cautiously to the spot, regained possession of his treasure, and abandoning his dog-cart and horse in a by-road near North Barningham, succeeded in getting over to Edgefield. Here, however, he was discovered and challenged by the sentries. He succeeded, nevertheless, in convincing them that he was not endeavouring to escape; otherwise he would undoubtedly have been shot there and then, as quite a dozen unfortunate persons had been at various points along the German line.

To obtain information of the enemy's position this brave old officer had risked his life, yet concealed in his golf-cap was the map which would condemn him as a spy. He knew the peril, but faced it boldly, as an English soldier should face it.

His meeting with Frölich had been most unfortunate, for he knew that he was now a marked man.

At first the sentries disbelieved him, but, speaking German fluently, he argued with them, and was at last allowed to go free. His one object was to get the map into the hands of the Intelligence Department, but the difficulties were, he soon saw, almost insurmountable. Picquets and sentries held every road and every bridge, while the railway line between Fakenham and Aylsham had been destroyed in several places, as well as that between Melton Constable and Norwich.

Through the whole night he wandered on, hoping to find some weak point in the cordon about Weybourne, but in vain. The Germans were everywhere keeping a sharp vigil to prevent anyone getting out with information, and taking prisoners all upon whom rested the slightest suspicion.

Near dawn, however, he found his opportunity, for at the junction of the three roads near the little hamlet of Stody, a mile south of Hunworth, he came upon a sleeping Uhlan, whose companions had evidently gone forward into Briningham village. The horse was grazing quietly at the roadside, and the man, tired out, lay stretched upon the bank, his helmet by his side, his sabre still at his belt.

Macdonald crept up slowly. If the man woke and discovered him he would be again challenged. Should he take the man's big revolver and shoot him as he lay?

No. That was a coward's action, an unjustifiable murder, he decided.

He would take the horse, and risk it by making a dash for life.

Therefore, on tiptoe he crept up, passing the prostrate man, till he approached the horse, and in a second, old though he was, he was nevertheless in the saddle. But none too soon. The jingle of the bit awakened the Uhlan suddenly, and he sprang up in time to see the stranger mount.

In an instant he took in the situation, and before the colonel could settle himself in the saddle he raised his revolver and fired.

The ball struck the colonel in the left shoulder, shattering it, but the gallant man who was risking his life for his country only winced, cursed his luck beneath his breath, set his teeth, and with the blood pouring from the wound, made a dash for life, and succeeded in getting clean away ere the alarm could be raised.

Twelve hours later the valuable information the colonel had so valiantly gained at such risk was in the hands of the Intelligence Department at Whitehall, and had been transmitted back to Norwich and Colchester.

That the Fourth German Army Corps were in a position as strong as those who had landed at Lowestoft could not be denied, and the military authorities could not disguise from themselves the extreme gravity of the situation.

V

Our Fleet Taken Unawares

The first news of the great naval battle, as generally happens in war, was confused and distorted. It did not clearly show how the victory had been gained by the one side, or what had brought defeat upon the other. Only gradually did the true facts appear. The following account, however, of the sudden attack made by the Germans upon the British Fleet represents as near an approach as can ever be made, writing after events, to the real truth:

On the fateful evening of September 1, it appears that the North Sea Fleet lay peacefully at anchor off Rosyth, in the Firth of Forth. It mustered sixteen battleships, four of them of the famous Dreadnought class, and all powerful vessels. With it, and attached to it, was a squadron of armoured cruisers eight ships strong, but no destroyers, as its torpedo flotilla was taking part in the torpedo manœuvres in the Irish Sea. Some excitement had been caused in the fleet by orders received on the previous day, directing it to remain under steam ready to put to sea at an hour's notice. Officers and men had read the reports in the papers announcing some friction with Germany, and had recalled with ironical amusement certain speeches of the Premier, in which he had declared that since his advent to power war was impossible between civilised nations. On the morning of the First, however, the orders to hold the fleet in readiness were cancelled, and Admiral Lord Ebbfleet was instructed to wait at his anchorage the arrival of reinforcements from the reserve divisions at the great naval ports. The Admiral had reported some shortage of coal and ammunition, and had asked for further supplies of both. A promise was made him that more coal should be sent to Rosyth, but ammunition, he was told, it would be inconvenient and unnecessary to forward at this juncture. There was no reason for precipitation or alarm, a cipher telegram from Whitehall ran: Any sign of either would irritate Germany and endanger the situation. He was peremptorily enjoined to refrain from any act of preparation for war. The estimates could not be exceeded without good reason, and the necessary economies of the Admiralty had left no margin for unexpected expenses. Even the commissioning of the reserve ships, he was told, was not to be considered in any sense as pointing to the imminence of war; it was merely a test of the readiness of the fleet.

This remarkable despatch and the series of telegrams which accompanied it were produced at the Parliamentary investigation after the war, and caused simple stupefaction. There was not a hint in them of the peril which menaced the North Sea Fleet. Not the safety of England, but the feelings of the enemy, were considered. And yet the same utter absence of precautions had characterised the policy of the Government during the Fashoda crisis, when Mr. Goschen indignantly denied to an approving House of Commons the suggestion that the dockyards had been busy or that special efforts to prepare for war had been needed. In the North Sea crisis again, the safety of England had been left to chance, and the British fleets carefully withdrawn from the waters of the North Sea, or placed in a position of such weakness that their defeat was a probability.

Lord Ebbfleet, the Admiral, however, was wiser than the Admiralty. There were too many busybodies about, and the ships were too plainly under observation, to make the full battle toilet. But all that afternoon his crews were active in removing the woodwork, which could not, unfortunately, be sent ashore or thrown into the water—that would have caused excessive suspicion. He would personally have preferred to weigh anchor and proceed to sea, but his instructions forbade this. A great admiral at such a juncture might have disobeyed, and acted on his own responsibility; but Lord Ebbfleet, though brave and capable, was not a Nelson. Still, as well as he could, he made ready for war, and far into the night the crews worked with a will.

Torpedo-nets were got out in all the large ships; the guns were loaded; the watch manned and armed ship; the ships' torpedo boats were hoisted out and patrolled the neighbouring waters; all ships had steam up ready to proceed to sea, though the Admiralty had repeatedly censured Lord Ebbfleet for the heinous offence of wasting coal. Unhappily, the fortifications on the Firth of Forth were practically unmanned and dismantled. Many of the guns had been sold in 1906 to effect economies. In accordance with the policy of trusting to luck and the kindness of the Germans, in fear, also, of provoking Germany, no steps had been taken to mobilise their garrisons. Under the latest scheme of defence which the experts in London had produced, it had been settled that fortifications were not needed to protect the bases used by the fleet. The garrison artillery had gone—sacrificed to the demand for economy. It was considered amply sufficient to man the works with mobilised Volunteers when the need arose. That the enemy might come like a thief in the night had seemingly not occurred to the Government, the House of Commons, or the Army reformers.

Thus the Admiral had to trust entirely to his own ships and guns. The very searchlights on the coast defences were not manned; everything after the usual English fashion was left to luck and the last minute. And, truth to tell, the pacific assurances of the Ministerial Press had lulled anxiety to rest everywhere, save, perhaps, in the endangered fleet. The nation wished to slumber, and it welcomed the leading articles which told it that all disquietude was ridiculous.

It was equally disastrous that no destroyers accompanied the fleet. The three North Sea flotillas of twenty-four boats were conducting exercises in the Irish Sea, whither they had been despatched after the grand naval manœuvres were over. No flotilla of destroyers, and not even a single one of those worn-out, broken-down torpedo boats which the Admiralty had persisted in maintaining as a sham defence for the British coast, was stationed in the Forth. For patrol work the Admiral had nothing but his armoured cruisers and the little launches carried in his warships, which were practically useless for the work of meeting destroyers. The mine defences on the coast had been abolished in 1905, with the promise that torpedo boats and submarines should take their place. Unluckily, the Admiralty had sold off the stock of mines for what it would fetch, before it had provided either the torpedo boats or the submarines, and now five years after this act of supreme wisdom and economy there was still no mobile defence permanently stationed north of Harwich.

At nightfall six of the battleships' steam torpedo boats were stationed outside the Forth Bridge, east of the anchorage, to keep a vigilant watch, while farther out to sea was the fast cruiser *Leicestershire* with all lights out, in mid-channel, just under the island of Inchkeith. Abreast of her and close inshore, where the approach of hostile torpedo craft was most to be feared, were three small ships' torpedo boats to the north and another three to the south, so that, in all, twelve torpedo boats and one cruiser were in the outpost line, to prevent any such surprise as that of the Russian fleet at Port Arthur on the night of February 8, 1904. Thus began this most eventful night in the annals of the British Navy.

Hour after hour passed, while the lieutenants in charge of the torpedo boats incessantly swept the horizon with night glasses; and on the bridge of the *Leicestershire* a small group of officers and signalmen directed their telescopes and glasses out to sea. The great cruiser in the darkness showed not a glimmer of light; gently her engines moved her to and fro upon her beat; she looked through the blackness like a monstrous destroyer herself; and as she went to and fro her guns were always kept trained out seawards, with the watch ready. Towards 2 A.M. the tide began to set strongly into the Forth, and at the same time the weather became misty. Captain Cornwall, noting with uneasiness that the horizon was becoming obscured, and that the field of vision was narrowing, exclaimed to his fellow-watchers on the bridge that it was an ideal night for destroyers—if they should come.

Barely had he spoken thus when he was called aft to the wireless telegraphy instruments. Out of the night Hertzian waves were coming in. The mysterious message was not in the British code; it was not in the international code; and it bore no intelligible meaning. It was in no language that could be recognised—was evidently a cipher. For two or three minutes the recorder rattled off dots and dashes, and then the aërial impulse ceased. Immediately, with a noise like the rattle of pistol shots, the *Leicestershire's* transmitters began to send the news of this strange signal back to the flagship at the anchorage. The special tuning of the British instruments kept for fleet work would prevent a stranger taking in her news.

While the *Leicestershire's* wireless instruments were signalling, a steamer was made out approaching Inchkeith. From her build she was a tramp; she carried the usual lights, and seemed to be heading for Queensferry. A flashlight signal was made to her to ask her name and nationality, and to direct her not to approach, as manœuvres were in progress. She made not the faintest response to these signals—a by no means unusual case with British and foreign merchant steamers. In the dim light she looked to be of about 2500 tons displacement as she steered straight for the *Leicestershire*. Captain Cornwall ordered one of the inshore torpedo boats to proceed to her, and examine her, and direct her, if she was not British, to go into Leith, thus taking upon his shoulders the considerable responsibility of interfering with a foreign ship in time of peace. But she paid no attention to the torpedo boat. She was about 3000 yards off the *Leicestershire* when the order to the boat was given, and she had now approached within 1500 yards. Disquieted by her proceedings, Captain Cornwall ordered one of the 3-pounders to fire a shot across her bow, and then, as this did not stop her, followed it up with two shots from a 3-pounder directed against her hull.

At the first shot across her bows she swung round, now little more than a thousand yards away from the British cruiser, bringing her broadside to bear. There was the noise of a dull report like the discharge of torpedo tubes, as an instant later the 3-pounder shells struck her hull. Immediately, at Captain Cornwall's order, the *Leicestershire* opened fire with all her guns that would bear. Through the water came two streaks of bubbles and foam, moving with lightning speed. One passed right ahead of the *Leicestershire*; the other swept towards the British cruiser's stern; there was a heavy explosion; the whole hull of the cruiser was violently shaken and lifted perceptibly up in the water; a spout of water and smoke rose up astern, and the engines ceased to work. The *Leicestershire* had been torpedoed by the stranger.

The stranger caught the cruiser's fire and reeled under it. The British gunners took their revenge. The searchlights came on; four 7.5's, in less time than it takes to tell, planted shell after shell upon her waterline, and the steamer began slowly to founder. Clouds of smoke and steam rose from her; her engine was apparently disabled, and the British launches closed about her to seize those of her crew that survived. In ten minutes all was over. The steamer had disappeared, her side torn open by a dozen 7.5-in. shells charged with lyddite. But the *Leicestershire* was in serious plight. The damage done by the German torpedo was of the gravest nature. The British cruiser was heavily down by the stern; her port engine and propeller would no longer revolve; two compartments on the port quarter had filled, and water was leaking into the port engine-room. Very slowly, with the help of the starboard engine, Captain Cornwall took her in towards Leith and beached his ship on the shoals near the new harbour.

The opening act had been cleverly thought out by the German staff. While the torpedo boats were picking up the crew of the steamer, three divisions of German torpedo craft, each six boats strong, had passed into the Forth under the shadow of the northern coast. They glided like shadows through the darkness, and they do not seem to have been seen by the British vessels off Inchkeith, whose crews' attention was riveted upon the *Leicestershire*. A fourth division, moving rapidly in the shadow of the southern coast, was seen by the *Leicestershire* and by the British launches about her and with her, and at once she opened fire upon the dim forms. But, bereft of motive power, she could not use her battery to advantage, and though it was thought that one of the destroyers disappeared in the water, the others sped up the estuary, towards the British fleet.

Warned by wireless telegraphy that destroyers had been sighted, the British crews were on the *qui vive*. There was not time at this eleventh hour to weigh and put out to sea; the only possible course was to meet the attack at anchorage. The fleet was anchored off Rosyth, the battleships in two lines ahead, headed by the flagships *Vanguard* and *Captain*. The *Vanguard* and *Captain*, the leading ships in the starboard and port lines respectively, were just abreast of the Beamer Rock and Port Edgar. The seven armoured cruisers were moored in the St. Margaret's Hope Anchorage. To torpedo craft coming from the sea and passing under the Forth Bridge, the fleet thus offered a narrow front, and comparatively few of its guns would bear.

About 2.30 A.M. on Sunday morning, the lookout of the *Vanguard* detected white foam, as from the bows of a destroyer, just under Battery Point; a few seconds later, the same sign was seen to the south of Inchgarvie, and as the bugles sounded and the 12-in. guns in the three forward turrets of the British flagship opened, and the searchlights played their steady glare upon the dark waters just under the Forth Bridge, the forms of destroyers or torpedo boats fast approaching were unmistakably seen.

In a moment the air trembled with the concussion of heavy guns; the quick-firers of the fleet opened a terrific fire; and straight at the battleships came eighteen German destroyers and large torpedo boats, keeping perfect station, at impetuous speed. The sea boiled about them; the night seemed ablaze with the flashing of the great guns and the brilliant flame of exploding shells. Now one destroyer careened and disappeared; now another flew into splinters, as the gunners sent home their huge projectiles. Above all the din and tumult could be heard the rapid hammering of the pom-poms, as they beat from the bridges with their steady stream of projectiles upon the approaching craft.

Four destroyers went to the bottom in that furious onrush; ten entered the British lines, and passed down them with the great ships on either side, not more than 200 yards away, and every gun depressed as much as it could be, vomiting flame and steel upon the enemy; the others turned back. The thud of torpedo firing followed; but the boats amid that tempest of projectiles, with the blinding glare of the searchlights in their gunners' eyes, aimed uncertainly. Clear and unforgettable the figures of officers and men stood out of the blackness, as the searchlights caught the boats. Some could be seen heaving heavy weights overboard; others were busy at the torpedo tubes; but in the blaze of light the pom-poms mowed them down, and tore the upper works of the destroyers to flinders. Funnels were cut off and vanished into space; a conning-tower was blown visibly away by a 12-in. shell which caught it fairly, and as the smitten boat sank there was a series of terrific explosions.

Fifth ship in the starboard British line from the *Vanguard* lay the great battleship *Indefatigable*, after the four "Dreadnoughts" one of the four powerful units in the fleet. Four torpedoes were fired at her by the German destroyers; three of the four missed her, two of them only by a hair's breadth, but the fourth cut through the steel net and caught her fairly abreast of the port engine-room, about the level of the platform deck. The Germans were using their very powerful 17.7-in. Schwartzkopf torpedo, fitted with net-cutters, and carrying a charge of 265 lb. of gun-cotton, the heaviest employed in any navy, and nearly a hundred pounds heavier than that of the largest British torpedo.

The effect of the explosion was terrific. Though the *Indefatigable* had been specially constructed to resist torpedo attack, her bulkheads were not designed to withstand so great a mass of explosive, and the torpedo breached the plating of the wing compartments, the wing passage, and the coal-bunker, which lay immediately behind it. The whole structure of the ship was shaken and much injured in the neighbourhood of the explosion, and water began to pour through the shattered bulkheads into the port engine-room.

The pumps got to work, but could not keep the inrush down; the ship rapidly listed to the port side, and though "out collision mat" was ordered at once, and a mat got over the huge, gaping hole in the battleship's side, the water continued to gain. Slipping her anchors, at the order of the Admiral, the *Indefatigable* proceeded a few hundred yards with her starboard screw to the shelving, sandy beach of Society Bank, where she dropped aground. Had the harbour works at Rosyth been complete, the value of them to the nation at this moment would have been inestimable, for there would have been plenty of time to get her into the dock which was under construction there. But in the desire to effect apparent economies the works since 1905 had been languidly pushed.

The calamities of the British fleet did not end with the torpedoing of the *Indefatigable*. A few seconds later some object drifting in the water, probably a mine—though in the confusion it was impossible to say what exactly happened—struck the *Resistance* just forward of the fore barbette. It must have drifted down inside the torpedo nets, between the hull and the network. There was an explosion of terrific violence, which rent a great breach in the side of the ship near the starboard fore torpedo tube, caused an irresistible inrush of water, and compelled her captain also to slip his anchors and beach his ship.

Two of the British battle squadron were out of action in the space of less than five minutes from the opening of fire.

Already the shattered remnants of the German torpedo flotilla were retiring; a single boat was steaming off as fast as she had come, but astern of her four wrecks lay in the midst of the British fleet devoid of motive power, mere helpless targets for the guns.

As they floated in the glare of the searchlights with the water sputtering about them, in the hail of projectiles, first one and then another, and finally all four, raised the white flag. Four German boats had surrendered; four more had been seen to sink in the midst of the fleet; one was limping slowly off under a rain of shells from the smaller guns of the *Vanguard*.

The British cruiser *Londonderry* was ordered to slip and give chase to her, and steamed off in pursuit down the Forth. A caution to "beware of mines" was flashed by the Admiral, and was needed. The German destroyers must have carried with them, and thrown overboard in their approach, a large number of these deadly agents, which were floating in all directions, greatly hampering the *Londonderry* in her chase.

But with the help of her searchlights she picked her way past some half-dozen mines which were seen on the surface, and she was so fortunate as not to strike any of those which had been anchored in the channel. Gathering speed, she overhauled the damaged destroyer. The crew could offer little resistance to the guns of a powerful cruiser.

A few shots from the three-pounders and a single shell from one of the *Londonderry's* 7.5's did the work. The German torpedo boat began to sink by the stern; her engines stopped; her rudder was driven by the explosion of the big projectile over to starboard, and the impulse of the speed at which she was travelling brought her head round towards the British vessel. The boat was almost flush with the water as one of her crew raised the white flag, and the fifth German boat surrendered.

The prisoners were rescued from the water with shaken nerves and quaking limbs, as men who had passed through the Valley of the Shadow of Death, who had endured the hail of shells and faced the danger of drowning.

So soon as the survivors of that most daring and gallant attack had been recovered from the water, and possession had been taken of the battered hulls in which they had made their onset, the Admiral ordered his torpedo launches to drag the channel for mines.

And while the dragging was proceeding, the prisoners were taken on board the flagship and interrogated. They would disclose little other than the fact that, according to them, war had been already declared. The ship which had attacked the *Leicestershire*, they said, was a tramp fitted for mine-laying and equipped with three torpedo tubes. Half of them were more or less seriously wounded; all admitted that the slaughter on board their boats caused by the British fire had been terrific. One lieutenant stated that all the men at one of his torpedo tubes had been mown down twice by the hail of small shells from the pom-poms, while a 12-in. shell which had hit the stern of his boat had blown it completely away. Yet the remnant of the boat had still floated.

Lord Ebbfleet surveyed the scene with rueful eyes. The *Indefatigable* and *Resistance*, two of his powerful battleships, were out of action, and could take no more part in operations for weeks. The *Leicestershire* was in the same plight. From sixteen battleships his force had fallen to fourteen; his armoured cruiser squadron was reduced from eight ships to seven. To remain in the anchorage without destroyers and torpedo boats to keep a lookout would be to court further torpedo attacks, and perhaps the even more insidious danger from German submarines, and might well imperil the safety of the British reserve ships. Only one course remained—to weigh and proceed to sea, endeavouring to pass south to meet the reserve ships.

Efforts to communicate his intention to the Admiralty failed. The roar of firing had awakened Leith and Edinburgh; people were pouring into the streets to know what this strange and sudden commotion meant, and what was the cause of the storm.

The windows at Queensferry had been shattered; the place was shaken as by a great earthquake. The three heavy bursts of firing, the continuous disquieting flashes of the searchlights, and the great hull of the *Leicestershire* ashore off Leith, indicated that something untoward had befallen the fleet.

For a moment it was thought that the Admiral had fallen to manœuvres at a most unseasonable hour, or that some accident had occurred on board the injured cruiser. Then suddenly the truth dawned upon the people. The crowd ashore, constantly increasing, as it gazed in alarm towards the anchorage, realised that war had begun, and that for the first time since the Dutch sailed up the Medway, more than two hundred years before, the sanctity of a British anchorage had been invaded by an enemy.

The coastguardsmen, who had been placed under the control of the civil authorities as the result of one of the numerous reforms effected in the interests of economy, had for the most part forgotten the art of quick signalling or quick reading of naval signals, else they might have interpreted to the crowd the history of that night, as it was flashed to the wireless station at Rosyth, for transmission to London.

But, as has been said, the attempt to despatch the news to headquarters failed. The private wire from the dockyard to Whitehall would not work, and though the post office wires were tried no answer could be obtained. It appeared that, as on the famous night of the North Sea outrage, there was no one at the Admiralty—not even a clerk. It was, therefore, impossible to obtain definite information.

Lord Ebbfleet had meantime received a report from his torpedo launches that a precarious passage had been cleared through the mines in the channel, and about four o'clock on Sunday morning he ordered the armoured cruiser squadron to put to sea and ascertain whether the coast was clear, preceding the battle squadron, which, minus the two damaged battleships, was to follow at six.

The interval of two hours was required to take on board ammunition from the damaged ships, to land woodwork and all the impedimenta that could possibly be discarded before battle, and also to complete the preparations for action.

It was now almost certain that a German fleet would be encountered, but, as has been said, the risk of remaining in the Forth was even greater than that of proceeding to sea, while the Commander-in-Chief realised the full gravity of the fact that upon his fleet and its activity would depend the safety of England from invasion.

He knew that the other main fleets were far distant; that the reserve ships were much too weak by themselves to meet the force of the German Navy, and that the best chance of averting a fresh disaster to them was to effect as speedily as possible a junction with them. Where exactly they were or whether they had moved from the Nore he was not yet aware; the absence of information from the Admiralty left him in the dark as to these two important points.

The armoured cruisers were ordered, if they encountered the German cruisers in approximately equal or inferior force, to drive them off and push through them, to ascertain the strength and whereabouts of the German battle fleet; if, however, the Germans were in much superior force, the British squadron was to fall back on the battle fleet. One by one the armoured cruisers steamed off, first the *Polyphemus*, with the Rear-Admiral's flag, then the *Olympia*, *Achates*, *Imperieuse*, *Aurora*, and *Londonderry*, and last of all the *Gloucester* bringing up the rear.

Upon these seven ships the duty of breaking through the enemy's screen was to devolve. As they went out they jettisoned their woodwork and formed a line ahead, in which formation they were to fight.

Unfortunately, the shooting of the squadron was very uneven. Three of its ships had done superbly at battle practice and in the gun-layers' test; but two others had performed indifferently, and two could scarcely be trusted to hit the target.

For years the uneven shooting of the fleet had been noted as a source of weakness; but what was needed to bring the bad ships up to the mark was a lavish expenditure of ammunition, and ammunition cost money. Therefore ammunition had to be stinted.

In the German Navy, on the other hand, a contrary course had been followed. For the two months before the war, as was afterwards disclosed by the German Staff History, the German ships had been kept constantly at practice, and if the best ships did not shoot quite so well as the best units in the British fleet, a far higher average level of gunnery had been attained.

Increasing the number of revolutions till the speed reached 18 knots, the cruiser squadron sped seawards. The east was flushed with the glow of dawn as the ships passed Inchcolm, but a grey mist lay upon the surface of the gently heaving sea and veiled the horizon. Leaving Inchkeith and the Kinghorn Battery soon after the Leith clocks had struck the half-hour, and steaming on a generally easterly course, the lookout of the *Polyphemus* saw right ahead and some ten or eleven miles away to the north-east the dark forms of ships upon the horizon. The British line turned slightly and headed towards these ships. All the telescopes on the *Polyphemus's* fore-bridge were directed upon the strangers, and the fact that they were men-of-war painted a muddy grey was ascertained as they drew nearer, and transmitted by wireless telegraphy to Lord Ebbfleet.

They were coming on at a speed which seemed to be about 17 knots, and were formed in line ahead, in a line perfectly maintained, so that, as they were approaching on almost exactly the opposite course, their number could not be counted. In another minute or two, as the distance between the two squadrons rapidly diminished, it was clear from her curious girdermasts that the ship at the head of the line was either the large German armoured cruiser *Waldersee*, the first of the large type built by Germany, or some other ship of her class. At six miles distance several squadrons of destroyers were made out, also formed in line ahead, and steaming alongside the German line, abaft either beam.

A battle was imminent; there was no time to issue elaborate orders, or make fresh dispositions.

The British Admiral signalled that he would turn to starboard, to reconnoitre the strange fleet, and reserve fire till closer quarters. He turned five points, which altered his course to an east-south-easterly one. For a fractional period of time the Germans maintained their original course, steering for the rear of the British line. Then the German flagship or leader of the line turned to port, steering a course which would bring her directly across the bows of the British line.

Simultaneously the two divisions of torpedo craft on the port beam of the German squadron increased speed, and, cutting across the loop, neared the head of the German line.

The German squadron opened fire as it began to turn, the *Waldersee* beginning the duel with the two 11-in. guns in her fore-turret.

A flash, a haze of smoke instantly dissipated, and a heavy shell passed screeching over the fore-turret of the *Polyphemus*.

Another flash an instant later, and a shell struck the British cruiser's third funnel, tearing a great hole in it, but failing to burst. Then every German gun followed, laid on the *Polyphemus*, which blew her steam siren and fired a 12-pounder, the prearranged signal to the British ships for opening, and an instant later, just after 5 A.M., both squadrons were exchanging the most furious fire at a distance which did not exceed 5000 yards.

As the two lines turned, the British were able at last to make out the strength and numbers of their enemy. There were ten German armoured cruisers in line—at the head of the line the fast and new *Waldersee*, *Caprivi*, and *Moltke*, each of 16,000 tons, and armed with four 11-in. and ten 9.4-in. guns, with astern of them the *Manteuffel*, *York*, *Roon*, *Friedrich Karl*, *Prince Adalbert*, *Prince Heinrich*, and *Bismarck*.

The last four did not follow the first six in the turn, but maintained their original course, and headed direct for the rear of the British line. Thus the position was this: One German squadron was manœuvring to pass across the head of the British line, and the other to cross the rear of that line. Each German squadron was attended by two torpedo divisions.

Retreat for the British Admiral was already out of the question, even if he had wished to retire. But as he stood in the *Polyphemus's* conning-tower and felt his great cruiser reel beneath him under the concussion of her heavy guns—as he saw the rush of splinters over her deck, and heard the officers at his side shouting down the telephones amid the deafening din caused by the crash of steel on steel, the violent explosion of the shells, the heavy roar of the great guns, and the ear-splitting crack and rattle of the 12-pounders and pom-poms—he realised that the German squadrons were manœuvring perfectly, and were trying a most daring move—one which it would need all his nerve and foresight to defeat.

VI

Fierce Cruiser Battle

Contrary to anticipation, in the interchange of fire the ships of the two combatants did not suffer any disabling injury. The armour on either side kept out the shells from the vitals, though great smoking gaps began to show where the unarmoured sides had been riven.

The *Waldersee's* turrets flashed and smoked incessantly as she closed; the whole German squadron of six ships, which included her and followed her, turned its concentrated fire upon the *Polyphemus*, and the British cruisers to the rear of the British line were at some disadvantage, since their weapons could only fire at extreme range. The Germans aimed chiefly at the *Polyphemus's* conning-tower, wherein, they knew, dwelt the brain that directed the British force.

Amidst the smoke and fumes of high-explosive shells, with the outlook obscured by the hail of splinters and the nerves shaken by the incessant blast of shells, it was difficult to keep a perfectly cool head.

The next move of the British Admiral has been bitterly criticised by those who forget that the resolutions of naval war may have to be reached in two seconds, under a strain to which no General on land is subjected.

Seeing that the main German squadron was gaining a position to execute the famous manœuvre of "crossing the T," and unable to turn away to starboard for want of sea-room, the British Admiral signalled to his fleet to turn simultaneously to port, reversing the direction of his movement and inverting the order of his fleet. His van became his rear, his rear his van.

Amidst all the uproar, the main German squadron replied with the same manœuvre, while the second German squadron instantly headed straight for the ships which had been to the rear of the British line, and now formed its van.

Simultaneously two of the four divisions of German destroyers attacked, one the rear and the other the head, of the British line, and the German ships let go their long-range torpedoes.

The range had fallen to a distance of not much over 3000 yards between the main German squadron and the *Polyphemus*. At the other extremity of the British line, as the four armoured cruisers forming the second German squadron closed on the British van, it rapidly decreased. The confusion was fearful on either side, and if the British had had destroyers with them the German official narrative acknowledges that it might have gone very hard with the German fleet. But here, as elsewhere, initial errors of disposition, in the famous words of the Archduke Charles, proved fatal beyond belief.

The smaller guns on board all the ships of both sides had been in many cases put out of action; even the heavier weapons had suffered. Several of the turrets no longer flashed and revolved. Funnels and bridges had sunk; wreckage of steel yawned where decks had been; dense clouds of smoke poured from blazing paint or linoleum, and the fires were incessantly renewed by fresh shell explosions. Blood covered the decks, the scuppers ran red; inside the fore barbette of the *Imperieuse*, which had been pierced by an 11-in. shell, was a scene of indescribable horror. The barbette had suddenly ceased firing.

An officer, sent to ascertain the cause, was unable to make his way in before he was swept away by a fresh projectile. Another volunteer climbed up through the top into the steel pent-house, for there was no other means of access—returned alive, and reported that the whole barbette crew were dead and that the place was like a charnel-house. There was no sign of disabling injury to the mechanism, but the problem was how to get a fresh crew of living men through the hail of shells to the guns.

The four German armoured cruisers of the second division turned within 1500 yards of the head of the British line, firing torpedoes and delivering and receiving a terrific shell fire. One torpedo boat followed each German cruiser closely, and as the four cruisers turned, the torpedo craft, instead of following them, charged home.

The manœuvre was so unexpected and so hazardous that it was difficult to meet. At twenty-five knots speed the German boats passed like a flash through the British line. A great hump of water rose under the British cruiser *Londonderry*, second in the inverted order of the line, and she reeled and settled heavily in the water. A torpedo had struck her abaft the fore-turret.

Almost at the same instant another German torpedo division attacked the rear of the British line, and a German torpedo boat made a hit upon the *Olympia*, last but one in the British line. She was struck abaft the starboard engine-room, and she too listed, and settled in the water.

As the German boats attempted to escape to the south they caught the fire of the British squadron's port broadsides, which sent two to the bottom and left two others in a sinking condition. Both the damaged British ships turned out of the British line and headed for the coast to the south. The only chance of saving the ships and crews was to beach the vessels and effect repairs. As they steered out of the battle, the tumult behind them increased, and their crews could see great tongues of flame shooting upwards from the *Bismarck*, which was held unmercifully by the British 9.2-in. shells. She was badly damaged and in sore trouble, but the rest of the German ships still appeared to be going well. The British torpedoes, fired from the cruisers' tubes, seemed to have made no hits.

The Germans offered no hindrance to the withdrawal of the injured ships. They closed on the remnant of the British force, now reduced to five ships, all much damaged. On their side, without the *Bismarck*, which had fallen out of the line, they had nine ships in action and two intact flotillas of torpedo craft to bring to bear.

The second German squadron had wheeled to join the other division, which was now steering a generally parallel course, though well astern of the British ships. The two fleets had drawn apart after the short but fierce torpedo action, and the British were now heading north. A fierce cruiser battle ensued.

In this sharp encounter at close quarters, at a range which did not exceed 2000 yards, a grave catastrophe had befallen the *Polyphemus*. As the Admiral was giving orders for his squadron to turn, two heavy projectiles in quick succession struck the conning-tower, inside which he was standing with the captain, a midshipman, a petty officer, and two boys at his side. The first shell struck the base of the conning-tower, causing a most violent shock, and filling the interior of the tower with smoke and fumes.

The Admiral leant against the side of the tower and strove to ascertain through the narrow opening in the steel wall what had happened, when the second shell hit the armour outside, and exploded against it with terrific violence. Admiral Hardy was instantly killed by the shock or by the bolts and splinters which the explosion or impact of the projectile drove into the conning-tower. The flag-captain was mortally wounded; the petty officer received an insignificant contusion. The midshipman and the two boys escaped without a scratch, though stunned and much shaken by the terrific blow.

For some seconds the ship passed out of control; then, dazed and bewildered, the midshipman took charge, and shouted to the chamber below, where the steering gear was placed with the voice-pipes and all other appliances,—an improvement introduced after the war in the Far East,—orders to communicate the death of the Admiral and disablement of the captain to the commander. For some minutes the British squadron was without a chief, though under the system of "follow my leader," which had been adopted for the cruiser squadron, the captain of the *Gloucester* which led the line was controlling the battle.

Some confusion resulted, and the opportunity of finishing off the *Bismarck* which undoubtedly offered at this moment was lost. Captain Connor, of the *Gloucester*, increased speed to eighteen knots, heading northward, to draw the German squadron away from the damaged British ships, and attempted to work across the head of the German line. The fleets now fought broadside to broadside, exchanging a steady fire, until Captain Connor, finding himself getting too close to the north coast, and with insufficient manœuvring room, turned southward, inverting the British line, and bringing the *Polyphemus* once more to its head.

The British squadron, after turning, steamed towards the *Bismarck*, which was crawling off eastwards, with a division of German torpedo boats near at hand to give her succour. The German squadrons had now formed up into one compact line, in which two of the ships appeared to be in serious difficulties. They copied the British manœuvre and steered a parallel course to the British cruisers, holding a position a little ahead of them. Simultaneously, their other intact torpedo division took station to leeward of their line near its rear, and the six remaining boats of the two divisions, which had executed the first attack, took station to leeward near the head of the line. The two fleets steamed 3500 yards apart, gradually closing, and fought an artillery battle, in which the greater gunpower, of the Germans, who had nine ships in action to the British five, speedily began to tell.

The *Gloucester* lost two of her four funnels; one of her masts fell with a resounding crash. The *Olympia* had a slight list; the *Aurora's* forward works were shot away; the *Achates* had lost one of her funnels.

In the German line the *Waldersee's* forward military mast tottered and could be seen swaying at each instant, the network of steel girders had been badly damaged. The *Caprivi* was on fire amidships, and smoke was pouring up from the fire. The *Moltke* was without one of her four funnels. The *Manteuffel's* stern had been wrecked till the structure of the ship above the armour looked like a tangle of battered girders. The *York* and *Roon* were less shattered, but gaping wounds could be seen in their sides. The *Friedrich Karl* had lost the upper portion of her after military mast. The *Prince Heinrich* was slightly down by the bow, and was drooping astern.

Sparks and splinters flew upwards from the steel sides of the great ships as the projectiles went home; the din was indescribable; mingled with the dull note of the heavy guns was the crackling of the smaller guns and the beating of the pom-poms, playing a devil's tattoo in this furious encounter of the mastodons.

The German Admiral saw that the two fleets were steadily nearing the *Bismarck*, and essayed once more the manœuvre which he had already tried, a manœuvre studiously practised in the German Navy, which had for ten years been daily experimenting with battle-evolutions, and testing its captains' nerves till they were of steel. In these difficult and desperate manœuvres, it was remarked then—and it has since been proved by experience—the Germans surpassed their British rivals, not because the German officer was braver or more capable, but because he was younger taught to display initiative to a higher degree than the personnel of the British fleet, and better trained for actual battle.

The four last cruisers in the German line suddenly altered course and steered straight at the British line, while behind them, as before, followed six torpedo boats. Through the intervals at the head of the German line came the other six boats—an evolution which they had constantly rehearsed in peace, and which they carried out with admirable precision and dash in the crisis of battle—and charged the head of the British line. The rest of the German squadron maintained its original course, and covered the attack with a terrific fire, all its guns accelerating the rapidity of their discharge till the air hummed with projectiles.

The attack was suddenly and vigorously delivered. The British ships at the rear of the line met it and countered it with success by turning together south and steaming away, so that the German effort in this quarter ended with a blow to the air.

But the flagship at the head of the line was not so alert; the death of the Admiral was at this critical moment severely felt, and the *Polyphemus*, though she eluded three torpedoes which were fired at her at about 3000 yards by the German battleships, found two torpedo boats closing in upon her from right ahead. She charged one with the ram; there was no time for thinking, and she caught the boat fair under her steel prow, which cut through the thin plating of the boat like a knife through matchwood. Her huge hull passed with a slight shudder over the boat, which instantly foundered with a violent explosion.

The other boat, however, passed her only a hundred yards away in the spray of shells and projectiles which seemed as if by enchantment just to miss it. Her crew had a vision of wild-looking officers and men busy at the boat's torpedo tubes; the flash of two torpedoes glinted in the sun as they leaped from the tubes into the water; then a great shell caught the boat and sent her reeling and sinking, but too late. The mischief had been done. One of the German torpedoes struck the *Polyphemus* full on the starboard engine-room, and, exploding with devastating effect, blew in the side and bulkheads. The engine-room filled at once, and bereft of half her power the great cruiser broke from the British line and headed for the shore with a heavy list. Almost at the same moment the fire on board the *Caprivi* blazed up so fiercely under the impact of the British shells that she, too, had to leave the line of battle.

The British line re-formed, heading east, now only four ships strong, faced by eight German ships. For some minutes both fleets steamed on a parallel course 4500 yards apart, the Germans, who had, on the whole, suffered less damage, since their injuries were distributed over a larger number of ships, steaming a little faster. Once more the German Admiral essayed a surprise. Suddenly the eight German ships made each simultaneously a quarter-turn, which brought them into line abreast. They stood in towards the four British survivors, to deal the culminating blow. End-on they caught the full vehemence of the British fire. But with forces so weakened, the British senior officer could not run the risk of a mêlée, and to avoid his antagonists he, too, turned away from the Germans in a line abreast, and at the same moment the *Achates*, *Imperieuse*, and *Aurora* fired their stern torpedo tubes. Realising the danger of pressing too closely in the course of a retiring fleet, the Germans again altered course to line ahead, and steered to cut the British ships off from their line of retreat up the Forth.

The four British cruisers now headed up the Forth, perceiving that victory was impossible and flight the only course. They again received the German fire, steering on a parallel course. At this juncture the *Gloucester*, the last ship in the British line, dropped far astern; she had received in quick succession half a dozen heavy German shells on her 6-in. armour and had sprung a serious leak. The German ships closed on her, coming in to less than 2000 yards, when their guns battered her with ever-increasing effect. She sank deeper in the water, heading for the coast, with the Germans in hot pursuit firing continuously at her. The other three cruisers were preparing to turn and go to her aid—a course which would certainly have involved the annihilation of the First Cruiser Squadron—when welcome help appeared.

To the west a column of great ships was made out coming up at impetuous speed from the Upper Forth. The new-comers were the British battleships steering to the scene of action.

At their approach the German cruisers wheeled and stood seaward, making off at a speed which did not exceed 16 knots, and leaving the *Gloucester* to beach herself. They were now in peril, in imminent danger of destruction—as it seemed to the British officers. Actually, however, the risk for them had not been great. Within touch of them the main German battle-fleet had waited off the Forth, linked to them by a chain of smaller cruisers and torpedo boats. It would have shown itself before, but for its commander's fear that its premature appearance might have broken off the battle and led to the retreat of the British squadron. As the British fleet came up, the German cruiser *Bismarck*, which had been for an hour in the gravest trouble, dropped astern of the other German ships, and it could be seen that one other German ship had been taken in tow and was falling astern.

Thus the preliminary cruiser action between the fleets had ended all to the disadvantage of the British, who had fought for two hours, and in that brief space lost four ships disabled. From seven ships on that disastrous morning, the British strength had been reduced to three. Impartial posterity will not blame the officers and men of the armoured cruiser squadron, who made a most gallant fight under the most unfavourable conditions.

The real criminals were the British Ministers, who neglected precautions, permitted the British fleet to be surprised, and compelled the British Admiral to play the most hazardous of games while they had left the coast without torpedo stations, and England without any military force capable of resisting an invading army.

Had there been a national army, even a national militia, the Commander-in-Chief could have calmly awaited the concentration of the remaining British fleets, which would have given the British Navy an overwhelming superiority. Had there been a fair number of destroyers always attached to his force, again, it is morally certain that he would have suffered no loss from the German torpedo attacks, while a number of torpedo stations disposed along the North Sea coast would have enabled him to call up torpedo divisions to his assistance, even if he had had none attached to his fleet.

Foresight would have provided for all the perils which menaced the British Navy on this eventful night; foresight had urged the rapid completion of the harbour at Rosyth, without which further strengthening of the North Sea fleet was difficult; foresight had pointed out the danger of neglecting the strengthening of the torpedo flotilla; foresight had called for a strong navy, and a nation trained to defend the fatherland.

It was the cry of the people and the politician for all manner of "reforms" at the expense of national security; the demand for old-age pensions, for feeding of children, for State work at preposterous wages for the work-shy; the general selfishness which asked everything of the State and refused to make the smallest sacrifice for it; the degenerate slackness of the Public and the Press, who refused to concern themselves with these tremendous interests, and riveted all their attention upon the trivialities of the football and cricket field, that worked the doom of England.

The nation was careless and apathetic; it had taken but little interest in its Fleet. Always it had assumed that the navy was perfect, that one British ship was a match for any two enemies. And now in a few hours it had been proved that the German Navy was as efficient; that its younger officers were better trained for war and more enterprising than the older British personnel; that its staff had perfectly thought out and prepared every move; and that much of the old advantage possessed by the British Navy had been lost by the too general introduction of short service.

The shooting of the British ships, it is true, had on the whole been good, and even the cruisers, which in battle practice had done badly, in action had improved their marksmanship to a remarkable degree. But it was in the art of battle manœuvring and in the scientific employment of their weapons that the British had failed.

The three surviving cruisers of the British squadron had all suffered much damage from the German fire, and had exhausted so much of their ammunition in the two hours' fight that they were practically incapable of taking further part in the operations. They had to proceed to Rosyth to effect hasty repairs and ship any further ammunition that might with luck be found in the insignificant magazines at that place.

WILLIAM LE QUEUX

The *Olympia* had been struck three times on her fore barbette, but though one of the 9.2-in. guns which it contained had been put out of action by splinters, the barbette still worked well. Twice almost the entire crew of the barbette had been put out of action and had been renewed. The scenes within the barbette were appalling. Two of her 7.5-in. barbettes had been jammed by the fire; her funnels were so much damaged that the draught had fallen and the coal consumption enormously increased. Below the armour deck, however, the vitals of the ship were intact.

The *Impérieuse* and *Aurora* had serious hits on the water-line astern, and each of them was taking on board a good deal of water. They, too, were much mauled about their funnels and upper works. As for the four beached cruisers, they were in a parlous condition, and it would take weeks to effect repairs. The losses in men of the cruisers had not been very heavy; the officers in the conning-towers had suffered most, as upon the conning-towers the Germans had directed their heaviest fire.

Most serious and trying in all the ships had been the outbreaks of fire. Wherever the shells struck they appeared to cause conflagrations, and this, though the hoses were spouting water and the decks drowned before the action began. Once a fire broke out, to get it under was no easy task. Projectiles came thick upon the fire-parties, working in the choking smoke. Shell-splinters cut down the bluejackets and tore the hoses. The difficulty of maintaining communications within the ships was stupendous; telephones were inaudible in the terrible din; voice-pipes were severed; mechanical indicators worked indifferently.

The battle-fleet had spent its respite at the anchorage in getting on board the intact ships much of the ammunition from the *Indefatigable* and *Triumph*, and stripping away all remaining impedimenta; in rigging mantlets and completing the work of preparation.

While thus engaged at five A.M. the heavy boom of distant firing came in towards it from the sea—the continuous thundering of a hundred large guns, a dull, sinister note, which alternately froze and warmed the blood. Orders were instantly issued to make ready for sea with all possible speed, and hoist in the boats. Meantime the ships' torpedo and picket boats had dragged carefully for mines, as Lord Ebbfleet dared to leave nothing to chance. Numerous mines were found floating on the water or moored in the channel, and it seemed a miracle that so many ships of the cruiser squadron had passed out to sea in safety.

Ten minutes later, at 5.10 A.M., Lord Ebbfleet signalled to weigh anchor, and the battle-fleet got under way and headed out to sea, its ships in a single line ahead, proceeding with the utmost caution. As it cleared the zone of danger, speed was increased to sixteen knots, and off Inchcolm the formation was modified.

Wishing to use to the utmost the high speed and enormous batteries of his four battleships of the "Dreadnought "class, Lord Ebbfleet had determined to manœuvre with them independently. They steamed three knots faster than the rest of his fleet; their armour and armament fitted them to play a decisive part in the approaching action. They took station to starboard, and to port steamed the other ten battleships, headed by the *Captain*, under Sir Louis Parker, the second in command, who was given full authority to control his division. Behind the *Captain* steamed the *Sultan*, *Defiance*, *Active*, *Redoubtable*, *Malta*, *Excellence*, *Courageous*, *Valiant*, and *Glasgow*—a magnificent array of two-funnelled, grey-painted monsters, keeping perfect station, with their crews at quarters, guns loaded, and battle-flags flying. To starboard were the enormous hulls of the four "Dreadnoughts," the *Vanguard* leading, with astern of her the *Thunderer*, *Devastation*, and *Bellerophon*. The great turrets, each with its pair of giant 45 ft. long 12-in. guns, caught the eye instantly; the three squat funnels in each ship emitted only a faint haze of smoke; on the lofty bridges high above the water stood white-capped officers, looking out anxiously to sea. Nearer and nearer came the roll of the firing; presently the four "Dreadnoughts" increased speed and drew fast ahead of the other line, while the spray flew from under their bows as the revolutions of the turbines rose and the speed went up to nineteen knots.

The other ten battleships maintained their speed, and fell fast astern. Off Leith a vast crowd gathered, watching the far-off fighting, and listening in disquietude to the roar of the firing of the cruiser battle, and cheered the great procession as it swiftly passed and receded from view, leaving behind it only a faint haze of smoke. A few minutes before 7 A.M. the group of officers on the *Vanguard's* bridge saw ahead of them three cruisers, evidently British, steaming towards them, and far away yet another British cruiser low in the water, smoking under the impact of shells, with about her a great fleet of armoured cruisers. The cruisers, as they approached, signalled the terrible news that Admiral Hardy was dead, three British cruisers out of action, and the *Gloucester* in desperate straits.

The battleships were just in time to effect the rescue. At 11,000 yards the *Vanguard's* fore-turret fired the first shot of the battleship encounter, and as the scream of the projectile filled the air, the German cruisers drew away from their prey. The "Dreadnoughts" were now two miles ahead of the main squadron. Steaming fast towards the *Bismarck*, which had been abandoned by her consorts, the *Vanguard* fired six shells at her from her fore and starboard 12-in. turrets. All the six 12-in. shells went home; with a violent explosion the German cruiser sank instantly, taking with her to the bottom most of her crew. Yet there was no time to think of saving men, for on the horizon ahead of the British Fleet, out to sea, could be seen a dense cloud of smoke, betokening the presence of a great assemblage of ships. Towards this cloud the German cruisers were steaming at their best pace.

Lord Ebbfleet reduced speed to permit his other battleships to complete their formation and take up their positions for battle. The ten battleships of the second division simultaneously increased speed from fifteen to sixteen knots, which was as much as their engines could be trusted to make without serious strain.

About 7.15 A.M. the British Fleet had resumed its original order, and was abreast of North Berwick, now fast nearing the cloud of smoke which indicated the enemy's presence, and rose from behind the cliffs of the Island of May.

The British admirals interchanged signals as the fleet steamed seaward, and Lord Ebbfleet instructed Vice-Admiral Parker and Rear-Admiral Merrilees to be prepared for the sudden charges of German torpedo craft.

That there would be many with the German Fleet was certain, for, although about twenty-four destroyers and torpedo boats had been sunk, damaged, or left without torpedoes as the result of the previous attacks during the night and early morning, the German torpedo flotilla had been enormously increased in the four years before the war, till it mustered 144 destroyers and forty large torpedo boats.

Even ruling thirty out of action and allowing for detachments, something like a hundred might have to be encountered.

Lord Ebbfleet was not one of those officers who expect the enemy to do the foolish thing, and he had no doubt but that the Germans would follow a policy of rigid concentration. They would bring all their force to bear against his fleet and strive to deal it a deadly blow.

Five minutes passed, and the smoke increased, while now at last the forms of ships could be made out far away. Rapidly approaching each other at the rate of some thirty knots an hour, the head ships of the two fleets were at 7.25 A.M. about nine miles apart. It could be seen that the German ships were in three distinct lines ahead, the starboard or right German line markedly in advance of the others, which were almost abreast. The German lines had wide intervals between them.

In the British ships the ranges were now coming down to the guns from the fire-control stations aloft: "18,000 yards!" "17,000 yards!" "16,000 yards!" "15,000 yards!" "14,000 yards!" followed in quick succession; the sights were quietly adjusted, and the tension of the crews grew almost unendurable. The hoses were all spouting water to wet the decks; every eye was turned upon the enemy. Far away to the south the Bass Rock and the cliffs near Tantallon Castle rose out of a heaving sea, and behind them loomed the upland country south of Dunbar, so famous in Scottish story. To the north showed the rocky coast of Fife. The sun was in the eyes of the British gunners.

The guns of the *Vanguard*, and, indeed, of all the British battleships, were kept trained upon the leading German. It could now be seen that she was of the "Kaiser" class, and that five others of the same class followed her. Her tier on tier of turrets showed against the sun; the grim brownish-grey hulls produced an impression of resolute force.

In the centre German line appeared to be stationed several ships of the "Braunschweig" and "Deutschland" classes—how many the British officers could not as yet make out, owing to the perfect order of the German line, and the fact that it was approaching on exactly the opposite course to the British Fleet.

The port or left German line was headed by one of the new monster battleships, built to reply to the *Dreadnought*, and of even greater size and heavier battery than that famous ship. It was, in fact, the *Sachsen*, flying Admiral Helmann's flag, armed with twelve of the new pattern 46 ft. long 11-in. guns, twenty-four 4-in. quick-firers, and ten pom-poms.

The monster German battleship could be plainly distinguished by the Eiffel Tower-like structure of her masts, each with its two platforms carried on an elaborate system of light steel girders, which rendered them less liable to be shot away. End-on she showed her four 11-in. turrets, each bristling with a pair of muzzles. She brought two more heavy guns to bear ahead and on the broadside than did the *Dreadnought*, while her stern fire was incomparably more powerful, delivered from eight 11-in. guns.

It was the completion of two ships of this class that had caused Lord Ebbfleet so much anxiety for his position. Yet there were four of the class in the German line of battle, two of which did not appear in the official lists as ready for sea, but were given out to be only completing.

The range-finders in the fire-control stations in the British flagship were still sending down the distance. "13,000 yards!" "12,000 yards!" and the tension augmented. The centre and port German columns of ships slowed and turned slightly in succession, while the starboard line increased speed and maintained its original course. By this manœuvre the German Fleet looked to be formed in one enormous irregular line, covering four miles of sea.

The numbers of the enemy could at last be counted; the British Fleet of fourteen battleships had twenty-two battleships against it, and of those twenty-two, four were as good ships as the *Vanguard*. The British Fleet turned a little to starboard to bring its batteries to bear with the best effect, and take advantage, as Lord Ebbfleet intended, of the dispersion of the German formation. "11,000 yards!" "10,000 yards!" came down to the barbettes. The *Vanguard* fired a 12-pounder, and as the flash was seen both Fleets opened with sighting shots, and the great battle began.

VII

CONTINUATION OF THE STRUGGLE AT SEA

B ut the German Admiral had anticipated the British move, and as the two fleets closed, replied with a daring and hazardous blow. His irregular line dissolved once more into its elements as the flashes came from every heavy gun that would bear in his twenty-two battleships. The Germans, as they drew abreast of the British Fleet, steaming on an opposite course, broke into three columns in three lines ahead, one of which steered straight for the British rear, one for the centre, and one for the van.

The *Vanguard* and the other three large battleships with Lord Ebbfleet had increased speed, and moved ahead of their original station till their broadsides bore and they practically belonged the British line. They circled at full battle speed of nineteen knots to pass across the German rear. Sheltering under the lee of the German battleships several destroyers or torpedo-boats could be discerned, and there were other destroyer or torpedo-boat divisions away to the north-east, moving gently apart and aloof from the battle out at sea.

The fire on either side had now become intense and accurate; the range varied from minute to minute, but it constantly fell. The tumult was indescribable. The German third division of six "Kaisers" passed round the rear of the main British division, executing against it the manœuvre of "crossing the T," but receiving serious injury in the process.

A stunning succession of blows rained upon the *Glasgow*, the sternmost battleship in the British line, and her excessively thin belt was pierced by three German 9.4-in. shells, one of which burst with dreadful effect inside the citadel, denting the armoured deck, driving bolts and splinters down into the boiler and engine-rooms, and for some instants rendering the ship uncontrollable. A great fire broke out where the shell had burst.

Almost at the same instant the *Glasgow's* fore barbette put two shells in succession home just above the upper level of the *Zahringen's* armour-belt amidships, and one of these shells bursting, wrecked and brought down the German battleship's after-funnel, besides putting two of her Schultz boilers out of action. The *Zahringen* took fire, but the flames were quickly got under; she carried no wood and nothing inflammable.

Dense clouds of smoke from funnels, from bursting shells, from burning ships, began to settle over the water, and the air was acrid with the taint of burnt cordite and nitrous fumes from the German powder. In the twilight of smoke the dim forms of monster ships marched and countermarched, aglow with red flame.

The four "Dreadnoughts" passed round the first German division containing the four battleships of the "Sachsen" class, interchanging with them a terrific fire at about 5000 yards. Each side made many hits, and some damage was done to unarmoured portions of the huge hulls. An 11-in. shell struck the *Thunderer's* centre 12-in. barbette, and jammed it for a few minutes; the *Vanguard*, at the head of the British division, received a concentrated fire, seven 11-in. shells striking her forward of her centre barbette. Several of her armour-plates were cracked; her port anchor gear was shot away, and her fore-funnel much shattered. Her whole structure vibrated under the terrific blows. Splinters swept her fore-bridge, and a hail of small projectiles from the German 40-pounder guns beat upon her conning-tower, rendering control of the battle exceedingly difficult.

The noise and concussion were terrible; the blast of the great 12-in. guns, when they fired ahead, shook the occupants of the tower, and extreme caution was needed to avoid serious injury. Lord Ebbfleet triumphantly achieved the manœuvre of "crossing the T," or passing across the head of the German line and raking it with all his ships, against the Germans, though the enormous bow-fire of the *Sachsen* served her well at this point.

But the German Admiral diminished the effectiveness of the manœuvre by turning away a little, and then, when the danger had passed, resuming his original course. The second German division rapidly came up on the port beam of the British main division, its head ships receiving a fearful fire from the British line. Closing upon the first German division, it formed up astern of it into one long line, and attacked the British rear.

Thus the Germans had surrounded the British ten battleships under Sir Louis Parker, and had concentrated against them twenty-two battleships. The fire of this great host of German ships told heavily upon the weak armour of the "Defiance" and "Valiant" classes. The "Sachsens," at about 4000 yards, put shot after shot from their 11-in. guns into the hull of the *Glasgow*, the last ship in the British line, and clouds of smoke and tongues of flame leapt up from her. She was now steaming slowly, and in evident distress.

The four "Dreadnoughts" worked to the north of the Germans, maintaining with them a long-range action, and firing with great effect. But seeing the German concentration against the other division of his fleet, Lord Ebbfleet turned and stood towards it, while at the same time Admiral Parker began to turn in succession and move to meet the "Dreadnoughts." As his line turned, the rearward ships received further injuries.

Outside the armour the structure of many ships on both sides was fast being reduced to a tangle of shattered beams and twisted and rent plating. Most of the smaller guns were out of action, though the 6-in. guns in the casemates of the British ships were still for the most part intact. The *Sultan's* 7.5's were firing with great effect; while the *Captain*, which headed the British main division, had resisted the battering superbly, and inflicted great injury on the *Preussen* by her fire. At moments, however, her guns were blanketed by the ships behind her, from the fact that the German columns were well astern. It was to bring his guns to bear as well as to rejoin his Commander-in-Chief that the British Vice-Admiral altered course and steamed south-westward.

The Germans now practised a masterly stroke.

Their third division of six "Kaisers" headed direct for the van of the British line, closing rapidly upon a generally opposite course. At the same time their other two divisions steered to prevent the British ships from making a countermarch and avoiding the charge which was now imminent.

Lord Ebbfleet saw the danger, and increased speed, closing on the "Kaisers," well astern of them, and plying them with a terrific fire from the three 12-in. turrets which bore ahead in his flagship. Smoke and sparks flew upwards from the *Friedrich III*, the last ship in the division. Her after-turret was out of action; her after-military mast fell amidst a rain of splinters; her stern sank slightly in the water.

At the same time the "Kaisers" began to catch the full fire of the other British division, and they were doubled upon. The head of their line was being raked by Sir Louis Parker; the *Captain* put shell after shell into the bows of the *Wilhelm II*; her 9.2's and 12-in. guns played with a steady stream of projectiles upon the German battleship, until, at 2000 yards, the *Wilhelm's* upper works appeared to be dissolving in smoke and flame as before some irresistible acid.

The bows of the German battleship sank a little, but she turned, brought her broadside to bear, and the five ships behind her did the same. The range was short; the position favourable for torpedoes; and the six Germans fired, first their bow tubes as they came round, and then twice in quick succession their two broadside tubes at the British line. The thirty torpedoes sped through the sea; the British replied with the two broadside tubes in each ship, as those tubes bore.

There was amidst all the din and turmoil and shooting flame a distinct pause in the battle as the crews of both fleets, or all those who could see what was happening, watched spell-bound the issue of this attack and counter-attack. They had not long to wait. One of the huge German torpedoes caught the *Excellent* right astern and wrecked her rudder and propellers. Another struck the *Sultan* almost amidships, inflicting upon her terrible injury, so that she listed heavily. The *Wilhelm II* was struck by a British torpedo right on her bows, and as she was already low in the water, began to fill and sink.

The scene at this point was one of appalling horror. One battleship, the *Wilhelm II*, was sinking fast, with none to rescue her crew; the men were rushing up on deck; the fire from her guns had ceased; she lay on the sea a shattered wreck, riddled with shell, and smoking with the fires which still burnt fiercely amidst the débris of her upper works.

Not far from her lay the *Excellent*, completely disabled, but still firing. Near the *Excellent*, again, moving very slowly, and clearly in a sinking condition, but still maintaining gallantly the battle, was the *Glasgow*, in a dense cloud of smoke caused by the bursting shell from the guns of sixteen enemies and the blazing fires on board.

Making off to the south to beach herself was the *Sultan*, in lamentable plight, with a heavy list. It was 8.40 A.M., or little more than an hour since the joining of battle, and the German Admiral at this moment signalled that victory was his.

The news was sent by wireless telegraphy to the German cruisers out at sea, and by them transmitted to Emden and Berlin.

At 11 that morning newspapers were selling in the streets of the German capital with the news that the British Fleet was beaten, and that Britain had lost the command of the sea. Five British battleships, it was added, in the brief wireless message, had been already sunk or put out of action.

The German lines closed upon the two injured British ships, *Exmouth* and *Glory*, showering shells upon them. At once the two British Admirals turned and moved to the rescue, through the clouds of smoke which had settled on the sea, and which were rendering

THE FIRST NEWS IN BERLIN OF THE GERMAN VICTORY.

shooting at long range more than ever difficult. Through the smoke German torpedo-boats could be made out on the move, but they did not attempt as yet to close on the intact battleships, and kept well out of the range of the British guns. The first and most powerful German battleship division covered the other German ships in their attack upon the disabled British battleships, and encountered the fire of the eleven British battleships which still remained in action. Meantime the other thirteen German battleships closed to about 1000 yards of the injured British ships. The 11-in. shells from the German turrets at this distance inflicted terrible injury. The German guns were firing three shots in two minutes, and under their fire and the storm of 6-in. and 6.7-in. shells which their smaller guns delivered it was impossible for the British gunners to shoot with any effect. Great explosions occurred on board the *Glory*; an 11-in. shell struck her fore barbette, where the plating had already been damaged by a previous hit, and, perforating, burst inside with fearful effect, blowing the crew of the barbette to pieces, and sending a blast of fire and gas down into the loading chamber under the barbette, where it exploded a cordite charge. Another shell struck the conning-tower, and disabled or killed all inside it. The funnels fell; both the masts, which were already tottering, came down; the ship lay upon the water a formless, smoking hulk. Yet still her crew fought on, a hopeless battle. Then several heavy shells caught her waterline, as the Germans closed a little, and must have driven in the armour or pierced it. More explosions followed; from the centre of the ship rose a column of smoke and flame and fragments of wreckage; the centre lifted visibly, and the ends dropped into the sea. The *Glory* parted amidships, and went to the bottom still firing her after barbette in that supreme moment, having proved herself worthy of her proud name. Several German torpedo-boats steamed towards the bubbles in the water, and fell to work to rescue the crew. Others had drawn near the *Wilhelm II*, and in neither case were they molested by the fire of the British fleet.

A scene as terrible took place on board the *Exmouth*. To save her was impossible, for only a few brief minutes were needed to complete the torpedo's work, and no respite was given by the German officers. They poured in a heavy fire from all their guns that remained battle-worthy upon the *Exmouth's* barbettes and conning-tower, raining such a shower of projectiles upon the ship that, as in the case of the *Glory*, it was impossible for the British crew to fight her with effect. Her 7-in. armour did not keep out the German 11-in. projectiles at short range, and the citadel of the ship became a perfect charnel-house.

Amid the tangled steel-work, amid the blaze of the fires which could no longer be kept under, amid the hail of splinters, in the choking fumes of smoke from burning wood and linoleum and exploding shells, officers and men clung manfully to their posts, while under them the hull sank lower and lower in the water. Then the *Braunschweig* headed in to 500 yards, and at this range fired her bow torpedo at the British ship amidships. The torpedo struck the British battleship and did its dreadful work. Exploding about the base of the after-funnel, it blew in the side, and immediately the British ship listed sharply, showed her deck to her enemy, and with a rattle of objects sliding across the deck and a rush of blue figures, capsized amid a cloud of steam.

While the two disabled battleships were being destroyed, and the *Swiftsure* was crawling off to the south in the hope of reaching the shore and beaching herself, the fight between the rest of the British Fleet and the German divisions had reached its full intensity. For some minutes, indeed, both fleets had been compelled by the smoke to cease fire, but the heavy thunder of the firing never altogether stopped. The four big German battleships were still seemingly undamaged in any vital respect, though all showed minor injuries. The four British "Dreadnoughts" had stood the stern test as well.

But the other battleships had all suffered grievously. The *Duncan* and *Russell* had lost, one both her funnels and the other both her masts, and the speed of the *Duncan* could scarcely be maintained in consequence. The *Montagu* had one of her barbettes out of action, and one of the *Albemarle's* 12-in. guns had either blown off its muzzle or else had it shot away. The *Albemarle* had received a shell forward below the waterline, and had a compartment full of water. In the German line the *Lothringen* was on fire amidships, had lost her fore and centre funnels, and was low in the water, but her heavy guns were still in action. On her the British line now concentrated most of its fire, while the Germans plied with shell the *Duncan* and *Russell*. The second and third German divisions used their port batteries against the British main fleet, while their starboard batteries were destroying the *Exmouth* and *Glory*.

At this juncture the *Duncan* fell astern and left the British line, and almost at the same moment the *Lothringen* quitted the German line. The British Admiral turned all his ships eight points simultaneously, inverting the order of his line, to rescue his injured vessel. To attempt an attack upon the *Lothringen* would have meant forcing his way through the German line, and with the ever-growing disparity of numbers he did not dare to risk so hazardous a venture. But before he could effect his purpose, the German Admiral closed on the *Duncan*, and from the *Sachsen's* and *Grosser Kurfuerst's* 11-in. turrets poured in upon her a broadside of twenty 11-in. shells, which struck her almost simultaneously—the range was now too short for the gunners to miss—and caused fearful slaughter and damage on board her. Two of the projectiles, which were alternately steel shell and capped armour-piercing shell, perforated her side-armour; two more hit her fore barbette; one exploded against the conning-tower; the others hulled her amidships; and when the smoke about her lifted for an instant in a puff of the wind, she was seen to be slowly sinking and motionless. One of her barbettes was still firing, but she was out of the battle and doomed. Four British battleships had gone and two German, though one of these was still afloat and moving slowly off to the north-east, towards two divisions of German destroyers, which waited the moment to close and deal a final blow against the British Fleet.

It was now about 10 A.M., and both fleets drew apart for some minutes. Another German battleship, the *Westfalien*, quitted the German line, and followed the *Lothringen* away from the fight. Her two turrets had been jammed temporarily by the British 12-in. shells, while most of her smaller guns had been put out of action by the *Agamemnon's* 9.2-in. weapons, which had directed upon her a merciless fire. The Germans could be seen re-forming their divisions, and one of the battleships moved from the second to the first division. With seven battleships in each of these two divisions and five in the third, the Germans once more approached the British line, which had also re-formed, the *Agamemnon* taking station to the rear. The battle was renewed off Dunbar. Astern of the Germans, now that the smoke had cleared away, could be seen fifteen or twenty torpedo craft. Other destroyer and torpedo divisions were farther away to sea.

The German battleships steamed direct towards the British battleships, repeating the manœuvre which they had employed at the opening of the battle, and forming their two first divisions in one line, which moved upon the port bow of the British, while the other division, the third, advanced against the starboard bow. Both fleets reopened fire, and to avoid passing between the two German lines, Lord Ebbfleet turned towards the main German force, hoping, at even this eleventh hour, to retrieve the fortunes of the disastrous day by the use of his big ships' batteries. Turning in succession in the attempt to cross his enemy's bows, his ships received a very heavy fire from both German lines; simultaneously the conning-towers of the *Vanguard* and the *Sachsen* were struck by several shells. Two British 12-in. projectiles caught the *Sachsen's* tower in succession; the first weakened the structure and probably killed every one inside, among them Admiral Helmann; the second practically demolished it, leaving it a complete wreck.

The blow of the German 11-in. shell upon the *Vanguard's* tower was equally fatal. Lord Ebbfleet was killed by a splinter, and his chief-of-the-staff received mortal injuries. Not a man in the tower escaped untouched. The brains of both fleets were paralysed, and the *Vanguard* steered wildly. The German destroyers saw their opportunity, and rushed in. Four boats came straight at the huge hull of the British flagship from ahead, and before she could be got under control, a torpedo fired from one of them hit her right forward, breaching two compartments and admitting a great quantity of water. Her bows sank in the sea somewhat, but she clung to her place in the line for some minutes, then dropped out, and, in manifest difficulty, headed for the shore, which was close at hand to the south. Another division of four destroyers charged on her, but her great turrets were still intact, and received them with a murderous fire of 12-in. shrapnel.

Two of the six guns made hits and wrecked two boats past recognition; the other four missed the swiftly moving targets, and two boats survived the first discharge and closed, one to port, and one to starboard. Her smaller guns were out of action, or unable to stop the boats with their fire. Both boats discharged two torpedoes; three torpedoes missed, but the fourth struck the flagship under the fore-turret. She took in so much water that she grounded, east of Dunbar, and lay there submerged up to the level of her main deck, and unable to use her big guns lest the concussion should shake her in this position to pieces. The Germans detached the battleship *Preussen* to wreck her with its fire. With the rest of their fleet they followed the remaining British ships, which were now heading seawards. Admiral Parker had determined to make a vigorous effort to escape to the south-east along the British coast, and surviving, to fight again on a less disastrous day, with the odds more even. Nothing could be achieved with nine ships against eighteen, even though many of the eighteen were much damaged. Moreover, on board some of the British ships ammunition was beginning to run low.

The seventeen German ships formed into a single line and pursued the British, steering a parallel course, the head of the German line somewhat overlapping the head of the British line, so that the four German battleships of the "Sachsen" class could bring their entire fire to bear upon the three remaining "Dreadnoughts." The other fourteen German battleships pounded the six older and weaker British battleships in the line. The distance between the two fleets was from 4500 to 6000 yards, and the fire of each fleet was slow, as the want of ammunition was beginning to be felt. For nearly five hours the two fleets had fought; it was now 11.30 A.M. Well out to sea, and some distance to leeward of the German battleships, the British captains could discern several German armoured cruisers, which, after having effected hasty repairs and shipped further ammunition from a store-ship in the offing, were closing once more. With them were at least four or five divisions of torpedo craft, shadowing and following the movements of the two fleets, prepared to rush in if a favourable opportunity offered. Both fleets were making about thirteen knots, for the worst damaged of the British battleships were not good for much more.

The fire of the *Thunderer's* 12-in. guns, concentrated on the hull of the *Sachsen*, at last began to produce some effect. The conning-tower had already been wrecked by the *Vanguard's* guns, which rendered the control and direction of the ship a matter of great difficulty. Two of her 11-in. turrets were also out of action, jammed by shells or completely disabled. She turned northward out of the German line, about twelve, leaving the *Bayern* at its head. About the same time the *Albemarle* signalled that she was in extreme difficulty; a great fire was raging on board her, her funnels were much damaged, both her masts were down, two compartments were full, and but few of her guns could fire. Looking down the British line from the battered afterbridge of the *Thunderer*, it was evident that other ships were finding difficulty in keeping station. Strange changes and transformations had been worked in their outward appearance. Funnels and cowls were gone, masts had been levelled, heaps of wreckage appeared in place of the trim lines of the grey-painted steel-work. The sea was red with the blood that poured from the scuppers. Great rents gaped everywhere in the unarmoured works.

In the German line the conditions were much the same. Certain ships were dropping from their stations and receding to the rear of the long procession; many of the German battleships had been grievously mauled; all showed evident traces of the British gunners' handiwork. The huge steel superstructures of the "Deutschland" class were wrecked beyond recognition. The *Braunschweig*, as the result of receiving a concentrated broadside from the *Bellerophon*, which caught her near the foot of her foremast, had an immense opening in the hull extending from the fore-turret to the foremast 6.7-in. gun turret, and her fore-funnel and foremast were completely shot away; her conning-tower, with its armoured support, stood up out of the gap, from which poured volumes of smoke and steam. She was clearly in a parlous condition, and only her after-turret still fired.

About 1 P.M. the *Albemarle* could keep up with the British line no longer. Admiral Parker signalled to her, with extreme difficulty, for most of his signalling appliances were shot away, and his message had to be conveyed by "flag-wagging," to beach herself if possible on the coast to the south. To have turned with his fleet to protect her would have meant annihilation of the rest of his force. She stood away to the south, and as the rest of the British fleet, now only six ships strong, increased speed to about fifteen knots, two German battleships were seen to follow her, shell her, and then rejoin the German fleet. The remnant of the British fleet, with the *Agamemnon* at the rear in the place of honour, began slowly to draw out of range, though still to the north the German torpedo craft followed in a sinister manner, and caused the more anxiety because, in view of the large quantity of ammunition that had been expended, and the great damage that had been done to all the smaller guns in the surviving British ships, their attacks would be extremely difficult to resist with success.

About 2 P.M. the German Admiral fired the last shot of the great battle of North Berwick at a range of 10,000 yards.

VIII

Situation in the North

Meanwhile let us turn to the state of affairs on land. When the intelligence of the invasion was received, Lancashire and Yorkshire were in a state of utter panic.

The first news, which reached Leeds, Bradford, Manchester, Liverpool, and the other great centres of commerce, about four o'clock on Sunday afternoon, was at once discredited.

Everyone declared the story to be a huge hoax. As the people assembled in the places of worship that evening, the amazing rumour was eagerly discussed; and later on, when the Sunday evening crowds promenaded the principal thoroughfares—Briggate in Leeds, Market Street in Manchester, Corporation Street in Birmingham, Cheapside in Barnsley, and the principal streets of Chester, Liverpool, Halifax, Huddersfield, Rochdale, Bolton, and Wigan—wild reports of the dash upon our east coast were upon everyone's tongue.

There was, however, no authentic news, and the newspapers in the various towns all hesitated to issue special editions—first because it was Sunday night, and secondly because the editors had no desire to spread a wider panic than that already created.

Upon the windows of the *Yorkshire Post* office in Leeds some of the telegrams were posted and read by large crowds, while the *Manchester Courier*, in Manchester, and the *Birmingham Daily Post*, in Birmingham, followed a similar example.

The telegrams were brief and conflicting, some from the London correspondents, and others from the Central News, the Press Association, and the Exchange Telegraph Company. Most of the news, however, in that early stage of the alarm was culled from the exclusive information obtained by the enterprise of the sub-editor of the *Weekly Dispatch*.

Leeds, the first city in Yorkshire, was the centre of most intense excitement on that hot, stifling Sunday night. The startling report spread like wildfire, first from the office of the *Yorkshire Post* among the crowds that were idling away their Sunday evening gossiping in Boar Lane, Briggate, and the Hunslett Road, and quickly the whole city from Burton Head to Chapel Town, and from Burmantofts to Armley Park, was in a ferment.

The sun sank with a misty, angry afterglow precursory of rain, and by the time the big clock in the tower of the Royal Exchange showed half-past seven the scene in the main streets was already an animated one. The whole city was agog. The astounding news, carried everywhere by eager, breathless people, had reached to even the remotest suburbs, and thousands of alarmed mill-hands and workers came flocking into town to ascertain the actual truth.

As at Leeds, so all through Lancashire and Yorkshire, Volunteers were assembling in breathless eagerness for the order to mobilise. But there was the same cry of unpreparedness everywhere. The Volunteer battalions of the Manchester Regiment at Patricroft, at Hulme, at Ashton-under-Lyne, at Manchester, and at Oldham; those of the Liverpool Regiment at Prince's Park, at St. Anne's, at Shaw Street, at Everton Brow, at Everton Road, and at Southport; those of the Lancashire Fusiliers at Bury, Rochdale, and Salford; the Hallamshire Volunteers at Sheffield; the York and Lancasters at Doncaster; the King's Own Light Infantry at Wakefield; the battalions of the Yorkshires at Northallerton and Scarborough, that of the East Yorkshires at Beverley, and those of the West Yorkshires at York and Bradford.

In Halifax great crowds assembled around the office of the *Yorkshire Daily Observer*, at the top of Russell Street, where the news received by telephone from Bradford was being constantly posted up. Huddersfield, with its cloth and woollen factories, was paralysed by the astounding intelligence. The electric trams brought in crowds from Cliff End, Oakes Fartown, Mold Green, and Lockwood, while telephone messages from Dewsbury, Elland, Mirfield, Wyke, Cleckheaton, Overdon, Thornton, and the other towns in the vicinity all spoke of the alarm and excitement that had so suddenly spread over the West Riding.

The mills would shut down. That was prophesied by everyone. And, if so, then before many days wives and families would most certainly be crying for food. Masters and operatives alike recognised the extreme gravity of the situation, and quickly the panic spread to every home throughout that densely populated industrial area.

The city of Bradford was, as may well be imagined, in a state of ferment. In the red, dusky sunset a Union Jack was flying from the staff above Watson's shop at the corner of Market Street, and the excited throngs, seeing it, cheered lustily. Outside the *Bradford Daily Telegraph*

By the King.

Proclamation

For Calling Out
The Army Reserve.

Edward R.

Whereas by the Reserve Forces Act, 1882, it is amongst other things enacted that in case of imminent national danger or of great emergency, it shall be lawful for Us, by Proclamation, the occasion being declared in Council and notified by the Proclamation, if Parliament be not then sitting, to order that the Army Reserve shall be called out on permanent service; and by any such Proclamation to order a Secretary of State from time to time to give, and when given, to revoke or vary such directions as may seem necessary or proper for calling out the forces or force mentioned in the Proclamation, or all or any of the men belonging thereto:

And Whereas Parliament is not sitting, and whereas We have declared in Council and hereby notify the present state of Public Affairs and the extent of the demands on our Military Forces for the protection of the interests of the Empire constitute a case of great emergency within the meaning of the said Act:

Now Therefore We do in pursuance of the said Act hereby order that Our Army Reserve be called out on permanent service, and We do hereby order the Right Honourable Charles Leonard Spencer Cotterell, one of our Principal Secretaries of State, from time to time to give, and when given, to revoke or vary such directions as may seem necessary or proper for calling out Our Army Reserve, or all or any of the men belonging thereto, and such men shall proceed to and attend at such places and at such times as may be respectively appointed by him to serve as part of Our Army until their services are no longer required.

Given at our Court at James', this fourth day of September, in the year of our Lord, one thousand nine hundred and ten, and in the tenth year of Our Reign.

GOD SAVE THE KING.

and the *Yorkshire Daily Observer* offices the latest intelligence was posted, the streets being blocked by the eager people who had come in by car from Manningham, Heaton, Tyersall, Dudley Hill, Eccleshill, Idle, Thackley, and other places.

Bolton, like the neighbouring towns, was ruled by Manchester, and the masters eagerly went there on Monday to go on 'Change and ascertain the exact situation. They knew, alas! that the alarm must have a disastrous effect upon the cotton trade, and more than one spinner when the astounding news had been told him on the previous night, knew well that he could not possibly meet his engagements, and that only bankruptcy was before him.

In every home, rich and poor, not only in Bolton but out at Farnworth, Kearsley, Over Hulton, Sharples, and Heaton the terrible catastrophe was viewed with abject terror. The mills would eventually close, without a doubt; if Manchester sent forth its mandate, then for the thousands of toilers it meant absolute starvation.

Those not at work assembled in groups in the vicinity of the Town Hall, and in Cheapside, Moor Street, Newport Street, Bridge Street, and the various central thoroughfares, eagerly discussing the situation, while outside Messrs. Tillotson's, the *Evening News* office in Mealhouse Lane, the latest telegrams from London and Manchester were posted, being read by a great crowd, which entirely blocked the thoroughfare. The *Evening News*, with characteristic smartness, was being published hourly, and copies were sold as fast as the great presses could print them, while a special meeting of the Town Council was summoned and met at twelve o'clock to discuss what steps should be taken in case the mills really did close and the great populace were thrown on the town in anger and idleness.

The cotton trade was already feeling the effect of the sudden crisis, for by noon startling reports were reaching Bolton from Manchester of unprecedented scenes on 'Change and of the utter collapse of business.

Most mill-owners were already in Manchester. All who were near enough at once took train—from Southport, Blackpool, Morecambe, and other places—and went on 'Change to learn what was intended. Meanwhile, through the whole of Monday authentic reports of the enemy's movements in Norfolk, Suffolk, Essex, and East Yorkshire were being printed by the *Evening News*, each edition increasing the panic in that level-headed, hard-working Lancashire town.

Across at smoky Wigan similar alarm and unrest reigned. On that Monday morning, bright and sunny, everyone re-started work, hoping for the best. Pearson and Knowles' and the Pemberton Collieries were running full time; Ryland's mills and Ekersley's spinning mills were also full up with work, for there was an era of as great a prosperity in Wigan as in Bolton, Rochdale, Oldham, and other Lancashire towns. Never for the past ten years had the cotton and iron industries been so prosperous; yet in one single day—nay, in a few brief hours—the blow had fallen, and trade had become paralysed.

Spy mania was rife everywhere. In Oldham an innocent German, agent of a well-known firm in Chemnitz, while walking along Manchester Street about one o'clock, was detected as a foreigner and compelled to seek protection inside a shop. From Chadderton to Lees, from Royton to Hollinwood, the crisis was on everyone's lips. Here again was the crucial question: Would the mills close?

Meanwhile, across at Liverpool, the wildest scenes were also taking place on 'Change. News over the wires from London became hourly more alarming, and this, combined with the rumour that German warships were cruising off the Mersey estuary, created a perfect panic in the city. The port was already closed, for the mouth of the river had been blocked by mines; yet the report quickly got abroad that the Germans would send in merchant ships to explode them and enter the Mersey after thus clearing away the deadly obstacles.

Liverpool knew too well the ridiculously weak state of her defences, which had so long been a reproach to the authorities, and if the German ships that had done such damage at Penarth, Cardiff, and Barry were now cruising north, as reported, it seemed quite within the bounds of probability that a demonstration would really be made before Liverpool.

Outside and within the great Exchange the excitement was at fever heat. The Bank Charter was suspended, and the banks had closed with one accord. Upon the "flags" the cotton-brokers were shouting excitedly, and many a ruined man knew that that would be his last appearance there. Every moment over the telephones came news from Manchester, each record more disastrous than the last. Hot, perspiring men who had lived, and lived well, by speculation in cotton for years, surged around the great pediment adorned by its allegorical group of sculpture, and saw each moment their fortunes falling away like ice in the sunshine.

Thus trade in Lancashire—cotton, wool, iron, and corn—was, in the course of one single morning, utterly paralysed, all awaiting the decision of Manchester.

Thousands were already face to face with financial disaster, even in those first moments of the alarm.

The hours passed slowly. What was Manchester doing? Her decision was now awaited with bated breath throughout the whole of Lancashire and Yorkshire.

In Manchester, the *Courier*, the *Daily Mail*, and the several other journals kept publishing edition after edition, not only through the day, but also through the night. Presses were running unceasingly, and hour after hour were printed accounts of the calm and orderly way in which the enemy were completing their unopposed landing at Goole, Grimsby, Yarmouth, Lowestoft, King's Lynn, and on the Blackwater.

Some British destroyers had interfered with the German plans at the latter place, and two German warships had been sunk, the *Courier* reported. But full details were not yet forthcoming.

There had been a good deal of skirmishing in the neighbourhood of Maldon, and again near Harleston, on the Suffolk border. The town of Grimsby had been half destroyed by fire, and the damage at Hull had been enormous. From a timber-yard there the wind had, it seemed, carried the flames across to the Alexandra Dock, where some stores had ignited and a quantity of valuable shipping in the dock had been destroyed at their moorings. The Paragon station and hotel had also been burned—probably by people of Hull themselves, in order to drive the German commander from his headquarters.

From Newcastle, Gateshead, and Tynemouth came harrowing details of bombardment, and the frightful result of those awful petrol bombs. Fire and destruction had been spread broadcast everywhere.

On the Manchester Exchange on Tuesday there was no longer any reason to doubt the accuracy of Sunday's report, and the feeling on 'Change became "panicky." It seemed as though the whole of the ten thousand members had made up their minds to be present. The main entrance in Cross Street was blocked for the greater part of the afternoon, and late comers dodged round to the two entrances in Market Street, and the third in Bank Street, in the hope of squeezing through into the vibrating mass of humanity that filled the floors, the corridors, and the telephone, reading, and writing rooms. The attendants found they had an impossible task set them to make their way to the many lanterns around the vast hall, there to affix the latest messages, recording astounding fluctuations of prices, and now and again some news of the invasion. The master and secretary in the end told the attendants to give up the struggle, and he made his way with difficulty to the topmost balcony, where, above the murmurings of the crowd below, he read the latest bulletins of commercial and general intelligence as they arrived.

But there were no efforts made to do business; and had any of the members felt so inclined, the crush and stress were so great that any attempt to book orders would have ended in failure. In the swaying of the crowd hats were lost and trampled under foot; men whose appearance on 'Change had always been immaculate were to be seen with torn collars and disarranged neckwear. Never before had such a scene been witnessed. Lancashire men had often heard of such a state of things having occurred in the "pit" of the New York Exchange, when wild speculation in cotton was indulged in, but they prided themselves that they were never guilty of such conduct. No matter how the market jumped, they invariably kept their heads, and waited until it assumed its normal condition, and became settled. It had often been said that nothing short of an earthquake would unnerve the Manchester commercial man; those who were responsible for the statement had evidently not turned a thought to a German invasion. That had done it completely.

In the cafés and the hotels, where the master-spinners and the manufacturers had been wont to forgather after high 'Change, there were the usual gatherings, but there was little or no discussion on business matters, except this: there was a common agreement that it would, in present circumstances, be inadvisable to keep the mills running. Work must be, and it was, completely suspended. The shippers, who had the manufacturers under contract to supply certain quantities of goods for transportation to their markets in India, China, and the Colonies, trembled at the very contemplation of the financial losses they would inevitably sustain by the non-delivery of the bales of cloth to their customers abroad; but, on the other hand, they also paid heed to the great danger of the vessels in which the goods were placed falling into the hands of the enemy when at sea. The whole question was full of grim perplexities, and even the most impatient among the shippers and the merchants had to admit that a policy of do-nothing seemed the safest course of procedure.

The chaotic scenes on 'Change in the afternoon were reproduced in the streets in the evening, and the Lord Mayor, towards eight o'clock, fearful of rioting, sent special messengers to the headquarters of three Volunteer corps for assistance in regulating street traffic. The officers in command immediately responded to the call. The 2nd V.B.M.R. took charge of Piccadilly and Market Street; the 4th were stationed in Cross Street and Albert Square; and the 5th lined Deansgate from St. Mary's Gate to Peter Street. Mounted constabulary, by the exercise of tact and good temper, kept the crowds on the move, and towards midnight the pressure became so light that the officers felt perfectly justified in withdrawing the Volunteers, who spent that night at their respective headquarters.

It was Wednesday, however, before Manchester people could thoroughly realise that the distressing news was absolutely true, and on the top of the confirmation came the startling report that the Fleet had been crippled, and immense troops of Germans were landing at Hull, Lowestoft, Yarmouth, Goole, and other places on the east, with the object of sweeping the country.

IX

State of Siege Declared

The authentic account of a further landing in Essex—somewhere near Maldon—was now published. The statement had been dictated by Mr. Henry Alexander, J.P.,—the Mayor of Maldon, who had succeeded in escaping from the town,—to Captain Wilfred Quare, of the Intelligence Department of the War Office. This Department had, in turn, given it to the newspapers for publication.

It read as follows:—

"On Sunday morning, September 2, I had arranged to play a round of golf with my friend Somers, of Beeleigh, before church. I met him at the Golf Hut about 8.30. We played one round, and were at the last hole but three in a second round when we both thought we heard the sound of shots fired somewhere in the town. We couldn't make anything at all of it, and as we had so nearly finished the round, we thought we would do so before going up to inquire about it. I was making my approach to the final hole when an exclamation from Somers spoilt my stroke. I felt annoyed, but as I looked round—doubtless somewhat irritably—my eyes turned in the direction in which I now saw my friend was pointing with every expression of astonishment in his countenance.

"'Who on earth are those fellows?' he asked. As for me, I was too dumbfounded to reply. Galloping over the links from the direction of the town came three men in uniform—soldiers, evidently. I had often been in Germany, and recognised the squat pickel-haubes and general get-up of the rapidly approaching horsemen at a glance.

"'I didn't know the Yeomanry were out!' was what my friend said.

"'Yeomanry be hanged! They're Germans, or I'm a Dutchman!' I answered; 'and what the dickens can they be doing here?'

"They were upon us almost as I spoke, pulling up their horses with a great spattering up of grass and mud, quite ruining one of our best greens. All three of them pointed big, ugly repeating pistols at us, and the leader, a conceited-looking ass in staff uniform, required us to 'surrender' in quite a pompous manner, but in very good English.

"'Do we look so very dangerous, Herr Lieutenant?' inquired I in German.

"He dropped a little of his frills when he heard me speak in his native language, asked which of us was the Mayor, and condescended to explain that I was required in Maldon by the officer at present in command of His Imperial Majesty the Kaiser's forces occupying that place.

"I was absolutely staggered.

"When I left my house a couple of hours back I had just as much expectation of finding the Chinese there on my return as the Germans. I looked at my captor in complete bewilderment. Could he be some fellow trying to take a rise out of me by masquerading as a German officer? But no, I recognised at once that he was the genuine article. Everything about him, from the badly-cut riding-boots to the sprouting moustache curled up in feeble imitation of the Emperor's characteristic adornment, bore witness to his identity. If anything were wanting, it was supplied by his aggressive manner.

"I suggested that he might point his pistol some other way. I added that if he wanted to try his skill as marksman it would be more sporting to aim at the flag at the Long Hole near Beeleigh Lock.

"He took my banter in good part, but demanded my parole, which I made no difficulty about giving, since I did not see any way of escape, and in any case was only too anxious to get back to town to see how things were.

"'But you don't want my friend, do you—he lives out the other way?' I queried.

"'I don't want him, but he will have to come all the same,' rejoined the German. 'It isn't likely we're going to let him get away to give the alarm in Colchester, is it?'

"Obviously it was not, and without more ado we started off at a sharp walk, holding on to the stirrup leathers of the horsemen.

"As we entered the town there was, on the bridge over the river, a small picket of blue-coated German infantry. The whole thing was a perfect nightmare. It was past belief.

"'How on earth did you get here?' I couldn't help asking. 'Did you come down from town in an excursion train or by balloon?'

"My German officer laughed.

"'By water,' he answered shortly, pointing down the river as he spoke, where I was still further astonished—if it were possible after such a morning—to see several steam pinnaces and boats flying the black and white German ensign.

"I was conducted straight to the Moot Hall. He already knew his way about, this German, it seemed. There I found a grizzled veteran waiting on the steps, who turned round and entered the building as we came up. We followed him inside, and I was introduced to him. He appeared to be a truculent old ruffian.

"'Well, Mr. Mayor,' he said, pulling viciously at his white moustache, 'do you know that I've a great mind to take you out into the street and have you shot?'

"I was not at all inclined to be browbeaten.

"'Indeed, Herr Hauptman?' I answered. 'And may I inquire in what way I have incurred the displeasure of the Hochwohlgeboren officer?'

"'Don't trifle with me, sir. Why do you allow your miserable Volunteers to come out and shoot my men?'

"'My Volunteers? I am afraid I don't understand what you mean,' I said. 'I'm not a Volunteer officer. Even if I were, I should have no cognisance of anything that has happened within the last two hours, as I have been down on the golf course. This officer will bear me out,' I added, turning to my captor. He admitted that he had found me there.

"'But, anyway, you are the Mayor,' persisted my interrogator. 'Why did you allow the Volunteers to come out?'

"'If you had been good enough to inform us of your visit, we might have made better arrangements,' I answered, 'but in any case you must understand that a mayor has little or no authority in this country. His job is to head subscription-lists, eat a dinner or two, and make speeches on public occasions.'

"He seemed to have some difficulty in swallowing this, but as another officer who was there, writing at a table, and who, it appears, had lived at some period in England, corroborated my statement, the choleric colonel seemed to be a little mollified, and contented himself with demanding my parole not to leave Maldon until he had reported the matter to the General for decision. I gave it without more ado, and then asked if he would be good enough to tell me what had happened. From what he told me, and what I heard afterwards, it seems that the Germans must have landed a few of their men about half an hour before I left home, down near the Marine Lake. They had not entered the town at once, as their object was to work round outside and occupy all the entrances, to prevent anyone getting away with the news of their presence. They had not noticed the little lane leading to the golf course, and so I had gone down without meeting any of them, although they had actually got a picket just beyond the railway arch at that time. They had completed their cordon before there was any general alarm in the town, but at the first reliable rumour it seems that young Shand, of the Essex Volunteers, had contrived to get together twenty or thirty of his men in their uniforms and foolishly opened fire on a German picket down by St. Mary's Church. They fell back, but were almost instantly reinforced by a whole company that had just landed, and our men, rushing forward, had been ridden into by some cavalry that came up a side street. They were dispersed, a couple of them were killed and several wounded, among them poor Shand, who was hit in the right lung. They had bagged four Germans, however, and their commanding officer was furious. It was a pity that it happened, as it could not possibly have been of any use. But it seems that Shand had no idea that it was more than a very small detachment that had landed from a gunboat that someone said they had seen down the river. Some of the Volunteers were captured afterwards and sent off as prisoners, and the Germans posted up a notice that all Volunteers were forthwith to surrender either themselves or their arms and uniforms, under pain of death. Most of them did the latter. They could do nothing after it was found that the Germans had a perfect army somewhere between Maldon and the sea, and were pouring troops into the town as fast as they could.

"That very morning a Saxon rifle battalion arrived from the direction of Mundon, and just afterwards a lot of spike-helmeted gentlemen came in by train from Wickford way. So it went on all day, until the whole town was in a perfect uproar. Another rifle battalion, then some sky-blue hussars and some artillery, then three more battalions of a regiment called the 101st Grenadiers, I believe. The infantry were billeted in the town, but the cavalry and guns crossed the river and canal at Heybridge, and went off in the direction of Witham. Later on, another infantry regiment came in by train and marched out after them.

"Maldon is built on a hill that slopes gradually towards the east and south, but rises somewhat abruptly on the west and north, humping up a shoulder, as it were, to the north-west. At this corner they started to dig entrenchments just after one o'clock, and soon officers and orderlies were busy all round the town, plotting, measuring, and setting up marks of one kind and another. Other troops appeared to be busy down in Heybridge, but what they were doing I could not tell, as no one was allowed to cross the bridge over the river.

"The German officer who had surprised me down on the golf course did not turn out to be a bad kind of youth on further acquaintance. He was a Captain von Hildebrandt, of the Guard Fusilier Regiment, who was employed on the Staff, though in what capacity he did not say. Thinking it was just as well to make the best of a bad job, I invited him to lunch. He said he had to be off. He, however, introduced me to three friends of his in the 101st Grenadiers, who, he suggested, should be billeted on me. I thought the idea a fairly good one, and Von Hildebrandt, having apparently arranged this with the billeting officer without any difficulty, I took them home with me to lunch.

"I found my wife and family in a great state of mind, both on account of the untoward happenings of the morning and my non-return from golf at the expected time. They had imagined all sorts of things which might have befallen me, but luckily seemed not to have heard of my adventure with the choleric colonel. Our three foreigners soon made themselves very much at home, but as they were undeniably gentlemen, they contrived to be about as agreeable as could be expected under the circumstances. Indeed, their presence was to a great extent a safeguard against annoyance, as the stable and back premises were stuffed full of soldiers, who might have been very troublesome had they not been there to keep them in order.

"Of what was happening up in London we knew nothing. Being Sunday, all the shops were shut; but I went out and contrived to lay in a considerable stock of provisions one way and another, and it was just as well I did, for I only just anticipated the Germans, who commandeered everything in the town and put everybody on an allowance of rations. They paid for them with bills on the British Government, which were by no means acceptable to the shopkeepers. However, it was 'Hobson's choice'—that or nothing. The Germans soothed them by saying that the British Army would be smashed in a couple of weeks, and the defrayment of such bills would be among the conditions of peace. The troops generally seemed to be well-behaved, and treated those inhabitants with whom they came in contact in an unexceptionable manner. They did not see very much of them, however, as they were kept hard at work all day with their entrenchments and were not allowed out of their billets after eight o'clock that evening. No one, in fact, was allowed to be about the streets after that hour.

On the other hand, a couple of poor young fellows in the Volunteers who had concealed their connection with the force and were trying to slip out of the town with their rifles after dark, were caught, and the next morning stood up against the three-cornered tower of All Saints' Church and shot without mercy. Two or three other people were shot by the sentries as they tried to break out in one direction or the other. These affairs produced a feeling of horror and indignation in the town, as Englishmen, having such a long experience of peace in their own country, have always refused to realise what war really means.

"The German fortifications went on at a rapid rate. Trenches were dug all round the northern and western sides of the town before dark on the first evening, and the following morning I woke up to find three huge gun-pits yawning in my garden, which looked to the northward. One was right in the middle of the lawn—or rather of where the lawn had been, for all the grass that had not been displaced in the digging had been cut up in sods to build up the insides of their parapets. During breakfast there was a great rattling and rumbling in the street without, and presently three big field howitzers were dragged in and planted in the pits. There they stood, their ugly snouts pointing skyward in the midst of the wreck of flowers and fruit.

"Afterwards I went out and found that other guns and howitzers were being put in position all along the north side of Beeleigh Road, and round the corner by the Old Barracks. The high tower of the disused Church of St. Peter's, now utilised for the safe custody of Dr. Plume's library, had been equipped as a lookout and signal station."

Such was the condition of affairs in the town of Maldon on Monday morning.

The excitement in London, and indeed all over the country, on Tuesday night was intense. Scotney's story of the landing at Weybourne was eagerly read everywhere.

As the sun sank blood-red into the smoke haze behind Nelson's Monument in Trafalgar Square, it was an ominous sign to the panic-stricken crowds that day and night were now assembled there.

The bronze lions facing the four points of the compass were now mere mocking emblems of England's departed greatness. The mobilisation muddle was known; for, according to the papers, hardly any troops had, as yet, assembled at their places of concentration. The whole of the East of England was helplessly in the invader's hands.

From Newcastle had come terrible reports of the bombardment. Half the city was in flames, the Elswick works were held by the enemy, and whole streets in Newcastle, Gateshead, Sunderland, and Tynemouth were still burning fiercely.

The Tynemouth fort had proved of little or no use against the enemy's guns. The Germans had, it appeared, used petrol bombs with appalling results, spreading fire, disaster, and death everywhere. The inhabitants, compelled to fly with only the clothes they wore, had scattered all over Northumberland and Durham, while the enemy had seized a quantity of valuable shipping that had been in the Tyne, hoisted the German flag, and converted the vessels to their own uses.

Many had already been sent across to Wilhelmshaven, Emden, Bremerhaven, and other places to act as transports, while the Elswick works—which surely ought to have been properly protected—supplied the Germans with quantities of valuable material.

Panic and confusion were everywhere. All over the country the railway system was utterly disorganised, business everywhere was at a complete deadlock, for in every town and city all over the kingdom the banks were closed.

Lombard Street, Lothbury, and other banking centres in the City had all day on Monday been the scene of absolute panic. There, as well as at every branch bank all over the metropolis, had occurred a wild rush to withdraw deposits by people who foresaw disaster. Many, indeed, intended to fly with their families away from the country.

The price of the necessities of life had risen further, and in the East End and poorer districts of Southwark the whole population were already in a state of semi-starvation. But worst of all, the awful truth with which London was now face to face was that the metropolis was absolutely defenceless.

Would not some effort be made to repel the invaders? Surely if we had lost our command of the sea the War Office could, by some means, assemble sufficient men to at least protect London? This was the cry of the wild, turbulent crowd surging through the City and West End, as the blood-red sun sank into the west, flooding London in its warm afterglow—a light in the sky that was prophetic of red ruin and of death to those wildly excited millions.

Every hour the papers were appearing with fresh details of the invasion, for reports were so rapidly coming in from every hand that the Press had difficulty in dealing with them.

FACSIMILE OF A PROCLAMATION POSTED BY
UNKNOWN HANDS ALL OVER THE COUNTRY.

Hull and Goole were known to be in the hands of the invaders, and Grimsby, where the Mayor had been unable to pay the indemnity demanded, had been sacked. But details were not yet forthcoming.

Londoners, however, learnt late that night more authentic news from the invaded zone, of which Beccles was the centre, and it was to the effect that those who had landed at Lowestoft were the IXth German Army Corps, with General von Kronhelm, the Generalissimo of the German Army. This Army Corps, consisting of about 40,000 men, was divided into the 17th Division, commanded by Lieutenant-General Hocker, and the 18th by Lieutenant-General von Rauch. The cavalry was under the command of Major-General von Heyden, and the motor infantry under Colonel Reichardt.

According to official information which had reached the War Office and been given to the Press, the 17th Division was made up of the Bremen and Hamburg Infantry Regiments, the Grand Duke of Mecklenburg's Grenadiers, the Grand Duke's Fusiliers, the Lübeck Regiment No. 162, the Schleswig-Holstein Regiment No. 163, while the cavalry brigade consisted of the 17th and 18th Grand Duke of Mecklenburg's Dragoons.

The 18th Division consisted of the Schleswig Regiment No. 84, and the Schleswig Fusiliers No. 86, the Thuringen Regiment, and the Duke of Holstein's Regiment, the two latter regiments being billeted in Lowestoft, while the cavalry brigade forming the screen across from Leiston by Wilby to Castle Hill were Queen Wilhelmina's Hanover Hussars and the Emperor of Austria's Schleswig-Holstein Hussars No. 16. These, with the smart motor infantry, held every communication in the direction of London.

As far as could be gathered, the German commander had established his headquarters in Beccles, and had not moved. It now became apparent that the telegraph cables between the East Coast and Holland and Germany, already described in the first chapter, had never been cut at all. They had simply been held by the enemy's advance agents until the landing had been effected. And now Von Kronhelm had actually established direct communication between Beccles and Emden, and on to Berlin.

Reports from the North Sea spoke of the enemy's transports returning to the German coast, escorted by cruisers; therefore the plan was undoubtedly not to move until a very much larger force had been landed.

Could England regain her command of the sea in time to prevent the completion of the blow?

The *Eastminster Gazette*, and similar papers of the Blue Water School, assured the public that there was but very little danger. Germany had made a false move, and would, in the course of a few days, be made to pay very dearly for it.

But the British public viewed the situation for itself. It was tired of these self-satisfied reassurances, and threw the blame upon the political party who had so often said that armed hostilities had been abolished in the twentieth century. Recollecting the Czar's proposals for universal peace, and the Russo-Japanese sequel, they had no further faith in the pro-German party or in its organs. It was they, cried the orators in the streets, that had prevented the critics having a hearing; they who were culpably responsible for the inefficient state of our defences; they who had ridiculed clever men, the soldiers, sailors, and writers who had dared to tell the plain, honest, but unpalatable truth.

We were at war, and if we were not careful the war would spell ruin for our dear old England.

That night the London streets presented a scene of panic indescribable. The theatres opened, but closed their doors again, as nobody would see plays while in that excited state. Every shop was closed, and every railway station was filled to overflowing with the exodus of terrified people fleeing to the country westward, or reserves on their way to join the colours.

The incredulous manner in which the country first received the news had now been succeeded by wild terror and despair. On that bright Sunday afternoon they laughed at the report as a mere journalistic sensation, but ere the sun set the hard, terrible truth was forced upon them, and now, on Tuesday night, the whole country, from Brighton to Carlisle, from Yarmouth to Aberystwyth, was utterly disorganised and in a state of terrified anxiety.

The Eastern counties were already beneath the iron heel of the invader, whose objective was the world's great capital—London.

Would they reach it? That was the serious question upon everyone's tongue that fevered, breathless night.

X

How the Enemy Dealt the Blow

The morning of Wednesday, September 5, dawned brightly, with warm sun and cloudless sky, a perfect day of English early autumn, yet over the land was a gloom and depression—the silence of a great terror. The fate of the greatest nation the world had ever known was now trembling in the balance.

When the first flush of dawn showed, the public clamoured for information as to what the War Office were doing to repel the audacious Teutons. Was London to be left at their mercy without a shot being fired? Was the whole of our military machinery a mere gold-braided farce?

Londoners expected that, ere this, British troops would have faced the foe, and displayed that dogged courage and grand heroism that had kept their reputation through centuries as the best soldiers in the world.

The Press, too, were loud in their demands that something should at once be done, but the authorities still remained silent, although they were in ceaseless activity.

They were making the best they could out of the mobilisation muddle.

So suddenly had the blow been struck that no preparation had been made for it. Although the printed forms and broadsides were, of course, in their dusty pigeon-holes ready to be filled up, yet where were the men? Many had read the proclamation which called them up for duty with their own corps, and in numberless cases, with commendable alacrity, they set out on a long and tiresome journey to join their respective units, which were stationed, as is the case in peace-time, all over the country.

A sturdy Scot, working in Whitechapel, was endeavouring to work his way up to Edinburgh; a broad-speaking Lancastrian from Oldham was struggling to get to his regiment down at Plymouth; while an easygoing Irishman, who had conducted an omnibus in London, gaily left for the Curragh, were a few examples of the hopeless confusion now in progress.

With the disorganised train and postal services, and with the railway line cut in various places by the enemy, how was it possible for these men to carry out the orders they received?

Meanwhile, the greatest activity was in progress in the regimental depôts in the Eastern counties, Norwich, Bury St. Edmunds, Bedford, Warley, Northampton, and Mill Hill. In London, at Wellington Barracks, Chelsea Barracks, and the Tower of London, were witnessed many stirring scenes. Veterans were rejoining, greeting their old comrades—many of whom had now become non-commissioned officers since they themselves left the ranks—while excited crowds pressed round the barrack squares, wildly cheering, and singing "God save the King."

There was bustle and movement on every hand, for the sight of English uniforms aroused the patriotic enthusiasm of the mob, who, having never been trained to arms themselves, now realised their own incompetency to defend their homes and loved ones.

Farther afield in the Home counties, the Regimental depôts at Guildford, Canterbury, Hounslow, Kingston, Chichester, and Maidstone were filling up quickly with surplus infantry, reservists, and non-efficients of all descriptions. At Guildford the Royal West Surrey Regiment were at Stoughton; at Canterbury were the old "Buffs"; at Hounslow the Royal Fusiliers; at Kingston the East Surrey Regiment; at Chichester the Royal Sussex, and at Maidstone the Royal West Kent.

Cavalry were assembling at the riding establishments, while veteran gunners and Army Service Corps men were making the best of their way by steamer, rail, and road to Woolwich.

Horses for both cavalry and artillery were urgently required, but owing to the substitution of the motor-omnibus for the horse-drawn vehicle in the London streets, there was no longer that supply of animals which held us in such good stead during the South African War.

At the depôts feverish excitement prevailed, now that every man was ordered on active service. All officers and men who had been on leave were recalled, and medical inspection of all ranks at once commenced. Rations and bedding, stores and equipment were drawn, but there was a great lack of uniforms. Unlike the German Army, where every soldier's equipment is complete even to the last button on the proverbial gaiter, and stowed away where the owner knows where to obtain it, our officers commanding depôts commenced indenting for clothing on the Royal Army Clothing Department, and the Army Corps Clothing Department.

A large percentage of men were, of course, found medically unfit to serve, and were discharged to swell the mobs of hungry idlers. The plain clothes of the reservists coming in were disposed of, no man daring to appear in the ranks unless in uniform, Von Kronhelm's proclamation having forbidden the tactics of the Boers of putting mere armed citizens into the field.

Horse-collecting parties went out all over the country, taking with them head-collars, head-ropes, bits, reins, surcingles, numnahs, horse-blankets, and nose-bags. These scoured every county in search of likely animals. Every farm, every livery stable, every hunting-box, all hound-kennels, and private stables were visited, and a choice made. All this, however, took time. Precious hours were thus being wasted while the enemy were calmly completing their arrangements for the long-contemplated blow at the heart of the British Empire.

While the War Office refused any information, special editions of the papers during Wednesday printed sensational reports of the ruthless completion of the impenetrable screen covering the operations of the enemy on the whole of the East Coast.

News had, by some means, filtered through from Yarmouth that a similar landing to those at Lowestoft and Weybourne had been effected. Protected as such an operation was, by its flanks being supported by the IVth and IXth Army Corps landing on either side, the Xth Army Corps under General von Wilburg had seized Yarmouth, with its many miles of wharves and docks, which were now crowded by the lighters' craft of flotilla from the Frisian Islands.

It was known that the landing had been effected simultaneously with that at Lowestoft. The large number of cranes at the fish-docks were of invaluable use to the enemy, for there they landed guns, animals, and stores, while the provisions they found at the various ship's chandlers, and in such shops as Blagg's and the International Stores in King Street, Peter Brown's, Doughty's, Lipton's, Penny's, and Barnes's, were at once commandeered. Great stores of flour were seized in Clarke's and Press's mills, while the horse-provender mills in the vicinity supplied them with valuable forage.

The hotels in the Market Place—the Bull, the Angel, the Cambridge, and Foulsham's—were full of men billeted, while officers occupied the Star, the Crown and Anchor, and Cromwell House, as well as the Queen's opposite the Britannia Pier, and the many boarding-houses along Marine Parade. And over all the effigy of Nelson looked down in silent contemplation!

Many men, it appeared, had also been landed at the red-brick little port of Gorleston, the Cliff and Pier Hotels being also occupied by officers remaining there to superintend the landing on that side of the Yare estuary.

Beyond these few details, as far as regarded the fate of Yarmouth nothing further was at present known.

The British division at Colchester, which comprised all the regular troops north of the Thames in the eastern command, was, no doubt, in a critical position, threatened so closely north and south by the enemy. None of the regiments, the Norfolks, the Leicestershire, and the King's Own Scottish Borderers of the 11th Infantry Brigade, were up to their strength. The 12th Infantry Brigade, which also belonged to the division, possessed only skeleton regiments stationed at Hounslow and Warley. Of the 4th Cavalry Brigade, some were at Norwich, the 21st Lancers were at Hounslow, while only the 16th Lancers were at Colchester. Other cavalry regiments were as far away as Canterbury, Shorncliffe, and Brighton, and although there were three batteries of artillery at Colchester, some were at Ipswich, others at Shorncliffe, and others at Woolwich.

Therefore it was quite evident to the authorities in London that unless both Colchester and Norwich were instantly strongly supported, they would soon be simply swept out of existence by the enormous masses of German troops now dominating the whole eastern coast, bent upon occupying London.

Helpless though they felt themselves to be, the garrison at Colchester did all they could. All available cavalry had been pushed out past Ipswich, north to Wickham Market, Stowmarket, and across to Bury St. Edmunds, only to find on Wednesday morning that they were covering the hasty retreat of the small body of cavalry who had been stationed at Norwich. They, gallantly led by their officers, had done everything possible to reconnoitre and attempt to pierce the enemy's huge cavalry screen, but in every instance entirely in vain. They had been outnumbered by the squadrons of independent cavalry operating in front of the Germans, and had, alas! left numbers of their gallant comrades upon the roads, killed and wounded.

Norwich had, therefore, on Wednesday morning, fallen into the hands of the German cavalry, utterly defenceless. Reports of the retiring troopers told a grim story of how the grand old city had fallen. From the Castle the German flag was now flying, the Britannia Barracks were being used by the enemy, food had all been seized, the streets were in a state of chaos, and a complete reign of terror had been created

CITY OF NORWICH.

CITIZENS—

AS IS WELL KNOWN, a hostile army has landed upon the coast of Norfolk, and has already occupied Yarmouth and Lowestoft, establishing their headquarters at Beccles.

IN THESE GRAVE CIRCUMSTANCES our only thought is for England, and our duty as citizens and officials is to remain at our post and bear our part in the defence of Norwich, our capital now threatened.

YOUR PATRIOTISM, of which you have on so many occasions in recent wars given proof, will, I have no doubt, again be shown. By your resistance you will obtain the honour and respect of your enemies, and by the individual energy of each one of you the honour and glory of England may be saved.

CITIZENS OF NORWICH, I appeal to you to view the catastrophe calmly, and bear your part bravely in the coming struggle.

CHARLES CARRINGTON,
Mayor.

NORWICH, *September 4, 1910.*

APPEAL ISSUED BY THE MAYOR OF NORWICH.

when a company of British infantry, having fired at some Uhlans, were ruthlessly shot down in the street close by the Maid's Head Hotel.

An attempt at a barricade had been erected at the top of Prince of Wales's Road, but the enemy, who came down the Aylsham Road, had soon cleared it. Many motor cars were seized from Howe's garage, and the Norfolk Imperial Yeomanry, who were assembled at their headquarters in Tombland, were quickly discovered, disarmed, and dispersed. Green

& Wright's wholesale provision stores in Upper King Street, as well as Chandler's in Prince of Wales's Road, Wood's in London Street, and many other grocers and provision-dealers were seized, the telegraph lines at the post-office were taken over by Germans, while, by reason of a shot fired from a window upon a German soldier who was passing, the whole block of buildings from the *East Anglia Daily Press* office, with Singer's and the railway receiving office, was deliberately set on fire, and produced an alarming state of things.

In addition to this, the Mayor of Norwich was taken prisoner, lodged in the Castle, and held as surety for the well-behaviour of the town.

Everywhere Von Kronhelm's famous proclamation was posted, and as the invaders poured into the city the inhabitants looked on in sullen silence, knowing that they were now under German military discipline, the most rigorous and drastic in the whole world.

The nation had, unfortunately, passed by unheeded the serious warnings of 1905–6. The authorities had remained impotent, and Mr. Haldane's Army Scheme had proved useless. The War Office had only one power within it, that of the man who represented the Cabinet. The rest were mere instruments.

There were many reports of sharp brushes between our cavalry vedettes and those of the enemy. The latter belonged to the corps who had established their headquarters in Maldon, and among those killed was an officer named Von Pabst, who was a prisoner, and who was shot while escaping, and in whose pocket was found a letter addressed to a friend, a certain Captain Neuhaus, of Lothringen Pioneer Battalion, stationed at Darmstadt.

It was interesting, for it threw some light upon the manner that particular corps of the invaders had embarked at Antwerp, and had apparently been hurriedly written in the intervals of the writer's duties with Prince Henry of Würtemburg's staff. Having been secured, it was sent to London, and was as follows:—

MALDON, ENGLAND,
Wednesday, September 5.

MY DEAR NEUHAUS,

Behold me, here at last in the 'tight little island,' by the English so greatly boasted! So far, we have had absolutely our own way, and have hardly seen an enemy. But you will be glad to have some account of my experience in this never-to-be-forgotten expedition. I was, of course, overjoyed to find myself appointed to the staff of His Highness Prince Henry of Würtemburg, and having obtained leave to quit my garrison, started for Treves without a moment's delay. Our troops were to enter Belgium ostensibly to quell the riots in Brussels. But the line was so continually blocked by troop-trains going west, that on arrival I found that he had gone with his army corps to Antwerp. There at last I was able to report myself—only just in time. My train got in at noon, and we sailed the same night.

"Antwerp might have been a German city. It was simply crammed with our troops. The Parc, the Pépinière, the Jardin Zoologique, the Parc du Palais de l'Industrie, the Boulevards, and every open space, was utilised as a bivouac. Prince Henry had his quarters in a very nice house on the Place Vert, opposite the Cathedral, and in the Place itself were picketed the horses belonging to the squadron of Jäegers zu Pferde, attached to the XIIth Corps. I rode round with the Prince in the afternoon, and saw the various regiments in the bivouacs, and the green-coated artillery, and the train in their sky-blue tunics hard at work all along the quays, getting their guns and waggons on board. The larger steamers lay two and three moored abreast alongside the quays, and astern of each a dozen flats or barges in two lots of six, each lashed together with a planked gangway leading to the outer ones. More barges, and the Rhine and other river steamers, and tugs to tow the lighters, lay outside in midstream. How all this had been arranged in the short time that had elapsed is more than I can imagine. Of course, our people had taken good care that no news should reach England by any of the many telegraph routes; the arrangements for that were most elaborate. There was no appearance of enthusiasm among the men. The gunners were too busy, and the infantry and cavalry destined for the expedition were not allowed to leave their bivouacs, and did not know that they were in for a sea voyage. The Belgian troops have all been disarmed and encamped on the other side of the river, between the older fortifications known as the Tête de Flandre and the outer lines. The populace for the most part have a sulky appearance, but as there is a very large German colony we found plenty of friends. The Burgomaster himself is a Bavarian, and most of the Councillors are also Germans, so that in the evening Prince Henry and his staff were entertained right royally at the Hôtel de Ville. I assure you, my friend, that I did justice to the civic hospitality. But the banquet was all too short.

"At eight o'clock we had to be on board. The steamer told off for us was the *Dresden*, which, with many other British vessels, had been commandeered that day. She lay alongside the pontoon, near the Steen Museum. As soon as she cast off, a gun was fired from the Citadel, followed by three rockets, which shot up into the darkness from the Tête de Flandre. This was the signal for the flotilla to start, and in succession one steamer after another slid out into the stream from the shadows of the quays, and, followed by her train of tugs and barges, began to glide down the Scheldt. Our arrangements had been perfected, and everything went without a hitch.

"The *Dresden* went dead slow along under the farther bank for a time, and we watched the head of the procession of transports pass down the river. It was an inspiring sight to see the densely-packed steamers and barges carrying their thousands of stout German hearts on their way to humble the pride of overbearing and threatening Albion. It brought to mind the highly prophetic utterance of our Emperor: 'Our Future lies on the Water.' The whole flotilla was off Flushing shortly before midnight, and after forming in four parallel columns, stood away to the north-west. It was a quiet night, not very dark, and the surface of the water, a shining, grey sheet, was visible for a considerable distance from the ship. The steamers carried the usual steaming lights, and the barges and lighters white lights at bow and stern. The scuttles were all screened, so that no other lights might confuse those who were responsible for the safe conduct of the armada. I had no inclination to turn in.

"The general excitement of the occasion, the fascination I found in watching the dim shades of the swarm of craft on all sides, the lines of red, white, and green lights slowly moving side by side with their flickering reflections in the gently-heaving waters, held me spellbound and wakeful as I leaned over the taffrail. Most of my comrades on the staff remained on deck, also muffled in their long cloaks, and talking for the most part in undertones. Prince Henry paced the bridge with the officer in command of the vessel. All of us, I think, were impressed with the magnitude of the venture on which our Fatherland had embarked, and although we felt that things had been so carefully thought out and so splendidly arranged that the chances were almost all in our favour, yet we could not but wonder what would be the end of it all. As Von der Bendt—whom you will doubtless remember when he was in the 3rd Horse Grenadiers at Bromberg, and who is also on the Prince's staff—said that night as he walked the deck, 'Where would we be if, despite our precautions, the English had contrived to get wind of our intentions, and half a dozen destroyers came tearing up out of the darkness, and in among our flotilla? Our own particular future would then probably lie under the water instead of on it.' I laughed at his croakings, but I confess I looked rather more intently at our somewhat limited horizon.

"About two in the morning the moon rose. Her light was but fitful and partial on account of a very cloudy sky, but I received rather a shock when her first rays revealed a long grey line of warships with all lights out, and with the darker forms of their attendant destroyers moving on their flanks, slowly crossing our course at right angles. As it turned out, they were only our own escorts, ordered to meet us at this point, and to convoy us and the other portions of the XIIth Corps, which were coming out from Rotterdam and other Dutch ports to join us. In a few minutes after meeting the ironclads, a galaxy of sparkling points of light approaching from the northward heralded their arrival, and by three o'clock the whole fleet was steaming due west in many parallel lines. Four battleships moved in line ahead on each flank, the destroyers seemed to be constantly coming and going in all directions, like dogs shepherding a flock of sheep, and I fancy there were several other men-o'-war ahead of us. The crossing proved entirely uneventful. We saw nothing of the much-to-be-dreaded British warships, nor indeed of any ships at all, with the exception of a few fishing-boats

GOD SAVE THE KING.

PROCLAMATION.

TO ALL WHOM IT MAY CONCERN.

In regard to the Decree of September 3rd of the present year, declaring a state of siege in the Counties of Norfolk and Suffolk.

In regard to the Decree of August 10th, 1906, regulating the public administration of all theatres of war and military servitude;

Upon the proposition of the Commander-in-Chief

IT IS DECREED AS FOLLOWS:

(1) There are in a state of war:

1st. In the Eastern Command, the counties of Northamptonshire, Rutlandshire, Cambridgeshire, Norfolk, Suffolk, Essex, Huntingdonshire, Bedfordshire, Hertfordshire, and Middlesex (except that portion included in the London Military District).

2nd. In the Northern Command, the counties of Northumberland, Durham, Cumberland, and Yorkshire, with the southern shore of the estuary of the Humber.

(2) I, Charles Leonard Spencer Cotterell, his Majesty's Principal Secretary of State for War, am charged with the execution of this Decree.

WAR OFFICE, WHITEHALL,
September the Fourth, 1910.

This proclamation was posted outside the War Office in London at noon on Wednesday, and was read by thousands. It was also posted upon the Town Hall of every city and town throughout the country.

WILLIAM LE QUEUX

and the Harwich-Antwerp boat, which, ablaze with lights, ran through the rear portion of our flotilla, luckily without colliding with any of our flats or lighters. What her crew and passengers must have thought of meeting such an array of shipping in mid-Channel can only be surmised. In any case, it was of no consequence, for by the time they arrived in Antwerp all our cards would be on the table.

"Towards morning I got very drowsy, and eventually fell asleep on a bench behind the after deck-house. I seemed hardly to have closed my eyes when Von der Bendt woke me up to inform me that land was in sight. It was just dawn. A wan light was creeping up out of the east, bringing with it a cold air that made one shiver. There was but little light in the west, but there right ahead a long black line was just discernible on the horizon. It was England!

"Our half of the fleet now altered course a few points to the southward, the remainder taking a more northerly course, and by five o'clock we were passing the Swin Lightship, and stood in the mouth of the river Crouch, doubtless to the amazement of a few fishermen who gazed open-mouthed from their boats at the apparition of our grey warships, with their bristle of guns and the vast concourse of shipping that followed them. By six we were at Burnham-on-Crouch, a quaint little town, evidently a yachting centre, for the river was absolutely covered with craft—small cutters, yawls, and the like, and hundreds upon hundreds of boats of all sizes. Many large, flat-bottomed barges, with tanned sails, lay alongside the almost continuous wooden quay that bordered the river. The boats of the squadron carrying a number of sailors and detachments from the 2nd Marine Battalion that formed part of the expedition had evidently preceded us, as the German ensign was hoisted over the coastguard station, which was occupied by our men. Several of our steam pinnaces were busily engaged in collecting the boats and small craft that were scattered all over the estuary, while others were hauling and towing some of the barges into position beside the quays to serve as landing-places. The method employed was to lash one outside the other till the uttermost one was outside the position of low-water mark.

Our lighter craft, at any rate, could then go alongside and disembark their men and stores at any time.

"The first men I saw land were the residue of the Marine Battalion, who were in the next transport to us. As soon as they were ashore, Prince Henry and his staff followed. We landed at a little iron pier, the planking of which was so rotten that it had given way in many places, and as the remainder of the flooring threatened to follow suit if one placed one's weight on it, we all marched gingerly along the edge, clutching tight hold of the railings. The carpenter's crew from one of the warships was, however, already at work on its repair. As we landed, I saw the *Odin*, followed by a steamer, towing several flats containing the 1st Battalion of the 177th Infantry, and a battery of artillery landing farther up the river. She did not go far, but anchored stem and stern. The steamer cast off her lighters close to the southern bank, and they ran themselves ashore, some on the river bank, and others in a little creek that here ran into the main stream. This detachment, I was informed, was to entrench itself in the little village of Canewdon, supposed to have been the site of Canute's camp, and situated on an eminence about three miles west of us, and about a mile south of the river. As it is the only high ground on that side the river within a radius of several miles of Burnham, its importance to us will be evident.

"While we were waiting for our horses to be landed, I took a turn through the village. It consists of one street, fairly wide in the central portion, with a curious red tower on arches belonging to the local Rath-haus on one side of it. At the western exit of the town is a red-brick drill hall for the Volunteers. Our Marines were in possession, and I noticed several of them studying with much amusement a gaudily-coloured recruiting poster on the post-office opposite, headed: 'Wanted, recruits for His Majesty's Army.' One of their number, who apparently understood English, was translating the letterpress, setting forth the joys and emoluments which awaited the difficult-to-find Englishman patriotic enough to become a soldier. As if such a system of raising an army could ever produce an efficient machine! Was it not the famous Admiral Coligny who perished in the massacre of St. Bartholomew who said, 'Rather than lead again an army of voluntaries, I would die a thousand times.'

"By this time our horses, and those of a couple of troops of the Jäegers zu Pferde had been put on shore. Then having seen that all the exits of the village were occupied, the Mayor secured, and the usual notices posted threatening death to any civilian who obstructed our operations, directly or indirectly, we started off for the high ground to the northward, where we hoped to get into touch with the Division which should now be landing at Bradwell, on the Blackwater. With us went as escort a troop of the Jäegers in their soft grey-green uniforms—for the descent being a surprise one we were in our ordinary uniforms—and a number of mounted signallers.

"The villagers were beginning to congregate as we left Burnham. They scowled at us, but said nothing. For the most part they appeared to be completely dumbfounded. Such an event as a real invasion by a real army of foreigners had never found any place in their limited outlook on life and the world in general. There were some good-looking girls here and there, with fresh, apple-red cheeks, who did not look altogether askance at our prancing horses and our gay uniforms. It was now about half-past eight, and the morning mists, which had been somewhat prevalent down by the river and the low-lying land on either bank, had thinned and drifted away under the watery beams of a feeble sun that hardly pierced the cloudy canopy above us. This, I suppose, is the English summer day of which we hear so much! It is not hot, certainly. The horses were fresh, delighted to escape from their cramped quarters on shipboard, and, trotting and cantering through the many turns of the muddy lanes, we soon skirted the village of Southminster, and began to mount the high ground between it and a little place called Steeple.

"Here, just north of a steading known as Batt's Farm, is the highest point on the peninsula formed by the Blackwater and Crouch Rivers. Though it is only 132 ft. above sea-level, the surrounding ground is so flat that a perfect panorama was spread before us. We could not distinguish Burnham, which was six miles or more to the southward, and hidden by slight folds of the ground and the many trees which topped the hedgerows, but the Blackwater and its creeks were in full view, and about seven miles to the north-west the towers and spires of Maldon, our principal objective in the first instance, stood up like grey pencillings on the sky-line. Our signallers soon got to work, and in a very few minutes picked up those of the Northern Division, who had established a station on a church tower about two miles to our north-east, at St. Lawrence. They reported a successful landing at Bradwell, and that the *Ægir* had gone up in the direction of Maldon with the 3rd Marine Battalion, who were being towed up in their flats by steam pinnaces.

"I think, my dear Neuhaus, that it would be as well if I now gave you some general idea of our scheme of operations, so far as it is known to me, in order that you may be the better able to follow my further experiences by the aid of the one-inch English ordnance map which you will have no difficulty in procuring from Berlin.

"As I have already said, Maldon is our first objective. It is situated at the head of the navigable portion of the Blackwater, and in itself—situated as it is on rising grounds suitable for defence, and surrounded to the north and north-west with a network of river and canal—offers a suitable position to check the preliminary attack that we may surely expect from the Colchester garrison. It is intended, then, to occupy this as quickly as possible, and place it in a state of defence. Our next move will be to entrench ourselves along a line extending southward from Maldon to the river Crouch, which has already been reconnoitred by our Intelligence Department, and the general positions selected and planned. Prince Henry will, of course, be able to make any modifications in the original design that he may consider called for by circumstances. The total length of our front will be nearly seven miles, rather long for the number of troops we have at our disposal, but as the English reckon that to attack troops in position a six-to-one force is required, and as they will be fully occupied elsewhere, I expect we shall be amply sufficient to deal with any attack they can make on us. The right half of the line—with the exception of Maldon itself—is very flat, and offers no very advantageous positions for defence, especially as the ground slopes upwards in the direction of the enemy's attack. It is, however, but a gradual slope. Towards the left, though, there is higher ground, affording fairly good gun positions, and this we must hold on to at all hazards. This, in fact, will be the real key of the position. Holding this, even if we are beaten out of Maldon and forced to abandon our defences in the flat ground to the south of the town, we can use it as a pivot, and fall back on a second position along a line of low hills that run in a north-east direction across the peninsula to St. Lawrence, which will quite well cover our landing-places. In order to further protect us from surprise, the three battalions of the 108th Sharpshooter Regiment belonging to the 32nd Division left Flushing somewhat in advance of us under convoy of some of the older battleships in three or four average-sized steamers that could get alongside the long pier at Southend, and have been ordered to occupy Hockley, Rayleigh, and Wickford, forming as it were a chain of outposts covering us from any early interruption by troops sent over from Chatham, or coming from London by either the southern branch of the Great Eastern Railway or the London, Tilbury, and Southend line. They took nothing with them but their iron ration, the ammunition in their pouches, and that usually carried in the company ammunition waggons (57.6 rounds per man). For the transport of this they were to impress carts and horses at Southend, and to move by a forced march to their positions. As soon as we are able, we also shall push forward advanced troops to South Hanningfield, East Hanningfield, Danebury, and Wickham Bishops, covering us in a similar manner to the west and north. Our flanks are well protected by the two rivers, which are tidal, very wide in parts, and difficult to cross, except at one or two places on the Crouch, which we shall make special arrangements to defend. Moreover—with the exception of Canewdon, which we have already occupied—there is no elevated ground within miles of them which would offer good positions from which the enemy might fire into the ground we occupy between them.

"So much for the military portion of our programme. Now for the part allotted to the Navy. As I have told you, we had eight warships as our convoy, not counting destroyers, etc. These were the eight little armour-clads of the "Ægir" class, drawing only 18 ft. of water and carrying three 9.4 guns apiece, besides smaller ones. The *Ægir* and *Odin* are operating in the rivers on our flanks as far as they are able. The remaining six are busy, three at the entrance of each river, laying down mine-fields and other obstacles to protect us from any inroad on the part of the British Navy, and arranging for passing through the store-ships, which we expect to-night or to-morrow morning from various German and Dutch ports, with the provisions, stores, and ammunition for the use of the Northern Army Corps, when they have penetrated sufficiently far to the south to get into touch with us. Except by these rivers, I do not think that the English naval commanders can get at us.

"What are known as the Dengie Flats extend for three miles seaward, all along the coast between the mouths of the two rivers, and broken marshy land extends for three miles more inland. Their big ships would have to lie at least seven or eight miles distant from our headquarters and store depôt, which we intend to establish at Southminster, and even if they were so foolish as to waste their ammunition in trying to damage us with their big guns firing at high elevations, they would never succeed in doing us any harm. I believe that the squadron of older battleships that escorted the 108th to Southend have orders to mine the mouth of the Thames, cover the mine-field with their guns as long as they can before being overpowered, and incidentally to try and capture Shoeburyness and destroy or bring off what guns they may find there. But this is not really in our particular section of the operations.

"But to return to my own experiences. I told you that Prince Henry and his staff had arrived at Steeple Hill, and that the signallers had got through to the other division that had landed at Bradwell. This was soon after nine o'clock. Not long afterwards the advanced guard of one of the Jäeger battalions, with their smart glazed shakoes, having the black plumes tied back over the left ear, and looking very workmanlike in their green red-piped tunics, came swinging along the road between St. Lawrence and the village of Steeple. They had some of their war-dogs with them in leashes. They were on their way to reinforce the 3rd Marine Battalion, which by this time we trusted had occupied Maldon and cut off all communication with the interior. They had a good nine miles before them. The Prince looked at his watch. 'If they're there before noon it's as much as we can expect,' he said. 'Go and see if they are coming up from Burnham now,' he added, turning sharply to me. Away I went at a gallop till I struck the main road out of Southminster. Here I just headed off the 1st Battalion of the 101st Grenadiers. Its Colonel informed me that the whole regiment was ashore and that the other two battalions were following close behind. When they left Burnham the three battalions of the 100th Body Grenadiers had nearly completed their disembarkation, and the horses of the Garde Reiter Regiment and the 17th Uhlans were being hoisted out by means of the big spritsail yards of the barges lying alongside the quays. The landing pontoons had been greatly augmented and improved during the last hour or two, and the disembarkation was proceeding more and more quickly. They had got two of the batteries of the 1st Brigade Division landed as well as the guns belonging to the Horse Artillery, but they were waiting for the horses. The Prince signalled to the officer superintending the disembarkation at Burnham to send forward the cavalry and horse artillery by batteries and squadrons as soon as they could be mounted.

"Nothing could be done in the meantime but trust that the marines had been successful in occupying Maldon and in stopping any news of our presence from leaking out to Colchester. Presently, however, the signallers reported communication with a new signal station established by the Jäegers zu Pferde on Kit's Hill, an eminence about six miles to the south-west. The officer in command of the troop reported: 'Have cut line at Wickham Ferrers. Captured train of eight coaches coming from Maldon, and have shunted it on to line to Burnham.' Prince Henry signalled back: 'Despatch train to Burnham'; and then also signalled to O.C.

23 Division at Burnham: 'Expect train of eight coaches at once. Entrain as many infantry as it will hold, and send them to Maldon with the utmost despatch.'

"While these signals were passing, I was employed in taking a careful survey with my glasses. This is what I saw, looking from right to left. The green and white lance pennons of a detachment of the hussars belonging to the 32nd Division came fluttering round the shoulder of the hill topped by the grey tower of St. Lawrence. Immediately below us a Jäeger battalion was winding through Steeple Village like a dark green snake. Away to my left front the helmets of the 101st Grenadier Regiment twinkled over the black masses of its three battalions as they wound downhill towards the village of Latchingdon, lying in a tree-shrouded hollow. Maldon was more distinct now, but there was nothing to indicate the presence of our men, though not so very far down the river the lofty mast of the *Ægir*, with its three military tops, was distinguishable over a line of willows. As I lowered my field-glasses the Prince beckoned me. 'Von Pabst,' ordered he, as I raised my hand to the salute, 'take half a dozen troopers, ride to Maldon, and report to me the situation there. I shall be at Latchingdon,' added he, indicating its position on the map, 'or possibly on the road between that and Maldon.'

"Followed by my six Jäegers in their big copper helmets, I dashed away on my mission, and before long was nearing my destination. Maldon perched on its knoll, with its three church towers and gabled houses, brought to my mind one of the old engravings of sixteenth-century cities by Merian. Nothing indicated the approach of war till we were challenged by a sentry, who stepped from behind a house at the entrance to a straggling street. We trotted on till just about to turn in the main street, when 'bang' went a straggling volley from the right. Shot after shot replied, and this told me that our marines had arrived. Then a score of khaki-clad men ran across the entrance of the side street up which we were approaching. 'The English at last!' thought I. It was too late to turn back. One or two of the enemy had caught sight of us as they rushed by, though most of them were too busily engaged in front to observe us. So with a shout of 'Vorwarts!' I stuck in my spurs, and with my six troopers charged into the middle of them, though I had no idea of how many there might be up the street. There was a tremendous clatter and banging of rifles. I cut down one fellow who ran his bayonet into my wallet. At the same time I heard a loud German 'Hoch!' from our right, and caught sight of a body of marines coming up the street at the double. It was all over in a moment. There were not more than thirty 'khakis' all told. Half a dozen lay dead or wounded on the ground, some disappeared up side alleys, and others were made prisoners by the marines. It appeared afterwards that on the first boat-load landing, about an hour previously, the alarm had reached a local Volunteer officer, who had managed to collect some of his men and get them into uniform. He then made the foolish attack on our troops which had ended in so unsatisfactory a manner for him. He, poor fellow, lay spitting blood on the kerbstone. The colonel of marines appeared a moment later, and at once gave orders for the Mayor of Maldon to be brought before him."

The letter ended abruptly, the German officer's intention being no doubt to give some further details of the operations before despatching it to his friend in Darmstadt. But it remained unfinished, for its writer lay already in his grave.

XI

Germans Landing at Hull and Goole

A special issue of the *Times* in the evening of 3rd September contained the following vivid account—the first published—of the happenings in the town of Goole, in Yorkshire:—

Goole, *September 3.*

"Shortly before five o'clock on Sunday morning the night operator of the telephone call-office here discovered an interruption on the trunk-line, and on trying the telegraphs was surprised to find that there was no communication in any direction. The railway station, being rung up, replied that their wires were also down.

"Almost immediately afterwards a well-known North Sea pilot rushed into the post-office and breathlessly asked that he might telephone to Lloyd's. When told that all communication was cut off he wildly shouted that a most extraordinary sight was to be seen in the river Ouse, up which was approaching a continuous procession of tugs, towing flats, and barges filled with German soldiers.

"This was proved to be an actual fact, and the inhabitants of Goole, awakened from their Sunday morning slumbers by the shouts of alarm in the streets, found to their abject amazement foreign soldiers swarming everywhere. On the quay they found activity everywhere, German being spoken on all hands. They watched a body of cavalry consisting of the 1st Westphalian Hussars and the Westphalian Cuirassiers land with order and ease at the Victoria Pier, whence, after being formed up on the quay, they advanced at a sharp trot up Victoria Street, Ouse Street, and North Street to the railway stations, where, as is generally known, there are large sidings of the North-East Lancashire and Yorkshire lines in direct communication both with London and the great cities of the north. The enemy here found great quantities of engines and rolling stock, all of which was at once seized, together with huge stacks of coal at the new sidings.

"Before long the first of the infantry of the 13th Division, which was commanded by Lieutenant-General Doppschutz, marched up to the stations. They consisted of the 13th and 56th Westphalian Regiments; and the cavalry on being relieved advanced out of the town, crossing the Dutch River by the railway bridge, and pushed on as far as Thorne and Hensall, near which they at once strongly held the several important railway junctions.

"Meanwhile cavalry of the 14th Brigade, consisting of Westphalian Hussars and Uhlans, were rapidly disembarking at Old Goole, and, advancing southwards over the open country of Goole Moors and Thorne Waste, occupied Crowle. Both cavalry brigades were acting independently of the main body, and by their vigorous action both south and west they were entirely screening what was happening in the port of Goole.

"Infantry continued to pour into the town from flats and barges, arriving in endless procession. Doppschutz's Division landed at Aldan Dock, Railway Dock, and Ship Dock; the 14th Division at the Jetty and Basin, also in the Barge Dock and at the mouth of the Dutch River; while some, following the cavalry brigade, landed at Old Goole and Swinefleet.

"As far as can be ascertained, the whole of the VIIth German Army Corps have landed, at any rate as far as the men are concerned. The troops, who are under the supreme command of General Baron von Bistram, appear to consist almost entirely of Westphalians, and include Prince Frederick of the Netherlands' 2nd Westphalians; Count Bulow von Dennewitz's 6th Westphalians; but one infantry brigade, the 79th, consisted of men from Lorraine.

"Through the whole day the disembarkation proceeded, the townsmen standing there helpless to lift a finger and watching the enemy's arrival. The Victoria Pleasure Grounds were occupied by parked artillery, which towards afternoon began to rumble through the streets. The German gunners, with folded arms, sat unconcernedly upon the ammunition boxes as the guns were drawn up to their positions. Horses were seized wherever found, the proclamation of Von

Kronhelm was nailed upon the church doors, and the terrified populace read the grim threat of the German field-marshal.

"The wagons, of which there were hundreds, were put ashore mostly at Goole, but others up the river at Hook and Swinefleet. When the cavalry advance was complete, as it was soon after midday, and when reports had come in to Von Bistram that the country was clear of the British, the German infantry advance began. By nightfall they had pushed forward, some by road, some by rail, and others in the numerous motor-wagons that had accompanied the force, until march-outposts were established south of Thorne, Askern, and Crowle, straddling the main road to Bawtry. These places, including Fishlake and the country between them, were at once strongly held, while ammunition and stores were pushed up by railway to both Thorne and Askern.

"The independent cavalry advance continued through Doncaster until dusk, when Rotherham was reached, during which advance scattered bodies of British Imperial Yeomanry were met and compelled to retreat, a dozen or so lives being lost. It appears that late in the afternoon of Sunday news was brought into Sheffield of what was in progress, and a squadron of Yeomanry donned their uniforms and rode forward to reconnoitre, with the disastrous results already mentioned.

"The sensation caused in Sheffield when it became known that German cavalry were so close as Rotherham was enormous, and the scenes in the streets soon approached a panic; for it was wildly declared that that night the enemy intended to occupy the town. The Mayor telegraphed to the War Office appealing for additional defensive force, but no response was received to the telegram. The small force of military in the town, which consisted of the 2nd Battalion Yorkshire Light Infantry, some Royal Artillery, and the local Volunteers, were soon assembled, and going out occupied the strong position above Sheffield between Catcliffe and Tinsley, overlooking the valley of the Rother to the east.

"The expectation that the Germans intended an immediate descent on Sheffield was not realised because the German tactics were merely to reconnoitre and report on the defences of Sheffield if any existed. This they did by remaining to the eastward of the river Rother, whence the high ground rising before Sheffield could be easily observed.

"Before dusk one or two squadrons of Cuirassiers were seen to be examining the river to find fords and ascertain the capacity of the bridges, while others appeared to be comparing the natural features of the ground with the maps with which they all appeared to be provided.

"As night fell, however, the cavalry retired towards Doncaster, which town was occupied, the Angel being the cavalry headquarters. The reason the Germans could not advance at once upon Sheffield was that the cavalry was not strongly enough supported by infantry from their base, the distance from Goole being too great to be covered in a single day. That the arrangements for landing were in every detail perfect could not be doubted, but owing to the narrow channel of the Ouse time was necessary, and it is considered probable that fully three days must elapse from Sunday before the Germans are absolutely established.

"An attempt has been made by the Yorkshire Light Infantry and the York and Lancaster Regiment, with three battalions of Volunteers stationed at Pontefract, to discover the enemy's strength and position between Askern and Snaith, but so far without avail, the cavalry screen across the whole country being impenetrable.

"The people of the West Riding, and especially the inhabitants of Sheffield, are stupefied that they have received no assistance—not even a reply to the Mayor's telegram. This fact has leaked out, and has caused the greatest dissatisfaction. An enemy is upon us, yet we are in ignorance of what steps, if any, the authorities are taking for our protection.

"There are wild rumours here that the enemy have burned Grimsby, but these are generally discredited, for telegraphic and telephonic communication has been cut off, and at present we are completely isolated. It has been gathered from the invaders that the VIIIth Army Corps of the Germans have landed and seized Hull, but at present this is not confirmed. There is, alas! no communication with the place, therefore the report may possibly be true.

"Dewsbury, Huddersfield, Wakefield, and Selby are all intensely excited over the sudden appearance of German soldiers, and were at first inclined to unite to stem their progress. But the German proclamation showing the individual peril of any citizen taking arms against the invaders having been posted everywhere, has held everyone scared and in silent inactivity.

"'Where is our Army?' everyone is asking. The whole country has run riot in a single hour, now that the Germans are upon us. On every hand it is asked: 'What will London do?'"

THE FOLLOWING ACCOUNT, WRITTEN BY a reporter of the *Hull Daily Mail*, appeared in the *London Evening News* on Wednesday evening, and was the first authentic news of what had happened on the Humber on Sunday:—

HULL, *Monday Night*.

"A great disaster has occurred here, and the town is in the hands of the Germans. The totally unexpected appearance in the river at dawn on Sunday of an extraordinary flotilla of all kinds of craft, filled with troops and being towed towards Goole, created the greatest alarm. Loud shouting in the street just before five o'clock awakened me, and I opened my window. Shouting to a seaman running past, I asked what was the matter, when the man's astounding reply was: 'The whole river is swarming with Germans!' Dressing hastily, I mounted my bicycle and ran along the Beverley road through Prospect Street to the dock office, where around the Wilberforce monument the excited crowd now already collected was impassable, and I was compelled to dismount.

"On eager inquiry I learnt that half an hour before men at work in the Alexandra Dock were amazed to discern through the grey mists still hanging across the Humber an extraordinary sight. Scores of ocean-going tugs, each laboriously towing great Dutch barges and lighters, came into sight, and telescopes being quickly borrowed revealed every boat in question to be literally crammed with grey-coated men, evidently soldiers. At first it was believed that they were about to enter Hull, but they kept out in the channel, on the New Holland side, and were accompanied, it was seen, by a quantity of tramp steamers of small tonnage, evidently of such capacity as might get up to the port of Goole. It was at once patent that Goole was their objective.

"The alarm was at once raised in the town. The police ran down to the quays and the Victoria Pier, while the townspeople hastily dressed and joined them to witness the amazing spectacle.

"Somebody at the pier who had a powerful glass recognised the grey uniforms and declared them to be Germans, and then like wildfire the alarming news spread into every quarter of the town that the Germans were upon us.

"The police ran to the telegraph office in order to give the alarm, but it was at once discovered that both telegraph and telephone systems had suddenly been interrupted. Repeated calls elicited no reply, for the wires running out of Hull in every direction had been cut.

"In endless procession the strange medley of queer-looking craft came up out of the morning mist only to be quickly lost again in the westward, while the onlookers, including myself—for I had cycled to the Victoria Pier—gazed at them in utter bewilderment.

"At the first moment of alarm the East Yorkshire Volunteers hurried on their uniforms and assembled at their regimental headquarters for orders. There were, of course, no regular troops in the town, but the Volunteers soon obtained their arms and ammunition, and after being formed, marched down Heddon road to the Alexandra Dock.

"On every side was the greatest commotion, already bordering upon panic. Along Spring Bank, the Hessle road, the Anlaby road, and all the thoroughfares converging into Queen Victoria Square, came crowds of all classes eager to see for themselves and learn the truth of the startling rumour. The whole riverside was soon black with the excited populace, but to the astonishment of everyone the motley craft sailed on, taking no notice of us and becoming fewer and fewer, until ships appeared through the grey bank of fog only at intervals.

"One thing was entirely clear. The enemy, whoever they might be, had destroyed all our means of appealing for help, for we could not telephone to the military at York, Pontefract, Richmond, or even to the regimental district headquarters at Beverley. They had gone on to Goole, but would they turn back and attack us?

"The cry was that if they meant to seize Goole they would also seize Hull! Then the terrified crowd commenced to collect timber and iron from the yards, furniture from neighbouring houses, tramway-cars, omnibuses, cabs; in fact, anything they could lay their hands upon to form barricades in the streets for their own protection.

"I witnessed the frantic efforts of the people as they built one huge obstacle at the corner of Queen Street, facing the pier. Houses were ruthlessly entered, great pieces of heavy furniture—wardrobes, pianos, and sideboards—were piled anyhow upon each other. Men got coils of barbed wire, and lashed the various objects together with seamanlike alacrity. Even paving-stones were prised up with pickaxes and crowbars, and placed in position. The women, in deadly terror of the Germans, helped the men in this hastily improvised barrier, which even as I watched grew higher across the street until it reached the height of the first-storey windows in one great heterogeneous mass of every article conceivable—almost like a huge rubbish heap.

"This was only one of many similar barricades. There were others in the narrow Pier Street, in Wellington Street, Castle Street, south of Prince's Dock, in St. John's Street, between Queen's Dock and Prince's Dock, while the bridges over the river Hull were all defended by hastily improvised obstructions. In Jennings Street, on Sculcoates Bridge, and also the two railway bridges of the Hull and Barnsley and North-Eastern Railways were similarly treated. Thus the whole of the town west of the river Hull was at any rate temporarily protected from any landing eastward.

"The whole town now seemed in a perfect ferment. Wildest rumours were afloat everywhere, and the streets by six o'clock that morning were so crowded that it was almost impossible to move.

"Hundreds found themselves outside the barriers; indeed, the people in the Southcoates, Drypool, and Alexandra

Wards were in the threatened zone, and promptly began to force their way into the town by escalading the huge barricades and scrambling over their crests.

"Foreigners—sailors and others—had a rough time of it, many of them being thrust back and threatened by the indignant townspeople. Each time a foreigner was discovered there was a cry of 'spy,' and many innocent men had fortunate escapes.

"The river seemed clear, when about seven o'clock there suddenly loomed up from seaward a great, ugly, grey-hulled warship flying the German flag. The fear was realised. Her sight caused absolute panic, for with a sudden swerve she calmly moored opposite the Alexandra Dock.

"Eager-eyed seamen, some of them Naval Reservists, recognised that she was cleared for action, and even while we were looking, two more similar vessels anchored in positions from which their guns could completely dominate the town.

"No sooner had these swung to their anchors than, from the now sunlit horizon, there rose the distant smoke of many steamers, and as the moments of terror dragged by, there came slowly into the offing a perfect fleet of all sizes of steamers, escorted by cruisers and destroyers.

"Standing behind the barricade in Queen Street I could overlook the Victoria Pier, and the next half-hour was the most exciting one in my whole life. Three dirty-looking steamers of, as far as I could judge, about 2500 tons each, anchored in a line almost midstream. From my coign of vantage I could hear the rattle of the cables in the hawse-pipes as many other vessels of about the same size followed their example farther down the river. No sooner had the anchors touched the bottom than boats were hoisted out, lowered from all the davits, and brought alongside, while into them poured hundreds upon hundreds of soldiers, all in a uniform dusky grey. Steam pinnaces quickly took these in charge, towing some of them to the Victoria Pier near where I stood, and others to the various wharves.

"Armed and accoutred, the men sprang ashore, formed up, and were quickly told off by their officers in guttural accents, when, from our barricade, close beside me, a Volunteer officer gave the order to fire, and a ragged volley rang sharply out.

"A young German infantry officer standing in Nelson Street, in the act of drawing his revolver from its pouch, pitched heavily forward upon his face with a British bullet through his heart. There were also several gaps in the German ranks. Almost instantly the order for advance was given. The defence was an ill-advised and injudicious one, having in view the swarm of invaders. Hundreds of boats were now approaching every possible landing-place right along the river front, and men were swarming upon every wharf and quay.

"Shots sounded in every direction. Then, quite suddenly, some unintelligible order was given in German, and the crowd of the enemy who had landed at our pier extended, and, advancing at the double, came straight for our barricade, endeavouring to take it by assault. It was an exciting moment. Our Volunteers poured volleys into them, and for a time were able to check them, although the Germans kept up a withering fire, and I found myself, a non-combatant, with bullets whistling about me everywhere, in unpleasant proximity.

"They were breathless moments. Men were continually falling on both sides, and one fierce-faced, black-haired woman, evidently a sailor's wife, who had helped to build the barricade, fell dead at my side, shot through the throat. From the very beginning our defence at this point seemed utterly hopeless. The Volunteers—many of them friends of mine—very gallantly endeavoured to do what they could in the circumstances, but they themselves recognised the utter futility of fighting against what seemed to be a veritable army. They did their utmost, but the sudden rush of an enormous number of supports to strengthen the enemy's advanced parties proved too much for them, and ten minutes later bearded Teutons came clambering over the barricades, ruthlessly putting to death all men in uniform who did not at once throw down their arms.

"As soon as I saw the great peril of the situation I confess that I fled, when behind me I heard a loud crash as a breach was at last made in the obstruction. I ran up Queen Street to Drypool Bridge, where at the barricade there I found desperate fighting in progress. The scene was terrible. The few

Volunteers were bravely trying to defend us. Many civilians, in their frantic efforts to guard their homes, were lying upon the pavement dead and dying. Women, too, had been struck by the hail of German bullets, and the enemy, bent upon taking the town, fought with the utmost determination. From the ceaseless rattle of musketry which stunned the ears on every side it was evident that the town was being taken by assault.

"For five minutes or so I remained in Salthouse Lane, but so thick came the bullets that I managed to slip round to Whitefriargate, and into Victoria Square.

"I was standing at the corner of King Edward Street when the air was of a sudden rent by a crash that seemed to shake the town to its very foundations, and one of the black cupolas of the dock office was carried away, evidently by a high explosive shell.

"A second report, no doubt from one of the cruisers lying in the river, was followed by a great jet of flame springing up from the base of one of the new shops on the left side of King Edward Street—caused, as I afterwards ascertained, by one of those new petrol shells, of which we had heard so much in the newspapers, but the practicability of which our unprogressive Government had so frequently refused to entertain.

"In a flash three shops were well alight, and even while I watched the whole block from Tyler's to the corner was furiously ablaze, the petrol spreading fire and destruction on every hand.

"Surely there is no more deadly engine in modern warfare than the terrible petrol bomb, as was now proved upon our unfortunate town. Within ten minutes came a veritable rain of fire. In all directions the houses began to flare and burn. The explosions were terrific, rapidly succeeding one another, while helpless men stood frightened and aghast, no man knowing that the next moment might not be his last.

"In those never-to-be-forgotten moments we realised for the first time what the awful horror of War really meant.

"The scene was frightful. Hull had resisted, and in retaliation the enemy were now spreading death and destruction everywhere among us."

Reports now reached London that the VIIth German Army Corps had landed at Hull and Goole, and taking possession of those towns, were moving upon Sheffield in order to paralyse our trade in the Midlands. Hull had been bombarded, and was in flames! Terrible scenes were taking place at that port.

The disaster was, alas! of our own seeking.

Lord Roberts, who certainly could not be called an alarmist, had in 1905 resigned his place on the Committee of National Defence in order to be free to speak his own mind. He had told us plainly in 1906 that we were in no better position than we were five or six years previous. Behind the Regular Army we had no practicable reserve, while military training was more honoured in the breach than in the observance. The outlook was alarming, and the reasons for reform absolutely imperative.

He had pointed out to the London Chamber of Commerce in December 1905 that it was most important that our present unpreparedness for war should not be allowed to continue. We should use every endeavour to prevent the feeling of anxiety as to our unpreparedness from cooling down. England's military hero, the man who had dragged us out of the South African muddle, had urged most strongly that a committee of the leading men of London should be formed to take the matter into their earnest consideration. The voice of London upon a question of such vital importance could not fail to carry great weight throughout the country.

A "citizen army," he had declared, was needed as well as the Regular Army. The only way by which a sufficient amount of training could be given—short of adopting the Continental practice—was by giving boys and youths such an amount of drill and practice in rifle shooting as was possible while they were at school, and by some system of universal training after they reached manhood. And that Lord Roberts had urged most strongly.

Yet what had been done? Ay, what?

A deaf ear had been turned to every appeal. And now, alas! the long prophesied blow had fallen.

On that memorable Sunday, when a descent had been made upon our shores, there were in German ports on the North Sea nearly a million tons gross of German shipping. Normally, in peace time, half a million tons is always to be found there, the second half having been quietly collected by ships putting in unobserved into such ports as Emden,

Bremen, Bremerhaven, and Geestemunde, where there are at least ten miles of deep-sea wharves, with ample railway access. The arrival of these crafts caused no particular comment, but they had already been secretly prepared for the transport of men and horses while at sea.

Under the cover of the Frisian Islands, from every canal, river, and creek had been assembled a huge multitude of flats and barges, ready to be towed by tugs alongside the wharves and filled with troops. Of a sudden, in a single hour it seemed, Hamburg, Altona, Cuxhaven, and Wilhelmshaven were in excited activity, and almost before the inhabitants themselves realised what was really in progress the embarkation had well commenced.

At Emden, with its direct cables to the theatre of war in England, was concentrated the brain of the whole movement. Beneath the lee of the covering screen of Frisian Islands, Borkum, Juist, Norderney, Langebog, and the others, the preparations for the descent upon England rapidly matured.

Troop-trains from every part of the Fatherland arrived with the punctuality of clockwork. From Düsseldorf came the VIIth Army Corps, the VIIIth from Coblenz, the IXth were already assembled at their headquarters at Altona, while many of them being stationed at Bremen embarked from there, the Xth came up from Hanover, the XIVth from Magdeburg, and the Corps of German Guards, the pride and flower of the Kaiser's troops, arrived eagerly at Hamburg from Berlin and Potsdam, among the first to embark.

Each army corps consisted of about 38,000 officers and men, 11,000 horses, 144 guns, and about 2000 motor-cars, wagons, and carts. But for this campaign—which was more of the nature of a raid than of any protracted campaign—the supply of wheeled transport, with the exception of motor-cars, had been somewhat reduced.

Each cavalry brigade attached to an army corps consisted of 1400 horses and men, with some thirty-five light machine-guns and wagons. The German calculation—which proved pretty correct—was that each army corps could come over to England in 100,000 tons gross of shipping, bringing with them supplies for twenty-seven days in another 3000 tons gross. Therefore about 618,000 tons gross conveyed the whole of the six corps, leaving an ample margin still in German ports for any emergencies. Half this tonnage consisted of about 100 steamers, averaging 3000 tons each, the remainder being the boats, flats, lighters, barges, and tugs previously alluded to.

The Saxons who, disregarding the neutrality of Belgium, had embarked at Antwerp, had seized the whole of the flat-bottomed craft in the Scheldt and the numerous canals, as well as the merchant ships in the port, finding no difficulty in commandeering the amount of tonnage necessary to convey them to the Blackwater and the Crouch.

As hour succeeded hour, the panic increased.

It was now also known that, in addition to the various corps who had effected a landing, the German Guards had, by a sudden swoop into the Wash, got ashore at King's Lynn, seized the town, and united their forces with Von Kleppen's corps, who, having landed at Weybourne, were now spread right across Norfolk. This picked corps of Guards was under the command of that distinguished officer the Duke of Mannheim, while the infantry divisions were under Lieutenant-Generals von Castein and Von Der Decken.

The landing at King's Lynn on Sunday morning had been quite a simple affair. There was nothing whatever to repel them, and they disembarked on the quays and in the docks, watched by the astonished populace. All provisions were seized at shops, including the King's Lynn and County Stores, the Star Supply Stores, Ladyman's and Lipton's in the High Street, while headquarters were established at the municipal buildings, and the German flag hoisted upon the old church, the tower of which was at once used as a signal station.

Old-fashioned people of Lynn peered out of their quiet, respectable houses in King Street in utter amazement, but soon, when the German proclamation was posted, the terrible truth was plain.

In half an hour, even before they could realise it, they had been transferred from the protection of the British flag to the militarism of the German.

The Tuesday Market Place, opposite the Globe Hotel, was one of the points of assembly, and from there and from other open spaces troops of cavalry were constantly riding out of town by the Downham Market and Swaffham Roads. The intention of this commander was evidently to join hands with Von Kleppen as soon as possible. Indeed, by that same evening the Guards and IVth Corps had actually shaken hands at East Dereham.

A few cavalry, mostly Cuirassiers and troopers of the Gardes du Corps, were pushed out across the flat, desolate country over Sutton Bridge to Holbeach and Spalding, while others, moving south-easterly, came past the old Abbey of Crowland, and even to within sight of the square cathedral tower of Peterborough. Others went south to Ely.

Ere sundown on Sunday, stalwart, grey-coated sentries of the Guards Fusiliers from Potsdam and the Grenadiers from Berlin were holding the roads at Gayton, East Walton, Narborough, Markham, Fincham, Stradsett, and Stow Bardolph. Therefore on Sunday night, from Spalding on the east, Peterborough, Chatteris, Littleport, Thetford, Diss, and Halesworth were faced by a huge cavalry screen protecting the landing and repose of the great German Army behind it.

Slowly but carefully the enemy were maturing their plans for the defeat of our defenders and the sack of London.

XII

Desperate Fighting in Essex

London was at a standstill. Trade was entirely stopped. Shopkeepers feared to open their doors on account of the fierce, hungry mobs parading the streets. Orators were haranguing the crowds in almost every open space. The police were either powerless, or feared to come into collision with the assembled populace. Terror and blank despair were everywhere.

There was unrest night and day. The banks, head offices and branches, unable to withstand the run upon them when everyone demanded to be paid in gold, had, by mutual arrangement, shut their doors, leaving excited and furious crowds of customers outside unpaid. Financial ruin stared everyone in the face. Those who were fortunate enough to realise their securities on Monday were fleeing from London south or westward. Day and night the most extraordinary scenes of frantic fear were witnessed at Paddington, Victoria, Waterloo, and London Bridge. The southern railways were badly disorganised by the cutting of the lines by the enemy, but the Great Western system was, up to the present, intact, and carried thousands upon thousands to Wales, to Devonshire, and to Cornwall.

In those three hot, breathless days the Red Hand of Ruin spread out upon London.

The starving East met the terrified West, but in those moments the bonds of terror united class with mass. Restaurants and theatres were closed, there was but little vehicular traffic in the streets, for of horses there were none, while the majority of the motor 'buses had been requisitioned, and the transit of goods had been abandoned. "The City," that great army of daily workers, both male and female, was out of employment, and swelled the idlers and gossips, whose temper and opinion were swayed each half-hour by the papers now constantly appearing night and day without cessation.

Cabinet Councils had been held every day, but their decisions, of course, never leaked out to the public. The King also held Privy Councils, and various measures were decided upon. Parliament, which had been hurriedly summoned, was due to meet, and everyone speculated as to the political crisis that must now ensue.

In St. James's Park, in Hyde Park, in Victoria Park, on Hampstead Heath, in Greenwich Park, in fact, in each of the "lungs of London," great mass meetings were held, at which resolutions were passed condemning the Administration and eulogising those who, at the first alarm, had so gallantly died in defence of their country.

It was declared that by the culpable negligence of the War Office and the National Defence Committee we had laid ourselves open to complete ruin, both financially and as a nation.

The man-in-the-street already felt the strain, for the lack of employment and the sudden rise in the price of everything had brought him up short. Wives and families were crying for food, and those without savings and with only a few pounds put by looked grimly into the future and at the mystery it presented.

Most of the papers published the continuation of the important story of Mr. Alexander, the Mayor of Maldon, which revealed the extent of the enemy's operations in Essex and the strong position they occupied.

It ran as below:—

"Of the events of the early hours of the morning I have no very clear recollection. I was bewildered, staggered, dumbfounded by the sights and sounds which beset me. Of what modern war meant I had till then truly but a very faint idea. To witness its horrid realities enacted in this quiet, out-of-the-way spot where I had pitched my tent for so many years, brought them home to me literally, as well as metaphorically. And to think that all this wanton destruction of property and loss of life was directly due to our apathy as a nation! The Germans had been the aggressors without a doubt, but as for us we had gone out of our way to invite attack. We had piled up riches and made no provision to prevent a stronger nation from gathering them. We had seen every other European nation, and even far-distant Japan, arm their whole populations and perfect their preparedness for the eventualities of war, but we had been content to scrape along with an apology for a military system—which was really no system at all—comforting ourselves with the excuse that nothing could possibly evade or compete with our magnificent navy. Such things as fogs, false intelligence, and the interruption of telegraphic and telephonic communication were not taken into account, and were pooh-poohed if any person, not content with living in a fool's paradise, ventured to draw attention to the possibility of such contingencies.

"So foolhardy had we become in the end, that we were content to see an immense and threatening increase in the German shipbuilding programme without immediately 'going one better.' The specious plea that our greater rapidity in construction would always enable us to catch up our rivals in the race was received with acclamation, especially as the argument was adorned with gilt lettering in the shape of promised Admiralty economies.

"As might have been foreseen, Germany attacked us at the psychological moment when her rapidly increasing fleet had driven even our *laissez faire* politicians to lay down new ships with the laudable idea of keeping our naval pre-eminence by the rapidity of our construction. Our wide-awake enemy, seeing that should these be allowed to attain completion the place he had gained in the race would be lost, allowed them to be half finished and then suddenly attacked us.

"But to return to my personal experiences on this never-to-be-forgotten day. I had run down Cromwell Hill, and seeing the flames of Heybridge, was impelled to get nearer, if possible, to discover more particularly the state of affairs in that direction. But I was reckoning without the Germans. When I got to the bridge over the river at the foot of the hill, the officer in charge there absolutely prevented my crossing. Beyond the soldiers standing or kneeling behind whatever cover was offered by the walls and buildings abutting on the riverside, and a couple of machine guns placed so as to command the bridge and the road beyond, there was nothing much to see. A number of Germans were, however, very busy in the big mill just across the river, but what they were doing I could not make out. As I turned to retrace my steps, the glare of the conflagration grew suddenly more and more intense. A mass of dark figures came running down the brightly-illuminated road towards the bridge, while the rifle fire became louder, nearer, and heavier than ever. Every now and again the air became alive with, as it were, the hiss and buzz of flying insects. The English must have fought their way through Heybridge, and these must be the bullets from their rifles. It was dangerous to stay down there any longer, so I took to my heels. As I ran I heard a thundering explosion behind me, the shock of which nearly threw me to the ground. Looking over my shoulder, I saw that the Germans had blown up the mill at the farther end of the bridge, and were now pushing carts from either side in order to barricade it. The two Maxims, too, began to pump lead with their hammering reports, and the men near them commenced to fall in twos and threes. I made off to the left, and passed into the High Street by the end of St. Peter's Church, now disused. At the corner I ran against Mr. Clydesdale, the optician, who looks after the library which now occupies the old building. He pointed to the tower, which stood darkly up against the blood-red sky.

"'Look at those infernal Germans!' he said. 'They can't even keep out of that old place. I wish we could have got the books out before they came.'

"I could not see any of our invaders where he was pointing, but presently I became aware of a little winking, blinking light at the very summit of the tower.

"'That's them,' said Clydesdale. 'They're making signals, I think. My boy says he saw the same thing on Purleigh Church tower last night. I wish it would come down with them, that I do. It's pretty shaky, anyway.'

"The street was fairly full of people. The Germans, it is true, had ordered that no one should be out of doors between eight in the evening and six in the morning; but just now they appeared to have their hands pretty full elsewhere, and if any of the few soldiers that were about knew of or thought anything of the interdiction, they said nothing. Wat Miller, the postman, came up and touched his cap.

"'Terrible times, sir,' he said, 'ain't they? There was a mort of people killed this afternoon by them shells. There was poor old Missis Reece in the London Road. Bed-ridden, she were, this dozen years. Well, sir, there ain't so much as the head on her left. A fair mash up she were, poor old lady! Then there was Jones the carpenter's three kids, as was left behind when their mother took the baby to Mundon with the rest of the women. The house was struck and come down atop of 'em. They got two out, but they were dead, poor souls! and they're still looking for the other one.'

"The crash of a salvo of heavy guns from the direction of my own house interrupted the tale of horrors.

"'That'll be the guns in my garden,' I said.

"'Yes, sir; and they've got three monstrous great ones in the opening between the houses just behind the church there,' said Clydesdale.

"As he spoke the guns in question bellowed out, one after the other.

"'Look—look at the tower!' cried the postman.

"The light at the top had disappeared, and the lofty edifice was swaying slowly, slowly, over to the left.

"'She's gone at last!' exclaimed Clydesdale.

"It was true. Down came the old steeple that had pointed heavenward for so many generations, with a mighty crash and concussion that swallowed up even the noise of the battle, though cannon of all sorts and sizes were now joining in the hellish concert, and shell from the English batteries began to roar over the town. The vibration and shock of the heavy guns had been too much for the old tower, which, for years in a tottery condition, had been patched up so often.

"As soon as the cloud of dust cleared off we all three ran towards the huge pile of débris that filled the little churchyard. Several other people followed. It was very dark down there, in the shadow of the trees and houses, despite the firelight overhead, and we began striking matches as we looked about among the heaps of bricks and beams to see if there were any of the German signal party among them. Why we should have taken the trouble under the circumstances I do not quite know. It was an instinctive movement of humanity on my part, and that of most of the others, I suppose. Miller, the postman, was, however, logical. 'I 'opes as they're all dead!' was what he said.

"I caught sight of an arm in a light blue sleeve protruding from the débris, and took hold of it in a futile attempt to

WILLIAM LE QUEUX

remove some of the bricks and rubbish which I thought were covering the body of its owner. To my horror, it came away in my hand. The body to which it belonged might be buried yards away in the immense heap of ruins. I dropped it with a cry, and fled from the spot.

"Dawn was now breaking. I do not exactly remember where I wandered to after the fall of St. Peter's Tower, but it must have been between half-past five and six when I found myself on the high ground at the north-western corner of the town, overlooking the golf links, where I had spent so many pleasant hours in that recent past that now seemed so far away. All around me were batteries, trenches, and gun-pits. But though the firing was still going on somewhere away to the right, where Heybridge poured black smoke skyward like a volcano, gun and howitzer were silent, and their attendant artillerymen, instead of being in cover behind their earthen parapets, were clustered on the top watching intently something that was passing in the valley below them. So absorbed were they that I was able to creep up behind them, and also get a sight of what was taking place. And this is what I saw:—

"Over the railway bridge which spanned the river a little to the left were hurrying battalion after battalion of green and blue clad German infantry. They moved down the embankment after crossing, and continued their march behind it. Where the railway curved to the right and left, about half a mile beyond the bridge, the top of the embankment was lined with dark figures lying down and apparently firing, while over the golf course from the direction of Beeleigh trotted squadron after squadron of sky-blue riders, their green and white lance pennons fluttering in the breeze. They crossed the Blackwater and Chelmer Canal, and cantered off in the direction of Langford Rectory.

"At the same time I saw line after line of the Germans massed behind the embankment spring over it and advance rapidly towards the lower portion of the town, just across the river. Hundreds fell under the fire from the houses, which must have been full of Englishmen, but one line after another reached the buildings. The firing was now heavier than ever—absolutely incessant and continuous—though, except for an occasional discharge from beyond Heybridge, the artillery was silent.

"I have but little knowledge of military matters, but it was abundantly evident, even to me, that what I had just seen was a very formidable counter-attack on the part of the Germans, who had brought up fresh troops either from the rear of the town or from farther inland, and launched them against the English under cover of the railway embankment. I was not able to see the end of the encounter, but bad news flies apace, and it soon became common knowledge in the town that our troops from Colchester had not only failed to cross the river at any point, but had been driven helter-skelter out of the lower town near the station and from the smoking ruins of Heybridge with great loss, and were now in full retreat.

"Indeed, some hundreds of our khaki-clad fellow-countrymen were marched through the town an hour or two later as prisoners, to say nothing of the numbers of wounded who, together with those belonging to the Germans, soon began to crowd every available building suitable for use as an hospital. The wounded prisoners with their escort went off towards Mundon, and are reported to have gone in the direction of Steeple. It was altogether a disastrous day, and our hopes, which had begun to rise when the British had penetrated into the northern part of the town, now fell below zero.

"It was a black day for us, and for England. During the morning the same officer who had captured me on the golf course came whirling into Maldon on a 24-h.p. Mercedes car. He drove straight up to my house, and informed me that he had orders to conduct me to Prince Henry, who was to be at Purleigh early in the afternoon.

"'Was it in connection with the skirmish with the Volunteers?' I asked.

"'I don't know,' was the reply. 'But I don't fancy so. In the meantime, could I write here for an hour or two?' he asked politely. 'I have much to write to my friends in Germany, and have not had a minute up to now.'

"I was very glad to be able to oblige the young man in such a small way, and left him in my study till midday, very busy with pens, ink, and paper.

"After a makeshift of a lunch, the car came round, and we got into the back seat. In front sat his orderly and the chauffeur, a fierce-looking personage in a semi-military uniform. We ran swiftly down the High Street, and in a few minutes were spinning along the Purleigh Road, where I saw much that amazed me. I then for the first time realised how absolutely complete were the German plans."

TUESDAY, *September 4*

"About six o'clock this morning I awoke rather suddenly. The wind had gone round to the northward, and I was certain that heavy firing was going on somewhere in that direction. I opened the window and looked out. The 'thud' and rumble of a cannonade, with the accompaniment of an occasional burst of musketry, came clearly and loudly on the wind from the hills by Wickham Bishops village. The church spire was in plain view, and little faint puffs and rings of grey smoke were just visible in its vicinity every now and again, sometimes high up in the air, at others among the trees at its base. They were exploding shells; I had no doubt of that. What was going on it was impossible to say, but I conjectured that some of our troops from Colchester had come into collision with the Germans, who had gone out in that direction the day of their arrival. The firing continued for about an hour, and then died away.

"Soon after eight Count von Ohrendorff, the general officer commanding the 32nd Division, who appeared to be the supreme authority here, sent for me, and suggested that I should take steps to arrange for the manufacture of lint and bandages by the ladies living in the town. I could see no reason for objecting to this, and so promised to carry out his suggestion. I set about the matter at once, and, with the assistance of my wife, soon had a couple of score of more or less willing workers busily engaged in the National Schoolroom. In the meantime, the roll of a terrible cannonade had burst forth again from Wickham Bishops. It seemed louder and more insistent than ever. As soon as I got away from the schools I hurried home and climbed out on the roof. The top of the Moot Hall, the tower of St. Peter's, and other better coigns of vantage had all been occupied by the Germans. However, with the aid of a pair of field-glasses I was able to see a good bit. Black smoke was now pouring from Wickham Bishops in clouds, and every now and again I fancied I could see the forked tongues of flame shooting up above the surrounding trees. A series of scattered black dots now came out on the open ground to the south of the church. The trees of Eastland Wood soon hid them from my sight, but others followed, mingled with little moving black blocks, which I took to be formed bodies of troops. After them came four or five guns, driven at breakneck pace towards the road that passes between Eastland and Captain's Woods, then more black dots, also in a desperate hurry. Several of these last tumbled, and lay still here and there all over the slope.

"Other dots followed at their heels. They were not quite so distinct. I looked harder. Hurrah! They were men in khaki. We were hustling these Germans at last. They also disappeared behind the woods. Then from the fringe of trees about Wickham half a dozen big brilliant flashes, followed after an interval by the loud detonation of heavy cannon. I could not distinguish much more, though the rattle of battle went on for some time longer. Soon after eleven four German guns galloped in from Heybridge. These were followed by a procession of maimed and limping humanity. Some managed to get along unaided, though with considerable difficulty. Others were supported by a comrade, some carried between two men, and others borne along on stretchers. A couple of ambulance carts trotted out and picked up more wounded. Our bandages and lint had not long to wait before being required. After this there was a cessation of firing.

"About one o'clock the German general sent word to me that he thought an attack quite possible during the afternoon, and that he strongly advised me to get all the women and children out of the town—for the time being, at any rate. This was evidently well meant, but it was a pretty difficult matter to arrange for, to say nothing of raising a panic among the inhabitants. However, in an hour and a half's time I had contrived to marshal several hundred of them together, and to get them out on to the road to Mundon. The weather was warm for the time of year, and I thought, if the worst came to the worst, they could spend the night in the old church. I left the sad little column of exiles—old, bent women helped along by their daughters, tiny children dragged along through the dust, clutching their mothers' skirts, infants in arms, and other older and sturdier children staggering beneath the weight of the most precious home adornments—and made the best of my way back to arrange for the forwarding to them of their rations.

"At every step on my homeward way I expected to hear the cannonade begin again. But beyond the twittering of the birds in the trees and hedgerows, the creak and rumble of a passing cart, and the rush of a train along the railway on my left—just the usual sounds of the countryside—nothing broke the stillness. As I stepped out on the familiar highway I could almost bring myself to believe that the events of the past twenty-four hours were but the phantasmagoria of a dream. After interviewing some of the town councillors who were going to undertake the transport of provisions to the women and children at Mundon, I walked round to my own house.

"My wife and family had driven over to Purleigh on the first alarm, and had arranged to stay the night with some friends, on whatever shakedowns could be improvised, since every house in the peninsula harboured some of the ubiquitous German officers and men. I wandered through the familiar rooms, and came out into the garden—or rather what had been the garden. There I saw that the Saxon gunners were all standing to their pieces, and one of my none too welcome guests accosted me as I left the house.

"'If you'll take my advice, sare, you'll get away out of this,' he said in broken English.

"'What! are you going to fire?' I asked.

"'I don't fancy so. It wouldn't hurt you if we were. But I think your English friends from Colchester are about to see if they can draw us.'

"As he spoke I became aware of a sharp, hissing noise like a train letting off steam. It grew louder and nearer, passed over our heads, and was almost instantly followed by a terrible crash somewhere behind the house. A deeper and more muffled report came up from the valley beyond Heybridge.

"'Well, they've begun now, and the best thing you can do is to get down into that gun epaulment there,' said the German officer.

"I thought his advice was good, and I lost no time in following it.

"'Here comes another!' cried he, as he jumped down into the pit beside me. 'We'll have plenty of them now.'

"So we did. Shell after shell came hissing and screaming at us over the tree-tops in the gardens lower down the hill. Each one of them sounded to me as if it were coming directly at my head, but one after another passed over us to burst beyond. The gunners all crouched close to the earthen parapet—and so did I. I am not ashamed to say so. My German officer, however, occasionally climbed to the top of the embankment and studied the prospect through his field-glasses. At length there was a loud detonation, and a column of dirt and smoke in the garden next below us. Then two shells struck the parapet of the gun-pit on our left almost simultaneously. Their explosion was deafening, and we were covered with the dust and stones they threw up.

"Immediately afterwards another shell passed so close over our heads that I felt my hair lift. It just cleared the parapet and plunged into the side of my house. A big hole appeared just to the right of the dining-room window, and through it came instantaneously the loud bang of the explosion. The glass was shattered in all the windows, and thick smoke, white and black, came curling from every one of them.

"'The house is on fire!' I shouted, and sprang madly from the pit. Heedless of the bombardment, I rushed into the building. Another crash sounded overhead as I entered, and a blaze of light shone down the stairway for an instant. Another projectile had found a billet in my home. I tried to make my way to my study, but found the passage blocked with fallen beams and ceiling. What with the smoke and dust, and the blocking of some of the windows, it was very dark in the hall, and I got quite a shock when, as I looked about me to find my way, I saw two red, glittering specks shining over the top of a heap of débris. But the howl that followed told me that they were nothing but the eyes of miserable Tim, the cat, who, left behind, had been nearly frightened out of his senses by the noise and concussion of the bursting shell. As I gazed at him another projectile struck the house quite close to us. Tim was simply smashed by a flying fragment. I was thrown down, and half buried under a shower of bricks and mortar. I think I must have lost consciousness for a time.

"The next thing I recollect was being dragged out into the garden by a couple of Saxons. I had a splitting headache, and was very glad of a glass of water that one of them handed me. Their officer, who appeared to be quite a decent fellow, offered me his flask.

"'The house is all right,' he said, with his strong accent. 'It caught fire once, but we managed to get it under. Your friends have cleared off—at any rate for the present. They got too bold at last, and pushed their guns down till they got taken in flank by the warship in the river. They had two of their pieces knocked to bits, and then cleared out. Best thing you can do is to do the same.'

"I was in two minds. I could not save the house by staying, and might just as well join my people at Purleigh Rectory. On the other hand, I felt that it would better become me, as Mayor, to stick to the town. Duty triumphed, and I decided to remain where I was—at least for the present. All was now quiet, and after an early supper I turned in, and, despite the excitement of the day and my aching head, was asleep the moment I touched the pillow."

WEDNESDAY, *September 5*.

"It must have been about three in the morning when I awoke. My head was much better, and for a minute or two I lay comfortably in the darkness, without any recollection of the events of the preceding day. Then I saw a bright reflection pass rapidly over the ceiling. I wondered vaguely what it was. Presently it came back again, paused a moment, and disappeared. By this time I was wide awake. I went to the window and looked out. It was quite dark, but from somewhere over beyond Heybridge a long white ray was sweeping all along this side of Maldon. Now the foliage of a tree in the garden below would stand out in pale green radiance against the blackness; now the wall of a house half a mile away would reflect back the moving beam, shining white as a sheet of notepaper.

"Presently another ray shone out, and the two of them moving backwards and forwards made the whole of our hillside caper in a dizzy dance. From somewhere far away to my right another stronger beam now streamed through the obscurity, directed apparently at the sources of the other two, and almost simultaneously came the crack of a rifle from the direction of Heybridge, sharp and ominous in the quiet darkness of the night. Half a dozen scattered shots followed; then a faint cheer. More and more rifles joined in, and presently the burring tap-tap-tap of a Maxim. I hurried on my clothes. The firing increased in volume and rapidity; bugles rang out here, there, and everywhere through the sleeping town, and above the rolling, rattling clamour of the drums I could distinguish the hurried tramp of hundreds of feet.

"I cast one glance from the window as I quitted the room. The electric searchlights had increased to at least half a dozen. Some reached out long, steady fingers into the vague spaces of the night, while others wandered restlessly up and down, hither and thither. Low down over the trees of the garden a dull red glare slowly increased in extent and intensity. The rattle of musketry was now absolutely continuous. As I ran out of the house into the street I was nearly carried off my feet by the rush of a battalion that was pouring down Cromwell Hill at the double. Hardly knowing what I did, I followed in their wake. The glare in front got brighter and brighter. A few steps, and I could see the cause of it. The whole of Heybridge appeared to be on fire, the flames roaring skywards from a dozen different conflagrations."

ENGLAND HALTED BREATHLESS. FIGHTING HAD commenced in real earnest.

The greatest consternation was caused by the publication in the *Times* of the description of the operations in Essex, written by Mr. Henry Bentley, the distinguished war correspondent, who had served that journal in every campaign since Kitchener had entered Khartum.

WILLIAM LE QUEUX

All other papers, without exception, contained various accounts of the British defence at the point nearest London, but they were mostly of the scrappy and sensational order, based more on report than upon actual fact. The *Times* account, however, had been written with calm impartiality by one of the most experienced correspondents at the front. Whether he had been afforded any special facilities was not apparent, but, in any case, it was the most complete and truthful account of the gallant attempt on the part of our soldiers to check the advance from Essex westward.

During the whole of that hot, stifling day it was known that a battle was raging, and the excitement everywhere was intense.

The public were in anxious terror as the hours crept by until the first authentic news of the result of the operations was printed in a special evening edition of the *Times* as follows:—

(From our War Correspondent.)

DANBURY, ESSEX, *September 8*

"To-day has been a momentous one for England. The great battle has raged since dawn, and though just at present there seems to be a lull, during which the opposing forces are, so to speak, regaining their breath, it can be by no means over.

"Dead and living alike will lie out on the battlefield the whole night through, for we must hold on to the positions so hardly won, and be ready to press forward at the first glimmer of daylight. Our gallant troops, Regular and Volunteer alike, have nobly vindicated the traditions of our race, and have fought as desperately as ever did their forebears at Agincourt, Albuera, or Waterloo. But while a considerable success—paid for, alas! by the loss of thousands of gallant lives—has been achieved, it will take at least another day's hard fighting before victory is in our grasp. Nowadays a soldier need not expect to be either victorious or finally defeated by nightfall, and although this battle, fought as it is between much smaller forces and extending over a much more limited area than the great engagement between the Russians and Japanese at Liaoyang, will not take quite so long a time to decide, the end is not yet in sight. I write this after a hard day's travelling backwards and forwards behind our advancing line of battle.

"I took my cycle with me in my motor-car, and whenever opportunity offered mounted it, and pushed forward as near to the fighting as I could get. Frequently I had to leave the cycle also, and crawl forward on hands and knees, sheltering in some depression in the ground, while the enemy's bullets whined and whistled overhead. As reported in a previous issue, the Army which had assembled at Brentwood moved forward early on the 5th.

"During the afternoon the advanced troops succeeded in driving the enemy out of South Hanningfield, and before sundown they were also in full retreat from the positions they had held at East Hanningfield and Danbury. There was some stiff fighting at the latter place, but after a pounding from the artillery, who brought several batteries into action on the high ground north-west of East Hanningfield, the Germans were unable to withstand the attack of the Argyll and Sutherlands and the London Scottish, who worked their way through Danbury Park and Hall Wood right into their position, driving them from their entrenchments by a dashing bayonet charge. Everything north and east of the enemy's main position, which is now known to lie north and south, between Maldon and the river Crouch, was now in our hands, but his troops still showed a stout front at Wickford, and were also reported to be at Rayleigh, Hockley, and Canewdon, several miles to the eastward. All preparations were made to assault the German position at Wickford at daybreak to-day, but our scouts found that the place had been evacuated. The news that Rayleigh and Hockley had also been abandoned by the enemy came in shortly afterwards. The German invaders had evidently completed their arrangements for the defence of their main position, and now said, in effect, 'Come on, and turn us out if you can.'

"It was no easy task that lay before our gallant defenders. Maldon, perched on a high knoll, with a network of river and canal protecting it from assault from the northward, fairly bristles with guns, many of them heavy field howitzers, and has, as we know to our cost, already repulsed one attack by our troops. Farther south there are said to be many guns on the knolls about Purleigh. This little out-of-the-way hamlet, by the way, is noteworthy as having had as its Rector from 1632–1643 the great-great-grandfather of the famous George Washington, and the father of the first Washingtons who emigrated to Virginia. Great Canney Hill, standing boldly up like an immense redoubt, is reported to be seamed with entrenchments mounting many heavy guns. The railway embankment south of Maldon forms a perfect natural rampart along part of the enemy's position, while the woods and enclosures south-west of Great Canney conceal thousands of sharpshooters. A sort of advanced position was occupied by the enemy at Edwin Hall, a mile east of Woodham Ferrers, where a pair of high kopjes a quarter of a mile apart offered command and cover to some of their field batteries.

"Our scouts have discovered also that an elaborate system of wire entanglements and other military obstacles protects almost the whole front of the somewhat extensive German position. On its extreme left their line is said to be thrown back at an angle, so that any attempt to outflank it would not only entail crossing the river Crouch, but would come under the fire of batteries placed on the high ground overlooking it. Altogether, it is a very tough nut to crack, and the force at our disposal none too strong for the work that lies before it.

"Further detail regarding our strength would be inadvisable for obvious reasons, but when I point out that the Germans are supposed to be between thirty and forty thousand strong, and that it is laid down by competent military authorities that to attack troops in an entrenched position a superiority of six to one is advisable, my readers can draw their own conclusions. For the same reason, I will not enumerate all the regiments and corps that go to compose our Army in Essex. At the same time there can be no harm in mentioning some of them which have particularly distinguished themselves in the hard fighting of the past twelve hours.

"Among these are the Grenadier and Irish Guards, the Inns of Court Volunteers, and the Honourable Artillery Company from London, and the Oxfordshire and two battalions of the Royal Marines from Chatham, which, with other troops from that place, crossed over at Tilbury and joined our forces. The last-mentioned are the most veteran troops we have here, as, besides belonging to a long-service corps, they have in their ranks a number of their Reservists who had joined at a day's notice. The Marines are in reality, though not nominally, the most territorial of our troops, since the greater number of their Reserve men settle down in the immediate neighbourhood of their headquarters. It is this fact which enabled them to mobilise so much quicker than the rest of our regiments. The Oxfordshire, for instance, coming from the same garrison, has very few Reservists as yet, while most of the others are in the same plight. And yet the fiat has gone forth that the Marine Corps, despite its past record, the excellence of its men, and its constant readiness for active service, is to lose its military status. Would that we had a few more of its battalions with us to-day. But to return to the story of the great battle.

"The repairs to the railway line between Brentwood and Chelmsford, that had been damaged by the enemy's cavalry on their first landing, were completed yesterday, and all night reinforcements had been coming in by way of Chelmsford and Billericay. The general headquarters had been established at Danbury, and thither I made my way as fast as my car could get along the roads, blocked as they were by marching horse, foot, and artillery. I had spent the night at South Hanningfield, so as to be on the spot for the expected attack on Wickford; but as soon as I found it was not to come off, I considered that at Danbury would be the best chance of finding out what our next move was to be.

"Nor was I mistaken. As I ran up to the village I found the roads full of troops under arms, and everything denoted action of some kind. I was lucky enough to come across a friend of mine on the staff—Captain B——, I will call him— who spared a moment to give me the tip that a general move forward was commencing, and that a big battle was imminent. Danbury is situated on the highest ground for many miles round, and as it bid fair to be a fine, clear day, I thought I could not do better than try and get a general look round from the summit of the church tower before proceeding farther. But I was informed that the General was up there with some of his staff and a signalling party, so that I could not ascend.

"However, no other newspaper correspondents were in the immediate vicinity, and as there was thus no fear of my case being quoted as a precedent, my pass eventually procured me admission to the little platform, which, by the way, the General left a moment after my arrival. It was now eight o'clock, the sun was fairly high in the heavens, and the light mists that hung about the low ground in the vicinity of Maldon were fast fading into nothingness. The old town was plainly distinguishable as a dark silhouette against the morning light, which, while it illumined the panorama spread out before me, yet rendered observation somewhat difficult, since it shone almost directly into my eyes. However, by the aid of my glasses I was able to see something of the first moves on the fatal chess-board where so many thousands of lives are staked on the bloody game of war.

"I noticed among other things that the lessons of the recent war in the East had not passed unobserved, for in all the open spaces on the eastern slope of the hill, where the roads were not screened by trees or coppices, lofty erections of hurdles and greenery had been placed overnight to hide the preliminary movements of our troops from the glasses of the enemy. Under cover of these regiment after regiment of khaki-clad soldiers, batteries of artillery, and ammunition carts, were proceeding to their allotted posts down the network of roads and lanes leading to the lower ground towards the south-east. Two battalions stood in quarter column behind Thrift Wood. They were kilted corps, probably the Argylls and the London Scottish. Several field batteries moved off to the left towards Woodham Walter. Other battalions took up their position behind Hyde Woods, farther away to the right, the last of them, the Grenadier Guards, I fancy, passing behind them and marching still farther southward.

"Finally two strong battalions, easily recognised as marines by their blue war-kit, marched rapidly down the main road and halted presently behind Woodham Mortimer Place. All this time there was neither sight nor sound of the enemy. The birds carrolled gaily in the old elms round my eyrie, the sparrows and martins piped and twittered in the eaves of the old church, and the sun shone genially on hill and valley, field and wood. To all appearance, peace reigned over the countryside, though the dun masses of troops in the shadows of the woodlands were suggestive of the autumn manœuvres. But for all this, the 'Real Thing' was upon us. As I looked, first one then another long and widely scattered line of crouching men in khaki issued from the cover of Hyde Woods and began slowly to move away towards the east. Then, and not till then, a vivid violet-white flash blazed out on the dim grey upland five miles away to the south-east, which had been pointed out to me as Great Canney, and almost at once a spout of earth and smoke sprang up a little way ahead of the advancing British. A dull boom floated up on the breeze, but was drowned in an ear-splitting crash somewhere close to me. I felt the old tower rock under the concussion, which I presently discovered came from a battery of big 4.7 guns established just outside the churchyard.

"There were at least six of them, and as one after another gave tongue, I descended from my rickety perch and went down to look at them. They were manned by a party of Bluejackets, who had brought them over from Chatham, and among the guns I found some of my acquaintances in the Boer War, 'Joe Chamberlain' and 'Bloody Mary,' to wit. But I must leave my own personal experiences, at least for the present, and endeavour to give a general account of the day's operations so far as I was able to follow them by observation and inquiry. The movement I saw developing below me was the first step towards what I eventually discovered was our main objective—Purleigh. The open ground, flat as a billiard-table to the north of this towards Maldon, presented the weakest front to our attack, but it was considered that if we penetrated there we should in a very short time be decimated and swept away by the cross fire from Maldon and Purleigh, to say nothing of that from other positions we might certainly assume the enemy had prepared in rear.

"Could we succeed in establishing ourselves at Purleigh, however, we should be beyond effective range from Maldon, and should also take Great Canney in reverse, as well as the positions on the refused left flank of the enemy. Maldon, too, would be isolated. Purleigh, therefore, was the key of the position. We have not got it yet, but have made a good stride in its direction, and if it is true that 'fortune favours the brave,' ought certainly to be in possession of it by to-morrow evening. Our first move was in this direction, as I have already indicated. The scouts were picked men from the Line battalions, but the firing lines were composed of Volunteers and, in some cases, Militiamen. It was considered more politic to reserve the Regulars for the later stages of the attack. The firing from Canney, and afterwards from Purleigh, was at first at rather too long a range to be effective, even from the heavy guns that were in use, and later on the heavy long-range fire from 'Bloody Mary' and her sisters at Danbury, and other heavy guns and howitzers in the neighbourhood of East Hanningfield, kept it down considerably, although the big, high-explosive shells were now and again most terribly destructive to the advancing British.

"When, however, the firing line—which as yet had not been near enough to fire a shot in reply—arrived in the neighbourhood of Loddard's Hill, its left came under a terrible rifle fire from Hazeleigh Wood, while its right and centre were all but destroyed by a tornado of shrapnel from some German field batteries to the north of Purleigh. Though dazed and staggered under the appalling sleet of projectiles, the Volunteers stuck doggedly to their ground, though unable to advance. They were intelligent men; and even if they had the inclination to fall back, they knew that there was no safety that way. Line after line was pushed forward, the men stumbling and falling over the thickly scattered bodies of their fallen comrades.

"It was a perfect holocaust. Some other card must be played at once, or the attack must fail."

THE SECOND OF MR. HENRY BENTLEY's descriptive articles in the *Times* told a terrible truth, and was as follows:—

(*From our War Correspondent.*)

CHELMSFORD, *September 7*

"When I sent off my despatch by motor-car last night it was with very different feelings to those with which I take my pen in hand this evening, in the Saracen's Head Hotel, which is the headquarters of my colleagues, the correspondents.

"Last night, despite the hard fighting and the heavy losses we had sustained, the promise of the morrow was distinctly a good one. But now I have little heart with which to commence the difficult and unpleasant task of chronicling the downfall of all our high hopes, the repulse—ay, and the defeat—it is no use mincing matters—of our heroic and sorely tried Army.

"Yes, our gallant soldiers have sustained a reverse which, but for their stubborn fighting qualities and a somewhat inexplicable holding back on the part of the Germans, might very easily have culminated in disaster. Defeat although it undoubtedly is, the darkness of the gloomy outlook is illuminated by the brilliancy of the conduct of our troops.

"From General down to the youngest Volunteer drummer boy, our brave soldiers did all, and more, than could be humanly expected of them, and on none of them can be laid the blame of our ill-success. The plan of attack is agreed on all hands to have been as good a one as could have been evolved; the officers led well, their men fought well, and there was no running short of ammunition at any period of the engagement.

"'Who, then, was responsible?' it may well be asked. The answer is simple. The British public, which, in its apathetic attitude towards military efficiency, aided and abetted by the soothing theories of the extremists of the 'Blue Water' school, had, as usual, neglected to provide an Army fitted to cope in numbers and efficiency with those of our Continental neighbours. Had we had a sufficiency of troops, more especially of regular troops, there is not the slightest doubt that the victory would have been ours. As it was, our General was obliged to attack the enemy's position with a force whose numbers, even if they had been all regular soldiers, were below those judged necessary by military experts for the task in hand.

"Having broken through the German lines, success was in his grasp, had he had sufficient reinforcements to have established him in the position he had won and to beat back the inevitable counter-attack. But it is best that I should continue my account of the fighting from the point at which I closed my letter of yesterday. I had arrived at the checking of our advance near Loddard's Hill by the blast of shrapnel from the German field batteries. It was plain that the Volunteer Brigade, though it held its ground, could not advance farther. But, unnoticed by them, the General had been preparing for this eventuality.

"On the left the two battalions of Marines that I noticed drawn up behind Woodham Mortimer Place suddenly debouched on Loddard's Hill, and, carrying forward with them the débris of the Volunteer firing line, hurled themselves into Hazeleigh Wood. There was a sanguinary hand-to-hand struggle on the wire-entangled border, but the new-comers were not to be denied, and after a quarter of an hour's desperate mêlée, which filled the sylvan glades with moaning and writhing wounded and stark dead bodies, we remained masters of the wood, and even obtained a footing on the railway line where it adjoins it.

"Simultaneously a long line of our field batteries came into action near Woodham Mortimer, some trying to beat down the fire of the German guns opposite, while others replied to a battery that had been established near West Maldon Station to flank the railway, and which was now beginning to open on Hazeleigh Wood. The latter were assisted by a battery of 4.7 guns manned by Volunteers, which took up a position behind Woodham Walter. The firing on Great Canney from our batteries at East Hanningfield redoubled, the whole summit of the hill being at times obscured by the clouds of smoke and débris from the explosions of the big, high-explosive projectiles.

"The main firing line, continually fed from the rear, now began slowly to gain ground, and when the Grenadiers and the Irish Guards, who had managed to work up through the series of plantations that run eastwards for nearly two miles from Woodham Hall without drawing any particular attention from the busily engaged enemy, came into action on the right, there was a distinct move forward. But the defence was too stubborn, and about midday the whole line again came to a standstill, its left still in Hazeleigh Wood, its right at Prentice Farm. Orders were passed that the men should try to entrench themselves as best they could, and spades and other tools were sent forward to those corps who were not provided with them already.

"Here we must leave the main attack to notice what was going on elsewhere. On the north the Colchester Garrison again brought their heavy artillery into action on the slopes south of Wickham Bishops, while others of our troops made a show of advancing against Maldon from the west. These movements were, however, merely intended to keep the German garrison occupied. But on the right a rather important flanking movement was in progress.

"We had a considerable body of troops at East Hanningfield, which lies in a hollow between two little ridges, both running from south-west to north-east, and about a mile apart. The most easterly ridge is very narrow for the most part, and behind it were stationed several batteries of our field howitzers, which fired over it at Great Canney at a range of about 5000 yards. A number of 4.7-inch guns, scattered over the western hill, were also concentrated on the same target. Although the range was an extremely long one, there is no doubt that they made a certain number of effective hits, since Great Canney offered a conspicuous and considerable target. But beyond this the flashes of their discharges drew off all attention from the howitzer batteries in front of them, and served to conceal their presence from the enemy. Otherwise, although invisible, their presence would have been guessed at. As it was, not a single German projectile came anywhere near them.

"When the fighting began, those troops who were not intended to be held in reserve or to co-operate with the right of the main attack moved off in the direction of Woodham Ferrers, and made a feint of attacking the German position astride the two kopjes at Edwin's Hall, their field guns coming into action on the high ground north of Rettendon, and engaging those of the enemy at long range. But the real attack on this salient of the German position came from a very different quarter.

"The troops detailed for this movement were those who had advanced against Wickford at daybreak, and had found it abandoned by the enemy. They consisted of the Oxfordshire Light Infantry, the Honourable Artillery Company, and the Inns of Court Volunteers, together with their own and three or four other machine-gun detachments, their Maxims being mounted on detachable legs instead of carriages. Co-operating with them were the Essex and the East Kent Yeomanry, who were scouting in the direction of Hockley.

"The troops had a long, wearisome march before them, the design being to take advantage of the time of low tide, and to move along out of sight of the enemy behind the northern bank of the river Crouch, as it had been discovered that the German line of defence turned back to the eastward at a mile or two north of the river at the point aimed at. Its guns still commanded it, and might be trusted to render abortive any attempt to throw a bridge across it. The Yeomanry had the task of occupying the attention of the enemy at Canewdon, and of preventing the passage of boats from the German warships. This part of our operations succeeded admirably. The long creeping lines of the Oxfordshires and the machine-gun detachments in their khaki uniforms were almost indistinguishable against the steep mud banks at any distance, and they escaped observation both from the German main lines and from their outpost at Canewdon until they had reached the entrances of the two branch creeks for which they were making.

"Then, and not till then, came the sound of artillery from the left rear of the German position. But it was too late. The Oxford companies pushed forward at the double. Five companies lined the embankments of Stow Creek, the easternmost of the two, while the remainder, ensconced in Clementsgreen Creek, aligned the whole of their machine-guns on the southern of the two kopjes against which the manœuvre had been directed. Their fire, which, coming from a little to the rear of the left flank of the southern kopje, completely enfiladed it, created such slaughter and confusion that the Honourable Artillery Company and the Inns of Court, who had been working up the railway line from

Battle Bridge, had little difficulty in establishing themselves at Woodham Ferrers Station and in an adjacent farm. Being almost immediately afterwards reinforced by the arrival of two regular battalions who had been pushed forward from Rettendon, a determined assault was made on the southern kopje. Its defenders, demoralised by the pelting shower of lead from the machine-gun battery, and threatened also by the advance from Woodham Ferrers village, gave way, and our people, forcing their way over every obstacle, seized the position amid frantic cheering.

"Meanwhile the Oxfordshires had been subjected to a determined counter-attack from North Frambridge. Preceded by a pounding from the guns on Kit's Hill, but aided by the fire of the Yeomanry on the south bank of the river, who galloped up and lined the embankment, thus flanking the defenders of Stow Creek, it was beaten back with considerable loss. The machine-guns were transferred to the neighbourhood of South Kopje, and used with such effect that its defenders, after repulsing several counter-attacks from the adjoining German entrenchment, were able to make themselves masters of the North Kopje also.

"Elsewhere the fighting still continued strenuous and deadly. The main attack had contrived to make some little shelter for itself; but though three several attempts were made to advance from this, all ended in failure, one nearly in disaster. This was the last of the three, when the advancing line was charged by a mass of cavalry which suddenly appeared from behind Great Canney Hill. I myself was a witness of this attack, the most picturesque incident of the day's fighting.

"I was watching the progress of the engagement through my glasses from the high ground about Wickhams Farm, when I saw line after line of the German horsemen in their sky-blue tunics and glittering helmets trot out into the open, canter, and one after another break into a mad gallop as they bore down upon the advancing lines of our citizen soldiers. Staunchly as these had withstood the murderous fire which for hours had been directed upon them, this whirlwind of lance and sabre, the thunder of thousands of hoofs, and the hoarse cries of the riders, were rather more than such partially trained soldiers could stand. A scattering discharge from their rifles was followed by something very much approaching a *sauve qui peut*.

"A large number of the Volunteers, however, sought shelter among the ruined houses of Cock Clarke's hamlet, from whence they opened a heavy fire on the adventurous horsemen. The Argyll and Sutherland Highlanders, who were by this time in Mosklyns Copse, and the Guards and other troops on the right, also opened a rapid and sustained fire on the German cavalry, which, seconded by the shrapnel from our guns on Loddard's Hill, caused them to turn and ride back for their lives. There was a tremendous outburst of firing from both sides after this, followed by quite a lull. One could well imagine that all the combatants were exhausted by the prolonged effort of the day. It was now between five and six in the evening. It was at this time that the news of the capture of the two kopjes reached me, and I made for Danbury to write my despatches.

"Shortly after my arrival I heard of the capture of Spar Hill, a detached knoll about 12,000 yards to the north-west of Purleigh. The Marines from Hazeleigh Wood and the Highlanders from Mosklyns Copse had suddenly and simultaneously assaulted it from opposite sides, and were now entrenching themselves upon it. What wonder, then, that I reported satisfactory progress, and reckoned—too confidently, as it proved—on a victory for the morrow?

"I spent a great part of that night under the stars on the hilltop near East Hanningfield, watching the weird play of the searchlights which swept over the country from a score of different positions, and listening to the crash of artillery and clatter of rifle fire which now and again told of some attempted movement under cover of the darkness. Just before daylight the continuous roar of battle began again, and when light dawned I found that our troops had cut right through the German lines, and had penetrated as far as Cop Kitchen's farm, on the Maldon-Mundon road. Reinforcements were being hurried up, and an attack was being pushed towards the rear of Purleigh and Great Canney, which was being heavily bombarded by some of our large guns, which had been mounted during the night on the two kopjes.

"But the reinforcements were not enough. The Germans held fast to Purleigh and to some reserve positions they had established about Mundon. After two or three hours of desperate effort, costing the lives of thousands, our attack was at a standstill. At this critical moment a powerful counter-attack was made from Maldon, and, outnumbered and almost surrounded, our gallant warriors had to give ground. But they fell back as doggedly as they had advanced, the Argylls, Marines, and Grenadiers covering the retreat on Danbury.

"The guns at East Hanningfield and the two kopjes checked the pursuit to a great extent, and the Germans seemed unwilling to go far from their works. The kopjes had to be abandoned later in the day, and we now occupy our former line from Danbury to Billericay, and are busily engaged in entrenching ourselves."

XIII

Defence at Last

L ate on Wednesday night came tardy news of the measures we were taking to mobilise.

The Aldershot Army Corps, so complete in the "Army List," consisted, as all the world knew, of three divisions, but of these only two existed, the other being found to be on paper. The division in question, located at Bordon, was to be formed on mobilisation, and this measure was now being proceeded with. The train service was practically suspended, owing to the damage done to the various lines south of London by the enemy's emissaries. Several of these men had been detected, and being in plain clothes were promptly shot out of hand. However, their work had, unfortunately for us, been accomplished, and trains could only run as far as the destroyed bridges, so men on their way to join their respective corps were greatly delayed in consequence.

In one instance, at about four o'clock in the morning, three men were seen by a constable acting suspiciously beneath the iron girder bridge of the South-Western Railway spanning the road on the London side of Surbiton Station. Of a sudden the men bolted, and a few moments later, with a terrific explosion, the great bridge crashed into the road.

The constable raised the alarm that the fugitives were German spies, whereupon a few unemployed workmen, rushing down Effingham Gardens, caught two of the men in Malpas Road. In the hands of these irate bricklayers the Germans were given short shrift, and, notwithstanding the protests of the constable, the two spies were dragged along the Portsmouth Road, pitched headlong into the Thames almost immediately opposite the water-works, and drowned.

All was confusion at Bordon, where men were arriving in hundreds on foot, and by the service of motor-omnibuses, which the War Office had on the day before established between Charing Cross and Aldershot. Perspiring staff officers strove diligently, without much avail, to sort out into their respective units this ever-increasing mass of reservists.

There was perfect chaos.

Before the chief constituent parts of the division—that is to say, regiments who were stationed elsewhere—had arrived little could be done with the reservists. The regiments in question were in many cases stationed at considerable distance, and although they had received orders to start, were prevented from arriving owing to the universal interruptions of the railway traffic south. By this, whole valuable days were lost—days when at any hour the invaders might make a sudden swoop on London.

Reports were alarming and conflicting. Some said that the enemy meant to strike a blow upon the capital just as suddenly as they had landed, while others reassured the alarmists that the German plans were not yet complete, and that they had not sufficient stores to pursue the campaign.

Reservists, with starvation staring them in the face, went eagerly south to join their regiments, knowing that at least they would be fed with regularity; while, in addition, the true patriotic spirit of the Englishman had been roused against the aggressive Teuton, and everyone, officer and man, was eager to bear his part in driving the invader into the sea.

The public were held breathless. What would happen?

Arrivals at Aldershot, however, found the whole arrangements in such a complete muddle that Army Service Corps men, who ought to have been at Woolwich, were presenting themselves for enrolment at Bordon, and infantry of the line were conducted into the camp of the Dragoons. The Motor Volunteer Corps were at this moment of very great use. The cars were filled with staff officers and other exalted officials, who were settling themselves in various offices, and passing out again to make necessary arrangements for dealing with such a large influx of men.

There were activity and excitement everywhere. Men were rapidly drawing their clothing, or as much of it as they could get, and civilians were quickly becoming soldiers on every hand. Officers of the Reserve were driving up in motor-cars and cabs, many of them with their old battered uniform-cases, that had seen service in the field in distant parts of the globe. Men from the "Junior" and the "Senior" wrung each other's hands on returning to active duty with their old regiments, and at once settled down into the routine work they knew so well.

The rumour, however, had now got about that a position in the neighbourhood of Cambridge had been selected by the General Staff as being the most suitable theatre of action where an effective stand could, with any hope of success, be made. It was evident that the

German tactics were to strike a swift and rapid blow at London. Indeed, nothing at present stood in their way except the gallant little garrison at Colchester, who had been so constantly driven back by the enemy's cavalry on attempting to make any reconnaissance, and who might be swept out of existence at any hour.

During Tuesday and Wednesday large gangs of workmen had been busy repairing the damaged lines. The first regiment complete for the field was the 2nd Battalion of the 5th Fusiliers, who carried upon their colours the names of a score of battles, ranging from Corunna and Badajoz, all through the Peninsula, Afghanistan, and Egypt, down to the Modder River. This regiment left by train for London on Tuesday evening, and was that same night followed by the 2nd Battalion King's Liverpool Regiment and the 1st King's Shropshire Light Infantry, while the Manchester Regiment got away soon after midnight.

These formed the second infantry brigade of the 1st Division, and were commanded by Brigadier-General Sir John Money. They were several hours getting up to London, whence from Clapham Junction their trains circled London on to the Great Eastern system to Braintree, where the Horn Hotel was made the headquarters. By other trains in the small hours of the morning the last of the Guards Brigade under Colonel (temporary Brigadier-General) Lord Wansford departed, and duly arrived at Saffron Walden, to join their comrades on the line of defence.

The divisional troops were also on the move early on Wednesday. Six batteries of artillery and the field company of Royal Engineers left by road. There was a balloon section accompanying this, and searchlights, wireless instruments, and cables for field-telegraphy were carried in the waggons.

The 2nd Division, under Lieutenant-General Morgan, C.B., was also active. The 3rd Infantry Brigade, commanded by Major-General Fortescue, composed of 2nd Battalion Northamptonshire Regiment, the 2nd Bedfordshire, the 1st Princess of Wales' Own, and the 1st Royal Welsh Fusiliers, were preparing, but had not yet moved. The 4th Infantry Brigade of the same division, consisting of the 3rd and 4th Battalions King's Royal Rifle Corps, the 2nd Sherwood Foresters, and the 2nd South Lancashire, with the usual smartness of those distinguished regiments, were quick and ready, now as ever, to go to the front. They were entrained to Baldock, slightly east of Hitchin, where they marched out on the Icknield Way. These were followed by Fortescue's Brigade, who were also bound for Baldock and the neighbourhood.

The bulk of the cavalry and field artillery of both divisions, together with the divisional troops, were compelled to set out by march-route from Aldershot for the line of defences. The single and all-sufficient reason of this delay in sending out the cavalry and artillery was owing to the totally inadequate accommodation on the railways for the transport of so many horses and guns. The troop-trains, which were, of course, necessary to transport the infantry, were not forthcoming in sufficient numbers, this owing to the fact that at several points the lines to London were still interrupted.

The orders to the cavalry who went by march-route were to get up to the line proposed to be taken up by the infantry as quickly as possible, and to operate in front of it to the east and north-east in screening and reconnoitring duties. The temporary deficiency of cavalry, who ought, of course, to have been the first to arrive at the scene, was made good as far as possible by the general employment of hordes of motor-cyclists, who scoured the country in large armed groups in order to ascertain, if possible, the dispositions of the enemy. This they did, and very soon after their arrival reported the result of their investigations to the general officers commanding the 1st and 2nd Divisions.

Meanwhile both cavalry and artillery in great bodies, and strings of motor-omnibuses filled with troops, were upon the white, dusty roads passing through Staines to Hounslow and Brentford, thence to London, St. Albans, *en route* to their respective divisions. Roughly, the distance was over fifty miles, therefore those marching were compelled to halt the night on the way, while those in the motor-omnibuses got through to their destination.

To cavalry, thirty-five miles is a long day's march, and in view of the heavy work before them, stringent orders had been given them to spare the horses as much as possible. The heads of the columns did not, therefore, pass beyond Hounslow on the first night, and in that neighbourhood the thousands of all ranks made themselves as comfortable as circumstances would permit. The majority of the men were fed and billeted by the all-too-willing inhabitants, and upon their hot march they met with ovations everywhere.

At last we were defending ourselves! The sight of British troops hurrying to the front swelled the hearts of the villagers and townsfolk with renewed patriotism, and everywhere, through the blazing, dusty day, the men were offered refreshment by even the poorest and humblest cottagers. In Bagshot, in Staines, and in Hounslow the people went frantic with excitement, as squadron after squadron rapidly passed along, with its guns, wagons, and ambulances rumbling noisily over the stones, in the rear.

Following these came pontoon troops with their long grey wagons and mysterious-looking bridging apparatus, telegraph troops, balloon sections, supply columns, field bakery, and field hospitals, the last-named packed in wagons marked with the well-known red cross of the Geneva Convention.

No sooner was Aldershot denuded of its army corps, however, than battalions began to arrive from Portsmouth on their way north, while troops from the great camp on Salisbury Plain were rapidly being pushed to the front, which, roughly speaking, extended through Hitchin, Royston, to Saffron Walden, across to Braintree, and also the high ground commanding the valley of the Colne to Colchester.

The line chosen by the General Staff was the natural chain of hills which presented the first obstacle to the enemy advancing on London from the wide plain stretching eastward beyond Cambridge to the sea.

If this could be held strongly, as was intended, by practically the whole of the British forces located in the South of England, including the Yeomanry, Militia, and Volunteers—who were now all massing in every direction—then the deadly peril threatening England might be averted.

But could it be held?

This was the appalling question on everyone's tongue all over the country, for it now became generally known that upon this line of defence four complete and perfectly equipped German army corps were ready to advance at any moment, in addition to the right flank being exposed to the attack of the XIIth Saxon Corps, entrenched on the Essex coast.

It was estimated that no fewer than two hundred thousand Germans were already upon English soil!

The outlook grew blacker every hour.

London was in a state of absolute stagnation and chaos. In the City, business was now at an entire standstill. The credit system had received a fatal blow, and nobody wanted to buy securities. Had people kept level heads in the crisis there would have been a moratorium, but, as it was, a panic had been created that nothing could allay. Even Consols

WE, WILHELM,

GIVE NOTICE to the inhabitants of those provinces occupied by the German Imperial Army, that—

I MAKE WAR upon the soldiers, and not upon English citizens. Consequently, it is my wish to give the latter and their property entire security, and as long as they do not embark upon hostile enterprise against the German troops they have a right to my protection.

GENERALS COMMANDING the various corps in the various districts in England are ordered to place before the public the stringent measures which I have ordered to be adopted against towns, villages, and persons who act in contradiction to the usages of war. They are to regulate in the same manner all the operations necessary for the well-being of our troops, to fix the difference between the English and German rate of exchange, and to facilitate in every manner possible the individual transactions between our Army and the inhabitants of England.

WILHELM

Given at POTSDAM, *September 4th, 1910.*

The above is a copy of the German Imperial Decree, printed in English, which was posted by unknown German agents in London, and which appeared everywhere throughout East Anglia and in that portion of the Midlands held by the enemy.

were now unsaleable. Some of the smaller banks were known to have failed, and traders and manufacturers all over the country had been ruined on account of credit, the foundation of all trade, having been swept away. Only persons of the highest financial standing could have dealt with the banks, even if they had remained open.

The opinion held in banking circles was that if the invasion should unfortunately prove disastrous to England, and Germany demand a huge indemnity, there was still hope, however small. The experience of the Franco-German War had proved that though in such circumstances the Bank, for a considerable period, might not be able to resume cash payments, yet, with sound finance, there was no reason that the currency should greatly depreciate. During the period of suspension of cash payments by the Bank of France the premium on gold never went above 1.5 per cent., and during most of the period was 5, 4, or even less per mille. Therefore what the French by sound banking had been able to do, there was no reason why English bankers could not also do.

At the outbreak of the war of 1870, on August 1 French Three per Cent. Rentes were at 60.85, and Four and a Half per Cents. at 98. On the memorable day of Sedan, September 2, they were at 50.80 and 88.50 respectively, and on January 2, 1871, Three per Cents. were down to 50.95. At the commencement of the Commune, on March 18, they were at 51.50 and 76.25, and on the 30th of that month down to 50.60 and 76.25 respectively.

With so little money in England as there now was, securities had fallen to the value at which holders would as soon not sell as sell at such a great discount. High rates and the heavy fall in the value of securities had brought business in every quarter all over London to a standstill. Firms all over the country were now hard put to it in order to find the necessary money to carry on their various trades. Instantly, after the report of the reverse at Sheffield, there was a wild rush to obtain gold, and securities dropped even a few more points.

Therefore, there was little or nothing for the banks to do, and Lombard Street, Lothbury, and the other banking centres were closed, as though it had been Sunday or Bank Holiday. Despair was, alas! everywhere, and the streets presented strange scenes.

Most of the motor-omnibuses had been taken off the road and pressed into the service of the military. The walls bore a dozen different broadsides and proclamations, which were read by the gaping, hungry crowds.

The Royal Standard was flying from St. Stephen's Tower, for Parliament had now met, and all members who were not abroad for their summer vacation had taken their places at the heated debates now hourly in progress. Over Buckingham Palace the Royal Standard also flew proudly, while upon every public building was displayed a Union Jack or a white ensign, many of which had done duty at the coronation of His Majesty King Edward. The Admiralty flew its own flag, and upon the War Office, the India Office, the Foreign Office, and all the dark, sombre Government buildings in Whitehall was bunting displayed.

The wild enthusiasm of Sunday and Monday, however, had given place to a dark, hopeless apprehension. The great mobs now thronging all the principal thoroughfares in London were already half-famished. Food was daily rising in price, and the East End was already starving. Bands of lawless men and women from the slums of Whitechapel were parading the West End streets and squares, and were camping out in Hyde Park and St. James's Park.

The days were stifling, for it was an unusually hot September following upon a blazing August, and as each breathless evening the sun sank, it shed its blood-red afterglow over the giant metropolis, grimly precursory of the ruin so surely imminent.

Supplies were still reaching London from the country, but there had been immediate panic in the corn and provision markets, with the result that prices had instantly jumped up beyond the means of the average Londoner. The poorer ones were eagerly collecting the refuse in Covent Garden Market and boiling it down to make soup in lieu of anything else, while wise fathers of families went to the shops themselves and made meagre purchases daily of just sufficient food to keep body and soul together.

For the present there was no fear of London being absolutely starved, at least the middle class and wealthier portion of it. At present it was the poor—the toiling millions now unemployed—who were the first to feel the pinch of hunger and its consequent despair. They filled the main arteries of London—Holborn, Oxford Street, the Strand, Regent Street, Piccadilly, the Haymarket, St. James's Street, Park Lane, Victoria Street, and Knightsbridge, overflowing northward into Grosvenor, Berkeley, Portman, and Cavendish Squares, Portland Place, and to the terraces around Regent's Park. The centre of London became congested. Day and night it was the same. There was no sleep. From across the river and from the East End the famished poor came in their bewildering thousands, the majority of them honest workers, indignant that by the foolish policy of the Government they now found themselves breadless.

Before the Houses of Parliament, before the fine new War Office, and the Admiralty, before Downing Street, and before the houses of known members of the Government, constant demonstrations were being made, the hungry crowds groaning at the authorities, and singing "God save the King." Though starving and in despair, they were nevertheless loyal, still confident that by the personal effort of His Majesty some amicable settlement would be arrived at. The French *entente cordiale* was remembered, and our Sovereign had long ago been declared to be the first diplomat in Europe. Every Londoner believed in him, and loved him.

Many houses of the wealthy, especially those of foreigners, had their windows broken. In Park Lane, in Piccadilly, and in Grosvenor Square, more particularly, the houses seemed to excite the ire of the crowds, who, notwithstanding special constables having been sworn in, were now quite beyond the control of the police. The German Ambassador had presented his letters of recall on Sunday evening, and together with the whole staff had been accorded a safe conduct to Dover, whence they had left for the Continent. The Embassy in Carlton House Terrace, and also the Consulate-General in Finsbury Square, had, however, suffered severely at the hands of the angry crowd, notwithstanding that both premises were under police protection.

All the German waiters employed at the Cecil, the Savoy, the Carlton, the Métropole, the Victoria, the Grand, and the other big London hotels, had already fled for their lives out into the country, anywhere from the vengeance of the London mob. Hundreds of them were trying to make their way within the German lines in Essex and Suffolk, and it was believed that many had succeeded—those, most probably, who had previously acted as spies. Others, it was reported, had been set upon by the excited populace, and more than one had lost his life.

Pandemonium reigned in London. Every class and every person in every walk of life was affected. German interests were being looked after by the Russian Ambassador, and this very fact caused a serious demonstration before Chesham House, the big mansion where lives the representative of the Czar. Audacious spies had, in secret, in the night actually posted copies of Von Kronhelm's proclamation upon the Griffin at Temple Bar, upon the Marble Arch, and upon the Mansion House. But these had been quickly torn down, and if the hand that had placed them there had been known, it would certainly have meant death to the one who had thus insulted the citizens of London.

Yet the truth was, alas! too plain. Spread out across Essex and Suffolk, making leisurely preparations and laughing at our futile defence, lay over one hundred thousand well-equipped, well-fed Germans, ready, when their plans were completed, to advance upon and crush the complex city which is the pride and home of every Englishman—London.

ON FRIDAY NIGHT AN OFFICIAL communication from the War Office was issued to the Press, showing the exact position of the invaders. It was roughly this:—

"The IXth German Corps, which had effected a landing at Lowestoft, had, after moving along the most easterly route, including the road through Saxmundham and Ipswich, at length arrived at a position where their infantry outposts had occupied the higher slopes of the rising ground overlooking the river Stour, near Manningtree, which town, as well as Ipswich, was held by them.

"The left flank of this corps rested on the river Stour itself, so that it was secure from any turning movement. Its front was opposed to and directly threatened Colchester, while its outposts, to say nothing of its independent cavalry, reached out in a northerly direction towards Stowmarket, where they joined hands with the left flank of the Xth Corps—those under Von Wilburg, who had landed at Yarmouth—whose headquarters were now at Bury St. Edmund's, their outposts being disposed south, overlooking the valley of the upper reaches of the Stour."

Nor was this all. From Newmarket there came information that the enemy who had landed at Weybourne and Cromer—viz., the IVth Corps under Von Kleppen—were now encamping on the racecourse and being billeted in the town and villages about, including Exning, Ashley, Moulton, and Kentford. Frölich's cavalry brigade had penetrated South, covering the advance, and had now scoured the country, sweeping away the futile resistance of the British Yeomanry, and scattering cavalry squadrons which they found opposed to them, all the time maintaining communication with the Xth Corps on their left, and the flower of the German Army, the Guards Corps, from King's Lynn, on their right. Throughout the advance from Holt, Von Dorndorf's motorists had been of the greatest utility. They had taken constantly companies of infantry hither and thither. At any threatened point, so soon as the sound of firing was heard in any cavalry skirmish or little engagement of outposts, the smart motor infantry were on the spot with the promptness of a fire brigade proceeding to a call. For this reason the field artillery, who were largely armed with quick-firing guns, capable of pouring in a hail of shrapnel on any exposed point, were enabled to push on much farther than would have been otherwise possible. They were always adequately supported by a sufficient escort of these up-to-date troops, who, although infantry, moved with greater rapidity than cavalry itself, and who, moreover, brought with them their Maxims, which dealt havoc far and near.

The magnificent troops of the Duke of Mannheim in their service uniforms, who had landed at King's Lynn, had come across the wide, level roads, some by way of Downham Market, Littleport, and Ely, and arrived at Cambridge. The 2nd Division, under Lieutenant-General von Kasten, protecting the exposed flanks, had marched *viâ* Wisbech, March, Chatteris, and St. Ives, while the masses of the cavalry of the Guard, including the famous White Cuirassiers, had been acting independently around the flat fen country, Spalding and Peterborough, and away to quaint old Huntingdon, striking terror into the inhabitants, and effectively checking any possible offensive movement of the British that might have been directed upon the great German Army during its ruthless advance.

Beyond this, worse remained. It was known that the VIIth Corps, under Von Bristram, had landed at Goole, and that General Graf Haeseler had landed at Hull, New Holland, and Grimsby. This revealed what the real strategy of the Generalissimo had been. Their function seemed twofold. First and foremost their presence, as a glance at the map will show, effectually prevented any attack from the British troops gathered from the north and elsewhere, and who were, as shown, concentrated near Sheffield and Birmingham, until these two corps had themselves been attacked and repulsed, which we were, alas! utterly unable to accomplish.

These were two fine German army corps, complete to the proverbial last button, splendidly equipped, well fed, and led by officers who had had lifelong training, and were perfectly well acquainted with every mile of the country they occupied, by reason of years of careful study given to maps of England. It was now entirely plain that the function of these two corps was to paralyse our trade in Yorkshire and Lancashire, to commit havoc in the big cities, to terrify the people, and to strike a crushing blow at our industrial centres, leaving the siege of London to the four other corps now so rapidly advancing upon the metropolis.

Events meanwhile were marching quickly in the North.

The town of Sheffield throughout Tuesday and Wednesday was the scene of the greatest activity. Day and night the streets were filled with an excited populace, and hour by hour the terror increased.

Every train arriving from the North was crowded with Volunteers and troops of the line from all stations in the Northern Command.

The 1st Battalion West Riding Regiment had joined the Yorkshire Light Infantry, who were already stationed in Sheffield, as had also the 19th Hussars, and from every regimental district and depot, including Scarborough, Richmond, Carlisle, Seaforth, Beverley, Halifax, Lancaster, Preston, Bolton, Warrington, Bury, Ashton-under-Lyne, came battalions of Militia and Volunteers. From Carlisle came the Reservists of the Border Regiment, from Richmond those of the Yorkshire Regiment, from Newcastle came what was left of the Reservists of the Durham Light Infantry, and the Northumberland Fusiliers, from Lancaster the Royal Lancashires, while field artillery came from Seaforth and Preston, and small bodies of Reservists of the Liverpool and the South Lancashire Regiments came from Warrington. Contingents of the East and North Lancashire Regiments arrived from Preston. The Militia, including battalions of the Liverpool Regiment, the South Lancashire Regiment, the Lancashire Fusiliers, and other regiments in the command, were hurried to the scene of action outside Sheffield. From every big town in the whole of the North of England and South of Scotland came straggling units of Volunteers. The mounted troops were almost entirely Yeomanry, and included the Duke of Lancaster's Own Imperial Yeomanry, the East Riding of Yorks, the Lancashire Hussars, Northumberland Yeomanry, Westmorland and Cumberland Yeomanry, the Queen's Own Yorkshire Dragoons, and the York Hussars.

These troops, with their ambulances, their baggage, and all their impedimenta, created the utmost confusion at both railway stations. The great concourse of idlers cheered and cheered again, the utmost enthusiasm being displayed when each battalion forming up was marched away out of the town to the position chosen for the defence, which now reached from Woodhouse on the south, overlooking and commanding the whole valley of the river Rother, through Catcliffe, Brinsworth, and Tinsley, previously alluded to, skirting Greasborough to the high ground north of Wentworth, also commanding the river Don and all approaches to it through Mexborough, and over the various bridges which spanned this stream—a total of about eight miles.

The south flank was thrown back another four miles to Norton, in an endeavour to prevent the whole position being turned, should the Germans elect to deliver their threatened blow from a more southerly point than was anticipated.

The total line then to be occupied by the defenders was about twelve miles, and into this front was crowded the heterogeneous mass of troops of all arms. The post of honour was at Catcliffe, the dominating key to the whole position, which was occupied by the sturdy soldiers of the 1st Battalion West Riding Regiment and the 2nd Battalion Yorkshire Light Infantry, while commanding every bridge crossing the rivers which lay between Sheffield and the invaders were concentrated the guns of the 7th Brigade Royal Horse Artillery, and of the Field Artillery, the 2nd, the 30th, the 37th, and 38th Brigades, the latter having hurriedly arrived from Bradford.

All along the crests of these slopes which formed the defence of Sheffield, rising steeply from the river at times up to five hundred feet, were assembled the Volunteers, all now by daybreak on Thursday morning busily engaged in throwing up shelter-trenches and making hasty earthwork defences for the guns. The superintendence of this force had merged itself into that of the Northern Command, which nominally had its headquarters in York, but which had now been transferred to Sheffield itself, for the best of reasons—that it was of no value at York, and was badly wanted farther south. General Sir George Woolmer, who so distinguished himself in South Africa, had therefore shifted his headquarters to the Town Hall in Sheffield, but as soon as he had begun to get the line of defence completed, he, with his staff, moved on to Handsworth, which was centrally situated.

In the command were to be found roughly twenty-three battalions of Militia and forty-eight of Volunteers; but owing to the supineness and neglect of the Government the former regiments now found themselves, at the moment when wanted, greatly denuded of officers, and, owing to any lack of encouragement to enlist, largely depleted in men. As regards the Volunteers, matters were even worse. During the past five years as much cold water as possible had been thrown upon all voluntary and patriotic military endeavour by the "antimilitant" Cabinets which had so long met at No. 10 Downing Street. The Volunteers, as a body, were sick to death of the slights and slurs cast upon their well-meaning efforts. Their "paper" organisation, like many other things, remained intact, but for a long time wholesale resignations of officers and men had been taking place. Instead, therefore, of a muster of about twenty-five thousand auxiliaries being available in this command, as the country would have anticipated, if the official tabulated statements had been any guide, it was found that only about fifteen thousand had responded to the call to arms. And upon these heroic men, utterly insufficient in point of numbers, Sheffield had to rely for its defence.

It might reasonably have been anticipated that in the majority of Volunteer regiments furnished by big manufacturing towns, a battalion would have consisted of at least five hundred efficient soldiers; but owing to the causes alluded to, in many cases it was found that from one hundred to two hundred only could "pass the doctor," after having trained themselves to the use of arms. The catchword phrase, "Peace, retrenchment, and reform," so long dinned into the ears of the electorate by the pro-German Party and by every socialistic demagogue, had sunk deeply into the minds of the people. Patriotism had been jeered at, and solemn warnings laughed to scorn, even when uttered by responsible and far-seeing statesmen. Yet the day of awakening had dawned—a rude awakening indeed!

Away to the eastward of Sheffield—exactly where was yet unknown—sixty thousand perfectly-equipped and thoroughly-trained German horse, foot and artillery, were ready at any moment to advance westward into our manufacturing districts!

XIV

British Success at Royston

Arrests of alleged spies were reported from Manchester, Birmingham, Liverpool, Sheffield, and other large towns. Most of the prisoners were, however, able to prove themselves naturalised British subjects; but several men in Manchester, Birmingham, and Sheffield were detained pending investigation and examination of correspondence found at their homes. In Manchester, where there are always a number of Germans, it is known that many slipped away on Sunday night after the publication of the news of the invasion. Several houses in Eccles and Patricroft, outside Manchester, a house in Brown Street in the City itself, one in Gough Street, Birmingham, and another in Sandon Place, Sheffield, were all searched, and from the reports received by Scotland Yard it was believed that certain important correspondence had been seized, correspondence which had betrayed a widespread system of German espionage in this country. Details were wanting, as the police authorities withheld the truth, for fear, it was supposed, of increasing the public alarm. At the house in Sheffield, where lived a young German who had come to England ostensibly as pupil at one of the large steelworks, an accumulation of newspaper cuttings was discovered, together with a quantity of topographical information concerning the country over which the enemy was now advancing from Goole.

In most of the larger Midland towns notices had been issued by the mayors deprecating hostility towards residents of foreign origin, and stating that all suspicious cases were already receiving the attention of the police.

In Stafford the boot factories were idle, and thousands of despairing men were lounging about in Greengate, Eastgate, and other thoroughfares. In the Potteries all work was at a standstill. At Stoke-on-Trent, at Hanley, at Burslem, Tunstall, and Congleton all was chaos. Minton's, Copeland's, Doulton's, and Brown Westhead's were closed, and thousands upon thousands were already wanting bread. The silk-thread industry at Leek was ruined, so was the silk industry at Macclesfield; the great breweries at Burton were idle, while the hosiery factories of Leicester and the boot factories of Northampton were all shut.

With the German troops threatening Sheffield, Nottingham was in a state of intense alarm. The lace and hosiery factories had with one accord closed on Tuesday, and the great Market Place was now filled day and night by thousands upon thousands of unemployed mill-hands of both sexes. On Friday, however, came the news of how Sheffield had built barricades against the enemy, and there ensued a frantic attempt at defence on the part of thousands of terrified and hungry men and women. In their frenzy they sacked houses in order to obtain material to construct the barricades, which were, however, built just where the fancy took the crowd. One was constructed in Clumber Street, near the Lion Hotel; another at Lister Gate; and a third, a much larger one, in Radford Road. Near the Carrington Station, on the road to Arnold, a huge structure soon rose, another at Basford, while the road in from Carlton and the bridges leading in from West Bridgford and Wilford were also effectually blocked.

The white, interminable North Road, that runs so straight from London through York and Berwick to Edinburgh, was, with its by-roads in the Midlands, now being patrolled by British cavalry, and here and there telegraphists around a telegraph post showed that those many wires at the roadside were being used for military communication.

At several points along the road between Wansford Bridge and Retford the wires had been cut and tangled by the enemy's agents, but by Friday all had been restored again. In one spot, between Weston and Sutton-on-Trent, eight miles south of Newark, a trench had actually been dug during the night, the tube containing the subterranean telegraph lines discovered, and the whole system to the North disorganised. Similar damage had been done by German spies to the line between London and Birmingham, two miles south of Shipston-on-Stour, and again the line between Loughborough and Nottingham had been similarly destroyed.

The Post Office linesmen had, however, quickly made good the damage everywhere in the country not already occupied by the enemy, and telegraph and telephone communication North and South was now practically again in its normal state.

Through Lincolnshire the enemy's advance patrols had spread South over every road between the Humber and the Wash, and in the city of Lincoln itself a tremendous sensation was caused when on Wednesday, market-day, several bodies of German motor-cyclists swept into the Stonebow and dismounted at the Saracen's Head amid the crowd of farmers and dealers who had assembled there, not, alas! to do business, but to discuss the situation. In a moment the city was panic-stricken. From mouth to mouth the dread truth spread that the Germans were upon them, and people ran indoors and barricaded themselves within their houses.

A body of Uhlans came galloping proudly through the Stonebow a quarter of an hour later, and halted in High Street, opposite Wyatt's clothing shop, as though awaiting orders. Then in rapid succession troops seemed to arrive from all quarters, many halting in the Cathedral Close and by Exchequer Gate, and others riding through the streets in order to terrify the inhabitants.

Von Kronhelm's famous proclamation was posted by German soldiers upon the police station, upon the Stonebow, and upon the door of the grand old Cathedral itself, and before noon a German officer accompanied by his staff called upon the Mayor and warned him that Lincoln was occupied by the German troops, and that any armed resistance would be punished by death, as the Generalissimo's proclamation stated. An indemnity was demanded, and then the powerless people saw upon the Cathedral and upon several of the public buildings the German flag rise and float out upon the summer wind.

Boston was full of German infantry, and officers had taken up temporary quarters in the Peacock and the other hotels in the market-place, while upon the "stump" the enemy's colours were flying.

No news came from London. People in Norwich, Ipswich, Yarmouth, and other places heard vaguely of the invasion in the North, and of fighting in which the Germans were careful to report that they were always successful. They saw the magnificently equipped army of the Kaiser, and, comparing it with our mere apology for military force, regarded the issue as hopeless from the very first. In every town the German colours were displayed, and all kinds of placards in German and in English made their appearance.

The *Daily Mail*, on September 10, published the following despatch from one of its war correspondents, Mr. Henry Mackenzie:—

ROYSTON, *September 9*

"Victory at last. A victory due not only to the bravery and exertion of our troops, regular and auxiliary, but also to the genius of Field-Marshal Lord Byfield, our Commander-in-Chief, ably seconded by the energy and resource with which

Sir William Packington, in command of the IVth Army Corps at Baldock, carried out that part of the programme entrusted to him.

"But though in this success we may hope that we are seeing the first glimmerings of dawn,—of deliverance from the nightmare of German invasion that is now oppressing our dear old England,—we must not be led into foolishly sanguine hopes. The snake has been scotched, and pretty badly into the bargain, but he is far from being killed. The German IVth Army Corps under the famous General Von Kleppen, their magnificent Garde Corps commanded by the Duke of Mannheim, and Frölich's fine Cavalry Division, have been repulsed in their attack on our positions near Royston and Saffron Walden, and driven back with great loss and confusion. But we are too weak to follow up our victory as it should be followed up.

"The menace of the IXth and Xth Corps on our right flank ties us to our selected position, and the bulk of our forces being composed of indifferently trained Volunteers and Militia, is much more formidable behind entrenchments than when attempting to manœuvre in a difficult and intricate country such as it is about here. But, on the other hand, we have given pause to the invaders, and have certainly gained a few days' time, which will be invaluable to us.

"We shall be able to get on with the line of fortifications that are being constructed to bar the approaches to London, and behind which it will be necessary for us to make our final stand. I do not conceive that it is possible for such an agglomeration of amateur troops as ours are in the main, to defeat in the open field such formidable and well-trained forces as the Germans have succeeded in throwing into this country. But when our Navy has regained command of the sea we hope that we may, before very long, place our unwelcome visitors 'between the devil and the deep sea'—the part of the devil being played by our brave troops finally concentrated behind the strong defences of the metropolis. In short, that the Germans may run out of ammunition and provisions. For if communication with the Fatherland is effectively cut, they must starve, unless they have previously compelled our submission, for it is impossible for an army of the size that has invaded us to live on the country.

"No doubt hundreds, nay thousands, of our non-militant countrymen—and, alas! women and children—will starve before the German troops are conquered by famine, that most terrible of enemies; but this issue seems to be the only possible one that will save the country.

"But enough of these considerations of the future. It is time that I should relate what I can of the glorious victory which our gallant defenders have torn from the enemy. I do not think that I am giving any information away if I state that the British position lay mainly between Saffron Walden and Royston, the headquarters respectively of the IInd and IIIrd Army Corps. The IVth Corps was at Baldock, thrown back to cover the left flank, and protect our communications by the Great Northern Railway. A detached force, from what command supplied it is not necessary or advisable to say, was strongly entrenched on the high ground north-west of Helions Bumpstead, serving to strengthen our right. Our main line of defence—very thinly held in some parts— began a little to the south-east of Saffron Walden, and ran westwards along a range of high ground through Elmdon and Chrishall to Heydon. Here it turned south through Great Chrishall to Little Chrishall, where it again turned west, and occupied the high range south of Royston, on which stands the village of Therfield.

"The night before the battle we knew that the greater portion of the German IVth and Garde Corps were concentrated, the former at Newmarket, the 1st Division of the latter at Cambridge, the 2nd on this side of St. Ives, while Frölich's Cavalry Division had been in constant contact with our outposts the greater part of the day previous. The Garde Cavalry Brigade was reported to be well away to the westward towards Kettering, as we suppose, on account of the reports which have been going about of a concentration of Yeomanry and Militia in the hilly country near Northampton. Our Intelligence Department, which appears to have been very well served by its spies, obtained early knowledge of the intention of the Germans to make an attack on our position. In fact, they talked openly of it, and stated at Cambridge and Newmarket that they would not manœuvre at all, and only hoped that we should hold on long enough to our position to enable them to smash up our IInd and IIIrd Corps by a frontal attack, and so clear the road to London. The main roads lent themselves admirably to such strategy, which rendered the reports of their intentions the more probable, for they all converged on our position from their main points of concentration.

"The letter 'W' will exactly serve to show the positions of the contending forces. St. Ives is at the top of the first stroke, Cambridge at the junction of the two shorter centre ones, Newmarket at the top of the last stroke, while the British positions at Royston and Saffron Walden are at the junctions of all four strokes at the bottom of the letter. The strokes also represent the roads, except that from Cambridge three good roads lead towards each of the British positions. The prisoners taken from the Germans in the various preliminary skirmishes also made no bones of boasting that a direct attack was imminent, and our Commander-in-Chief eventually, and rightly as it proved, determined to take the risk of all this information having been specially promulgated by the German Staff to cover totally different intentions, as was indeed quite probable, and to accept it as true. Having made up his mind, he lost no time in taking action. He ordered the IVth Corps under Sir William Packington to move on Potton, twelve miles to the north-west, as soon as it was dark. As many cavalry and mounted infantry as could possibly be spared from Royston were placed at his disposal.

"It ought to be stated that while the auxiliary troops had been busily employed ever since their arrival in entrenching the British position, the greater part of the regular troops had been occupying an advanced line two or three miles to the northward on the lower spurs of the hills, and every possible indication of a determination to hold this as long as possible was afforded to the German reconnoitrers. During the night these troops fell back to the position which had been prepared, the outposts following just before daylight. About 6 A.M. the enemy were reported to be advancing in force along the Icknield Way from Newmarket, and also by the roads running on either bank of the river Cam. Twenty minutes later considerable bodies of German troops were reported at Fowlmere and Melbourn on the two parallel Royston-Cambridge roads. They must have followed very close on the heels of our retiring outposts. It was a very misty morning,—down in the low ground over which the enemy were advancing especially so,—but about seven a gust of wind from the westward dispelled the white fog-wreaths that hung about our left front and enabled our look-outs to get a glimpse along the famous Ermine Street, which runs straight as an arrow from Royston for twenty or thirty miles to the N.N.W.

"Along this ancient Roman way, far as the eye could reach, poured a steady stream of marching men, horse, foot, and artillery. The wind dropped, the mists gathered again, and once more enveloped the invaders in an impenetrable screen. But by this time the whole British line was on the *qui vive*. Regulars, Militia, and Volunteers were marching down to their chin-deep trenches, while those who were already there busied themselves in improving their loopholes and strengthening their head cover. Behind the ridges of the hills the gunners stood grouped about their 'Long Toms' and heavy howitzers, while the field batteries waited, ready horsed, for orders to gallop under cover of the ridge to whichever set of emplacements should first require to be manned and armed. We had not enough to distribute before the movements of the enemy should, to a certain extent, show his hand.

"About seven o'clock a series of crackling reports from the outskirts of Royston announced that the detachment of Mounted Infantry, who now alone held it, was exchanging shots with the advancing enemy, and in a few minutes, as the morning mistiness cleared off, the General and his staff, who were established at the northern edge of the village of Therfield, three or four hundred feet higher up than the German skirmishers, were able to see the opening of the battle spread like a panorama before them. A thick firing line of drab-costumed Germans extended right across from Holland Hall to the Coach and Horses on the Fowlmere Road. On their left moved two or three compact masses of cavalry, while the infantry reserves were easily apparent in front of the village of Melbourn. Our Mounted Infantry in the village were indistinguishable, but away on the spur to the north-east of Royston a couple of batteries of Horse Artillery were unlimbered and were pushing their guns up to the brow of the hill by hand. In two minutes they were in action, and hard at work.

"Through the glasses the shrapnel could be seen bursting, half a dozen together, in front of the advancing Germans, who began to fall fast. But almost at once came an overwhelming reply from somewhere out of sight behind Melbourn. The whole hilltop around our guns was like a spouting volcano. Evidently big high-explosive shells were being fired from the German field-howitzers. In accordance with previous orders, our horse-gunners at once ran down their guns, limbered up, and started to gallop back towards our main position. Simultaneously a mass of German cavalry deployed into attack formation near the Coach and Horses, and swept down in their direction with the evident intention of cutting off and capturing them. But they reckoned without their escort of Mounted Infantry, who had been lying low behind the long, narrow line of copse north of Lowerfield Farm. Safely ensconced behind this—to cavalry—impassable barrier, the company, all good shots, opened a terrible magazine fire on the charging squadrons as they passed at close range. A Maxim they had with them also swept horses and men away in swathes. The charge was checked, and the guns saved, but we had not finished with the German reiters. Away to the north-east a battery of our 4.7 guns opened on the disorganised cavalry, firing at a range of four thousand yards. Their big shells turned the momentary check into a rout, both the attacking cavalry and their supports galloping towards Fowlmere to get out of range. We had scored the first trick!

"The attacking lines of German Infantry still pressed on, however, and after a final discharge the Mounted Infantry in Royston sprang on their horses and galloped back over Whitely Hill, leaving the town to be occupied by the enemy. To the eastward the thunder of heavy cannon, gradually growing in intensity, proclaimed that the IInd Corps was heavily attacked. Covered by a long strip of plantation, the German IVth Corps contrived to mass an enormous number of guns on a hill about two miles north of the village of Elmdon, and a terrific artillery duel began between them and our artillery entrenched along the Elmdon-Heydon ridge. Under cover of this the enemy began to work his infantry up towards Elmdon, obtaining a certain amount of shelter from the spurs which ran out towards the north-east of our line. Other German troops with guns put in an appearance on the high ground to the north-east of Saffron Walden, near Chesterton Park.

"To describe the fortunes of this fiercely-contested battle, which spread along a front of nearly twenty miles, counting from the detached garrison of the hill at Helions Bumpstead—which, by the way, succeeded in holding its ground all day, despite two or three most determined assaults by the enemy—to Kelshall on the left of the British position, would be an impossibility in the space at my disposal. The whole morning it raged all along the northern slopes of the upland held by our gallant troops. The fiercest fighting was, perhaps, in the neighbourhood of Elmdon, where our trenches were more than once captured by the Magdeburg battalions, only to be themselves hurled out again by the rush of the 1st Coldstream Guards, who had been held in reserve near the threatened point. By noon the magnificent old palace at Audley End was in flames. Art treasures which were of inestimable value and absolutely unreplaceable perished in this shocking conflagration. Desperate fighting was going on in the streets of the little town of Saffron Walden, where a mingled mass of Volunteers and Militia strove hard to arrest the advance of a portion of the German Army which was endeavouring to work round the right of our position.

"On our left the Foot Guards and Fusiliers of the 1st German Guard Division, after receiving a terrible pounding from our guns when they poured into Royston at the heels of our Mounted Infantry, had fought their way up the heights to within fifteen hundred yards of our trenches on the upper slopes of the ridge. Farther than that they had been unable to advance. Their close formations offered an excellent target to the rifles of the Volunteers and Militia lining our entrenchments. The attackers had lost men in thousands, and were now endeavouring to dig themselves in as best they could under the hail of projectiles that continually swept the hillside. About noon, too, the 2nd Division of the Garde Corps, after some skirmishing with the Mounted Infantry away on our left front, got into attack formation along the line of the Hitchin and Cambridge Railway, and after pouring a deluge of projectiles from field guns and howitzers upon our position, advanced upon Therfield with the greatest bravery and determination. They had succeeded by 2 P.M. in driving our men from the end of the spur running northward near Therfield Heath, and managed to get a number of their howitzers up there, and at once opened fire from the cover afforded by several copses out of which our men had been driven.

"In short, things were beginning to look very bad for old England, and the watchers on the Therfield heights turned their glasses anxiously northward in search of General Sir William Packington's force from Potton. They had not long to wait. At 2.15 the winking flash of a heliograph away near Wendy Place, about eight miles up Ermine Street, announced that the advance guard, consisting of the 1st Royal Welsh Fusiliers, was already at Bassingbourn, and that the main body was close behind, having escaped detection by all the enemy's patrols and flank guards. They were now directly in the rear of the right of the German reserves, who had been pushed forward into the neighbourhood of Royston to support the attack of their main body on the British position. A few minutes later it was evident that the enemy had also become aware of their advent. Two or three regiments hurriedly issued from Royston and deployed to the north-west. But the guns of the Baldock Corps turned such a 'rafale' fire upon them that they hesitated and were lost.

"Every long-range gun in the British entrenchments that would bear was also turned upon them, leaving the infantry and field guns to deal with the troops assaulting their position. The three battalions, as well as a fourth that was sent to their assistance, were simply swept out of existence by this terrible cross-fire. Their remnants streamed away, a disorganised crowd of scattered stragglers, towards Melbourn; while, still holding on to Bassingbourn, the Baldock force moved down on Royston, driving everything before it.

"The most advanced German troops made a final effort to capture our position when they saw what was going on behind them, but it was half-hearted; they were brought to a standstill, and our men, fixing bayonets, sprang from their trenches and charged down upon them with cheers, which were taken up all along the line for miles. The Germans here and there made a partial stand, but in half an hour they were down on the low ground, falling back towards the north-east in the greatest confusion, losing men in thousands from the converging fire of our guns. Their cavalry made a gallant attempt to save the day by charging our troops to the north of Royston. It was a magnificent sight to see their enormous masses sweeping over the ground with an impetus which looked capable of carrying everything before it, but our men, clustering behind the hedges of Ermine Street, mowed them down squadrons at a time. Not one of them reached the roadway. The magnificent Garde Corps was routed.

"The combined IIIrd and IVth Corps now advanced on the exposed right flank of the German IVth Corps, which, fighting gallantly, fell back, doing its best to cover the retreat of its comrades, who, on their part, very much hampered its movements. By nightfall there was no unwounded German south of Whittlesford, except as a prisoner. By this time, too, we were falling back on our original position."

XV

British Abandon Colchester

On Tuesday, 10th September, the *Tribune* published the following telegram from its war correspondent, Mr. Edgar Hamilton:—

Chelmsford, *Monday, September 9*

"I sit down, after a sleepless night, to indite the account of our latest move. We hear that Sheffield has fallen, and our troops are in flight. As, by the time this appears in print, the enemy will of necessity be aware of our abandonment of Colchester, the censor will not, I imagine, prevent the despatch of my letter.

"For our move has been one of a retrograde nature, and I do not doubt that the cavalry of the German IXth Corps are close behind us and in touch with our own. But I must not, in using the word 'retrograde,' be supposed to criticise in any way the strategy of our generals. For everyone here is, I am sure, fully persuaded of the wisdom of the step. Colchester, with its plucky little garrison, was altogether too much 'in the air,' and stood a great risk of being isolated by a converging advance of the IXth and Xth Corps of the German invaders, to say nothing of the XIIth (Saxon) Corps at Maldon, which since the unfortunate battle of Purleigh has shown itself very active to the north and east.

"The Saxons have refrained from attacking our Vth Corps since its repulse, and it has been left almost in peace to entrench its position from Danbury to the southward; but, on the other hand, while not neglecting to further strengthen their already formidable defences between the Blackwater and the Crouch, their cavalry have scoured the country up to the very gates of Colchester. Yesterday morning the 16th Lancers and the 17th Hussars—who had fallen back from Norwich— together with some of the local Yeomanry, moved out by the Tolleshunt d'Arcy and Great Totham roads, and drove in their patrols with some loss. At Tiptree Heath there was a sharp cavalry engagement between our red Lancers and several squadrons of a sky-blue hussar regiment. Our people routed them, but in the pursuit that followed would have fared badly, as they fell in with the four remaining squadrons supported by another complete regiment, had it not been for the opportune arrival of the Household Cavalry Brigade, which had moved north-east from Danbury to co-operate. This completely changed the aspect of affairs. The Germans were soundly beaten, with the loss of a large number of prisoners, and galloped back to Maldon in confusion. In the meantime the 2nd King's Own Royal Lancaster Regiment and the 5th Battery R.F. Artillery had been sent down to Witham by train, whence they marched up to the high ground near Wickham Bishops. They and the Yeomanry were left there in a position to cover the main London road and the Great Eastern Railway, and at the same time threaten any movement of the enemy by the Great Totham road. When the news of our success reached Colchester soon after midday, we were all very jubilant. In fact, I fear that a great many people spent the afternoon in a species of fool's paradise. And when towards the evening the announcement of our splendid victory at Royston was posted up on the red walls of the fine town hall, and outside the Cups, there was an incipient outbreak of that un-English excitement known as 'Mafficking.' Gangs of youths paraded the High Street, Head Street, and the principal thoroughfares, shouting, yelling, and hustling passers-by, and even respectable members of society seemed bitten by the desire to throw up their hats and make idiots of themselves.

"The hotels, the Lamb, the Red Lion, and other places, did a roaring trade, and altogether the town was more or less demoralised. But all this exultation was fated to be but short-lived, even though the Mayor appeared on the balcony of the town hall and addressed the crowd, while the latest news was posted outside the offices of the *Essex Telegraph*, opposite the post-office. The wind was in the north, and about 5.45 in the afternoon the sound of a heavy explosion was heard from the direction of Manningtree. I was in the Cups Hotel at the time arranging for an early dinner, and ran out into the street. As I emerged from the archway of the hotel I distinctly heard a second detonation from the same direction. A sudden silence, ominous and unnatural, seemed to fall on the yelping jingoes in the street, in the midst of which the rumble of yet another explosion rolled down on the wind, this time from a more westerly direction. Men asked their neighbours breathlessly as to what all this portended. I myself knew no more than the most ignorant of the crowd, till in an officer who rushed hastily by me in Head Street, on his way into the hotel, I recognised my friend Captain Burton, of the Artillery.

"I buttonholed him at once.

"'Do I know what those explosions were?' repeated he in answer to my inquiry. 'Well, I don't *know*, but I'm open to bet you five to one that it's the sappers blowing up the bridges over the Stour at Manningtree and Stratford St. Mary.'

"'Then the Germans will have arrived there?' I queried.

"'Most probably. And look here,' he continued, taking me aside by the arm, and lowering his voice, 'you take my tip. We shall be out of this to-night. So you'd best pack up your traps and get into marching order.'

"'Do you know this?' said I.

"'Not officially, or I shouldn't tell you anything about it. But I can put two and two together. We all knew that the General wouldn't be fool enough to try and defend an open town of this size with such a small garrison against a whole army corps, or perhaps more. It would serve no good purpose, and expose the place to destruction and bring all sorts of disaster on the civil population. You could have seen that for yourself, for no attempt whatever has been made to erect defences of any kind, neither have we received any reinforcements at all. If they had meant to defend it they would certainly have contrived to send us some Volunteers and guns at any rate. No, the few troops we have here have done their best in assisting the Danbury Force against the Saxons, and are much too valuable to be left here to be cut off without being able to do much to check the advance of the enemy. If we had been going to try anything of that kind, we should have now been holding the line of the river Stour; but I know we have only small detachments at the various bridges, sufficient only to drive off the enemy's cavalry patrols. By now, having blown up the bridges, I expect they are falling back as fast as they can get. Besides, look here,' he added, 'what do you think that battalion was sent to Wickham Bishops for this morning?'

"I told him my theories as set forth above.

"'Oh yes, that's all right,' he answered. 'But you may bet your boots that there's more in it than that. In my opinion, the General has had orders to clear out as soon as the enemy are preparing to cross the Stour, and the Lancasters are planted there to protect our left flank from an attack from Maldon while we are retreating on Chelmsford.'

"'But we might fall back on Braintree?' I hazarded.

"'Don't you believe it. We're not wanted there—at least, I mean, not so much as elsewhere. Where we shall come in is to help to fill the gap between Braintree and Danbury. I think, myself, we might just as well have done it before. We have been sending back stores by rail for the last two days. Well, goodbye,' he said, holding out his hand. 'Keep all this to yourself, and mark my words, we'll be off at dusk.'

"Away he went, and convinced that his prognostications were correct—as, indeed, in the main they proved—I hastened to eat my dinner, pay my bill, and get my portmanteau packed and stowed away in my motor. As soon as the evening began to close in I started and made for the barracks, going easy. The streets were still full of people, but they were very quiet, and mostly talking together in scattered groups. A shadow seemed to have fallen on the jubilant crowd of the afternoon, though, as far as I could ascertain, there were no definite rumours of the departure of the troops and the close advent of the enemy. Turning out of the main street, I had a very narrow escape of running over a drunken man. Indeed, I regret to say that there were a good many intoxicated people about, who had celebrated the day's victory 'not wisely but too well.'

"When I arrived at the barracks, I saw at once that there was something in the wind, for there was a great coming and going of orderlies; all the men I could see were in marching order, and the Volunteers, who had been encamped on the drill-ground since the outbreak of hostilities, were falling in, surrounded by an agitated crowd of their relations and friends. I pulled up alongside the barrack railings, and determined to watch the progress of events. I had not long to wait. In about ten minutes a bugle sounded, and the scattered assemblage of men on the barrack-square closed together and solidified into a series of quarter columns. At the same time, the Volunteer battalion moved across from the other side of the road and joined the Regular troops. I heard a sharp clatter and jingling behind me, and looking round, saw the General and his staff with a squad of cavalry canter up the road. They turned into the barrack gate, greeted by a sharp word of command and the rattle of arms from the assembled battalions. As far as I could make out, the General made them some kind of address, after which I heard another word of command, upon which the regiment nearest to the gate formed fours and marched out.

"It was the 2nd Dorsetshire. I watched anxiously to see which way they turned. As I more than expected, they turned in the direction of the London road. My friend had been right so far, but till the troops arrived at Mark's Tey, where the road forked, I could not be certain whether they were going towards Braintree or Chelmsford. The Volunteers followed; then the Leicestershires, then a long train of artillery, field batteries, big 4.7 guns, and howitzers. The King's Own Scottish Borderers formed the rearguard. With them marched the General and his staff. I saw no cavalry. I discovered afterwards that the General, foreseeing that a retirement was imminent, had ordered the 16th Lancers and the 7th Hussars, after their successful morning performance, to remain till further orders at Kelvedon and Tiptree respectively, so that their horses were resting during the afternoon.

"During the night march the former came back and formed a screen behind the retiring column, while the latter were in a position to observe and check any movement northwards that might be made by the Saxons, at the same time protecting its flank and rear from a possible advance by the cavalry of Von Kronhelm's Army, should they succeed in crossing the river Stour soon enough to be able to press after us in pursuit by either of the two eastern roads leading from Colchester to Maldon. After the last of the departing soldiers had tramped away into the gathering darkness through the mud, which after yesterday's downpour still lay thick upon the roads, I bethought me that I might as well run down to the railway station to see if anything was going on there. I was just in time.

"The electric lights disclosed a bustling scene as the last of the ammunition and a certain proportion of stores were being hurried into a long train that stood with steam up ready to be off. The police allowed none of the general public to enter the station, but my correspondent's pass obtained me admission to the departure platform. There I saw several detachments of the Royal Engineers, the Mounted Infantry—minus their horses, which had been already sent on—and some of the Leicestershire Regiment. Many of the men had their arms, legs, or heads bandaged, and bore evident traces of having been in action. I got into conversation with a colour-sergeant of the Engineers, and learned these were the detachments who had been stationed at the bridges over the Stour. It appears that there was some sharp skirmishing with the German advanced troops before the officers in command had decided that they were in sufficient force to justify them in blowing up the bridges. In fact, at the one at which my informant was stationed, and that the most important one of all, over which the main road from Ipswich passed at Stratford St. Mary, the officer in charge delayed just too long, so that a party of the enemy's cavalry actually secured the bridge, and succeeded in cutting the wires leading to the charges which had been placed in readiness to blow it up. Luckily, the various detachments present rose like one man to the occasion, and despite a heavy fire, hurled themselves upon the intruders with the bayonet with such determination and impetus that the bridge was swept clear in a moment. The wires were reconnected, and the bridge cleared of our men just as the Germans, reinforced by several of their supporting squadrons, who had come up at a gallop, dashed upon it in pursuit. The firing key was pressed at this critical moment, and, with a stunning report, a whole troop was blown into

Notice.

Concerning Wounded British Soldiers.

In compliance with an order of the Commander-in-Chief of the German Imperial Army, the Governor-General of East Anglia decrees as follows:—

(1) Every inhabitant of the counties of Norfolk, Suffolk, Essex, Cambridge, Lincolnshire, Yorkshire, Nottingham, Derby, Leicester, Northampton, Rutland, Huntingdon, and Hertford, who gives asylum to or lodges one or more ill or wounded British soldier, is obliged to make a declaration to the mayor of the town or to the local police within 24 hours, stating name, grade, place of birth, and nature of illness or injury.

Every change of domicile of the wounded is also to be notified within 24 hours.

In absence of masters, servants are ordered to make the necessary declarations.

The same order applies to the directors of hospitals, surgeries, or ambulance stations, who receive the British wounded within our jurisdiction.

(2) All mayors are ordered to prepare lists of the British wounded, showing the number, with their names, grade, and place of birth in each district.

(3) The mayor, or the superintendent of police, must send on the 1st and 15th of each month a copy of his lists to the headquarters of the Commander-in-Chief. The first list must be sent on the 15th September.

(4) Any person failing to comply with this order will, in addition to being placed under arrest for harbouring British troops, be fined a sum not exceeding £20.

(5) This decree is to be published in all towns and villages in the Province of East Anglia.

Count Von Schonburg-Waldenburg,
Lieutenant-General,
Governor of German East Anglia.

Ipswich, *September 6, 1910.*

Copy of One of the Enemy's Proclamations.

the air, the remaining horses, mad with fright, stampeding despite all that their riders could do. The road was cut, and the German advance temporarily checked, while the British detachment made off as fast as it could for Colchester.

"I asked the sergeant how long he thought it would be before the Germans succeeded in crossing it. 'Bless you, sir, I expect they're over by now,' he answered. 'They would be sure to have their bridging companies somewhere close up, and it would not take them more than an hour or two to throw a bridge over that place.' The bridges at Boxted Mill and Nayland had been destroyed previously.

"The railway bridge and the other one at Manningtree were blown up before the Germans could get a footing, and their defenders had come in by rail. But my conversation was cut short, the whistle sounded, the men were hustled on board the train, and it moved slowly out of the station. As for me, I hurried out to my car. As I came out I noticed that it had begun to rain. However, I was fully equipped for it, and, except for the chance of skidding and the splashing of the flying mud, did not mind it. But I could not help thinking of the poor soldiers trudging along on their night march over the weary miles that lay before them. I determined to follow in their steps, and putting on speed, was soon clear of the town, and spinning along for Mark's Tey. It is about five miles, and shortly before I got there I overtook the marching column. The men were halted, and in the act of putting on their greatcoats. I was stopped here by the rearguard, who took charge of me, and would not let me proceed until permission was obtained from the General.

"Eventually this officer ordered me to be brought to him. I presented my pass; but he said, 'I am afraid that I shall have to ask you either to turn back, or to slow down and keep pace with us. In fact, you had better do the latter. I might, indeed, have to exercise my powers and impress your motor, should the exigencies of the Service require it.' I saw that it was best to make a virtue of necessity, and replied that it was very much at his service, and that I was very well content to accompany the column. In point of fact, the latter was strictly true, for I wanted to see what was to be seen, and there were no points about going along with no definite idea of where I wanted to get to, with a possible chance of falling into the hands of the Saxons into the bargain. So a Staff officer, who was suffering from a slight wound, was placed alongside me, and the column, having muffled itself in its greatcoats, once more began to plug along through the thickening mire. My position was just in front of the guns, which kept up a monotonous rumble behind me. My companion was talkative, and afforded me a good deal of incidental and welcome information. Thus, just after we started, and were turning to the left at Mark's Tey, a bright glare followed by a loudish report came from the right of the road. 'What's that?' I naturally exclaimed. 'Oh, that will be the sappers destroying the junction with the Sudbury line,' he replied. 'There's the train waiting for them just beyond.'

"So it was. The train that I had seen leaving had evidently stopped after passing the junction, while the line was broken behind it. 'They will do the same after passing the cross line at Witham,' volunteered he.

"A mile or two farther on we passed between two lines of horsemen, their faces set northwards, and muffled to the eyes in their long cloaks, 'That's some of the 16th,' he said, 'going to cover our rear.'

"So we moved on all night through the darkness and rain. The slow, endless progress of the long column of men and horses seemed like a nightmare. We passed through the long street of Kelvedon, scaring the inhabitants, who rushed to their windows to see what was happening, and with the first glimmer of dawn halted at Witham. We had about nine miles still to go to reach Chelmsford, which I learned was our immediate destination, and it was decided to rest here for an hour, while the men made the best breakfast they could from the contents of their haversacks. But the villagers brought out hot tea and coffee, and did the best they could for us, so we did not fare so badly after all. As for me, I got permission to go on, taking with me my friend the Staff officer, who had despatches to forward from Chelmsford. I pushed on at full speed. We were there in a very short space of time, and during the morning I learned that the Braintree Army was falling back on Dunmow, and that the Colchester garrison was to assist in holding the line of the river Chelmer."

Another despatch from Mr. Edgar Hamilton, of the *Tribune*, was published in that journal on Friday, the 14th September:—

BRENTWOOD, *Thursday, September 13, 1910*
"The events of the last three days have been so tremendous, so involved, and so disastrous to us as a nation, that I hardly know how to deal with them. It is no news now that we have again been beaten, and beaten badly. The whole right of our line of defence has been driven back in disorder, and we are now practically at the 'last ditch.' The remnants of that fine force which has, up to now, not only been able to hold the Saxon Army in check, but even to be within an ace of beating it at the memorable battle of Purleigh, less than a week ago, is now occupying the entrenchments which have been under construction ever since the landing of the Germans, and which form a section of the works that have been planned for the defence of the metropolis.

"Here, too, are portions of the Braintree Army Corps and some of the troops lately constituting the garrison of Colchester, whom I accompanied on their night march out of that city when it had been decided to abandon it. We have only the vaguest rumours as to what has happened to the other portion of the 1st Army Corps that was occupying

Dunmow and the upper part of the river Chelmer. We can only hope that these troops, or at any rate a considerable portion of them, have been able to gain the shelter of the defensive enceinte to the north-westward. It is to be feared this reverse will necessitate the retreat of the Second, Third, and Fourth Armies from Saffron Walden, Royston, and Baldock, that position which they so gallantly defended against the flower of the German Army, emerging victorious from the glorious battle of Royston. For to stay where they are, in the face of the combined forward movement of the IXth, Xth, and XIIth Corps of the invaders, and the rumoured resumption of the offensive by the two corps defeated before Royston, would be to court being outflanked and cut off from the rest of our forces at a time when every single soldier is urgently required to man the northern portion of the defences of London.

"But to return to the relation of our latest and most disastrous defeat, which I must preface by saying that my readers must not be deceived by the words 'Army Corps' as applied to the various assemblages of our troops. As a matter of fact, 'Divisions,' or even 'Brigades,' would be nearer the mark. The 'Army Corps' at Braintree had only four, or perhaps later six, regular infantry regiments, with a very small force of cavalry and not too many guns. Compare that with the Xth German Army Corps under General von Wilberg, which was more immediately opposed to it. This formidable fighting unit may be taken as a representative one, observing that the Garde Corps is yet stronger. Von Wilberg's Corps is a Hanoverian one, and comprises no less than twenty-three battalions of infantry, four regiments of cavalry, twenty-five batteries of artillery, a train battalion, and a pioneer battalion. What chance has a so-called army corps of half a dozen regular infantry battalions, perhaps a dozen Volunteer and Militia Corps, a scratch lot of cavalry, and half the number of guns, against such a powerful, well-organised, and well-trained force as this?

"In the recent fighting about Chelmsford we have had at the outside thirty regular battalions to oppose the onslaught of three complete German Army Corps such as that described above. We have had a number of auxiliary troops in addition, as well as a preponderance in heavy long-ranging artillery, but the former cannot be manœuvred in the same way as regular soldiers, however brave and devoted they may be; while, if weaker in big guns, the enemy outnumbered our mobile horse and field artillery by five or six to one. So it must be understood that while a defeat is deplorable and heartbreaking, yet a victory against such odds would have been little less than a miracle. No blame can be attached either to our officers or their men. All did as much, or more, than could be humanly expected of them. The long and short of it is that since we, as a nation, have not chosen to have a sufficient and up-to-date Army, we must take the rub when an invasion comes.

"We knew well enough—though most of us pretended ignorance—that we could not afford to pay for such an Army at a rate comparable to the current labour market rates, even if we had been twice as rich, and if shoals of recruits had been forthcoming. We were aware, in consequence, that some form of universal service was the only possible method of raising a real Army, but we shrank from making the personal sacrifices required. We were too indolent, too careless, too unpatriotic. Now we have got to pay for the pleasures of living in a fool's paradise, and pay through the nose into the bargain. We have no right to grumble, whatever may be the outcome, and God only knows what the bitter end of this war may be, what final defeat may mean for our future as a nation. But I must quit moralising and betake myself to my narrative.

"In my letter of the 9th I left the Colchester garrison making their breakfast at Witham. I had understood that they were coming on to Chelmsford, but, as it turned out, the Leicestershires and Dorsets got orders to turn off to the right just before reaching Boreham, and to take up a position on the high ground east of Little Waltham, which is about four miles due north of Chelmsford. With them went a number of the heavy 4.7-inch guns we brought away with us. The Volunteers, Scottish Borderers, and the Lancasters—the latter of whom had been covering the flank of the retreat at Wickham Bishops—came in to Chelmsford, and during the evening were marched out and billeted in the houses thickly scattered along the Braintree road. The cavalry, after some slight skirmishing with the advanced patrols of Von Kronhelm's Army, who came up with them near Hatfield Peverell, turned up in the afternoon.

"In Chelmsford, when I halted at the Saracen's Head, I found there were the 2nd Lincolnshire and the 2nd Royal Scots Fusiliers, who had come up from Salisbury Plain, the 1st Hampshire and the 1st Royal Fusiliers from Portsmouth and the Isle of Wight. The 2nd South Wales Borderers from Tidworth and the 1st Border Regiment from Bordon Camp arrived in the afternoon, and were marched out to Great Baddow, half-way to Danbury. The 14th Hussars from Shorncliffe and the 20th from Brighton had also come in the day previously, and they at once moved out to the front to relieve the 16th Lancers and 7th Hussars, who had been covering the retiral from Colchester. The town was crowded with Volunteers in khaki, green, red, blue—all the colours of the rainbow—and I noticed two very smart corps of Yeomanry marching out to support the two regular cavalry regiments. Everyone seemed in good spirits on account of the news from Royston and the successful issue of the cavalry skirmish of the morning before. As Chelmsford lies in a kind of hollow, I could not see much from there, so in the afternoon I thought I would run out to the high ground near Danbury and see if I could get any idea of what was going on.

"As I passed Danbury Place I heard the deafening report of heavy guns close at hand. I found that the firing came from some of the Bluejackets' 4.7's near the church, where I had seen them at work at the opening of Purleigh Battle. I got out of my car and went up to the officer in charge, whom I met on that occasion. I asked him at what he was firing. 'Look over there,' he said, pointing towards Maldon. I saw nothing at first. 'Look higher,' said the sailor. I raised my eyes, and there, floating hundreds of feet over and on this side of the old town, a great yellow sausage-like something glistened in the sunlight. I recognised it at once from the photographs I had seen of the German manœuvres. It was their great military balloon, known as the 'Wurst,' or sausage, from its elongated shape. Its occupants were doubtless hard at work reconnoitring our position.

"Another gun gave tongue with an ear-splitting report, and then a second one, its long chase sticking up into the air like a monster telescope. They were firing high explosive shell at the balloon, hoping that the detonation would tear it if near enough. I saw the big shell explode apparently close to their target, but the distance was deceptive, and no apparent injury was done. After another round, however, it began slowly to descend, and soon disappeared behind the huddled roofs of the town. 'Might have got her,' remarked Akers, the commander in charge of the guns, 'but I fancy not. But I reckon they thought it too warm to stay up. We had our balloon up this morning,' he continued, 'and I expect she'll go up again before dark. They had a few slaps at her, but didn't get within a mile of her. She's in a field behind the woods at Twitty Fee, about half a mile over there, if you want to see her.'

"I thanked him and motored slowly off in the direction indicated. I noticed great changes on Danbury Hill since my last visit. Entrenchments and batteries had sprung up on every side, and men were still as busy as bees improving and adding to them. I found the balloon, filled with gas and swaying about behind a mass of woodland that effectually concealed it from the enemy, but as I was informed that there would be no ascent before half-past five, I continued my tour round the summit of the hill. When I arrived at the northern end I found that fresh defences were being constructed right away round to the westward side. The northern edge of Blake's Wood had been felled and made into a formidable abattis, the sharpened branches of the felled trees being connected together with a perfect web of barbed wire.

"The same process was being carried out in the woods and copses at Great Graces. New Lodge had been placed in a state of defence. The windows, deprived of glass and sashes, were being built up with sand bags; the flower garden was trampled into a chaos; the grand piano stood in the back yard, forming a platform for a Maxim gun that peered over the wall. The walls were disfigured with loop-holes. Behind the house were piled the arms of a Volunteer Battalion who, under the direction of a few officers and N.C.O.'s of the Royal Engineers, were labouring to turn the pretty country house into a scarred and hideous fortress. Their cooks had dug a Broad Arrow kitchen in the midst of the tennis lawn, and were busied about the big black kettles preparing tea for the workers. New Lodge was the most suggestive picture of the change brought about by the war that I had yet seen. From the corner of Great Graces Wood I could see through my glasses that the outskirts of Great Baddow were also alive with men preparing it for defence. I got back to the balloon just in time to see it rising majestically above the trees. Either on account of their failure to reach it in the morning, or for some other reason, the enemy did not fire at it, and the occupants of the car were able to make their observations in peace, telephoning them to a non-commissioned officer at the winding engine below, who jotted them down in shorthand. From what I afterwards heard, it seems that a long procession of carts was seen moving northwards from Maldon by way of Heybridge.

"It was presumed that these contained provisions and stores for the IXth and Xth Corps from the big depôt which it had been discovered that the Saxons had established near Southminster. A few long-range shots were fired at the convoy from the big guns, but without any appreciable effect. The procession stopped though. No more carts came from the town, and those already out disappeared behind the woods about Langford Park. I understand that, apprised of this by signal from the balloon, the 14th Hussars made a gallant effort to attack the convoy, but they found the country east of the Maldon-Witham Railway to be full of the enemy, both infantry and cavalry, came under a heavy fire from concealed troops, and sustained considerable loss without being able to effect anything. It is believed that the movement of stores continued after dark, for our most advanced outposts and patrols reported that the rumble of either artillery or wagons was heard coming from the direction of the roads leading north out of Maldon almost the whole night through.

"On my return to Chelmsford I visited Springfield, where I found the Scots Fusiliers, a Militia, and a Volunteer Regiment entrenching themselves astride the railway.

"I dined with three brother newspaper men at the Red Lion Hotel. One of them had come from Dunmow, and reported that the First Army was busily entrenching itself on a long ridge a couple of miles to eastward of the town. He said he had heard also that the high ground about Thaxted had been occupied by some troops who had come up from the South on Sunday night, though he could not say what regiments they were. They had detrained at Elsenham, and marched the rest of the way by road. If his information is correct, the British Army on Monday night occupied an almost continuous line stretching from Baldock on the west to South Hanningfield, or perhaps Billericay on the south. A very extensive front, but necessary to be held if the forward march of the five German Army Corps operating in the Eastern Counties was to be checked. For though it would, of course, have been desirable to take the offensive and attack the Xth Corps during the temporary discomfiture of the Garde and IVth Corps, we were compelled in the main to adopt the tactics pursued by the Boers in South Africa and act almost entirely on the defensive on account of the poor quality of the bulk of our forces. There was this exception, however, that the few regular battalions were as far as possible placed in such positions that they would be available for local counter-attacks and offensive action. Our generals could not be altogether guided by the generally-accepted rules of tactics and strategy, but had to do the best they could with the heterogeneous material at their disposal.

"As to what the enemy were doing during this day we had no information worth speaking of, although there was a rumour going about late in the afternoon that Braintree had been occupied by the Hanoverians, and that the head of General Von Kronhelm's Army Corps had arrived at Witham. However this may have been, we neither saw nor heard anything of them during the night, and I much enjoyed my slumbers after the fatigues of the last twenty-four hours. But this was but the lull before the storm. About ten A.M. the low growl of artillery rolled up from the south-east, and it began to be bruited about that the Saxons were attacking South Hanningfield in force, doubtless with the object of turning our right flank. I ordered out my motor, thinking I would run down to the high ground at Stock, five miles to the southward, and see if I could get an inkling of how matters were progressing. That heavy fighting was in progress I felt certain, for the cannonade grew momentarily louder and heavier. Hardly had I cleared the town, when a fresh outburst of firing boomed out from a northerly direction. I stopped irresolute.

"Should I go on or turn back and set my face towards Dunmow? I eventually decided to go on, and arrived at Stock about eleven. I could not get much information there, or see what was going on, so I decided to make for South Hanningfield. At the foot of the hill leading up to Harrow Farm I came across a battalion of infantry lying down in quarter column behind the woods on the left of the road. From some of the officers I ascertained that it was the 1st Buffs, and that they were in support of two Militia battalions who were holding the ridge above. The Saxons, they said, had come up from the direction of Woodham Ferris in considerable force, but had not been able to advance beyond the Rettendon-Battles-Bridge Road on account of the heavy fire of our artillery, which comprised several heavy guns, protected both from fire and sight, and to which their field batteries in the open ground below could make no effective reply.

"I had noticed for some little time that the firing had slackened, so I thought I might as well get to the top of the hill and get a view of the enemy. I did not see much of them. By the aid of my glass I fancied I could distinguish green uniforms moving about near the copses in front of Rettendon Hall, but that was about all. I looked towards Danbury and saw our big balloon go up, and I also observed the big German sausage wobbling about over Purleigh. But there was no sign of military movement on either side. All the time, however, I was conscious of the distant rumble of guns away to the northward, and as there was apparently nothing more to be seen at South Hanningfield for the present, I regained my car and started back for Chelmsford. I found the town buzzing like a hive of bees.

"The troops were falling in under arms, the station was full of people trying to get away by train, while the inhabitants were tramping away in crowds by the Brentwood and Ongar roads. The booming of the still distant guns sounded louder and faster, and rumour had it that the Hanoverians were trying to force the passage of the river at Ford Mill. I replenished my flask and luncheon basket, and started off in the direction of the firing.

"All along the road to Little Waltham I caught glimpses of khaki uniforms in the trenches that zig-zagged about on the river slopes, while I passed two or three regiments stepping northwards as fast as they could get over the ground. There was a grim, set look on the men's faces that betokened both anger and determination."

XVI

Fierce Fighting at Chelmsford

The continuation of the despatch from Brentwood, as follows, was published on Saturday, 15th September:

"At Little Waltham I found myself close to the scene of action. About a mile ahead of me the hamlet of Howe Street was in flames and burning furiously. I could see the shells bursting in and all over it in perfect coveys. I could not make out where they were coming from, but an officer I met said he thought the enemy must have several batteries in action on the high ground about Littley Green, a mile and a half to the north on the opposite side of the river. I crossed over myself, and got up on the knoll where the Leicestershires and Dorsets had been stationed, together with a number of the 4.7-inch guns brought from Colchester.

"This piece of elevated ground is about two miles long, running almost north and south, and at the top of it I got an extensive view to the eastward right away to beyond Witham, as the ground fell all the way. The country was well wooded, and a perfect maze of trees and hedgerows. If there were any Germans down there in this plain they were lying very low indeed, for my glasses did not discover the least indication of their presence. Due east my view was bounded by the high wooded ground about Wickham Bishops and Tiptree Heath, which lay a long blue hummock on the horizon, while to the south-east Danbury Hill, with our big war-balloon floating overhead, was plainly discernible.

"While I gazed on the apparently peaceful landscape I was startled by a nasty sharp, hissing sound, which came momentarily nearer. It seemed to pass over my head, and was followed by a loud bang in the air, where now hung a ring of white smoke. It was a shell from the enemy. Just ahead of me was a somewhat extensive wood; and, urged by some insane impulse of seeking shelter, I left the car, which I ordered my chauffeur to take back for a mile and wait, and made for the close-standing trees. If I had stopped to think I should have realised that the wood gave me actually no protection whatever, and I had not gone far when the crashing of timber and noise of the bursting projectiles overhead and in the undergrowth around made me understand clearly that the Germans were making a special target of the wood, which, I imagine, they thought might conceal some of our troops. I wished heartily that I was seated beside my chauffeur in his fast-receding car.

"However, my first object was to get clear of the wood again, and after some little time I emerged on the west side, right in the middle of a dressing station for the wounded, which had been established in a little hollow. Two surgeons, with their assistants, were already busily engaged with a number of wounded men, most of whom were badly hit by shrapnel bullets about the upper part of the body. I gathered from one or two of the few most slightly wounded men that our people had been, and were, very hardly put to it to hold their own. 'I reckon,' said one of them, a bombardier of artillery, 'that the enemy must have got more than a hundred guns firing at us, and at Howe Street village. If we could only make out where the foreign devils were,' continued my informant, 'our chaps could have knocked a good many of them out with our four-point-sevens, especially if we could have got a go at them before they got within range themselves. But they must have somehow contrived to get them into position during the night, for we saw nothing of them coming up. They are somewhere about Chatley, Fairstead Lodge, and Little Leighs, but as we can't locate them exactly and only have ten guns up here, it don't give us much chance, does it?' Later I saw an officer of the Dorsets, who confirmed the gunner's story, but added that our people were well entrenched and the guns well concealed, so that none of the latter had been put out of action, and he thought we should be able to hold on to the hill all right. I regained my car without further adventure, bar several narrow escapes from stray shell, and made my way back as quickly as possible to Chelmsford.

"The firing went on all day, not only to the northward, but also away to the southward, where the Saxons, while not making any determined attack, kept the Vth Corps continually on the alert, and there was an almost continuous duel between the heavy pieces. As it appeared certain that the knoll I had visited in the forenoon was the main objective of the enemy's attack, reinforcements had been more than once sent up there, but the German shell fire was so heavy that they found it almost impossible to construct the additional cover required. Several batteries of artillery were despatched to Pleshy and Rolphy Green to keep down, if possible, the fire of the Germans, but it seemed to increase rather than diminish. They must have had more guns in action than they had at first. Just at dusk their infantry made the first openly offensive movement.

"Several lines of skirmishers suddenly appeared in the valley between Little Leighs and Chatley, and advanced towards Lyonshall Wood, at the north end of the knoll east of Little Waltham. They were at first invisible from the British gun positions on the other side of the Chelmer, and when they cleared the spur on which Hyde Hall stands they were hardly discernible in the gathering darkness. The Dorsetshire and the other battalions garrisoning the knoll manned their breastworks as they got within rifle range, and opened fire, but they were still subjected to the infernal rafale from the Hanoverian guns on the hills to the northward, and to make matters worse at this critical moment the Xth Corps brought a long line of guns into action between Flacks Green and Great Leighs Wood, in which position none of the British guns except a few on the knoll itself could reach them. Under this cross hurricane of projectiles the British fire was quite beaten down, and the Germans followed up their skirmishers by almost solid masses, which advanced with all but impunity save for the fire of the few British long-range guns at Pleshy Mount. There they were firing almost at random, as the gunners could not be certain of the exact whereabouts of their objectives. There was a searchlight on the knoll, but at the first sweep of its ray it was absolutely demolished by a blizzard of shrapnel. Every German gun was turned upon it. The Hanoverian battalions now swarmed to the assault, disregarding the gaps made in their ranks by the magazine fire of the defenders as soon as their close advance masked the fire of their own cannon.

"The British fought desperately. Three several times they hurled back at the attackers, but, alas! we were overborne by sheer weight of numbers. Reinforcements summoned by telephone, as soon as the determined nature of the attack was apparent, were hurried up from every available source, but they only arrived in time to be carried down the hill again in the rush of its defeated defenders, and to share with them the storm of projectiles from the quick-firers of General Von Kronhelm's artillery, which had been pushed forward during the assault. It was with the greatest difficulty that the shattered and disorganised troops were got over the river at Little Waltham. As it was, hundreds were drowned in the little stream, and hundreds of others killed and wounded by the fire of the Germans. They had won the first trick. This was indisputable, and as ill news travels apace, a feeling of gloom fell upon our whole force, for it was realised that the possession of the captured knoll would enable the enemy to mass troops almost within effective rifle range of our river line of defence. I believe that it was proposed by some officers on the staff that we should wheel back our left and take up a fresh position during the night. This was overruled, as it was recognised that to do so would enable the enemy to push in between the Dunmow force and our own, and so cut our general line in half. All that could be done was to get up every available gun and bombard the hill during the night, in order to hamper the enemy in his preparations for further forward movement and in his entrenching operations.

"Had we more men at our disposal I suppose there is little doubt that a strong counter attack would have been made on the knoll almost immediately; but in the face of the enormous numbers opposed to us, I imagine that General Blennerhasset did not feel justified in denuding any portion of our position of its defenders. So all through the dark hours the thunder of the great guns went on. In spite of the cannonade the Germans turned on no less than three searchlights from the southern end of the knoll about midnight. Two were at once put out by our fire, but the third managed to exist for over half an hour, and enabled the Germans to see how hard we were working to improve our defences along the river bank. I am afraid that they were by this means able to make themselves acquainted with the positions of a great number of our trenches. During the night our patrols reported being unable to penetrate beyond Pratt's Farm, Mount Maskell, and Porter's Farm on the Colchester Road. Everywhere they were forced back by superior numbers. The enemy were fast closing in upon us. It was a terrible night in Chelmsford.

"There was a panic on every hand. A man mounted the Tindal statue and harangued the crowd, urging the people to rise and compel the Government to stop the war. A few young men endeavoured to load the old Crimean cannon in front of the Shire Hall, but found it clogged with rust and useless. People fled from the villa residences in Brentwood Road into the town for safety, now that the enemy were upon them. The banks in High Street were being barricaded, and the stores still remaining in the various grocers' shops, Luckin Smith's, Martin's, Cramphorn's, and Pearke's, were rapidly being concealed from the invaders. All the ambulance wagons entering the town were filled with wounded, although as many as possible were sent south by train. By one o'clock in the morning, however, most of the civilian inhabitants had fled. The streets were empty, but for the bivouacking troops and the never-ending procession of wounded men. The General and his Staff were deliberating to a late hour in the Shire Hall, at which he had established his headquarters. The booming of the guns waxed and waned till dawn, when a furious outburst announced that the second act of the tragedy was about to open.

"I had betaken myself at once to the round tower of the church, next the Stone-bridge, from which I had an excellent view both east and north. The first thing that attracted my eye was the myriad flashings of rifle fire in the dimness of the breaking day. They reached in a continuous line of coruscations from Boreham Hall, opposite my right hand, to the knoll by Little Waltham, a distance of three or four miles, I should say. The enemy were driving in all our outlying and advanced troops by sheer weight of numbers. Presently the heavy batteries at Danbury began pitching shell over in the direction of the firing, but as the German line still advanced, it had not apparently any very great effect. The next thing that happened was a determined attack on the village of Howe Street made from the direction of Hyde Hall. This is about two miles north of Little Waltham. In spite of our incessant fire, the Germans had contrived to mass a tremendous number of guns and howitzers on and behind the knoll they captured last night, and there were any quantity more on the ridge above Hyde Hall. All these terrible weapons concentrated their fire for a few moments on the blackened ruins of Howe Street. Not a mouse could have lived there. The little place was simply pulverised.

"Our guns at Pleshy Mount and Rolphy Green, aided by a number of field batteries, in vain endeavoured to make head against them. They were outnumbered by six to one. Under cover of this tornado of iron and fire, the enemy pushed several battalions over the river, making use of the ruins of the many bridges about there which had been hastily destroyed, and which they repaired with planks and other materials they brought along with them. They lost a large number of men in the process, but they persevered, and by ten o'clock were in complete possession of Howe Street, Langley's Park, and Great Waltham, and moving in fighting formation against Pleshy Mount and Rolphy Green, their guns covering their advance with a perfectly awful discharge of shrapnel. Our cannon on the ridge at Partridge Green took the attackers in flank, and for a time checked their advance, but, drawing upon themselves the attention of the German artillery, on the south end of the knoll, were all but silenced.

"As soon as this was effected another strong column of Germans followed in the footsteps of the first, and deploying to the left, secured the bridge at Little Waltham, and advanced against the gun positions on Partridge Green. This move turned all our river bank entrenchments right down to Chelmsford. Their defenders were now treated to the enfilade fire of a number of Hanoverian batteries that galloped down

Decree

Concerning The Power of Councils of War.

We, Governor-General of East Anglia, in virtue of the powers conferred upon us by His Imperial Majesty the German Emperor, Commander-in-Chief of the German Armies, order, for the maintenance of the internal and external security of the counties of the Government-General:—

Article I—Any individual guilty of incendiarism or of wilful inundation, of attack, or of resistance with violence against the Government-General or the agents of the civil or military authorities, of sedition, of pillage, of theft with violence, of assisting prisoners to escape, or of exciting soldiers to treasonable acts, shall be Punished By Death.

In the case of any extenuating circumstances, the culprit may be sent to penal servitude with hard labour for twenty years.

Article II—Any person provoking or inciting an individual to commit the crimes mentioned in Article I will be sent to penal servitude with hard labour for ten years.

Article III—Any person propagating false reports relative to the operations of war or political events will be imprisoned for one year, and fined up to £100.

In any case where the affirmation or propagation may cause prejudice against the German army, or against any authorities or functionaries established by it, the culprit will be sent to hard labour for ten years.

Article IV—Any person usurping a public office, or who commit any act or issues any order in the name of a public functionary, will be imprisoned for five years, and fined £150.

ARTICLE V—Any person who voluntarily destroys or abstracts any documents, registers, archives, or public documents deposited in public offices, or passing through their hands in virtue of their functions as government or civic officials, will be imprisoned for two years, and fined £150.

ARTICLE VI—Any person obliterating, damaging, or tearing down official notices, orders, or proclamations of any sort issued by the German authorities will be imprisoned for six months, and fined £80.

ARTICLE VII—Any resistance or disobedience of any order given in the interests of public security by military commanders and other authorities, or any provocation or incitement to commit such disobedience, will be punished by one year's imprisonment, or a fine of not less than £150.

ARTICLE VIII—All offences enumerated in Articles I–VII are within the jurisdiction of the Councils of War.

ARTICLE IX—It is within the competence of Councils of War to adjudicate upon all other crimes and offences against the internal and external security of the English provinces occupied by the German Army, and also upon all crimes against the military or civil authorities, or their agents, as well as murder, the fabrication of false money, of blackmail, and all other serious offences.

ARTICLE X—Independent of the above, the military jurisdiction already proclaimed will remain in force regarding all actions tending to imperil the security of the German troops, to damage their interests, or to render assistance to the Army of the British Government.

Consequently, there will be PUNISHED BY DEATH, and we expressly repeat this, all persons who are not British soldiers and—

(*a*) Who serve the British Army or the Government as spies, or receive British spies, or give them assistance or asylum.

(*b*) Who serve as guides to British troops, or mislead the German troops when charged to act as guides.

(*c*) Who shoot, injure, or assault any German soldier or officer.

(*d*) Who destroy bridges or canals, interrupt railways or telegraph lines, render roads impassable, burn munitions of war, provisions, or quarters of the troops.

(*e*) Who take arms against the German troops.

Article XI—The organisation of Councils of War mentioned in Articles VIII and IX of the Law of May 2, 1870, and their procedure are regulated by special laws which are the same as the summary jurisdiction of military tribunals. In the case of Article X there remains in force the Law of July 21, 1867, concerning the military jurisdiction applicable to foreigners.

Article XII—The present order is proclaimed and put into execution on the morrow of the day upon which it is affixed in the public places of each town and village.

The Governor-General of East Anglia,

Count von Schonburg-Waldenburg,
Lieutenant-General.

Norwich, *September 7th, 1910.*

to Little Waltham. They stuck to their trenches gallantly, but presently when the enemy obtained a footing on Partridge Green they were taken in reverse, and compelled to fall back, suffering terrible losses as they did so. The whole of the infantry of the Xth Corps, supported—as we understand—by a division which had joined them from Maldon, now moved down on Chelmsford. In fact, there was a general advance of the three combined armies stretching from Partridge Green on the west to the railway line on the east. The defenders of the trenches facing east were hastily withdrawn, and thrown back on Writtle. The Germans followed closely with both infantry and guns, though they were for a time checked near Scot's Green by a dashing charge of our cavalry brigade, consisting of the 16th Lancers and the 7th, 14th, and 20th Hussars, and the Essex and Middlesex Yeomanry. We saw nothing of their cavalry, for a reason that will be apparent later. By one o'clock fierce fighting was going on all round the town, the German hordes enveloping it on all sides but one. We had lost a great number of our guns, or at anyrate had been cut off from them by the German successes around Pleshy Mount, and in all their assaults on the town they had been careful to keep out of effective range of the heavy batteries on Danbury Hill. These, by the way, had their own work cut out for them, as the Saxon artillery were heavily bombarding the hill with their howitzers. The British forces were in a critical situation. Reinforcements—such as could be spared—were hurried up from the Vth Army Corps, but they were not very many in numbers, as it was necessary to provide against an attack by the Saxon Corps. By three o'clock the greater part of the town was in the hands of the Germans, despite the gallant way in which our men fought them from street to street, and house to house. A dozen fires were spreading in every direction, and fierce fighting was going on at Writtle. The overpowering numbers of the Germans, combined with their better organisation, and the number of properly trained officers at their disposal, bore the British mixed Regular and Irregular forces back, and back again.

"Fearful of being cut off from his line of retreat, General Blennerhasset, on hearing from Writtle soon after three that the Hanoverians were pressing his left very hard, and endeavouring to work round it, reluctantly gave orders for the troops in Chelmsford to fall back on Widford and Moulsham. There was a lull in the fighting for about half an hour, though firing was going on both at Writtle and Danbury. Soon after four a terrible rumour spread consternation on every side. According to this, an enormous force of cavalry and motor infantry was about to attack us in the rear. What had actually happened was not quite so bad as this, but quite bad enough. It seems, according to our latest information, that almost the whole of the cavalry belonging to the three German Army Corps with whom we were engaged—something like a dozen regiments, with a proportion of horse artillery and all available motorists, having with them several of the new armoured motors carrying light, quick-firing and machine guns—had been massed during the last thirty-six hours behind the Saxon lines extending from Maldon to the River Crouch. During the day they had worked round to the southward, and at the time the rumour reached us were actually attacking Billericay, which was held by a portion of the reserves of our Vth Corps. By the time this news was confirmed the Germans were assaulting Great Baddow, and moving on Danbury from east, north, and west, at the same time resuming the offensive all along the line. The troops at Danbury must be withdrawn, or they would be isolated. This difficult manœuvre was executed by way of West Hanningfield. The rest of the Vth Corps conformed to the movement, the Guards Brigade at East Hanningfield forming the rearguard, and fighting fiercely all night through with the Saxon troops, who moved out on the left flank of our retreat. The wreck of the Ist Corps and the Colchester Garrison was now also in full retirement. Ten miles lay between it and the lines at Brentwood, and had the Germans been able to employ cavalry in pursuit, this retreat would have been even more like a rout than it was. Luckily for us the Billericay troops mauled the German cavalry pretty severely, and they were beset in the close country in that neighbourhood by Volunteers, motorists and every one that the officer commanding at Brentwood could get together in this emergency.

"Some of them actually got upon our line of retreat, but were driven off by our advance guard; others came across the head of the retiring Vth Corps, but the terrain was all against cavalry, and after nightfall most of them had lost their way in the maze of lanes and hedgerows that covered the countryside. Had it not been for this we should probably have been absolutely smashed. As it was, rather more than half our original numbers of men and guns crawled into Brentwood in the early morning, worn out and dead-beat."

XVII

In the Enemy's Hands

We must now turn to the position of Sheffield on Saturday, September 8. It was truly critical.

It was known that Lincoln had been occupied without opposition by General Graf Haesler, who was in command of the VIIIth Corps, which had landed at New Holland and Grimsby. The enemy's headquarters had been established in the old cathedral city, and it was reported in Sheffield that the whole of this force was on the move westward. In fact, on Saturday afternoon the head of the advance-guard coming by way of Saxilby and Tuxford had arrived at East Retford, and during the night the rest of the main body, following closely on its heels, disposed itself for bivouac in rear of that sloping ground which reaches from Clarborough, through Grove and Askham, to Tuxford, on the south.

In advance was Major-General von Briefen's splendid cavalry brigade, who, during the march, had scoured the county almost as far west as the River Rother itself. Chesterfield, with its crooked spire, had been approached by the 7th Westphalian Dragoons, supported by the Grand Duke of Baden's Hussars and a company of smart motor infantry. Finding, however, that no resistance was offered, they had extended, forming a screen from that place to Worksop, examining and reconnoitring every road, farmstead, and hamlet, in order that the advance of the main body behind them could not be interfered with.

The cavalry brigade of the other division, the Cuirassiers of the Rhine No. 8, and the 7th Rhine Hussars, scouted along to the northward as far as Bawtry, where they were able to effect a junction with their comrades of the VIIth Corps, who, it will be remembered, had landed at Goole, and had now pushed on.

During Saturday afternoon a squadron of British Yeomanry had been pushed out from Rotherham as far as the high ground at Maltby, and hearing from the contact patrols that nothing appeared to be in front of them, moved on to Tickhill, a small village four miles west of Bawtry. Unknown to them, however, a force of Westphalian Dragoons, having had information of their presence, crept up by the lower road through Blythe and Oldcoats, effectively taking them in rear, passing as they did through the grounds of Sandbeck Hall.

The Yeomanry, at the alarm, pulled up, and, dismounting under cover, poured in a rattling volley upon the invaders, emptying more than one Westphalian saddle. Next instant the Germans, making a dash, got between them and their line of retreat on Maltby. It was palpable to the officer in charge of the Yeomanry that he must get back to Sheffield some other way. It would not do to stay and fight where he was, as there was every prospect of his small troop being annihilated, nor did he desire himself to be taken prisoner. His business was to report what he had seen. This latter he was bound to accomplish at all risks. So, hastily leaping into his saddle in the middle of a perfect hail of bullets—the result of which was that several horses went down and left their riders at the mercy of the invaders—the little band set off to regain their camp outside Rotherham, by the cross-country roads through Stainton and Braithwell. Here again they narrowly escaped falling into the hands of some cavalry, who evidently belonged to the VIIth Corps, and who had come down from the direction of Goole and Doncaster.

Eventually, however, they crossed the River Don at Aldwark, and brought in the first definite news which General Sir George Woolmer at Sheffield had yet received. It was thus proved that the German cavalry were now within the sphere of operations, and that in all probability they formed a screen covering the advance of the two great German corps, which it was quite certain now intended to make an attack upon the position he had selected for defence.

Night fell. On every road British yeomanry, cavalry, motor-cyclists, motor-infantry, and independent groups of infantry were endeavouring to penetrate the secret of the exact whereabouts of the enemy. Yet they found every road, lane, and pathway, no matter how carefully approached, held by Germans. Ever and anon, as they crept near the line of German outposts, came the low, guttural demand as sentries challenged the intruder.

Here and there in the hot night shots rang out, and some daring spirit fell dead, while more than once a dying scream was heard as a German bayonet ended the career of some too inquisitive patriot.

Away in Sheffield the town awaited, in breathless tension and hot unrest, what was felt by everyone to be the coming onslaught. Through the night the heavy clouds that had gathered after sunset culminated in a terrific thunderstorm. The heavens seemed rent asunder by the vivid lightning, the thunder crashed and rolled, and rain fell in torrents upon the excited populace, who, through the dark hours, crowded around the barricades in the Sheffield streets. In the murky dawn, grey and dismal, portentous events were impending.

Information from the enemy's camp—which was subsequently made public—showed that well before daylight the advance of the VIIth German Corps had begun from Doncaster, while along the main road through Warmsworth and Conisborough sturdily tramped the 13th Division, all Westphalians, formed into three infantry brigades and commanded by Lieut.-General Doppschutz. The 14th Division, under Lieut.-General von Kehler, moving through Balby and Wadworth, prolonged the flank to the south. The advance of both divisions was thus steadily continued south-westward parallel to the River Rother, which lay between themselves and the British. It was therefore plain that the plan of the senior officer—General Baron von Bistram, commanding the VIIth Corps—was that the attack should be carried out mainly by that corps itself, and that strong support should be given to it by the VIIIth Corps, which was coming, as has already been shown, from East Retford, and which could effectively assist either to strike the final blow against our Army, or, keeping well to the south, could threaten Sheffield from the direction of Staveley.

No one knew what resistance the British were prepared to offer. Full of courage and patriotism, they were dominated by the proud traditions of English soldiers; still, it was to be remembered that they consisted mainly of raw levies, and that they were opposed by a force whose training and equipment were unequalled in the world, and who outnumbered them in proportion of about four to one.

What was to be expected? Sheffield knew this—and was breathless and terrified.

The great thunderstorm of the night helped to swell the Rivers Don and Rother, and as the invaders would have to cross them, doubtless under a terrific fire, the battle must result in enormous casualties.

Early on Sunday morning it was evident that the all-important blow, so long threatened, was about to be struck. During the night great masses of German artillery had been pushed up to the front, and these now occupied most of the dominating hills, commanding not only all approaches to the British position over the River Rother, but they were even within effective range of the key of the British position itself.

Hundreds of guns—many of them coming under the head of siege-artillery—were concentrated a little to the east of Whiston, whence they were able to pour in an oblique fire upon the defences. This artillery belonged evidently to the VIIth German Corps, and had, with great labour and difficulty, been hauled by all available horses, and even by traction-engines, right across the country to where they were now placed. The heaviest metal of all had been posted on Bricks Hill, an eminence of some four hundred feet, immediately above the Rother, and about six thousand yards from Catcliffe, already referred to as the key of our defences.

Suddenly, at sunrise, a low boom was heard from this point. This was the opening German gun of the artillery preparation for the attack, which was now evidently developing, and although the distance was nearly six thousand yards, yet the bursts of the huge shells were seen to have been well timed. Another and another followed, and presently these huge projectiles, hurtling through the air and bursting with a greenish-yellow smoke, showed that they were charged with some high explosive. No sooner had this terrific tornado of destruction opened in real earnest from the enemy, than the field artillery, massed as has already been described, commenced their long-distance fire at a range of about three thousand five hundred yards, and for a period, that seemed hours, but yet was in reality only about fifty minutes, the awful cannonade continued.

The British guns had already come into action, and intermittent firing of shrapnel and other projectiles was now directed against the German batteries.

These latter, however, were mostly carefully concealed, effective cover having, by means of hard spade-work, been thrown up during the night. The British guns were mostly served by Volunteers and Militia-Artillerymen, who, although burning with patriotism, were—owing to the little real practice they had had in actually firing live shell, having mostly been drilled with dummy guns—utterly incompetent to make any impression upon the enemy's lines of concealed artillery.

It was plain, then, that the Germans had adopted the principle of massing the bulk of the guns of their two divisions of the VIIth Corps at such a point that they might strike the heaviest blow possible at the defence, under cover of which, when resistance had been somewhat beaten down, the infantry might advance to the attack. This was now being done. But away to the south was heard the distant roar of other artillery, no doubt that of Haesler's Corps, which had apparently crossed the river somewhere in the neighbourhood of Renishaw, and advancing via Eckington had established themselves on the high ground, about five hundred and twenty feet in altitude, just north of Ridgeway, whence they were able to pour in an enfilading fire all along the British position from its centre at Woodhouse almost to Catcliffe itself. This rendered our position serious, and although the German guns had opposed to them the southernmost flank from Woodhouse to Norton Woodseats, yet it was plain that the main portion of the British defence was in process of being "turned."

The heavy firing continued, and at last, under cover of it, the rear attack now began some two hours after the opening of the fight.

The 13th Division, under Doppschutz, were evidently advancing by the main Doncaster road. Their advance guard, which had already occupied Rotherham, had also seized the bridge which the invaders had neither time nor material to demolish, and now swept on across it, although exposed to a heavy onslaught from that line of the British position between Tinsley and Brinsworth. Those sturdy, stolid Westphalians and bearded men of Lorraine still kept on. Numbers dropped, and the bridge was quickly strewn with dead and dying. Yet nothing checked the steady advance of that irresistible wave of humanity.

Down the River Rother, at Kanklow Bridge, a similar scene was being enacted. The railway bridge at Catcliffe was also taken by storm, and at Woodhouse Mill the 14th Division, under Von Kehler, made a terrific and successful dash, as they also did at Beighton.

The river itself was about an average distance of a mile in front of the British position, and although as heavy a fire as possible was directed upon all approaches to it, yet the Germans were not to be denied. Utterly indifferent to any losses, they still swept on in an overwhelming tide, leaving at the most not more than ten per cent. of casualties to be dealt with by the perfectly equipped ambulances in their rear. So, for the most part, the various regiments constituting the divisions of the two German commanders found themselves shaken, but by no means thwarted. On the west bank of the river, the steep slopes rising from Beighton to Woodhouse gave a certain amount of dead ground, under cover of which the foreign legions took refuge, in order to dispose themselves for the final assault.

A similar state of things had taken place to the south. General Graf Haesler had flung both his divisions across the river, with but little opposition. The 15th, composed mainly of men of the Rhine, under Von Kluser, crossed at Killamarsh and Metherthorpe Station, while the 16th, under Lieut.-General Stolz, crossed at Renishaw, and, striking north-easterly in the direction of Ridgeway, closed in as they advanced, till at length they were enabled to be within effective reach of their comrades on the right.

The German attack had now developed into an almost crescent-shaped formation, and about noon Von Bistram, the commander-in-chief, issued his final orders for the assault.

The cavalry of the VIIth German Corps under Major-General von Landsberg, commanding the 13th Cavalry Brigade, and the 14th Cavalry Brigade, consisting of Westphalian Hussars and Uhlans, under Major-General von Weder, were massed in the neighbourhood of Greasborough, whence it might be expected that at the critical stage of the engagement if the British defences gave way they might be launched upon the retiring Englishmen. Similarly in the valley over by Middle Handley, a little south of Eckington, were found the 15th and 16th Cavalry Brigades of the VIIIth Corps, consisting of the 15th of Cuirassiers and Hussars of the Rhine, and the 16th of Westphalians, and the Grand Duke of Baden's Hussars, under that well-known soldier, Major-General von Briefen. All these were equally ready to advance in a northerly direction to strike the crushing blow at the first of the many important cities which was their objective.

Unless the scheme of von Bistram, the German generalissimo in the North, was ill-conceived, then it was plain, even to the defenders, that Sheffield must eventually give way before the overpowering force opposed to it.

Within the city of Sheffield the excitement now rose to fever-heat.

It was known that the enemy had closed in upon the defences, and were now across the river, ready at any moment to continue their advance, which, as a matter of fact, had developed steadily without intermission, notwithstanding the heroic efforts of the defenders.

In these days of smokeless powder it was hard for the Germans to see where the British lines of defence were actually located, but the heavy pounding of the artillery duel, which had been going on since early morning, was now beginning to weaken as the German infantry, company by company, regiment by regiment, and brigade by brigade, were calmly launched to the attack. They were themselves masking the fire of the cannon of their own comrades as, by desperate rushes, they gradually ascended the slopes before them.

The objective of the VIIth Corps seemed to be the strongpoint which has already been referred to as dominating the position a little west of

Catcliffe, and the VIIIth Corps were clearly directing their energies on the salient angle of the defence which was to be found a little south of Woodhouse. From this latter point the general line of the British position from Woodhouse north to Tinsley would then be turned.

The British stood their ground with the fearless valour of Englishmen. Though effective defence seemed from the very first futile, steady and unshaken volleys rang out from every knoll, hillock, and shelter-trench in that long line manned by the sturdy Yorkshire heroes. Machine-guns rattled and spat fire, and pom-poms worked with regularity, hurling their little shells in a ceaseless stream into the invaders, but all, alas! to no purpose. Where one German fell, at least three appeared to take his place. The enemy seemed to rise from the very ground. The more stubborn the defence, the more numerous the Germans seemed to become, gaps in their fighting line being reinforced in that ruthless manner which is such a well-known principle in German tactics— namely, that the commander must not be sparing in his men, but fling forward reinforcements at whatever cost.

Thus up the storm-swept glacis reaching from the Rother struggled thousands of Germans in a tide that could not be stemmed, halting and firing as they advanced, until it became clear that an actual hand-to-hand combat was imminent.

The British had done all that men could. There was no question of surrender. They were simply swept away as straws before a storm. Dead and dying were on every hand, ambulances were full, and groaning men were being carried by hundreds to the rear. General Woolmer saw that the day was lost, and at last, with choking emotion, he was compelled to give that order which no officer can ever give unless to save useless bloodshed—"Retire!—Retire upon Sheffield itself!"

Bugles rang out, and the whistles of the officers pierced the air. Then in as orderly a manner as was possible in the circumstances, and amid the victorious shouts from thousands of German throats, the struggling units fell back upon the city.

The outlook was surely black enough. Worse was, however, yet to follow. In the line of retreat all roads were blocked with endless masses of wagons and ambulances, and in order to fall back at all men had to take to the open fields and clamber over hedges, so that all semblance of order was very quickly lost.

Thus the retreat became little short of a rout.

Presently a shout rang out. "The cavalry! The cavalry!"

And then was seen a swarm of big Uhlans riding down from the north at a hand-gallop, evidently prepared to cut off the routed army.

By Tinsley Park a body of Volunteers were retreating in an orderly manner, when the alarm of the cavalry advance reached their ears. Their colonel, a red-faced, bearded old gentleman, wearing the green ribbon of the V.D., and who in private life was a brewery's manager at Tadcaster, rose in his stirrups and, turning round towards the croup of his somewhat weedy steed, exclaimed the words in a hoarse and raucous bellow: "Soaky Poo!"

His men wondered what he meant. Some halted, believing it to be a new order which demanded further attention, until a smart young subaltern, smiling behind his hand, shouted out, "Sauve qui peut— Every man for himself!"

And at this there was a helter-skelter flight on the part of the whole battalion.

The Uhlans, however, were not to be denied, and, circling round through Attercliffe, and thence south towards Richmond Park, they effectively placed themselves across the line of retreat of many of the fugitives.

The latter practically ran straight into the lines of the Germans, who called to them to lay down their arms, and in half an hour along the cordon over two thousand five hundred British of all arms found themselves prisoners in the hands of Von Landsberg, upon whose brigade the brunt of this attack had fallen.

General von Wedel, of the 14th Cavalry Brigade, was not inactive. He pursued the flying columns along all the roads and country north-east of the city. From the south came news of the cavalry of the VIIIth Corps, which had circled through Dronfield, Woodhouse, Totley, along Abbey Dale, till they made an unresisted entry into Sheffield from the south.

Within the town it was quickly seen that the day was lost. All resistance had been beaten down by the victorious invaders, and now, at the Town Hall, the British flag was hauled down, and the German ensign replaced it. From every street leading out of the city to the west poured a flying mob of disorganised British troops, evidently bent upon making the best of their way into the hilly district of the Peak of Derbyshire, where, in the course of time, they might hope to reorganise and re-establish themselves.

The German pursuit, although very strenuous on the part of the cavalry as far as effecting the occupation of the city was concerned, did not extend very much beyond it. Clearly the invaders did not want to be burdened with a large number of British prisoners whom they had no means of interning, and whom it would be difficult to place on parole. What they wanted was to strike terror in the great cities of the north.

Sheffield was now theirs. Nearly all the ammunition and stores of the defenders had fallen into their hands, and they were enabled to view, with apparent equanimity, the spectacle of retreating masses of British infantry, yeomanry, and artillery. Westwards along the network of roads leading in the direction of the High Peak, Derwent Dale, Bradfield, Buxton, and on to Glossop, the British were fast retreating, evidently making Manchester their objective.

Sheffield was utterly dumbfounded. The barricades had been broken down and swept away. The troops, of whom they had hoped so much, had been simply swept away, and now the streets were full of burly foreigners. George Street swarmed with Westphalian infantry and men of Lorraine; in Church Street a squadron of Uhlans were drawn up opposite the Sheffield and Hallamshire Bank, while the sidewalk was occupied by piled arms of the 39th Fusilier Regiment. In the space around the Town Hall the 6th Infantry Regiment of the Rhine and a regiment of Cuirassiers were standing at ease. Many of the stalwart sons of the Fatherland were seen to light their pipes and stolidly enjoy a smoke, while officers in small groups stood here and there discussing the events of the victorious day.

The saddest scenes were to be witnessed at the Royal Infirmary, in Infirmary Road, at the Royal Hospital in West Street, and even in some of the vacant wards in the Jessop Hospital for Women in Victoria Street, which had to be requisitioned for the accommodation of the crowds of wounded of both nations, so constantly being brought in by carts, carriages, motor-cars, and even cabs.

The St. John's Ambulance Brigade, with many ladies, were doing all they could to render aid, while the Queen Victoria Jubilee Institute for Nurses was called upon for all available help. Every place where sick could be accommodated, including the well-known George Woofindin Convalescent Home, was crowded to overflowing with sufferers, while every doctor in Sheffield bore his part in unceasing surgical work. But the number of dead on both sides it was impossible to estimate.

At the Town Hall the Lord Mayor, aldermen, and councillors assembled, and met the German General, who sternly and abruptly demanded the payment of half a million pounds sterling in gold as an indemnity, together with the production of all stores that the German Army should require in order that they could re-victual.

In reply the Lord Mayor, after consulting with the Council, stated that he would call a meeting of all bank managers and heads of the great manufacturing firms in order that the demand might be, as far as possible, complied with. This answer was promised at five P.M.

Meanwhile, on the notice-board outside the Town Hall, a proclamation was affixed by the Chief of the German Staff, a sentry being posted on either side of it to prevent it being torn down.

Copies were sent to the offices of the local newspapers, and within half an hour its tenor was known in every part of the city. Throughout the night German cavalry patrolled all the main streets, most of the infantry being now reassembled into their brigades, divisions, and army corps on the southern outskirts of the city, and in Norton, Coal Aston, Dronfield, and Whittington were being established the headquarters of the four different divisions of which the VII and VIII Corps respectively were composed.

XVIII

The Feeling in London

Reports from Sheffield stated that on Sunday the gallant defence of the town by General Sir George Woolmer had been broken. We had suffered a terrible reverse. The British were in full flight, and the two victorious Corps now had the way open to advance to the metropolis of the Midlands, for they knew that they had left behind them only a shattered remnant of what the day before had been the British Army of the North.

In both Houses of Parliament, hastily summoned, there had been memorable scenes. In the Commons, the Government had endeavoured to justify its suicidal actions of the past, but such speeches were howled down, and even the Government organs themselves were now compelled to admit that the party had committed very grave errors of judgment.

Each night the House had sat until early morning, every member who had been in England on the previous Sunday being in his place. In response to the ever-repeated questions put to the War Minister, the reply was each day the same. All that could be done was being done.

Was there any hope of victory? That was the question eagerly asked on every hand—both in Parliament and out of it. At present there seemed none. Reports from the theatres of war in different parts of the country reaching the House each hour were ever the same—the British driven back by the enemy's overwhelming numbers.

The outlook was indeed a black one. The lobby was ever crowded by members eagerly discussing the situation. The enemy were at the gates of London. What was to be done?

In the House on Friday, September 7, in view of the fact that London was undoubtedly the objective of the enemy, it was decided that Parliament should, on the following day, be transferred to Bristol, and there meet in the great Colston Hall. This change had actually been effected, and the whole of both Houses, with their staff, were hurriedly transferred to the west, the Great Western Railway system being still intact.

The riff-raff from Whitechapel, those aliens whom we had so long welcomed and pampered in our midst—Russians, Poles, Austrians,

WILLIAM LE QUEUX

Swedes, and even Germans—the latter, of course, now declared themselves to be Russians—had swarmed westward in lawless, hungry multitudes, and on Monday afternoon serious rioting occurred in Grosvenor Square and the neighbourhood, and also in Park Lane, where several houses were entered and pillaged by the alien mobs.

The disorder commenced at a great mass meeting held in the Park, just behind the Marble Arch. Orators were denouncing the Government and abusing the Ministers in unmeasured terms, when someone, seeing the many aliens around, set up the cry that they were German spies. A free fight at once ensued, with the result that the mob, uncontrolled by the police, dashed across into Park Lane and wrecked three of the largest houses—one of which was deliberately set on fire by a can of petrol brought from a neighbouring garage. Other houses in Grosvenor Square shared the same fate.

In every quarter of London shops containing groceries, provisions, or flour were broken open by the lawless bands and sacked. From Kingsland and Hoxton, Lambeth and Camberwell, Notting Dale and Chelsea, reports received by the police showed that the people were now becoming desperate. Not only were the aliens lawless, but the London unemployed and lower classes were now raising their voices. "Stop the war! Stop the war!" was the cry heard on every hand. Nearly all the shops containing provisions in Whitechapel Road, Commercial Road East, and Cable Street were, during Monday, ruthlessly broken open and ransacked. The police from Leman Street were utterly incompetent to hold back the rush of the infuriated thousands, who fought desperately with each other for the spoils, starving men, women, and children all joining in the fray.

The East End had indeed become utterly lawless. The big warehouses in the vicinity of the docks were also attacked and most of them emptied of their contents, while two at Wapping, being defended by the police, were deliberately set on fire by the rioters, and quantities of wheat burned.

Fierce men formed themselves into raiding bands and went westward that night, committing all sorts of depredations. The enemy were upon them, and they did not mean to starve, they declared. Southwark and Bermondsey, Walworth and Kennington had remained quiet and watchful all the week, but now, when the report spread of this latest disaster to our troops at Sheffield, and that the Germans were already approaching London, the whole populace arose, and the shopbreaking, once started in the Walworth and Old Kent Roads, spread everywhere throughout the whole of South London.

In vain did the police good-humouredly cry to them to remain patient; in vain did the Lord Mayor address the multitude from the steps of the Royal Exchange; in vain did the newspapers, inspired from headquarters, with one accord urge the public to remain calm, and allow the authorities to direct their whole attention towards repelling the invaders. It was all useless. The public had made up its mind.

At last the bitter truth was being forced home upon the public, and in every quarter of the metropolis those very speakers who, only a couple of years before, were crying down the naval and military critics who had dared to raise their voices in alarm, were now admitting that the country should have listened and heeded.

London, it was plain, had already abandoned hope. The British successes had been so slight. The command of the sea was still in German hands, although in the House the Admiralty had reassured the country that in a few days we should regain the supremacy.

A few days! In a few days London might be invested by the enemy, and then would begin a reign of terror unequalled by any in the history of the civilised world.

By day the streets of the city presented a scene of turmoil and activity, for it seemed as though City workers clung to their old habit of going there each morning, even though their workshops, offices, and warehouses were closed. By night the West End, Pall Mall, Piccadilly, Oxford Street, Regent Street, Portland Place, Leicester Square, Whitehall, Victoria Street, and around Victoria Station were filled with idle, excited crowds of men, women, and children, hungry, despairing, wondering.

At every corner men and boys shouted the latest editions of the newspapers. "'Nother great Battle! 'Nother British Defeat! Fall of Sheffield!" rose above the excited chatter of the multitude. The cries fell upon the ears of defenceless Londoners, darkening the outlook as hour after hour wore on.

The heat was stifling, the dust suffocating, now that the roads were no longer cleaned. The theatres were closed. Only the churches and chapels remained open—and the public-houses, crowded to overflowing. In Westminster Abbey, in St. Paul's Cathedral, in St. Martin's-in-the-Fields, and in Westminster Cathedral special prayers were that night being offered for the success of the British arms. The services were crowded by all sorts and conditions of persons, from the poor, pinched woman in a shawl from a Westminster slum, to the lady of title who ventured out in her electric brougham. Men from the clubs stood next half-starved working men, and more than one of the more fortunate slipped money unseen into the hand of his less-favoured brother in adversity.

War is a great leveller. The wealthy classes were, in proportion, losing as much as the workers. It was only the grip of hunger that they did not feel, only the cry of starving children that did not reach their ears. For the rest, their interests were equal.

Meanwhile, from every hand rose the strident cries of the newsboys:

"'Nother great Battle! British routed at Sheffield! Extrur spe-shall!—spe'shall!"

British routed! It had been the same ominous cry the whole week through.

Was London really doomed?

BOOK II
THE SIEGE OF LONDON

I

The Lines of London

The German successes were continued in the North and Midlands, and notwithstanding the gallant defence of Sir George Woolmer before Manchester and Sir Henry Hibbard before Birmingham, both cities were captured and occupied by the enemy after terrible losses. London, however, was the chief objective of Von Kronhelm, and towards the Metropolis he now turned his attention.

After the defeat of the British at Chelmsford on that fateful Wednesday Lord Byfield decided to evacuate his position at Royston and fall back on the northern section of the London defence line, which had been under construction for the last ten days. These hasty entrenchments, which would have been impossible to construct but for the ready assistance of thousands of all classes of the citizens of London and the suburbs, extended from Tilbury on the east to Bushey on the west, passing by the Laindon Hills, Brentwood, Kelvedon, North Weald, Epping, Waltham Abbey, Cheshunt, Enfield Chase, Chipping Barnet, and Elstree. They were more or less continuous, consisting for the most part of trenches for infantry, generally following the lines of existing hedgerows or banks, which often required but little improvement to transform them into well-protected and formidable cover for the defending troops. Where it was necessary to cross open ground they were dug deep and winding, after the fashion adopted by the Boers in the South African War, so that it would be difficult, if not impossible, to enfilade them.

Special bomb-proof covers for the local reserves were also constructed at various points, and the ground in front ruthlessly cleared of houses, barns, trees, hedges, and everything that might afford shelter to an advancing enemy. Every possible military obstacle was placed in front of the lines that time permitted, abattis, military pits, wire entanglements, and small ground mines. At the more important points along the fifty miles of entrenchments field-works and redoubts for infantry and guns were built, most of them being armed with 4.7 or even 6 and 7.5 in. guns, which had been brought from Woolwich, Chatham, Portsmouth, and Devonport, and mounted on whatever carriages could be adapted or improvised for the occasion.

The preparation of the London lines was a stupendous undertaking, but the growing scarceness and dearness of provisions assisted in a degree, as no free rations were issued to any able-bodied man unless he went out to work at the fortifications. All workers were placed under military law. There were any number of willing workers who proffered their services in this time of peril. Thousands of men came forward asking to be enlisted and armed. The difficulty was to find enough weapons and ammunition for them, to say nothing of the question of uniform and equipment, which loomed very large indeed. The attitude of the Germans, as set forth in Von Kronhelm's proclamations, precluded the employment of fighting men dressed in civilian garb, and their attitude was a perfectly natural and justifiable one by all the laws and customs of war.

It became necessary, therefore, that all men sent to the front should be dressed as soldiers in some way or another. In addition to that splendid corps, the Legion of Frontiersmen, many new armed organisations had sprung into being, some bearing the most fantastic names, such as the "Whitechapel War-to-the-Knifes," the "Kensington Cowboys," the "Bayswater Braves," and the "Southwark Scalphunters." All the available khaki and blue serge was used up in no time; even though those who were already in possession of ordinary lounge suits of the latter material were encouraged to have them altered into uniform by the addition of stand-up collars and facings of various colours, according to their regiments and corps.

Only the time during which these men were waiting for their uniforms was spent in drill in the open spaces of the metropolis. As soon as they were clothed, they were despatched to that portion of the entrenchments to which their corps had been allocated, and there, in the intervals of their clearing and digging operations, they were hustled through a brief musketry course, which consisted for the most part in firing. The question of the provision of officers and N.C.O.s was an almost insuperable one. Retired men came forward on every side, but the supply was by no means equal to the demand, and they themselves in many instances were absolutely out of date as far as knowledge of modern arms and conditions were concerned. However, every one, with but very few exceptions, did his utmost, and by the 11th or 12th of the month the entrenchments were practically completed, and manned by upwards of 150,000 "men with muskets" of stout heart and full of patriotism, but in reality nothing but an army "pour rire" so far as efficiency was concerned.

The greater part of the guns were also placed in position, especially on the north and eastern portions of the lines, and the remainder were being mounted as fast as it was practicable. They were well manned by Volunteer and Militia artillerymen, drawn from every district which the invaders had left accessible. By the 13th the eastern section of the fortifications was strengthened by the arrival of the remnants of the Ist and Vth Army Corps, which had been so badly defeated at Chelmsford, and no time was lost in reorganising them and distributing them along the lines, thereby, to a certain extent, leavening the unbaked mass of their improvised defenders. It was generally expected that the enemy would follow up the success by an immediate attack on Brentwood, the main barrier between Von Kronhelm and his objective—our great metropolis. But, as it turned out, he had a totally different scheme in hand. The orders to Lord Byfield to evacuate the position he had maintained with such credit against the German Garde and IVth Corps have already been referred to. Their reason was obvious. Now that there was no organised resistance on his right, he stood in danger of being cut off from London, the defences of which were now in pressing need of his men. A large amount of rolling stock was at once despatched to Saffron Walden and Buntingford by the G.E.R., and to Baldock by the G.N.R., to facilitate the withdrawal of his troops and stores, and he was given an absolutely free hand as to how these were to be used, all lines being kept clear and additional trains kept waiting at his disposal at their London termini.

The 13th of September proved a memorable date in the history of England.

The evacuation of the Baldock-Saffron Walden position could not possibly have been carried out in good order on such short notice, had not Lord Byfield previously worked the whole thing out in readiness. He could not help feeling that, despite his glorious victory on the ninth, a turn of Fortune's wheel might necessitate a retirement on London sooner or later, and, like the good General that he was, he made every preparation both for this, and other eventualities. Among other details, he had arranged that the mounted infantry should be provided with plenty of strong light wire. This was intended for the express benefit of Frölich's formidable cavalry brigade, which he foresaw would be most dangerous to his command in the event of a retreat. As soon, therefore, as the retrograde movement commenced, the mounted infantry began to stretch their wires across every road, lane, and byway leading to the north and north-east. Some wires were laid low, within a foot of the ground, others high up where they could catch a rider about the neck or breast. This operation they carried out again and again, after the troops had passed, at various points on the route of the retreat. Thanks to the darkness, this device well fulfilled its purpose. Frölich's brigade was on the heels of the retreating British soon after midnight, but as it was impossible for them to move over the enclosed country at night his riders were confined to the roads, and the accidents and delays occasioned by the wires were so numerous and disconcerting, that their advance had to be conducted with such caution that as a pursuit it was of no use at all. Even the infantry and heavy guns of the retiring British got over the ground nearly twice as fast. After two or three hours of this, only varied by occasional volleys from detachments of our mounted infantry, who sometimes waited in rear of their snares to let fly at the German cavalry before galloping back to lay others, the enemy recognised the fact, and, withdrawing their cavalry till daylight, replaced them by infantry, but so much time had been lost that the British had got several miles' start.

As has been elsewhere chronicled, the brigade of four regular battalions with their guns, and a company of Engineers, which were to secure the passage of the Stort and protect the left flank of the retirement, left Saffron Walden somewhere about 10.30 P.M. The line was clear, and they arrived at Sawbridgeworth in four long trains in a little under an hour. Their advent did not arouse the sleeping village, as the station lies nearly three-quarters of a mile distant on the further side of the river. It may be noted in passing that while the Stort is but a small stream, easily fordable in most places, yet it was important, if possible, to secure the bridges to prevent delay in getting over the heavy guns and wagons of the retiring British. A delay and congestion at the points selected for passage might, with a close pursuit, easily lead to disaster. Moreover, the Great Eastern Railway crossed the river by a wooden bridge just north of the village of Sawbridgeworth, and it was necessary to ensure the safe passage of the last trains over it before destroying it to preclude the use of the railway by the enemy.

There were two road bridges on the Great Eastern Railway near the village of Sawbridgeworth, which might be required by the Dunmow force, which was detailed to protect the same flank rather more to the northward. The most important bridge, that over which the main body of the Saffron Walden force was to retire, with all the impedimenta it had had time to bring away with it, was between Sawbridgeworth and

Harlow, about a mile north of the latter village, but much nearer its station. Thither, then, proceeded the leading train with the Grenadiers, four 4.7 guns, and half a company of Royal Engineers with bridging materials. Their task was to construct a second bridge to relieve the traffic over the permanent one. The Grenadiers left one company at the railway station, two in Harlow village, which they at once commenced to place in a state of defence, much to the consternation of the villagers, who had not realised how close to them were trending the red footsteps of war. The remaining five companies with the other four guns turned northward, and after marching another mile or so occupied the enclosures round Durrington House and the higher ground to its north. Here the guns were halted on the road. It was too dark to select the best position for them, for it was now only about half an hour after midnight. The three other regiments which detrained at Sawbridgeworth were disposed as follows, continuing the line of the Grenadiers to the northward. The Rifles occupied Hyde Hall, formerly the seat of the Earls of Roden, covering the operations of the Engineers, who were preparing the railway bridge for destruction, and the copses about Little Hyde Hall on the higher ground to the eastward.

The Scots Guards with four guns were between them and the Grenadiers, and distributed between Sheering village and Gladwyns House, from the neighbourhood of which it was expected that the guns would be able to command the Chelmsford Road for a considerable distance. The Seaforth Highlanders for the time being were stationed on a road running parallel to the railway, from which branch roads led to both the right, left, and centre of the position. An advanced party of the Rifle Brigade was pushed forward to Hatfield Heath with instructions to patrol towards the front and flanks, and, if possible, establish communication with the troops expected from Dunmow. By the time all this was completed it was getting on for 3 A.M. on the 13th. At this hour the advanced guard of the Germans coming from Chelmsford was midway between Leaden Roding and White Roding, while the main body was crossing the small River Roding by the shallow ford near the latter village. Their few cavalry scouts were, however, exploring the roads and lanes some little way ahead. A collision was imminent. The Dunmow force had not been able to move before midnight, and, with the exception of one regular battalion, the 1st Leinsters, which was left behind to the last and crowded into the only train available, had only just arrived at the northern edge of Hatfield Forest, some four miles directly north of Hatfield Heath. The Leinsters, who left Dunmow by train half an hour later, had detrained at this point at one o'clock, and just about three had met the patrols of the Rifles. A Yeomanry corps from Dunmow was also not far off, as it had turned to its left at the crossroads east of Takely, and was by this time in the neighbourhood of Hatfield Broad Oak. In short, all three forces were converging, but the bulk of the Dunmow force was four miles away from the point of convergence.

It was still profoundly dark when the Rifles at Hatfield Heath heard a dozen shots cracking through the darkness to their left front. Almost immediately other reports resounded from due east. Nothing could be seen beyond a very few yards, and the men of the advanced company drawn up at the crossroads in front of the village inn fancied they now and again saw figures dodging about in the obscurity, but were cautioned not to fire till their patrols had come in, for it was impossible to distinguish friend from foe. Shots still rattled out here and there to the front. About ten minutes later the captain in command, having got in his patrols, gave the order to fire at a black blur that seemed to be moving towards them on the Chelmsford Road. There was no mistake this time. The momentary glare of the discharge flashed on the shiny "pickel-haubes" of a detachment of German infantry, who charged forward with a loud "Hoch!" The Riflemen, who already had their bayonets fixed, rushed to meet them, and for a few moments there was a fierce stabbing affray in the blackness of the night. The Germans, who were but few in number, were overpowered, and beat a retreat, having lost several of their men. The Rifles, according to their orders, having made sure of the immediate proximity of the enemy, now fell back to the rest of their battalion at Little Hyde Hall, and all along the banks and hedges which covered the British front, our men, rifle in hand, peered eagerly into the darkness ahead of them.

Nothing happened for quite half an hour, and the anxious watchers were losing some of their alertness, when a heavy outburst of firing re-echoed from Hatfield Heath. To explain this we must return to the Germans. Von der Rudesheim, on obtaining touch with the British, at once reinforced his advanced troops, and they, a whole battalion strong, advanced into the hamlet, meeting with no resistance. Almost simultaneously two companies of the Leinsters entered it from the northward. There was a sudden and unexpected collision on the open green, and a terrible fire was exchanged at close quarters, both sides losing very heavily. The British, however, were borne back by sheer weight of numbers, and, through one of those unfortunate mistakes that insist on occurring in warfare, were charged as they fell back by the leading squadrons of the Yeomanry who were coming up from Hatfield Broad Oak. The officer commanding the Leinsters decided to wait till it was a little lighter before again attacking the village. He considered that, as he had no idea of the strength of the enemy, he had best wait till the arrival of the troops now marching through Hatfield Forest. Von der Rudesheim, on his part, mindful of his instructions, determined to try to hold the few scattered houses on the north side of the heath which constituted the village, with the battalion already in it, and push forward with the remainder of his force towards Harlow. His first essay along the direct road viâ Sheering, was repulsed by the fire of the Scots Guards lining the copses about Gladwyns. He now began to have some idea of the British position, and made his preparations to assault it at daybreak.

To this end he sent forward two of his batteries into Hatfield Heath, cautiously moved the rest of his force away to the left, arranged his battalions in the valley of the Pincey Brook ready for attacking Sheering and Gladwyns, placed one battalion in reserve at Down Hall, and stationed his remaining battery near Newman's End. By this time there was beginning to be a faint glimmer of daylight in the east, and, as the growing dawn began to render vague outlines of the nearer objects dimly discernible, hell broke loose along the peaceful countryside. A star shell fired from the battery at Newman's End burst and hung out a brilliant white blaze that fell slowly over Sheering village, lighting up its walls and roofs and the hedges along which lay its defenders, was the signal for the Devil's Dance to begin. Twelve guns opened with a crash from Hatfield Heath, raking the Gladwyns enclosures and the end of Sheering village with a deluge of shrapnel, while an almost solid firing line advanced rapidly against it, firing heavily. The British replied lustily with gun, rifle, and maxim, the big, high-explosive shells bursting amid the advancing Germans and among the houses of Hatfield Heath with telling effect. But the German assaulting lines had but six or seven hundred yards to go. They had been trained above all things to ignore losses and to push on at all hazards. The necessity for this had not been confused in their minds by maxims about the importance of cover, so the south side of the village street was taken at a rush. Von der Rudesheim continued to pile on his men, and, fighting desperately, the Guardsmen were driven from house to house and from fence to fence. All this time the German battery at Newman's End continued to fire star shells with rhythmical regularity, lighting up the inflamed countenances of the living combatants, and the pale upturned faces of the dead turned to heaven as if calling for vengeance on their slayers. In the midst of this desperate fighting the Leinsters, supported by a Volunteer and a Militia regiment, which had just come up, assaulted Hatfield Heath. The Germans were driven out of it with the loss of a couple of their guns, but hung on to the little church, around which such a desperate conflict was waged that the dead above ground in that diminutive God's acre outnumbered the "rude forefathers of the hamlet" who slept below.

It was now past five o'clock in the morning, and by this time strong reinforcements might have been expected from Dunmow, but, with the exception of the Militia and Volunteer battalions just referred to, who had pushed on at the sound of the firing, none were seen coming up. The fact was that they had been told off to certain positions in the line of defence they had been ordered to take up, and had been slowly and carefully installing themselves therein. Their commanding officer, Sir Jacob Stellenbosch, thought that he must carry out the exact letter of the orders he had received from Lord Byfield, and paid little attention to the firing except to hustle his battalion commanders, to try to get them into their places as soon as possible. He was a pig-headed man into the bargain, and would listen to no remonstrance. The two battalions which had arrived so opportunely had been at the head of the column, and had pushed forward "on their own" before he could prevent them. At this time the position was as follows: One German battalion was hanging obstinately on to the outskirts of Hatfield Heath; two were in possession of the copses about Gladwyns; two were in Sheering village, or close up to it, and the sixth was still in reserve at Down Hall. On the British side the Rifles were in their original position at Little Hyde Hall, where also were three guns, which had been got away from Gladwyns. The Seaforths had come up, and were now firing from about Quickbury, while the Scots Guards, after suffering fearful losses, were scattered, some with the Highlanders, others with the five companies of the Grenadiers, who with their four guns still fought gallantly on between Sheering and Durrington House.

II

Repulse of the Germans

The terrible fire of the swarms of Germans who now lined the edges of Sheering village became too much for the four 4.7 guns on the open ground to the south.

Their gunners were shot down as fast as they touched their weapons, and when the German field battery at Newman's End, which had been advanced several hundred yards, suddenly opened a flanking fire of shrapnel upon them, it was found absolutely impossible to serve them. A gallant attempt was made to withdraw them by the Harlow Road, but their teams were shot down as soon as they appeared. This enfilade fire, too, decimated the Grenadiers and the remnant of the Scots, though they fought on to the death, and a converging attack of a battalion from Down Hall and another from Sheering drove them down into the grounds of Durrington House, where fighting still went on savagely for some time afterwards.

Von der Rudesheim had all but attained a portion of his object, which was to establish his guns in such a position that they could fire on the main body of the British troops when they entered Sawbridgeworth by the Cambridge Road. The place where the four guns with the Grenadiers had been stationed was within 3000 yards of any part of that road between Harlow and Sawbridgeworth. But this spot was still exposed to the rifle fire of the Seaforths who held Quickbury. Von der Rudesheim therefore determined to swing forward his left, and either drive them back down the hill towards the river, or at least to so occupy them that he could bring up his field-guns to their chosen position without losing too many of his gunners.

By six o'clock, thanks to his enormous local superiority in numbers, he had contrived to do this, and now the opposing forces with the exception of the British Grenadiers, who still fought with a German battalion between Durrington House and Harlow, faced each other north and south, instead of east and west, as they were at the beginning of the fight. Brigadier-General Lane-Edgeworth, who was in command of the British, had been sending urgent messages for reinforcements to the Dunmow Force, but when its commanding officer finally decided to turn his full strength in the direction of the firing, it took so long to assemble and form up the Volunteer regiments who composed the bulk of his command, that it was past seven before the leading battalion had deployed to assist in the attack which it was decided to make against the German right. Meantime, other important events had transpired.

Von der Rudesheim had found that the battalion which was engaged with the Grenadiers could not get near Harlow village, or either the river or railway bridge at that place, both of which he wished to destroy. But his scouts had reported a lock and wooden footbridge immediately to the westward between Harlow and Sawbridgeworth, just abreast of the large wooded park surrounding Pishobury House on the farther side. He determined to send two companies over by this, their movements being hidden from the English by the trees. After crossing, they found themselves confronted by a backwater, but, trained in crossing rivers, they managed to ford and swim over, and advanced through the park towards Harlow Bridge. While this was in progress, a large force was reported marching south on the Cambridge Road.

While Von der Rudesheim, who was at the western end of Sheering hamlet, was looking through his glasses at the new arrivals on the scene of action—who were without doubt the main body of the Royston command, which was retiring under the personal supervision of Lord Byfield—a puff of white smoke rose above the trees about Hyde Hall, and at top speed four heavily loaded trains shot into sight going south. These were the same ones that had brought down the Regular British troops, with whom he was now engaged. They had gone north again, and picked up a number of Volunteer battalions belonging to the retreating force just beyond Bishop's Stortford. But so long a time had been taken in entraining the troops in the darkness and confusion of the retreat, that their comrades who had kept to the road arrived almost simultaneously. Von der Rudesheim signalled, and sent urgent orders for his guns to be brought up to open fire on them, but by the time the first team had reached him the last of the trains had disappeared from sight into the cutting at Harlow Station. But even now it was not too late to open fire on the troops entering Sawbridgeworth.

Things were beginning to look somewhat bad for Von der Rudesheim's little force. The pressure from the north was increasing every moment, his attack on the retreating troops had failed, he had not so far been able to destroy the bridges at Harlow, and every minute the likelihood of his being able to do so grew more remote. To crown all, word was brought him that the trains which had just slipped by were disgorging men in hundreds along the railway west of Harlow Station, and that these troops were beginning to move forward as if to support the British Grenadiers, who had been driven back towards Harlow. In fact, he saw that there was even a possibility of his being surrounded. But he had no intention of discontinuing the fight. He knew he could rely on the discipline and mobility of his well-trained men under almost any conditions, and he trusted, moreover, that the promised reinforcements would not be very long in turning up. But he could not hold on just where he was. He accordingly, by various adroit manœuvres, threw back his right to Down Hall, whose copses and plantations afforded a good deal of cover, and, using this as a pivot, gradually wheeled back his left till he had taken up a position running north and south from Down Hall to Matching Tye. He had not effected this difficult manœuvre without considerable loss, but he experienced less difficulty in extricating his left than he had anticipated, since the newly arrived British troops at Harlow, instead of pressing forward against him, had been engaged in moving into a position between Harlow and the hamlet of Foster Street, on the somewhat elevated ground to the south of Matching, which would enable them to cover the further march of the main body of the retreating troops to Epping.

But he had totally lost the two companies he had sent across the river to attack Harlow Bridge. Unfortunately for them, their arrival on the Harlow-Sawbridgeworth Road synchronised with that of the advanced guard of Lord Byfield's command. Some hot skirmishing took place in and out among the trees of Pishobury, and finally the Germans were driven to earth in the big square block of the red-brick mansion itself.

Here they made a desperate stand, fighting hard as they were driven from one storey to another. The staircases ran with blood, the woodwork smouldered and threatened to burst into flame in a dozen places. At length the arrival of a battery of field guns, which, unlimbered at close range, induced the survivors to surrender, and they were disarmed and carried off as prisoners with the retreating army.

BY THE TIME VON DER Rudesheim had succeeded in taking up his new position it was past ten o'clock, and he had been informed by despatches carried by motor-cyclists that he might expect assistance in another hour and a half.

The right column, consisting of the 39th Infantry Brigade of five battalions, six batteries, and a squadron of Dragoons, came into collision with the left flank of the Dunmow force, which was engaged in attacking Von der Rudesheim's right at Down Hall, and endeavouring to surround it. Sir Jacob Stellenbosch, who was in command, in vain tried to change front to meet the advancing enemy. His troops were nearly all Volunteers, who were incapable of quickly manœuvring under difficult circumstances; they were crumpled up and driven back in confusion towards Hatfield Heath. Had Von Kronhelm been able to get in the bulk of his cavalry from their luckless pursuit of the Ist and Vth British Army Corps, who had been driven back on Brentwood the evening previous, and so send a proportion with the 20th Division, few would have escaped to tell the tale. As it was, the unfortunate Volunteers were shot down in scores by the "feu d'enfer" with which the artillery followed them up, and lay in twos and threes and larger groups all over the fields, victims of a selfish nation that accepted these poor fellows' gratuitous services merely in order that its citizens should not be obliged to carry out what in every other European country was regarded as the first duty of citizenship—that of learning to bear arms in the defence of the Fatherland.

By this time the greater portion of the retreating British Army, with all its baggage, guns, and impedimenta, was crawling slowly along the road from Harlow to Epping. Unaccustomed as they were to marching, the poor Volunteers, who had already covered eighteen or twenty miles of road, were now toiling slowly and painfully along the highway. The regular troops, who had been engaged since early morning, and who were now mostly in the neighbourhood of Moor Hall, east of Harlow, firing at long ranges on Von der Rudesheim's men to keep them in their places while Sir Jacob Stellenbosch attacked their right, were now hurriedly withdrawn and started to march south by a track running parallel to the main Epping Road, between it and that along which the covering force of Volunteers, who had come in by train, were now established in position. The 1st and 2nd Coldstreamers, who had formed Lord Byfield's rear-guard during the night, were halted in Harlow village.

Immediately upon the success obtained by his right column, General Richel von Sieberg, who commanded the 20th Hanoverian Division, ordered his two centre and left columns, consisting respectively of the three battalions 77th Infantry and two batteries of Horse Artillery, then at Matching Green, and the three battalions 92nd Infantry, 10th Pioneer Battalion, and five batteries Field Artillery, then between High Laver and Tilegate Green, to turn to their left and advance in fighting formation in a south-westerly direction, with the object of attacking the sorely harassed troops of Lord Byfield on their way to Epping.

THE FINAL PHASE OF THIS memorable retreat is best told in the words of the special war correspondent of the *Daily Telegraph*, who arrived on the scene at about one o'clock in the afternoon:

EPPING, 5 P.M., *September 9*

"Thanks to the secrecy preserved by the military authorities, it was not known that Lord Byfield was falling back from the Royston-Saffron Walden position till seven this morning. By eight, I was off in my car for the scene of action, for rumours of fighting near Harlow had already begun to come in. I started out by way of Tottenham and Edmonton, expecting to reach Harlow by 9.30 or 10. But I reckoned without the numerous military officials with whom I came in contact, who constantly stopped me and sent me out of my way on one pretext or another. I am sure I hope that the nation has benefited by their proceedings. In the end it was close on one before I pulled up at the Cock Inn, Epping, in search of additional information, because for some time I had been aware of the rumbling growl of heavy artillery from the eastward, and wondered what it might portend. I found that General Sir Stapleton Forsyth, who commanded the Northern section of the defences, had made the inn his headquarters, and there was a constant coming and going of orderlies and staff-officers at its portals. Opposite, the men of one of the new irregular corps, dressed in dark green corduroy, blue flannel cricketing caps, and red cummerbunds, sat or reclined in two long lines on either side of their piled arms on the left of the wide street. On inquiry I heard that the enemy were said to be bombarding Kelvedon Hatch, and also that the head of our retreating columns was only three or four miles distant.

"I pushed on, and, after the usual interrogations from an officer in charge of a picket, where the road ran through the entrenchments about a mile farther on, found myself spinning along through the country in the direction of Harlow. As I began to ascend the rising ground towards

Potter Street I could hear a continuous roll of artillery away to my right. I could not distinguish anything except the smoke of shells bursting here and there in the distance, on account of the scattered trees which lined the maze of hedgerows on every side. Close to Potter Street I met the head of the retreating army. Very tired, heated, and footsore looked the hundreds of poor fellows as they dragged themselves along through the heat. It was a sultry afternoon and the roads inches deep in dust.

"Turning to the right over Harlow Common, I met another column of men. I noticed that these were all Regulars, Grenadiers, Scots Guards, a battalion of Highlanders, another of Riflemen, and, lastly, two battalions of the Coldstreamers. These troops stepped along with rather more life than the citizen soldiers I had met previously, but still showed traces of their hard marching and fighting. Many of them were wearing bandages, but all the more seriously wounded had been left behind to be looked after by the Germans. All this time the firing was still resounding heavy and constant from the north-east, and from one person and another whom I questioned I ascertained that the enemy were advancing upon us from that direction. Half a mile farther on I ran into the middle of the fighting. The road ran along the top of a kind of flat ridge or upland, whence I could see to a considerable distance on either hand.

"Partially sheltered from view by its hedges and the scattered cottages forming the hamlet of Foster Street was a long, irregular line of guns facing nearly east. Beyond them were yet others directed north. There were field batteries and big 4.7's. All were hard at work, their gunners working like men possessed, and the crash of their constant discharge was ear-splitting. I had hardly taken this in when "Bang! Bang! Bang! Bang!"—four dazzling flashes opened in the air overhead, and shrapnel bullets rattled on earth, walls, and roofs, with a sound as of handfuls of pebbles thrown on a marble pavement. But the hardness with which they struck was beyond anything in my experience.

"It was not pleasant to be here, but I ran my car behind a little public-house that stood by the wayside, and, dismounting, unslung my glasses and determined to get what view of the proceedings I could from the corner of the house. All round khaki-clad Volunteers lined every hedge and sheltered behind every cottage, while farther off, in the lower ground, from a mile to a mile and a half away I could distinguish the closely packed firing lines of the Germans advancing slowly but steadily, despite the gaps made in their ranks by the fire of our guns. Their own guns, I fancied I could make out near Tilegate Green, to the north-east. Neither side had as yet opened rifle fire. Getting into my car I motored back to the main road, but it was so blocked by the procession of wagons and troops of the retreating army that I could not turn into it. Wheeling round I made my way back to a parallel lane I had noticed, and turning to the left again at a smithy, found myself in a road bordered by cottages and enclosures. Here I found the Regular troops I had lately met lining every hedgerow and fence, while I could see others on a knoll further to their left. There was a little church here, and, mounting to the roof, I got a comparatively extensive view. To my right the long, dusty column of men and wagons still toiled along the Epping Road. In front, nearly three miles off, an apparently solid line of woods stretched along the horizon, surmounting a long, gradual, and open slope. This was the position of our lines near Epping, and the haven for which Lord Byfield's tired soldiery were making. To the left the serried masses of drab-clad German infantry still pushed aggressively forward, their guns firing heavily over their heads.

"As I watched them three tremendous explosions took place in their midst, killing dozens of them. Fire, smoke, and dust rose up twenty feet in the air, while three ear-splitting reports rose even above the rolling thunder of the gunfire. More followed. I looked again towards the woodland. Here I saw blaze after blaze of fire among the dark masses of trees. Our big guns in the fortifications had got to work, and were punishing the Germans most severely, taking their attack in flank with their big 6-inch and 7.5-inch projectiles. Cheers arose all along our lines, as shell after shell, fired by gunners who knew to an inch the distances to every house and conspicuous tree, burst among the German ranks, killing and maiming the invaders by hundreds. The advance paused, faltered, and, being hurriedly reinforced from the rear, once more went forward.

"But the big high explosive projectiles continued to fall with such accuracy and persistence that the attackers fell sullenly back, losing heavily as they did so. The enemy's artillery now came in for attention, and also was driven out of range with loss. The last stage in the retreat of Lord Byfield's command was now secured. The extended troops and guns gradually drew off from their positions, still keeping a watchful eye on the foe, and by 4.30 all were within the Epping entrenchments. All, that is to say, but the numerous killed and wounded during the running fight that had extended along the last seven or eight miles of the retreat, and the bulk of the Dunmow force under Sir Jacob Stellenbosch, which, with its commander, had, it was believed, been made prisoners. They had been caught between the 39th German Infantry Brigade and several regiments of cavalry, that it was said had arrived from the northward soon after they were beaten at Hatfield Heath. Probably these were the advanced troops of General Frölich's Cavalry Brigade."

III

Battle of Epping

The following is extracted from the *Times* of 15th September:—

EPPING, *14th September, Evening*.

"I have spent a busy day, but have no very important news to record. After the repulse of the German troops attacking Lord Byfield's retreating army and the arrival of our sorely harassed troops behind the Epping entrenchments, we saw no more of the enemy that evening. All through the night, however, there was the sound of occasional heavy gun firing from the eastward. I have taken up my quarters at the Bell, an inn at the south end of the village, from the back of which I can get a good view to the north-west for from two to four miles. Beyond that distance the high ridge known as Epping Upland limits the prospect. The whole terrain is cut up into fields of various sizes and dotted all over with trees. Close by is a lofty red brick water-tower, which has been utilised by Sir Stapleton Forsyth as a signal station. Away about a mile to my left front as I look from the back of the Bell a big block of buildings stands prominently out on a grassy spur of high ground. This is Copped Hall and Little Copped Hall.

"Both mansions have been transformed into fortresses, which, while offering little or no resistance to artillery fire, will yet form a tough nut for the Germans to crack, should they succeed in getting through our entrenchments at that point. Beyond, I can just see a corner of a big earthwork that has been built to strengthen the defence line, and which has been christened Fort Obelisk, from a farm of that name, near which it is situated. There is another smaller redoubt on the slope just below this hostelry, and I can see the gunners busy about the three big khaki-painted guns which are mounted in it. There are a 6-inch and two 4.7-inch guns, I believe. This morning our cavalry, consisting of a regiment of yeomanry and some mounted infantry, who had formed a portion of

Lord Byfield's force, went out to reconnoitre towards the north and east. They were not away long, as they were driven back in every direction in which they attempted to advance, by superior forces of the enemy's cavalry, who seemed to swarm everywhere.

"Later on, I believe, some of the German reiters became so venturesome that several squadrons exposed themselves to the fire of the big guns in the fort at Skip's Corner, and suffered pretty severely for their temerity. The firing continued throughout the morning away to the eastward, and about noon I thought I would run down and see if I could find out anything about it. I therefore mounted my car and ran off in that direction. I found that there was a regular duel going on between our guns at Kelvedon Hatch and some heavy siege guns or howitzers that the enemy had got in the neighbourhood of the high ground about Norton Heath, only about 3000 yards distant from our entrenchments. They did not appear to have done us much damage, but neither, in all probability, did we hurt them very much, since our gunners were unable to exactly locate the hostile guns.

"When I got back to Epping, about three o'clock, I found the wide single street full of troops. They were those who had come in the previous afternoon with Lord Byfield, and who, having been allowed to rest till midday after their long fighting march, were now being told off to their various sections of the defence line. The Guard regiments were allocated to the northernmost position between Fort Royston and Fort Skips. The rifles were to go to Copped Hall, and the Seaforths to form the nucleus of a central reserve of Militia and Volunteers, which was being established just north of Gaynes Park. Epping itself and the contiguous entrenchments were confided to the Leinster Regiment, which alone of Sir Jacobs Stellenbosch's brigade had escaped capture, supported by two Militia battalions. The field batteries were distributed under shelter of the woods on the south, east, and north-east of the town.

"During the afternoon the welcome news arrived that the remainder of Lord Byfield's command from Baldock, Royston, and Elmdon had safely arrived within our entrenchments at Enfield and New Barnet. We may now hope that what with Regulars, Militia, Volunteers, and the new levies, our lines are fully and effectively manned, and will suffice to stay the further advance of even such a formidable host as is that at the disposal of the renowned Von Kronhelm. It is reported, too, from Brentwood that great progress has already been made in reorganising and distributing the broken remnants of the 1st and 5th Armies that got back to that town after the great and disastrous battle of Chelmsford. Victorious as they were, the Germans must also have suffered severely, which may give us some breathing time before their next onslaught."

THE FOLLOWING ARE EXTRACTS FROM a diary picked up by a *Daily Mirror* correspondent, lying near the body of a German officer after the fighting in the neighbourhood of Enfield Chase. It is presumed that the officer in question was Major Splittberger, of the Kaiser Franz Garde Grenadier Regiment, since that was the name written inside the cover of the diary.

From inquiries that have since been instituted, it is probable that the deceased officer was employed on the staff of the General commanding the IVth Corps of the invading Army, though it would seem from the contents of his diary that he saw also a good deal of the operations of the Xth Corps. Our readers will be able to gather from it the general course of the enemy's strategy and tactics during the time immediately preceding the most recent disasters which have befallen our brave defenders. The first extract is dated September 15, and was written somewhere north of Epping:

Sept. 15

So far the bold strategy of our Commander-in-Chief, in pushing the greater part of the Xth Corps directly to the west immediately after our victory at Chelmsford, has been amply justified by results. Although we just missed cutting off Lord Byfield and a large portion of his command at Harlow, we gained a good foothold inside the British defences north of Epping, and I don't think it will be long before we have very much improved our position there. The IVth Corps arrived at Harlow about midday yesterday in splendid condition, after their long march from Newmarket, and the residue of the Xth joined us about the same time.

As there is nothing like keeping the enemy on the move, no time was lost in preparing to attack him at the very earliest opportunity. As soon as it was dark the IVth Corps got its heavy guns and howitzers into position along the ridge above Epping Upland, and sent the greater portion of its field batteries forward to a position from which they were within effective range of the British fortifications at Skip's Corner.

"The IXth Corps, which had arrived from Chelmsford that evening, also placed its field artillery in a similar position, from which its fire crossed that of the IVth Corps. This corps also provided the assaulting troops. The Xth Corps, which had been engaged all day on Thursday, was held in reserve. The howitzers on Epping Upland opened fire with petrol shell on the belt of woods that lies immediately in rear of the position to be attacked, and with the assistance of a strong westerly wind succeeded in setting them on fire and cutting off the most northerly section of the British defences from reinforcement. This was soon after midnight. The conflagration not only did us this service, but it is supposed so attracted the attention of the partially trained soldiers of the enemy that they did not observe the IXth Corps massing for the assault.

"We then plastered their trenches with shrapnel to such an extent that they did not dare to show a finger above them, and finally carried the northern corner by assault. To give the enemy their due, they fought well, but we outnumbered them five to one, and it was impossible for them to resist the onslaught of our well-trained soldiers. News came to-day that the Saxons have been making a demonstration before Brentwood with a view of keeping the British employed down there so that they cannot send any reinforcements up here. At the same time they have been steadily bombarding Kelvedon Hatch from Norton Heath.

"We hear, too, that the Garde Corps have got down south, and that their front stretches from Broxbourne to Little Berkhamsted, while Frölich's Cavalry Division is in front of them, spread all over the country, from the River Lea away to the westward, having driven the whole of the British outlying troops and patrols under the shelter of their entrenchments. Once we succeed in rolling up the enemy's troops in this quarter, it will not be long before we are entering London."

Sept. 16

Fighting went on all yesterday in the neighbourhood of Skip's Corner. We have taken the redoubt at North Weald Basset and driven the English back into the belt of burnt woodland, which they now hold along its northern edge. All day long, too, our big guns, hidden away behind the groves and woods above Epping Upland, poured their heavy projectiles on Epping and its defences. We set the village on fire three times, but the British contrived to extinguish the blaze on each occasion.

"I fancy Epping itself will be our next point of attack.

Sept. 17

We are still progressing, fighting is now all but continuous. How long it may last I have no idea. Probably there will be no suspension of the struggle until we are actually masters of the metropolis. We took advantage of the darkness to push forward our men to within three thousand yards of the enemy's lines, placing them as far as possible under cover of the numerous copses, plantations, and hedgerows which cover the face of this fertile country. At 4 A.M. the General ordered his staff to assemble at Latton Park, where he had established his headquarters. He unfolded to us the general outline of the attack, which, he now announced, was to commence at six precisely.

"I thought myself that it was a somewhat inopportune time, as we should have the rising sun right in our eyes; but I imagine that the idea was to have as much daylight as possible before us. For although we had employed a night attack against Skip's Corner, and successfully too, yet the general feeling in our Army has always been opposed to operations of this kind. The possible gain is, I think, in no way commensurable with the probable risks of panic and disorder. The principal objective was the village of Epping itself; but simultaneous attacks were to be carried out against Copped Hall, Fort Obelisk, to the west of it, and Fort Royston, about a mile north of the village. The IXth Corps was to co-operate by a determined attempt to break through the English lining the burnt strip of woodland and to assault the latter fort in rear. It was necessary to carry out both these flanking attacks in order to prevent the main attack from being enfiladed from right and left. At 5.30 we mounted, and rode off to Rye Hill about a couple of miles distant, from which the General intended to watch the progress of the operations. The first rays of the rising sun were filling the eastern sky with a pale light as we cantered off, the long wooded ridge on which the enemy had his position standing up in a misty silhouette against the growing day.

"As we topped Rye Hill I could see the thickly-massed lines of our infantry crouching behind every hedge, bank, or ridge, their rifle-barrels here and there twinkling in the feeble rays of the early sun, their shadows long and attenuated behind them. Epping with its lofty red water-tower was distinctly visible on the opposite side of the valley, and it is probable that the movement of the General's cavalcade of officers, with the escort, attracted the attention of the enemy's lookouts, for half-way down the hillside on their side of the valley a blinding violet-white flash blazed out, and a big shell came screaming along just over our heads, the loud boom of a heavy gun following fast on its heels. Almost simultaneously another big projectile hurtled up from the direction of Fort Obelisk, and burst among our escort of Uhlans with a deluge of livid flame and thick volumes of greenish brown smoke. It was a telling shot, for no fewer than six horses and their riders lay in a shattered heap on the ground.

"At six precisely our guns fired a salvo directed on Epping village. This was the preconcerted signal for attack, and before the echoes of the thunderous discharge had finished reverberating over the hills and forest our front lines had sprung to their feet and were moving at a racing pace towards the enemy. For a moment the British seemed stupefied by the suddenness of the advance. A few rifle shots crackled out here and there, but our men had thrown themselves to the ground after their first rush before the enemy seemed to wake up. But there was no mistake about it when they did. Seldom have I seen such a concentrated fire. Gun, pom-pom, machine gun, and rifle blazed out from right to left along more than three miles of entrenchments. A continuous lightning-like line of fire poured forth from the British trenches, which still lay in shadow. I could see the bullets raising perfect sand-storms in places, the little pom-pom shells sparkling about all over our prostrate men, and the shrapnel bursting all along their front, producing perfect swathes of white smoke, which hung low down in the still air in the valley.

"But our artillery was not idle. The field guns, pushed well forward, showered shrapnel upon the British position, the howitzer shells hurtled over our heads on their way to the enemy in constantly increasing numbers as the ranges were verified by the trial shots, while a terrible and unceasing reverberation from the north-east told of the supporting attack made by the IXth and Xth Corps upon the blackened woods held by the English. The concussion of the terrific cannonade that now resounded from every quarter was deafening; the air seemed to pulse within one's ears, and it was difficult to hear one's nearest neighbour speak. Down in the valley our men appeared to be suffering severely. Every forward move of the attacking lines left a perfect litter of prostrate forms behind it, and for some time I felt very doubtful in my own mind if the attack would succeed. Glancing to the right, however, I was encouraged to see the progress that had been made by the troops detailed for the assault on Copped Hall and Obelisk Fort, and, seeing this, it occurred to me that it was not intended to push the central attack on Epping home before its flank had been secured from molestation from this direction. Copped Hall itself stood out on a bare down almost like some mediæval castle, backed by the dark masses of forest, while to the west of it the slopes of Fort Obelisk could barely be distinguished, so flat were they and so well screened by greenery.

"But its position was clearly defined by the clouds of dust, smoke, and débris constantly thrown up by our heavy high-explosive shells, while ever and anon there came a dazzling flash from it, followed by a detonation that made itself heard even above the rolling of the cannonade, as one of its big 7.5-in. guns was discharged. The roar of their huge projectiles, too, as they tore through the air, was easily distinguishable. None of our epaulments were proof against them, and they did our heavy batteries a great deal of damage before they could be silenced.

"To cut a long story short, we captured Epping after a tough fight, and by noon were in possession of everything north of the Forest, including the war-scarred ruins that now represented the mansion of Copped Hall, and from which our pom-poms and machine guns were firing into Fort Obelisk. But our losses had been awful. As for the enemy, they could hardly have suffered less severely, for though partially protected by their entrenchments, our artillery fire must have been utterly annihilating."

Sept. 18.

Fighting went on all last night, the English holding desperately on to the edge of the Forest, our people pressing them close, and working round their right flank. When day broke the general situation was pretty much like this. On our left the IXth Corps were in possession of the Fort at Toothill, and a redoubt that lay between it and Skip's Fort. Two batteries were bombarding a redoubt lower down in the direction of Stanford Rivers, which was also subjected to a cross fire from their howitzers near Ongar.

"As for the English, their position was an unenviable one. From Copped Hall—as soon as we have cleared the edge of the Forest of the enemy's sharp-shooters—we shall be able to take their entrenchments in reverse all the way to Waltham Abbey. They have, on the other hand, an outlying fort about a mile or two north of the latter place, which gave us some trouble with its heavy guns yesterday, and which it is most important that we should gain possession of before we advance further. The Garde Corps on the western side of the River Lea is now, I hear, in sight of the enemy's lines, and is keeping them busily employed, though without pushing its attack home for the present.

"At daybreak this morning I was in Epping and saw the beginning of the attack on the Forest. It is rumoured that large reinforcements have reached the enemy from London, but as these must be merely scratch soldiers they will do them more harm than good in their cramped position. The Xth Corps had got a dozen batteries in position a little to the eastward of the village, and at six o'clock these guns opened a tremendous fire upon the north-east corner of the Forest, under cover of which their infantry deployed down in the low ground about Coopersale, and advanced to the attack. Petrol shells were not used against the Forest, as Von Kronhelm had given orders that it was not to be burned if it could possibly be avoided. The shrapnel was very successful in keeping down the fire from the edge of the trees, but our troops received a good deal of damage from infantry and guns that were posted to the east of the Forest on a hill near Theydon Bois. But about seven o'clock these troops were driven from their position by a sudden flank attack made by the IXth Corps from Theydon Mount. Von Kleppen followed this up by putting some of his own guns up there, which were able to fire on the edge of the Forest after those of the Xth Corps had been masked by the close advance of their infantry. To make a long story short, by ten the whole of the Forest east of the London Road, as far south as the cross roads near Jack's Hill, was in our hands. In the meantime the IVth Corps had made itself master of Fort Obelisk, and our gunners were hard at work mounting guns in it with which to fire on the outlying fort at Monkham's Hall. Von Kleppen was at Copped Hall about this time, and with him I found General Von Wilberg, commanding the Xth Corps, in close consultation. The once fine mansion had been almost completely shot away down to its lower storey. A large portion of this, however, was still fairly intact, having been protected to a certain extent by the masses of masonry that had fallen all around it, and also by the thick ramparts of earth that the English had built up against its exposed side.

"Our men were still firing from its loopholes at the edge of the woods, which were only about 1200 yards distant, and from which bullets were continually whistling in by every window. Two of our battalions had dug themselves in in the wooded park surrounding the house, and were also exchanging fire with the English at comparatively close ranges. They had, I was told, made more than one attempt to rush the edge of the Forest, but had been repulsed by rifle fire on each occasion. Away to the west I could see for miles, and even distinguish our shells bursting all over the enemy's fort at Monkham's Hall, which was being subjected to a heavy bombardment by our guns on the high ground to the north of it. About eleven Frölich's Cavalry Brigade, whose presence was no longer required in front of the Garde Corps, passed through Epping, going south-east. It is generally supposed that it is either to attack the British at Brentwood in the rear, or, which I think is more probable, to intimidate the raw levies by its presence between them and London, and to attack them in flank should they attempt to retreat.

"Just after eleven another battalion arrived at Copped Hall from Epping, and orders were given that the English position along the edge of the Forest was to be taken at all cost. Just before the attack began there was a great deal of firing somewhere in the interior of the Forest, presumably between the British and the advanced troops of the Xth Corps. However this may have been, it was evident that the enemy were holding our part of the Forest much less strongly, and our assault was entirely successful, with but small loss of men. Once in the woods, the superior training and discipline of our men told heavily in their favour. While the mingled mass of Volunteers and raw free-shooters, of which the bulk of their garrison was composed, got utterly disorganised and out of hand under the severe strain on them that was imposed by the difficulties of wood fighting, and hindered and broke up the regular units, our people were easily kept well in hand, and drove the enemy steadily before them without a single check. The rattle of rifle and machine gun was continuous through all the leafy dells and glades of the wood, but by two o'clock practically the whole Forest was in the hands of our Xth Corps. It was then the turn of the IVth Corps, who in the meantime, far from being idle, had massed a large number of their guns at Copped Hall, from which, aided by the fire from Fort Obelisk, the enemy's lines were subjected to a bombardment that rendered them absolutely untenable, and we could see company after company making their way to Waltham Abbey.

"At three the order for a general advance on Waltham Abbey was issued. As the enemy seemed to have few, if any, guns at this place, it was determined to make use of some of the new armoured motors that accompanied the Army. Von Kronhelm, who was personally directing the operations from Copped Hall, had caused each corps to send its motors to Epping, so that we had something like thirty at our disposal. These quaint, grey monsters came down through the Forest and advanced on Epping by two parallel roads, one passing by the south of Warlies Park, the other being the main road from Epping. It was a weird sight to see these shore-going armour-clads flying down upon the enemy. They got within 800 yards of the houses, but the enemy contrived to block their further advance by various obstacles which they placed on the roads.

"There was about an hour's desperate fighting in the village. The old Abbey Church was set on fire by a stray shell, the conflagration spreading to the neighbouring houses, and both British and Germans being too busy killing each other to put it out, the whole village was shortly in flames. The British were finally driven out of it, and across the river by five o'clock. In the meantime every heavy gun that could be got to bear was directed on the fort at Monkham's Hall, which, during the afternoon, was also made the target for the guns of the Garde Corps, which co-operated with us by attacking the lines at Cheshunt, and assisting us with its artillery fire from the opposite side of the river. By nightfall the fort was a mass of smoking earth, over which fluttered our black cross flag, and the front of the IVth Corps stretched from this to Gillwell Park, four miles nearer London.

"The Xth Corps was in support in the Forest behind us, and forming also a front to cover our flank, reaching from Chingford to Buckhurst Hill. The enemy was quite demoralised in this direction, and showed no indication of resuming the engagement. As for the IXth Corps, its advanced troops were at Lambourne End, in close communication with General Frölich, who had established his headquarters at Haveringatte-Bower. We have driven a formidable wedge right into the middle of the carefully elaborated system of defence arranged by the English Generals, and it will now be a miracle if they can prevent our entry into the capital.

"We had not, of course, effected this without great loss in killed and wounded, but you can't make puddings without breaking eggs, and in the end a bold and forward policy is more economical of life and limb than attempting to avoid necessary losses as our present opponents did in South Africa, thereby prolonging the war to an almost indefinite period, and losing many more men by sickness and in driblets than would have been the case if they had followed a more determined line in their strategy and tactics. Just before the sun sank behind the masses of new houses which the monster city spreads out to the northward I got orders to carry a despatch to General von Wilberg, who was stated to be at Chingford, on our extreme left. I went by the Forest road, as the parallel one near the river was in most parts under fire from the opposite bank.

"He had established his headquarters at the Foresters' Inn, which stands high up on a wooded mound, and from which he could see a considerable distance and keep in touch with his various signal stations. He took my despatch, telling me that I should have a reply to take back later on. 'In the meanwhile,' said he, 'if you will fall in with my staff you will have an opportunity of seeing the first shots fired into the biggest city in the world.' So saying, he went out to his horse, which was waiting outside, and we started off down the hill with a great clatter. After winding about through a somewhat intricate network of roads and by-lanes we arrived at Old Chingford Church, which stands upon a species of headland, rising boldly up above the flat and, in some places, marshy land to the westward.

"Close to the church was a battery of four big howitzers, the gunners grouped around them silhouetted darkly against the blood-red sky. From up here the vast city, spreading out to the south and west, lay like a grey, sprawling octopus spreading out ray-like to the northward, every rise and ridge being topped with a bristle of spires and chimney-pots. An ominous silence seemed to brood over the teeming landscape, broken only at intervals by the dull booming of guns from the northward. Long swathes of cloud and smoke lay athwart the dull, furnace-like glow of the sunset, and lights were beginning to sparkle out all over the vast expanse which lay before us mirrored here and there in the canals and rivers that ran almost at our feet. 'Now,' said Von Wilberg at length, 'commence fire.' One of the big guns gave tongue with a roar that seemed to make the church tower quiver above us. Another and another followed in succession, their big projectiles hurtling and humming through the quiet evening air on their errands of death and destruction in I know not what quarter of the crowded suburbs. It seemed to me a cruel and needless thing to do, but I am told that it was done with the set purpose of arousing such a feeling of alarm and insecurity in the East End that the mob might try to interfere with any further measures for defence that the British military authorities might undertake. I got my despatch soon afterwards and returned with it to the General, who was spending the night at Copped Hall. There, too, I got myself a shakedown and slumbered soundly till the morning.

To-day we have, I think, finally broken down all organised military opposition in the field, though we may expect a considerable amount of street fighting before reaping the whole fruits of our victories. At daybreak we began by turning a heavy fire from every possible quarter on the wooded island formed by the river and various back-waters just north of Waltham Abbey. The poplar-clad islet, which was full of the enemy's troops, became absolutely untenable under this concentrated fire, and they were compelled to fall back over the river. Our Engineers soon began their bridging operations behind the wood, and our infantry, crossing over, got close up to a redoubt on the further side and took it by storm. Again we were able to take a considerable section of the enemy's lines in reverse, and as they were driven out by our fire, against which they had no protection, the Garde Corps advanced, and by ten were in possession of Cheshunt.

"In the meanwhile, covered by the fire of the guns belonging to the IXth and Xth Corps, other bridges had been thrown across the Lea at various points between Waltham and Chingford, and in another hour the crossing began. The enemy had no good positions for his guns, and seemed to have very few of them. He had pinned his faith upon the big weapons he had placed in his entrenchments, and these were now of no further use to him. He had lost a number of his field guns, either from damage or capture, and with our more numerous artillery firing from the high ground on the eastern bank of the river we were always able to beat down any attempt he made to reply to their fire.

"We had a day of fierce fighting before us. There was no manœuvring. We were in a wilderness of scattered houses and occasional streets, in which the enemy contested our progress foot by foot. Edmonton, Enfield Wash, and Waltham Cross were quickly captured; our artillery commanded them too well to allow the British to make a successful defence; but Enfield itself, lying along a steepish ridge, on which the British had assembled what artillery they could scrape together, cost us dearly. The streets of this not too lovely suburban town literally ran with blood when at last we made our way into it. A large part of it was burnt to ashes, including unfortunately the ancient palace of Queen Elizabeth, and the venerable and enormous cedar tree that overhung it.

"The British fell back to a second position they had apparently prepared along a parallel ridge further to the westward, their left being between us and New Barnet and their right at Southgate.

"We did not attempt to advance further to-day, but contented ourselves in reorganising our forces and preparing against a possible counter-attack, by barricading and entrenching the further edge of Enfield Ridge.

Sept. 20

We are falling in immediately, as it has been decided to attack the British position at once. Already the artillery duel is in progress. I must continue to-night, as my horse is at the door."

The writer, however, never lived to complete his diary, having been shot half-way up the green slope he had observed the day previous.

IV

Bombardment of London

Day broke. The faint flush of violet away eastward beyond Temple Bar gradually turned rose, heralding the sun's coming, and by degrees the streets, filled by excited Londoners, grew lighter with the dawn. Fevered night thus gave place to day—a day that was, alas! destined to be one of bitter memory for the British Empire.

Alarming news had spread that Uhlans had been seen reconnoitring in Snaresbrook and Wanstead, had ridden along Forest Road and Ferry Lane at Walthamstow, through Tottenham High Cross, up High Street, Hornsey, Priory Road, and Muswell Hill. The Germans were actually upon London!

The northern suburbs were staggered. In Fortis Green, North End, Highgate, Crouch End, Hampstead, Stamford Hill, and Leyton the quiet suburban houses were threatened, and many people, in fear of their lives, had now fled southward into central London. Thus the huge population of greater London was practically huddled together in the comparatively small area from Kensington to Fleet Street, and from Oxford Street to the Thames Embankment.

People of Fulham, Putney, Walham Green, Hammersmith, and Kew had, for the most part, fled away to the open country across Hounslow Heath to Bedfont and Staines; while Tooting, Balham, Dulwich, Streatham, Norwood, and Catford had retreated farther south into Surrey and Kent.

For the past three days thousands of willing helpers had followed the example of Sheffield and Birmingham, and constructed enormous barricades, obstructing at various points the chief roads leading from the north and east into London. Detachments of Engineers had blown up several of the bridges carrying the main roads out eastwards—for instance, the bridge at the end of Commercial Road, East, crossing the Limehouse Canal, while the six other smaller bridges spanning the canal between that point and the Bow Road were also destroyed. The bridge at the end of Bow Road itself was shattered, and those over the Hackney Cut at Marshall Hill and Hackney Wick were also rendered impassable.

WILLIAM LE QUEUX

Most of the bridges across the Regent's Canal were also destroyed, notably those in Mare Street, Hackney, the Kingsland Road, and New North Road, while a similar demolition took place in Edgware Road and the Harrow Road. Londoners were frantic, now that the enemy were really upon them. The accounts of the battles in the newspapers had, of course, been merely fragmentary, and they had not yet realised what war actually meant. They knew that all business was at a standstill, that the City was in an uproar, that there was no work, and that food was at famine prices. But not until German cavalry were actually seen scouring the northern suburbs did it become impressed upon them that they were really helpless and defenceless.

London was to be besieged!

This report having got about, the people began building barricades in many of the principal thoroughfares north of the Thames. One huge obstruction, built mostly of paving-stones from the footways, overturned tramcars, wagons, railway trollies, and barbed wire, rose in the Holloway Road, just beyond Highbury Station. Another blocked the Caledonian Road a few yards north of the police-station, while another very large and strong pile of miscellaneous goods, bales of wool and cotton stuffs, building material, and stones brought from the Great Northern Railway depôt, obstructed the Camden Road at the south corner of Hildrop Crescent. Across High Street, Camden Town, at the junction of the Kentish Town and other roads, five hundred men worked with a will, piling together every kind of ponderous object they could pillage from the neighbouring shops—pianos, iron bedsteads, wardrobes, pieces of calico and flannel, dress stuffs, rolls of carpets, floorboards, even the very doors wrenched from their hinges—until, when it reached to the second storey window and was considered of sufficient height, a pole was planted on top, and from it hung limply a small Union Jack.

The Finchley Road, opposite Swiss Cottage Station, in Shoot Up-hill, where Mill Lane runs into it; across Willesden Lane, where it joins the High Road in Kilburn; the Harrow Road close to Willesden Junction Station; at the junction of the Goldhawk and Uxbridge roads; across the Hammersmith Road in front of the Hospital, other similar obstructions were placed with a view to preventing the enemy from entering London. At a hundred other points, in the narrower and more obscure thoroughfares, all along the north of London, busy workers were constructing similar defences, houses and shops being ruthlessly broken open and cleared of their contents by the frantic and terrified populace.

London was in a ferment. Almost without exception the gunmakers' shops had been pillaged, and every rifle, sporting gun, and revolver seized. The armouries at the Tower of London, at the various barracks, and the factory out at Enfield had long ago all been cleared of their contents; for now, in this last stand, every one was desperate, and all who could obtain a gun, did so. Many, however, had guns but no ammunition; others had sporting ammunition for service rifles, and others cartridges, but no gun.

Those, however, who had guns and ammunition complete mounted guard at the barricades, being assisted at some points by Volunteers who had been driven in from Essex. Upon more than one barricade in North London a Maxim had been mounted, and was now pointed, ready to sweep away the enemy should they advance.

Other thoroughfares barricaded, beside those mentioned, were the Stroud Green Road, where it joins Hanley Road; the railway bridge in the Oakfield Road in the same neighbourhood; the Wightman Road, opposite Harringay Station, the junction of Archway Road and Highgate Hill; the High Road, Tottenham, at its junction with West Green Road, and various roads around the New River reservoirs, which were believed to be one of the objectives of the enemy. These latter were very strongly held by thousands of brave and patriotic citizens, though the East London reservoirs across at Walthamstow could not be defended, situated so openly as they were. The people of Leytonstone threw up a barricade opposite the schools in the High Road, while in Wanstead a hastily constructed but perfectly useless obstruction was piled across Cambridge Park, where it joins the Blake Road.

Of course, all the women and children in the northern suburbs had now been sent south. Half the houses in those quiet, newly-built roads were locked up, and their owners gone; for as soon as the report spread of the result of the final battle before London and our crushing defeat, people living in Highgate, Hampstead, Crouch End, Hornsey, Tottenham, Finsbury Park, Muswell Hill, Hendon, and Hampstead saw that they must fly southward, now the Germans were upon them.

Think what it meant to those suburban families of City men! The ruthless destruction of their pretty, long-cherished homes, flight into the turbulent, noisy, distracted, hungry city, and the loss of everything they possessed. In most cases the husband was already bearing his part in the defence of the metropolis with gun or with spade, or helping to move heavy masses of material for the construction of the barricades. The wife, however, was compelled to take a last look at all those possessions that she had so fondly called "home," lock her front door, and with her children join in those long mournful processions moving ever southward into London, tramping on and on—whither she knew not where.

Touching sights were to be seen everywhere in the streets that day.

Homeless women, many of them with two or three little ones, were wandering through the less frequented streets, avoiding the main roads with all their crush, excitement, and barricade-building, but making their way westward, beyond Kensington and Hammersmith, which was now become the outlet of the metropolis.

All trains from Charing Cross, Waterloo, London Bridge, Victoria, and Paddington had for the past three days been crowded to excess. Anxious fathers struggled fiercely to obtain places for their wives, mothers, and daughters—sending them away anywhere out of the city which must in a few hours be crushed beneath the iron heel.

The South-Western and Great Western systems carried thousands upon thousands of the wealthier away to Devonshire and Cornwall—as far as possible from the theatre of war; the South-Eastern and Chatham took people into the already crowded Kentish towns and villages, and the Brighton line carried others into rural Sussex. London overflowed southward and westward until every village and every town within fifty miles was so full that beds were at a premium, and in various places, notably at Chartham, near Canterbury, at Willesborough, near Ashford, at Lewes, at Robertsbridge, at Goodwood Park, and at Horsham, huge camps were formed, shelter being afforded by poles and rick-cloths. Every house, every barn, every school, indeed every place where people could obtain shelter for the night, was crowded to excess, mostly by women and children sent south, away from the horrors that it was known must come.

Central London grew more turbulent with each hour that passed. There were all sorts of wild rumours, but, fortunately the Press still preserved a dignified calm. The Cabinet were holding a meeting at Bristol, whither the Houses of Commons and Lords had moved, and all depended upon its issue. It was said that Ministers were divided in their opinions whether we should sue for an ignominious peace, or whether the conflict should be continued to the bitter end.

Disaster had followed disaster, and iron-throated orators in Hyde and St. James's Parks were now shouting "Stop the war! Stop the war!" The cry was taken up but faintly, however, for the blood of Londoners, slow to rise, had now been stirred by seeing their country slowly, yet completely, crushed by Germany. All the patriotism latent within them was now displayed. The national flag was shown everywhere, and at every point one heard "God Save the King!" sung lustily.

Two gunmakers' shops in the Strand, which had hitherto escaped notice, were shortly after noon broken open, and every available arm and all the ammunition seized. One man, unable to obtain a revolver, snatched half a dozen pairs of steel handcuffs, and cried with grim humour as he held them up: "If I can't shoot any of the sausage-eaters, I can at least bag a prisoner or two!"

The banks, the great jewellers, the diamond merchants, the safe-deposit offices, and all who had valuables in their keeping, were extremely anxious as to what might happen. Below those dark buildings in Lothbury and Lombard Street, behind the black walls of the Bank of England, and below every branch bank all over London, were millions in gold and notes, the wealth of the greatest city the world has ever known. The strong rooms were, for the most part, the strongest that modern engineering could devise, some with various arrangements by which all access was debarred by an inrush of water; but, alas! dynamite is a great leveller, and it was felt that not a single strong room in the whole of London could withstand an organised attack by German engineers.

A single charge of dynamite would certainly make a breach in concrete upon which a thief might hammer and chip day and night for a month without making much impression. Steel doors must give to blasting force, while the strongest and most complicated locks would also fly to pieces.

The directors of most of the banks had met, and an endeavour had been made to co-operate and form a corps of special guards for the principal offices. In fact, a small armed corps was formed, and were on duty day and night in Lothbury, Lombard Street, and the vicinity. Yet what could they do if the Germans swept into London? There was but little to fear from the excited populace themselves, because matters had assumed such a crisis that money was of little use, as there was practically very little to buy. But little food was reaching London from the open ports on the west. It was the enemy that the banks feared, for

WILLIAM LE QUEUX

they knew that the Germans intended to enter and sack the metropolis, just as they had sacked the other towns that had refused to pay the indemnity demanded.

Small jewellers had, days ago, removed their stock from their windows and carried it away in unsuspicious-looking bags to safe hiding in the southern and western suburbs, where people for the most part hid their valuable plate, jewellery, etc., beneath a floor-board, or buried them in some marked spot in their small gardens.

The hospitals were already full of wounded from the various engagements of the past week. The London, St. Thomas's, Charing Cross, St. George's, Guy's, and Bartholemew's were overflowing; and the surgeons, with patriotic self-denial, were working day and night in an endeavour to cope with the ever-arriving crowd of suffering humanity. The field hospitals away to the northward were also reported full.

The exact whereabouts of the enemy was not known. They were, it seemed, everywhere. They had practically overrun the whole country, and the reports from the Midlands and the North showed that the majority of the principal towns had now been occupied.

The latest reverses outside London, full and graphic details of which were now being published hourly by the papers, had created an immense sensation. Everywhere people were regretting that Lord Roberts' solemn warnings in 1906 had been unheeded, for had we adopted his scheme for universal service such dire catastrophe could never have occurred. Many had, alas! declared it to be synonymous with conscription, which it certainly was not, and by that foolish argument had prevented the public at large from accepting it as the only means of our salvation as a nation. The repeated warnings had been disregarded, and we had, unhappily, lived in a fool's paradise, in the self-satisfied belief that England could not be successfully invaded.

Now, alas! the country had realised the truth when too late.

That memorable day, September 20, witnessed exasperated struggles in the northern suburbs of London, passionate and bloody collisions, an infantry fire of the defenders overwhelming every attempted assault; and a decisive action of the artillery, with regard to which arm the superiority of the Germans, due to their perfect training, was apparent.

A last desperate stand had, it appears, been made by the defenders on the high ridge north-west of New Barnet, from Southgate to near Potter's Bar, where a terrible fight had taken place. But from the very first it was utterly hopeless. The British had fought valiantly in defence of London, but here again they were outnumbered, and after one of the most desperate conflicts in the whole campaign—in which our losses were terrible—the Germans at length had succeeded in entering Chipping Barnet. It was a difficult movement, and a fierce contest, rendered the more terrible by the burning houses, ensued in the streets and away across the low hills southward—a struggle full of vicissitudes and alternating successes, until at last the fire of the defenders was silenced, and hundreds of prisoners fell into the German hands.

Thus the last organised defence of London had been broken, and the barricades alone remained.

The work of the German troops on the lines of communication in Essex had for the past week been fraught with danger. Through want of cavalry the British had been unable to make cavalry raids; but, on the other hand, the difficulty was enhanced by the bands of sharpshooters—men of all classes from London who possessed a gun and who could shoot. In one or two of the London clubs the suggestion had first been mooted a couple of days after the outbreak of hostilities, and it had been quickly taken up by men who were in the habit of shooting game, but had not had a military training.

Within three days about two thousand men had formed themselves into bands to take part in the struggle and assist in the defence of London. They were practically similar to the Francs-tireurs of the Franco-German War, for they went forth in companies and waged a guerilla warfare, partly before the front and at the flanks of the different armies, and partly at the communications at the rear of the Germans. Their position was one of constant peril in face of Von Kronhelm's proclamation, yet the work they did was excellent, and only proved that if Lord Roberts' scheme for universal training had been adopted the enemy would never have reached the gates of London with success.

These brave, adventurous spirits, together with "The Legion of Frontiersmen," made their attacks by surprise from hiding-places or from ambushes. Their adventures were constantly thrilling ones. Scattered all over the theatre of war in Essex and Suffolk, and all along the German lines of communication, the "Frontiersmen" rarely ventured on an open conflict, and frequently changed scene and point of attack. Within one week their numbers rose to over 8000, and, being well served by the villagers, who acted as scouts and spies for them, the Germans found them very difficult to get at. Usually they kept their arms concealed in thickets and woods, where they would lie in wait for the Germans. They never came to close quarters, but fired at a distance. Many a smart Uhlan fell by their bullets, and many a sentry dropped, shot by an unknown hand.

Thus they harassed the enemy everywhere. At need they concealed their arms and assumed the appearance of inoffensive non-combatants. But when caught red-handed, the Germans gave them "short shrift", as the bodies now swinging from telegraph poles on various high roads in Essex testified.

In an attempt to put a stop to the daring actions of the "Frontiersmen", the German authorities and troops along the lines of communication punished the parishes where German soldiers were shot, or where the destruction of railways and telegraphs had occurred, by levying money contributions, or by burning the villages.

The guerilla war was especially fierce along from Edgware up to Hertford, and from Chelmsford down to the Thames. In fact, once commenced, it never ceased. Attacks were always being made upon small patrols, travelling detachments, mails of the field post-office, posts or patrols at stations on the lines of communication, while field-telegraphs, telephones, and railways were everywhere destroyed.

In consequence of the railway being cut at Pitsea, the villages of Pitsea, Bowers Gifford, and Vange had been burned. Because a German patrol had been attacked and destroyed near Orsett, the parish were compelled to pay a heavy indemnity. Upminster near Romford, Theydon Bois, and Fyfield, near High Ongar, had all been burned by the Germans for the same reason; while at the Cherrytree Inn, near Rainham, five "Frontiersmen" being discovered by Uhlans in a hay loft asleep, were locked in and there burned alive. Dozens were, of course, shot at sight, and dozens more hanged without trial. But they were not to be deterred. They were fighting in defence of London, and around the northern suburbs the patriotic members of the "Legion" were specially active, though they never showed themselves in large bands.

Within London every man who could shoot game was now anxious to join in the fray, and on the day that the news of the last disaster reached the metropolis, hundreds left for the open country out beyond Hendon.

The enemy, having broken down the defence at Enfield and cleared the defenders out of the fortified houses, had advanced and occupied the northern ridges of London in a line stretching roughly from Pole Hill, a little to the north of Chingford, across Upper Edmonton, through Tottenham, Hornsey, Highgate, Hampstead, and Willesden, to Twyford Abbey. All the positions had been well reconnoitred, for at grey of dawn the rumbling of artillery had been heard in the streets of those places already mentioned, and soon after sunrise strong batteries were established upon all the available points commanding London.

These were at Chingford Green, on the left-hand side of the road opposite the inn at Chingford; on Devonshire Hill, Tottenham; on the hill at Wood Green; in the grounds of the Alexandra Palace; on the high ground above Churchyard Bottom Wood; on the edge of Bishop's Wood, Highgate; on Parliament Hill, at a spot close to the Oaks on the Hendon road; at Dollis Hill, and at a point a little north of Wormwood Scrubs, and at Neasden, near the railway works.

The enemy's chief object was to establish their artillery as near London as possible, for it was known that the range of their guns even from Hampstead—the highest point, 441 feet above London—would not reach into the actual city itself. Meanwhile, at dawn the German cavalry, infantry, motor-infantry, and armoured motor-cars—the latter mostly 35–40 h.p. Opel-Darracqs, with three quick-firing guns mounted in each, and bearing the Imperial German arms in black—advanced up the various roads leading into London from the north, being met, of course, with a desperate resistance at the barricades.

On Haverstock Hill, the three Maxims, mounted upon the huge obstruction across the road, played havoc with the Germans, who were at once compelled to fall back, leaving piles of dead and dying in the roadway, for the terrible hail of lead poured out upon the invaders could not be withstood. Two of the German armoured motor-cars were presently brought into action by the Germans, who replied with a rapid fire, this being continued for a full quarter of an hour without result on either side. Then the Germans, finding the defence too strong, again retired into Hampstead, amid the ringing cheers of the valiant men holding that gate of London. The losses of the enemy had been serious, for the whole roadway was now strewn with dead; while behind the huge wall of paving-stones, overturned carts, and furniture, only two men had been killed and one wounded.

Across in the Finchley Road a struggle equally as fierce was in progress; but a detachment of the enemy, evidently led by some German who had knowledge of the intricate side-roads, suddenly appeared in the rear of the barricade, and a fierce and bloody hand-to-hand conflict ensued. The defenders, however, stood their ground, and with the aid of some petrol bombs which they held in readiness, they destroyed the venturesome detachment almost to a man, though a number of houses in the vicinity were set on fire, causing a huge conflagration.

In Highgate Road the attack was a desperate one, the enraged Londoners fighting valiantly, the men with arms being assisted by the populace themselves. Here again deadly petrol bombs had been distributed, and men and women hurled them against the Germans. Petrol was actually poured from windows upon the heads of the enemy, and tow soaked in paraffin and lit flung in among them, when in an instant whole areas of the streets were ablaze, and the soldiers of the Fatherland perished in the roaring flames.

Every device to drive back the invader was tried. Though thousands upon thousands had left the northern suburbs, many thousands still remained bent on defending their homes as long as they had breath. The crackle of rifles was incessant, and ever and anon the dull roar of a heavy field gun and the sharp rattle of a Maxim mingled with the cheers, yells, and shrieks of victors and of vanquished.

The scene on every side was awful. Men were fighting for their lives in desperation.

Around the barricade in Holloway Road the street ran with blood; while in Kingsland, in Clapton, in West Ham, and Canning Town the enemy were making an equally desperate attack, and were being repulsed everywhere. London's enraged millions, the Germans were well aware, constituted a grave danger. Any detachments who carried a barricade by assault—as, for instance, they did one in the Hornsey Road near the station—were quickly set upon by the angry mob and simply wiped out of existence.

Until nearly noon desperate conflicts at the barricades continued. The defence was even more effectual than was expected; yet, had it not been that Von Kronhelm, the German generalissimo, had given orders that the troops were not to attempt to advance into London before the populace were cowed, there was no doubt that each barricade could have been taken in the rear by companies avoiding the main roads and proceeding by the side streets.

Just before noon, however, it was apparent to Von Kronhelm that to storm the barricades would entail enormous losses, so strong were they. The men holding them had now been reinforced in many cases by regular troops, who had come in in flight, and a good many guns were now manned by artillerymen.

Von Kronhelm had established his headquarters at Jack Straw's Castle, from which he could survey the giant city through his field-glasses. Below lay the great plain of roofs, spires, and domes, stretching away into the grey mystic distance, where afar rose the twin towers and double arches of the Crystal Palace roof.

London—the great London—the capital of the world—lay at his mercy at his feet.

The tall, thin-faced General, with the grizzled moustache and the glittering cross at his throat, standing apart from his staff, gazed away in silence and in thought. It was his first sight of London, and its gigantic proportions amazed even him. Again he swept the horizon with his glass, and knit his grey brows. He remembered the parting woods of his Emperor as he backed out of that plainly—furnished little private cabinet at Potsdam:

"You must bombard London, and sack it. The pride of those English must be broken at all costs. Go, Kronhelm—go—and may the best of fortune go with you!"

The sun was at the noon causing the glass roof of the distant Crystal Palace to gleam. Far down in the grey haze stood Big Ben, the Campanile, and a thousand church spires, all tiny and, from that distance, insignificant. From where he stood the sound of crackling fire at the barricades reached him, and a little behind him a member of his staff was kneeling on the grass with his ear bent to the field telephone. Reports were coming in fast of the desperate resistance in the streets, and these were duly handed to him.

He glanced at them, gave a final look at the outstretched city that was the metropolis of the world, and then gave rapid orders for the withdrawal of the troops from the assault of the barricades, and the bombardment of London.

In a moment the field-telegraphs were clicking, the telephone bell was ringing, orders were shouted in German in all directions, and next second, with a deafening roar, one of the howitzers of the battery in the close vicinity to him gave tongue and threw its deadly shell somewhere into St. John's Wood.

The rain of death had opened! London was surrounded by a semicircle of fire.

The great gun was followed by a hundred others as, at all the batteries along the northern heights, the orders were received. Then in a few minutes, from the whole line from Chingford to Willesden, roughly about twelve miles, came a hail of the most deadly of modern projectiles directed upon the most populous parts of the metropolis.

Though the Germans trained their guns to carry as far as was possible, the zone of fire did not at first, it seemed, extend farther south than a line roughly taken from Notting Hill through Bayswater, past Paddington Station, along the Marylebone and Euston Roads, then up to Highbury, Stoke Newington, Stamford Hill, and Walthamstow.

When, however, the great shells began to burst in Holloway, Kentish Town, Camden Town, Kilburn, Kensal Green, and other places lying within the area under fire, a frightful panic ensued. Whole streets were shattered by explosions, and fires were breaking out, the dark clouds of smoke obscuring the sunlit sky. Roaring flames shot up everywhere, unfortunate men, women, and children were being blown to atoms by the awful projectiles, while others distracted sought shelter in any cellar or underground place they could find, while their houses fell about them like packs of cards.

The scenes within that zone of terror were indescribable.

When Paris had been bombarded years ago, artillery was not at the perfection it now was, and there had been no such high explosive known as in the present day. The great shells that were falling everywhere, on bursting filled the air with poisonous fumes, as well as with deadly fragments. One bursting in a street would wreck the rows of houses on either side, and tear a great hole in the ground at the same moment. The fronts of the houses were torn out like paper, the iron railings twisted as though they were wire, and paving-stones hurled into the air like straws.

Anything and everything offering a mark to the enemy's guns was shattered. St. John's Wood and the houses about Regent's Park suffered seriously. A shell from Hampstead, falling into the roof of one of the houses near the centre of Sussex Place, burst and shattered nearly all the houses in the row; while another fell in Cumberland Terrace, and wrecked a dozen houses in the vicinity. In both cases the houses were mostly empty, for owners and servants had fled southward across the river as soon as it became apparent that the Germans actually intended to bombard.

At many parts in Maida Vale shells burst with appalling effect. Several of the houses in Elgin Avenue had their fronts torn out, and in one, a block of flats, there was considerable loss of life in the fire that broke out, escape being cut off owing to the stairs having been demolished by the explosion. Abbey Road, St. John's Wood Road, Acacia Road, and Wellington Road were quickly wrecked.

In Chalk Farm Road, near the Adelaide, a terrified woman was dashing across the street to seek shelter with a neighbour when a shell burst right in front of her, blowing her to fragments; while in the early stage of the bombardment a shell bursting in the Midland Hotel at St. Pancras caused a fire which in half an hour resulted in the whole hotel and railway terminus being a veritable furnace of flame. Through the roof of King's Cross Station several shells fell, and burst close to the departure platform. The whole glass roof was shattered, but beyond that little other material damage resulted.

Shots were now falling everywhere, and Londoners were staggered. In dense, excited crowds they were flying southward towards the Thames. Some were caught in the streets in their flight, and were flung down, maimed and dying. The most awful sights were to be witnessed in the open streets: men and women blown out of recognition, with their clothes singed and torn to shreds, and helpless, innocent children lying white and dead, their limbs torn away and missing.

Euston Station had shared the same fate as St. Pancras, and was blazing furiously, sending up a great column of black smoke that could be seen by all London. So many were the conflagrations now breaking out that it seemed as though the enemy were sending into London shells filled with petrol, in order to set the streets aflame. This, indeed, was proved by an eye-witness, who saw a shell fall in Liverpool Road, close to the Angel. It burst with a bright red flash, and next second the whole of the roadway and neighbouring houses were blazing furiously.

Thus the air became black with smoke and dust, and the light of day obscured in Northern London. And through that obscurity came those whizzing shells in an incessant hissing stream, each one, bursting in these narrow, thickly-populated streets, causing havoc indescribable, and a loss of life impossible to accurately calculate. Hundreds of people were blown to pieces in the open, but hundreds more were buried beneath the débris of their own cherished homes, now being so ruthlessly destroyed and demolished.

On every side was heard the cry: "Stop the war—stop the war!"

But it was, alas! too late—too late.

Never in the history of the civilised world were there such scenes of reckless slaughter of the innocent and peace-loving as on that never-to-be-forgotten day when Von Kronhelm carried out the orders of his Imperial master, and struck terror into the heart of London's millions.

V

The Rain of Death

Through the whole afternoon the heavy German artillery roared, belching forth their fiery vengeance upon London.

Hour after hour they pounded away, until St. Pancras Church was a heap of ruins, and the Foundling Hospital a veritable furnace, as well as the Parcel Post offices and the University College in Gower Street. In Hampstead Road many of the shops were shattered, and in Tottenham Court Road both Maple's and Shoolbred's suffered severely, for shells bursting in the centre of the roadway had smashed every pane of glass in the fronts of both buildings.

The quiet squares of Bloomsbury were, in some cases, great yawning ruins—houses with their fronts torn out revealing the shattered furniture within. Streets were, indeed, filled with tiles, chimney pots, fallen telegraph wires, debris of furniture, stone steps, paving stones, and fallen masonry. Many of the thoroughfares, such as the Pentonville Road, Copenhagen Street, and Holloway Road, were, at points, quite impassable on account of the ruins that blocked them. Into the Northern Hospital, in the Holloway Road, a shell fell, shattering one of the wards, and killing or maiming every one of the patients in the ward in question, while the church in Tufnell Park Road was burning fiercely. Upper Holloway, Stoke Newington, Highbury, Kingsland, Dalston, Hackney, Clapton, and Stamford Hill were being swept at long range by the guns on Muswell Hill and Churchyard Bottom Hill, and the terror caused in those densely populated districts was awful. Hundreds upon hundreds lost their lives, or else had a hand, an arm, a leg blown away, as those fatal shells fell in never-ceasing monotony, especially in Stoke Newington and Kingsland. The many side roads lying between Holloway Road and Finsbury Park, such as Hornsey Road, Tollington Park, Andover, Durham, Palmerston, Campbell, and Forthill Roads, Seven Sisters Road, and Isledon Road were all devastated, for the guns for a full hour seemed to be trained upon them.

The German gunners in all probability neither knew nor cared where their shells fell. From their position, now that the smoke of the hundreds of fires was now rising, they could probably discern but little. Therefore the batteries at Hampstead Heath, Muswell Hill, Wood Green, Cricklewood, and other places simply sent their shells as far distant south as possible into the panic-stricken city below. In Mountgrove and Riversdale Roads, Highbury Vale, a number of people were killed, while a frightful disaster occurred in the church at the corner of Park Lane and Milton Road, Stoke Newington. Here a number of people had entered, attending a special service for the success of the British arms, when a shell exploded on the roof, bringing it down upon them and killing over fifty of the congregation, mostly women.

The air, poisoned by the fumes of the deadly explosives and full of smoke from the burning buildings, was ever and anon rent by explosions as projectiles frequently burst in mid-air. The distant roar was incessant, like the noise of thunder, while on every hand could be heard the shrieks of defenceless women and children, or the muttered curses of some man who saw his home and all he possessed swept away with a flash and a cloud of dust. Nothing could withstand that awful cannonade. Walthamstow had been rendered untenable in the first half-hour of the bombardment, while in Tottenham the loss of life had been very enormous, the German gunners at Wood Green having apparently turned their first attention upon that place. Churches, the larger buildings, the railway station, in fact anything offering a mark, was promptly shattered, being assisted by the converging fire from the batteries at Chingford.

On the opposite side of London, Notting Hill, Shepherd's Bush, and Starch Green were being reduced to ruins by the heavy batteries above Park Royal Station, which, firing across Wormwood Scrubs, put their shots into Notting Hill, and especially into Holland Park, where widespread damage was quickly wrought.

A couple of shells falling into the generating station of the Central London Railway, or "Tube", as Londoners usually call it, unfortunately caused a disaster and loss of life which were appalling. At the first sign of the bombardment many thousands of persons descended into the "tube" as a safe hiding-place from the rain of shell. At first the railway officials closed the doors to prevent the inrush, but the terrified populace in Shepherd's Bush, Bayswater, Oxford Street, and Holborn, in fact, all along the subterranean line, broke open the doors, and descending by the lifts and stairs found themselves in a place which at least gave them security against the enemy's fire.

The trains had long ago ceased running, and every station was crowded to excess, while many were forced upon the line itself and actually into the tunnels. For hours they waited there in eager breathlessness, longing to be able to ascend and find the conflict over. Men and women in all stations of life were huddled together, while children clung to their parents in wonder; yet as hour after hour went by, the report from above was still the same—the Germans had not ceased.

Of a sudden, however, the light failed. The electric current had been cut off by the explosion of the shells in the generating station at Shepherd's Bush, and the lifts were useless! The thousands who, in defiance of the orders of the company, had gone below at Shepherd's Bush for shelter, found themselves caught like rats in a hole. True, there was the faint glimmer of an oil light here and there, but, alas! that did not prevent an awful panic.

Somebody shouted that the Germans were above and had put out the lights, and when it was found that the lifts were useless a panic ensued that was indescribable. The people could not ascend by the stairs, as they were blocked by the dense crowd, therefore they pressed into the narrow semi-circular tunnels in an eager endeavour to reach the next station, where they hoped they might escape; but once in there women and children were quickly crushed to death, or thrown down and trampled upon by the press behind.

In the darkness they fought with each other, pressing on and becoming jammed so tightly that many were held against the sloping walls until life was extinct. Between Shepherd's Bush and Holland Park Stations the loss of life was worst, for being within the zone of the German fire the people had crushed in frantically in thousands, and with one accord a move had unfortunately been made into the tunnels, on account of the foolish cry that the Germans were waiting above.

The railway officials were powerless. They had done their best to prevent anyone going below, but the public had insisted, therefore no blame could be laid upon them for the catastrophe.

At Marble Arch, Oxford Circus, and Tottenham Court Road Stations, a similar scene was enacted, and dozens upon dozens, alas! lost their lives in the panic. Ladies and gentlemen from Park Lane, Grosvenor Square, and Mayfair had sought shelter at Marble Arch Station rubbing shoulders with labourers' wives and costerwomen from the back streets of Marylebone. When the lights failed, a rush had been made into the tunnel to reach Oxford Circus, all exit by the stairs being blocked, as at Shepherd's Bush, on account of the hundreds struggling to get down.

As at Holland Park, the terrified crowd fighting with each other became jammed and suffocated in the narrow space. The catastrophe was a frightful one, for it was afterwards proved that over four hundred and twenty persons, mostly weak women and children, lost their lives in those twenty minutes of darkness before the mains at the generating station, wrecked by the explosions, could be repaired.

Then, when the current came up again, the lights revealed the frightful mishap, and people struggled to emerge from the burrows wherein they had so narrowly escaped death.

Upon the Baker Street and Waterloo and other "tubes" every station had also been beseiged. The whole of the first-mentioned line from north to south was the refuge of thousands, who saw in it a safe place for retreat. The tunnels of the District Railway, too, were filled with terror-stricken multitudes, who descended at every station and walked away into a subterranean place of safety. No trains had been running for several days, therefore there was no danger from that cause.

Meanwhile the bombardment continued with unceasing activity.

The Marylebone station of the Great Central Railway, and the Great Central Hotel, which seemed to be only just within the line of fire, were wrecked, and about four o'clock it was seen that the hotel, like that at St. Pancras, was well alight, though no effort could be made to save it. At the first two or three alarms of fire the Metropolitan Fire Brigade had turned out, but now that fresh alarms were reaching the chief station every moment, the brigade saw themselves utterly powerless to even attempt to save the hundred buildings, great and small, now furiously blazing.

Gasometers, especially those of the Gas Light and Coke Company at Kensal Green, were marked by the German gunners, who sent them into the air; while a well-directed petrol bomb at Wormwood Scrubs Prison set one great wing of the place alight, and the prisoners were therefore released. The rear of Kensington Palace, and the fronts of a number of houses in Kensington Palace Gardens were badly damaged, while in the dome of the Albert Hall was a great, ugly hole.

Shortly after five o'clock occurred a disaster which was of national consequence. It could only have been a mishap on the part of the Germans, for they would certainly never have done such irreparable damage willingly, as they destroyed what would otherwise have been the most valuable of loot.

Shots suddenly began to fall fast in Bloomsbury, several of them badly damaging the Hotel Russell and the houses near, and it was therefore apparent that one of the batteries which had been firing from near Jack Straw's Castle had been moved across to Parliament Hill, or even to some point south of it, which gave a wider range to the fire.

Presently a shell came high through the air and fell full upon the British Museum, striking it nearly in the centre of the front, and in exploding carried away the Grecian-Ionic ornament, and shattering a number of the fine stone columns of the dark façade. Ere people in the vicinity had realised that the national collection of antiques was within the range of the enemy's destructive projectiles, a second shell crashed into the rear of the building, making a great gap in the walls. Then, as although all the guns of that particular battery had converged in order to destroy our treasure-house of art and antiquity, shell after shell crashed into the place in rapid succession. Before ten minutes had passed, grey smoke began to roll out from beneath the long colonnade in front, and growing denser, told its own tale. The British Museum was on fire.

Nor was that all. As though to complete the disaster—although it was certain that the Germans were in ignorance—there came one of those terrible shells filled with petrol, which, bursting inside the manuscript room, set the whole place ablaze. In a dozen different places the building seemed to be now alight, especially the library, and thus the finest collection of books, manuscripts, Greek and Roman and Egyptian antiques, coins, medals, and prehistoric relics, lay at the mercy of the flames.

The fire brigade was at once alarmed, and at imminent risk of their lives, for shells were still falling in the vicinity, they, with the Salvage Corps and the assistance of many willing helpers—some of whom unfortunately lost their lives in the flames—saved whatever could be saved, throwing the objects out into the railed-off quadrangle in front.

The left wing of the Museum, however, could not be entered, although after most valiant efforts on the part of the firemen the conflagrations that had broken out in other parts of the building were at length subdued. The damage was, however, irreparable, for many unique collections, including all the prints and drawings, and many of the mediæval and historic manuscripts, had already been consumed.

Shots now began to fall as far south as Oxford Street, and all along that thoroughfare from Holborn as far as Oxford Circus, widespread havoc was being wrought. People fled for their lives back towards Charing Cross and the Strand. The Oxford Music Hall was a hopeless ruin, while a shell crashing through the roof of Frascati's restaurant, carried away a portion of the gallery and utterly wrecked the whole place. Many of the shops in Oxford Street had their roofs damaged or their fronts blown out, while a huge block of flats in Great Russell Street was practically demolished by three shells striking in rapid succession.

Then, to the alarm of all who realised it, shots were seen to be passing high over Bloomsbury, south towards the Thames. The range had been increased, for, as was afterwards known, some heavier guns had now been mounted upon Muswell Hill and Hampstead Heath, which, carrying to a distance of from six to seven miles, placed the City, the Strand, and Westminster within the zone of fire. The zone in question stretched roughly from Victoria Park through Bethnal Green and Whitechapel, across to Southwark, the Borough, Lambeth, and Westminster to Kensington, and while the fire upon the northern suburbs slackened, great shells now came flying through the air into the very heart of London.

The German gunners at Muswell Hill took the dome of St. Paul's as a mark, for shells fell constantly in Ludgate Hill, in Cheapside, in Newgate Street, and in the churchyard itself. One falling upon the steps of the Cathedral tore out two of the columns of the front, while another striking the clock tower just below the face, brought down much of the masonry and one of the huge bells, with a deafening crash, blocking the road with débris. Time after time the great shells went over the splendid Cathedral, which the enemy seemed bent upon destroying, but the dome remained uninjured, though about ten feet of the top of the second tower was carried away.

On the Cannon Street side of St. Paul's a great block of drapery warehouses had caught fire, and was burning fiercely, while the drapers' and other shops on the Paternoster Row side all had their windows shattered by the constant detonations. Within the cathedral two shells that had fallen through the roof had wrought havoc with the beautiful reredos and choir-stalls, many of the fine windows being also wrecked by the explosions.

Whole rows of houses in Cheapside suffered, while both the Mansion House, where the London flag was flying, and the Royal Exchange were severely damaged by a number of shells which fell in the vicinity. The equestrian statue in front of the Exchange had been overturned, while the Exchange itself showed a great yawning hole in the corner of the façade next Cornhill. At the Bank of England a fire had occurred, but had fortunately been extinguished by the strong force of Guards in charge, though they gallantly risked their lives in so doing. Lothbury, Gresham Street, Old Broad Street, Lombard Street, Gracechurch Street, and Leadenhall Street were all more or less scenes of fire, havoc, and destruction. The loss of life was not great in this neighbourhood, for most people had crossed the river or gone westward, but the high explosives used by the Germans were falling upon the shops and warehouses with appalling effect.

Masonry was torn about like paper, ironwork twisted like wax, woodwork shattered to a thousand splinters as, time after time, a great projectile hissed in the air and effected its errand of destruction. A number of the wharves on each side of the river were soon alight, and both Upper and Lower Thames Streets were soon impassable on account of huge conflagrations. A few shells fell in Shoreditch, Houndsditch, and Whitechapel, and these, in most cases, caused loss of life in those densely populated districts.

Westward, however, as the hours went on, the howitzers at Hampstead began to drop high explosive shells into the Strand, around Charing Cross, and in Westminster. This weapon had a calibre of 4.14 inches, and threw a projectile of 35 lb. The tower of St. Clement Dane's Church crashed to the ground and blocked the roadway opposite Milford Lane; the pointed roof of the clock-tower of the Law Courts was blown away, and the granite fronts of the two banks opposite the Law Courts entrance were torn out by a shell which exploded in the footpath before them.

Shells fell, time after time, in and about the Law Courts themselves, committing immense damage to the interior, while a shell bursting upon the roof of Charing Cross Station, rendered it a ruin as picturesque as it had been in December 1905. The National Liberal Club was burning furiously; the Hotel Cecil and the Savoy did not escape, but no material damage was done them. The Garrick Theatre had caught fire, a shot carried away the globe above the Coliseum, and the Shot Tower beside the Thames crashed into the river.

The front of the Grand Hotel in Trafalgar Square showed, in several places, great holes where the shell had struck, and a shell bursting at the foot of Nelson's monument turned over one of the lions—overthrowing the emblem of Britain's might!

The clubs in Pall Mall were, in one or two instances, wrecked, notably the Reform, the Junior Carlton, and the Athenæum, into each of which shells fell through the roof and exploded within.

From the number of projectiles that fell in the vicinity of the Houses of Parliament it was apparent that the German gunners could see the Royal Standard flying from the Victoria Tower, and were making it their mark. In the west front of Westminster Abbey several shots crashed, doing enormous damage to the grand old pile. The hospital opposite was set alight, while the Westminster Palace Hotel was severely damaged, and two shells falling into St. Thomas's Hospital created a scene of indescribable terror in one of the overcrowded casualty wards.

Suddenly one of the German high explosive shells burst on the top of the Victoria Tower, blowing away all four of the pinnacles, and bringing down the flagstaff. Big Ben served as another mark for the artillery at Muswell Hill, for several shots struck it, tearing out one of the huge clock faces and blowing away the pointed apex of the tower. Suddenly, however, two great shells struck it right in the centre, almost simultaneously, near the base, and made such a hole in the huge pile of masonry that it was soon seen to have been rendered unsafe, though it did not fall.

Shot after shot struck other portions of the Houses of Parliament, breaking the windows and carrying away pinnacles.

One of the twin towers of Westminster Abbey fell a few moments later, and another shell, crashing into the choir, completely wrecked Edward the Confessor's shrine, the Coronation chair, and all the objects of antiquity in the vicinity.

The old Horse Guards escaped injury, but one of the cupolas of the new War Office opposite was blown away, while shortly afterwards a fire broke out in the new Local Government Board and Education Offices. Number 10 Downing Street, the chief centre of the Government, had its windows all blown in—a grim accident, no doubt—the same explosion shattering several windows in the Foreign Office.

Many shells fell in St. James's and Hyde Parks, exploding harmlessly, but others, passing across St. James's Park, crashed into that high building, Queen Anne's Mansions, causing fearful havoc. Somerset House, Covent Garden Market, Drury Lane Theatre, and the Gaiety Theatre and Restaurant all suffered more or less, and two of the bronze footguards guarding the Wellington Statue at Hyde Park Corner were blown many yards away. Around Holborn Circus immense damage was being caused, and several shells bursting on the Viaduct itself blew great holes in the bridge.

So widespread, indeed, was the havoc, that it is impossible to give a detailed account of the day's terrors. If the public buildings suffered, the damage to property of householders and the ruthless wrecking of quiet English homes may well be imagined. The people had been driven out from the zone of fire, and had left their possessions to the mercy of the invaders.

South of the Thames very little damage was done. The German howitzers and long-range guns could not reach so far. One or two shots fell in York Road, Lambeth, and in the Waterloo and Westminster Bridge Roads, but they did little damage beyond the breaking of all the windows in the vicinity.

When would it end? Where would it end?

Half the population of London had fled across the bridges, and from Denmark Hill, Champion Hill, Norwood, and the Crystal Palace they could see the smoke issuing from the hundred fires.

London was cowed. Those northern barricades, still held by bodies of valiant men, were making a last desperate stand, though the streets ran with blood. Every man fought well and bravely for his country, though he went to his death. A thousand acts of gallant heroism on the part of Englishmen were done that day, but, alas! all to no purpose. The Germans were at our gates, and were not to be denied.

As daylight commenced to fade the dust and smoke became suffocating. And yet the guns pounded away with a monotonous regularity that appalled the helpless populace. Overhead there was a quick whizzing in the air, a deafening explosion, and as masonry came crashing down the atmosphere was filled with poisonous fumes that half asphyxiated all those in the vicinity.

Hitherto the enemy had treated us, on the whole, humanely, but finding that desperate resistance in the northern suburbs, Von Kronhelm was carrying out the Emperor's parting injunction. He was breaking the pride of our own dear London, even at the sacrifice of thousands of innocent lives.

The scenes in the streets within that zone of awful fire baffled description. They were too sudden, too dramatic, too appalling. Death and destruction were everywhere, and the people of London now realised for the first time what the horrors of war really meant.

Dusk was falling. Above the pall of smoke from the burning buildings the sun was setting with a blood-red light. From the London streets, however, this evening sky was darkened by the clouds of smoke and dust. Yet the cannonade continued, each shell that came hurtling through the air exploding with deadly effect and spreading destruction on all hands.

Meanwhile the barricades at the north had not escaped Von Kronhelm's attention. About four o'clock he gave orders by field telegraph for certain batteries to move down and attack them.

This was done soon after five o'clock, and when the German guns began to pour their deadly rain of shell into those hastily improvised defences there commenced a slaughter of the gallant defenders that was horrible. At each of the barricades shell after shell was directed, and very quickly breaches were made. Then upon the defenders themselves the fire was directed—a withering, awful fire from quick-firing guns which none could withstand. The streets, with their barricades swept away, were strewn with mutilated corpses. Hundreds upon hundreds had attempted to make a last stand, rallied by the Union Jack they waved above, but a shell exploding in their midst had sent them to instant eternity.

Many a gallant deed was done that day by patriotic Londoners in defence of their homes and loved ones—many a deed that should have earned the V.C.—but in nearly all cases the patriot who had stood up and faced the foe had gone to straight and certain death.

Till seven o'clock the dull roar of the guns in the north continued, and people across the Thames knew that London was still being destroyed, nay pulverised. Then with one accord came a silence—the first silence since the hot noon.

Von Kronhelm's field telegraph at Jack Straw's Castle had ticked the order to cease firing.

All the barricades had been broken.

London lay burning—at the mercy of the German eagle.

And as the darkness fell the German Commander-in-Chief looked again through his glasses, and saw the red flames leaping up in dozens of places, where whole blocks of shops and buildings, public institutions, whole streets in some cases, were being consumed.

London—the proud capital of the world, the "home" of the Englishman—was at last ground beneath the iron heel of Germany!

And all, alas! due to one cause alone—the careless insular apathy of the Englishman himself!

VI

Fall of London

Outside London the September night had settled down on the blood-stained field of battle. With a pale light the moon had risen, partly hidden by chasing clouds, her white rays mingling with the lurid glare of the fires down in the great terrified metropolis below. Northward, from Hampstead across to Barnet—indeed, over that wide district where the final battle had been so hotly fought—the moonbeams shone upon the pallid faces of the fallen.

Along the German line of investment there had now followed upon the roar of battle an uncanny silence.

Away to the west, however, there was still heard the growling of distant conflict, now mounting into a low crackling of musketry fire, and again dying away in muffled sounds. The last remnant of the British Army was being hotly pursued in the direction of Staines.

London was invested and bombarded, but not yet taken.

For a long time the German Field-Marshal had stood alone upon Hampstead Heath apart from his staff, watching the great tongues of flame leaping up here and there in the distant darkness. His grey, shaggy brows were contracted, his thin aquiline face thoughtful, his hard mouth twitching nervously, unable to fully conceal the strain of his own feelings as conqueror of the English. Von Kronhelm's taciturnity had long ago been proverbial. The Kaiser had likened him to Moltke, and declared that "he could be silent in seven languages." His gaze was one of musing, and yet he was the most active of men, and perhaps the cleverest strategist in all Europe. Often during the campaign he had astonished his aides-de-camp by his untiring energy, for sometimes he would even visit the outposts in person. On many occasions he had actually crept up to the most advanced posts at great personal risk to himself, so anxious had he been to see with his own eyes. Such visits from the Field-Marshal himself were not always exactly welcome to the German outposts, who, as soon as they showed the least sign of commotion consequent upon the visit, were at once swept by a withering English fire.

Yet he now stood there—the conqueror. And while many of his officers were installing themselves in comfortable quarters in houses about North End, North Hill, South Hill, Muswell Hill, Roslyn Hill, Fitzjohn's Avenue, Netherhall, and Maresfield Gardens, and other roads in that vicinity, the great Commander was still alone upon the Heath, having taken nothing save a nip from his flask since his coffee at dawn.

Time after time telegraphic despatches were handed to him from Germany, and telephonic reports from his various positions around London, but he received them all without comment. He read, he listened, but he said nothing.

For a full hour he remained there, strolling up and down alone in quick impatience. Then, as though suddenly making up his mind, he called three members of his staff, and gave orders for the entry into London.

This, as he knew, was the signal for a terrible and bloody encounter. Bugles sounded. Men and officers, who had believed that the storm and stress of the day were over, and that they were entitled to rest, found themselves called upon to fight their way into the city that they knew would be defended by an irate and antagonistic populace.

Still, the order had been given, and it must be obeyed. They had expected that the advance would be at least made at dawn, but evidently Von Kronhelm feared that six hours' delay might necessitate more desperate fighting. He intended, now that London was cowed, that she should be entirely crushed. The orders of his master the Kaiser were to that effect.

Therefore, shortly before nine o'clock the first detachments of German Infantry marched along Spaniards Road, and down Roslyn Hill to Haverstock Hill, where they were at once fired upon from behind the débris of the great barricade across the junction of Prince of Wales Road and Haverstock Hill. This place was held strongly by British Infantry, many members of the Legion of Frontiersmen,— distinguished only by the little bronze badge in their buttonholes,— and also by hundreds of citizens armed with rifles.

Twenty Germans dropped at the first volley, and next instant a Maxim, concealed in the first floor of a neighbouring house, spat forth its fire upon the invaders with deadly effect. The German bugle sounded the "Advance rapidly," and the men emulously ran forward, shouting loud hurrahs. Major von Wittich, who had distinguished himself very conspicuously in the fighting around Enfield Chase, fell, being shot through the lung when just within a few yards of the half-ruined barricade. Londoners were fighting desperately, shouting and cheering. The standard-bearer of the 4th Battalion of the Brunswick

Infantry Regiment, No. 92, fell severely wounded, and the standard was instantly snatched from him in the awful hand-to-hand fighting which that moment ensued.

Five minutes later the streets were running with blood, for hundreds, both Germans and British, lay dead and dying. Every Londoner struggled valiantly until shot down; yet the enemy, already reinforced, pressed forward, until ten minutes later the defenders were driven out of their position, and the house from which the Maxim was sending forth its deadly hail had been entered and the gun captured. Volley after volley was still, however, poured out on the heads of the storming party, but already the pioneers were at work clearing a way for the advance, and very soon the Germans had surmounted the obstruction and were within London.

For a short time the Germans halted, then, at a signal from their officers, they moved forward along both roads, again being fired upon from every house in the vicinity, many of the defenders having retired to continue their defence from the windows. The enemy therefore turned their attention to these houses, and after desperate struggles house after house was taken, those of the defenders not wearing uniform being shot down without mercy. To such no quarter was given.

The contest now became a most furious one. Britons and Germans fought hand to hand. A battalion of the Brunswick Infantry with some riflemen of the Guard took several houses by rush in Chalk Farm Road; but in many cases the Germans were shot by their own comrades. Quite a number of the enemy's officers were picked off by the Frontiersmen, those brave fellows who had seen service in every corner of the world, and who were now in windows and upon roofs. Thus the furious fight from house to house proceeded.

This exciting conflict was practically characteristic of what was at that moment happening in fifty other spots along the suburbs of North London. The obstinate resistance which we made against the Germans was met with equally obstinate aggression. There was no surrender. Londoners fell and died fighting to the very last.

Against those well-trained Teutons in such overwhelming masses we, however, could have no hope of success. The rushes of the infantry and rifles of the Guards were made skilfully, and slowly but surely broke down all opposition.

The barricade in the Kentish Town Road was defended with valiant heroism. The Germans were, as in Chalk Farm Road, compelled to fight their way foot by foot, losing heavily all the time. But here, at length, as at other points, the barricade was taken, and the defenders chased, and either taken prisoner or else ruthlessly shot down. A body of citizens armed with rifles were, after the storming of the barricades in question, driven back into Park Street, and there, being caught between two bodies of Germans, slaughtered to a man. Through those unlit side-streets between the Kentish Town and Camden Roads—namely, the Lawford, Bartholomew, Rochester, Caversham, and Leighton Roads, there was much skirmishing, and many on both sides fell in the bloody encounter. A thousand deeds of bravery were done that night, but were unrecorded. Before the barricade in the Holloway Road—which had been strongly repaired after the breach made in it by the German shells—the enemy lost very heavily, for the three Maxims which had there been mounted did awful execution. The invaders, however, seeing the strong defence, fell back for full twenty minutes, and then, making another rush, hurled petrol bombs into the midst of our men.

A frightful holocaust was the result. Fully a hundred of the poor fellows were literally burned alive; while the neighbouring houses being set in flames, compelled the citizen free-shooters to quickly evacuate their position. Against such terrible missiles even the best-trained troops cannot stand, therefore no wonder that all opposition at that point was soon afterwards swept away, and the pioneers quickly opened the road for the victorious legions of the Kaiser.

And so in that prosaic thoroughfare, the Holloway Road, brave men fought gallantly and died, while a Scotch piper paced the pavement sharply, backwards and forwards, with his colours flying. Then, alas! came the red flash, the loud explosions in rapid succession, and next instant the whole street burst into a veritable sea of flame.

High Street, Kingsland, was also the scene of several fierce conflicts; but here the Germans decidedly got the worst of it. The whole infuriated population seemed to emerge suddenly from the side streets of the Kingsland Road on the appearance of the detachment of the enemy, and the latter were practically overwhelmed, notwithstanding the desperate fight they made. Then ringing cheers went up from the defenders.

The Germans were given no quarter by the populace, all of whom were armed with knives or guns, the women mostly with hatchets, crowbars, or edged tools.

Many of the Germans fled through the side streets towards Mare Street, and were hotly pursued, the majority of them being done to death by the maddened mob. The streets in this vicinity were literally a slaughter-house.

The barricades in Finchley Road and in High Road, Kilburn were also very strongly held, and at the first named it was quite an hour before the enemy's pioneers were able to make a breach. Indeed, then only after a most hotly contested conflict, in which there were frightful losses on both sides. Petrol bombs were here also used by the enemy with appalling effect, the road being afterwards cleared by a couple of Maxims.

Farther towards Regent's Park the houses were, however, full of sharpshooters, and before these could be dislodged the enemy had again suffered severely. The entry into London was both difficult and perilous, and the enemy suffered great losses everywhere.

After the breaking down of the defences in High Road, Kilburn, the men who had held them retired to the Town Hall, opposite Kilburn Station, and from the windows fired at the passing battalions, doing much execution. All efforts to dislodge them proved unavailing, until the place was taken by storm, and a fearful hand-to-hand fight was the outcome. Eventually the Town Hall was taken, after a most desperate resistance, and ten minutes later wilfully set fire to and burned.

In the Harrow Road and those cross streets between Kensal Green and Maida Vale the advancing Germans shared much the same fate as about Hackney. Surrounded by the armed populace, hundreds upon hundreds of them were killed, struck down by hatchets, stabbed by knives, or shot with revolvers, the crowd shouting, "Down with the Germans! Kill them! Kill them!"

Many of the London women now became perfect furies. So incensed were they at the wreck of their homes and the death of their loved ones that they rushed wildly into the fray with no thought of peril, only of bitter revenge. A German, whenever caught, was at once killed. In those bloody street fights the Teutons got separated from their comrades and were quickly surrounded and done to death.

Across the whole of the northern suburbs the scenes of bloodshed that night were full of horror, as men fought in the ruined streets, climbing over the smouldering débris, over the bodies of their comrades, and shooting from behind ruined walls. As Von Kronhelm had anticipated, his Army was compelled to fight its way into London.

The streets all along the line of the enemy's advance were now strewn with dead and dying. London was doomed.

The Germans now coming on in increasing, nay, unceasing, numbers, were leaving behind them everywhere the trail of blood. Shattered London stood staggered.

Though the resistance had been long and desperate, the enemy had again triumphed by reason of his sheer weight of numbers.

Yet even though he were actually in our own dear London, our people did not mean that he should establish himself without any further opposition. Therefore, though the barricades had been taken, the Germans found in every unexpected corner men who shot at them, and Maxims which spat forth their leaden showers beneath which hundreds upon hundreds of Teutons fell.

Yet they advanced, still fighting. The scenes of carnage were awful and indescribable, no quarter being given to any armed citizens not in uniform, be they men, women, or children.

The German Army was carrying out the famous proclamation of Field-Marshal von Kronhelm to the very letter!

They were marching on to the sack of the wealthiest city of the world.

It wanted still an hour of midnight, London was a city of shadow, of fire, of death. The silent streets, whence all the inhabitants had fled in panic, echoed to the heavy tread of German infantry, the clank of arms, and the ominous rumble of guns. Ever and anon an order was shouted in German as the Kaiser's legions went forward to occupy the proud capital of the world. The enemy's plans appeared to have been carefully prepared. The majority of the troops coming from the direction of Hampstead and Finchley entered Regent's Park, whence preparations were at once commenced for encampment; while the remainder, together with those who came down the Camden, Caledonian, and Holloway Roads turned along Euston Road and Oxford Street to Hyde Park, where a huge camp was formed, stretching from the Marble Arch right along the Park Lane side away to Knightsbridge.

Officers were very soon billeted in the best houses in Park Lane and about Mayfair,—houses full of works of art and other valuables that had only that morning been left to the mercy of the invaders. From the windows and balconies of their quarters in Park Lane they could overlook the encampment—a position which had evidently been purposely chosen.

Other troops who came in never-ending procession by Bow Road, Roman Road, East India Dock Road, Victoria Park Road, Mare Street, and Kingsland Road all converged into the City itself, except those who had come from Edmonton down the Kingsland Road, and who, passing along Old Street and Clerkenwell, occupied the Charing Cross and Westminster districts.

At midnight a dramatic scene was enacted when, in the blood-red glare of some blazing buildings in the vicinity, a large body of Prince Louis Ferdinand of Prussia's 2nd Magdeburg Regiment suddenly swept up Threadneedle Street into the great open space before the Mansion House, whereon the London flag was still flying aloft in the smoke-laden air. They halted across the junction of Cheapside with Queen Victoria Street when, at the same moment, another huge body of the Uhlans of Altmark and Magdeburg Hussars came clattering along Cornhill, followed a moment later by battalion after battalion of the 4th and 8th Thuringen Infantry out of Moorgate Street, whose uniforms showed plain traces of the desperate encounters of the past week.

The great body of Germans had halted before the Mansion House, when General von Kleppen, the commander of the IVth Army Corps—who, it will be remembered, had landed at Weybourne—accompanied by Lieutenant-General von Mirbach of the 8th Division, and Frölich, commander of the cavalry brigade, ascended the steps of the Mansion House and entered.

Within, Sir Claude Harrison, the Lord Mayor, who wore his robes and jewel of office, received them in that great, sombre room wherein so many momentous questions concerning the welfare of the British Empire had been discussed. The representative of the City of London, a short, stout, grey-haired man, was pale and agitated. He bowed, but he could not speak.

Von Kleppen, however, a smart, soldierly figure in his service uniform and many ribbons, bowed in response, and in very fair English said:

"I regret, my Lord Mayor, that it is necessary for us to thus disturb you, but as you are aware, the British Army have been defeated, and the German Army has entered London. I have orders from Field-Marshal von Kronhelm to place you under arrest, and to hold you as hostage for the good behaviour of the City during the progress of the negotiations for peace."

"Arrest!" gasped the Lord Mayor. "You intend to arrest me?"

"It will not be irksome, I assure you," smiled the German commander grimly. "At least, we shall make it as comfortable as possible. I shall place a guard here, and the only restriction I place upon you is that you shall neither go out nor hold any communication with anyone outside these walls."

"But my wife?"

"If her ladyship is here I would advise that she leave the place. It is better that, for the present, she should be out of London."

The civic officials, who had all assembled for the dramatic ceremonial, looked at each other in blank amazement.

The Lord Mayor was a prisoner!

Sir Claude divested himself of his jewel of office, and handed it to his servant to replace in safe keeping. Then he took off his robe, and having done so, advanced closer to the German officers, who, treating him with every courtesy, consulted with him, expressing regret at the terrible loss of life that had been occasioned by the gallant defence of the barricades.

Von Kleppen gave the Lord Mayor a message from Von Kronhelm, and urged him to issue a proclamation forbidding any further opposition on the part of the populace of London. With the three officers Sir Claude talked for a quarter of an hour, while into the Mansion House there entered a strong guard of men of the 2nd Magdeburg, who quickly established themselves in the most comfortable quarters. German double sentries stood at every exit and in every corridor, and when a few minutes later the flag was hauled down and the German Imperial Standard run up, wild shouts of triumph rang from every throat of the densely packed body of troops assembled outside.

The joyous "hurrahs!" reached the Lord Mayor, still in conversation with Von Kleppen, Von Mirbach, and Frölich, and in an instant he knew the truth. The Teutons were saluting their own standard. The civic flag had, either accidentally or purposely, been flung down into the roadway below, and was trampled in the dust. A hundred enthusiastic Germans, disregarding the shouts of their officers, fought for the flag, and it was instantly torn to shreds, and little pieces preserved as souvenirs.

Shout after shout in German went up from the wildly excited troops of the Kaiser when the light wind caused their own flag to flutter out, and then as with one voice the whole body of troops united in singing the German National Hymn.

The scene was weird and most impressive. London had fallen.

Around were the wrecked buildings, some still smouldering, some emitting flame. Behind lay the Bank of England with untold wealth locked within; to the right, the damaged façade of the Royal Exchange was illuminated by the flickering light, which also shone upon the piled arms of the enemy's troops, causing them to flash and gleam.

WILLIAM LE QUEUX

In those silent, narrow City streets not an Englishman was to be seen. Everyone save the Lord Mayor and his official attendants had fled.

The Government offices in Whitehall were all in the hands of the enemy. In the Foreign Office, the India Office, the War Office, the Colonial Office, the Admiralty and other minor offices were German guards. Sentries stood at the shattered door of the famous No. 10 Downing Street, and all up Whitehall was lined with infantry.

German officers were in charge of all our public offices, and all officials who had remained on duty were firmly requested to leave. Sentries were stationed to guard the archives of every department, and precautions were taken to guard against any further outbreaks of fire.

Across at the Houses of Parliament, with their damaged towers, the whole great pile of buildings was surrounded by triumphant troops, while across at the fine old Abbey of Westminster was, alas! a different scene. The interior had been turned into a temporary hospital, and upon matresses placed upon the floor were hundreds of poor maimed creatures, some groaning, some ghastly pale in the last moments of agony, some silent, their white lips moving in prayer.

On one side in the dim light lay the men, some in uniform, others inoffensive citizens, who had been struck by cruel shells or falling débris; on the other side lay the women, some mere girls, and even children.

Flitting everywhere in the half light were nurses, charitable ladies, and female helpers, with numbers of doctors, all doing their best to alleviate the terrible sufferings of that crowded place, the walls of which showed plain traces of the severe bombardment. In places the roof was open to the angry sky, while many of the windows were gaunt and shattered.

A clergyman's voice somewhere was repeating a prayer in a low, distinct voice, so that all could hear, yet above all were the sighs and groans of the sufferers, and as one walked through that prostrate assembly of victims more than one was seen to have already gone to that land that lies beyond the human ken.

The horrors of war were never more forcibly illustrated than in Westminster Abbey that night, for the grim hand of Death was there, and men and women lying with their faces to the roof looked into Eternity.

Every hospital in London was full, therefore the overflow had been placed in the various churches. From the battlefields along the northern defences, Epping, Edmonton, Barnet, Enfield, and other places where the last desperate stand had been made, and from the barricades in the northern suburbs ambulance wagons were continually arriving full of wounded, all of whom were placed in the churches and in any large public buildings which had remained undamaged by the bombardment.

St. George's, Hanover Square, once the scene of many smart weddings, was now packed with unfortunate wounded soldiers, British and Germans lying side by side, while in the Westminster Cathedral and the Oratory at Brompton the Roman Catholic priests made hundreds of poor fellows as comfortable as they could, many members of the religious sisterhoods acting as nurses. St. James's Church in Piccadilly, St. Pancras Church, Shoreditch Church, and St. Mary Abbotts', Kensington, were all improvised hospitals, and many grim and terrible scenes of agony were witnessed during that long eventful night.

The light was dim everywhere, for there were only paraffin lamps, and by their feeble illumination many a difficult operation had to be performed by those London surgeons who one and all had come forward, and were now working unceasingly. Renowned specialists from Harley Street, Cavendish Square, Queen Anne Street, and the vicinity were directing the work in all the improvised hospitals, men whose names were world-famous kneeling and performing operations upon poor unfortunate private soldiers or upon some labourer who had taken up a gun in defence of his home.

Of lady helpers there were hundreds. From Mayfair and Belgravia, from Kensington and Bayswater, ladies had come forward offering their services, and their devotion to the wounded was everywhere apparent. In St. Andrew's, Wells Street, St. Peter's, Eaton Square, in the Scottish Church in Crown Court, Covent Garden, in the Temple Church, in the Union Chapel in Upper Street, in the Chapel Royal, Savoy, in St. Clement Danes in the Strand, and in St. Martin's-in-the-Fields there were wounded in greater or less numbers, but the difficulties of treating them were enormous owing to the lack of necessaries for the performance of operations.

Weird and striking were the scenes within those hallowed places, as, in the half darkness with the long, deep shadows, men struggled for life or gave to the women kneeling at their side their name, their address, or a last dying message to one they loved.

London that night was a city of shattered homes, of shattered hopes, of shattered lives.

The silence of death had fallen everywhere. The only sounds that broke the quiet within those churches were the sighs, the groans, and the faint murmurings of the dying.

VII

Two Personal Narratives

Some adequate idea of the individual efforts made by the citizens of London to defend their homes against the invader may be gathered from various personal narratives afterwards printed in certain newspapers. All of them were tragic, thrilling, and struck that strong note of patriotism which is ever latent in the breast of every Englishman, and more especially the Londoner.

The story told to a reporter of the *Observer* by a young man named Charles Dale, who in ordinary life was a clerk in the employ of the Royal Mail Steam Packet Company, in Moorgate Street, depicted, in graphic details, the frightful conflict. He said:

"When the Hendon and Cricklewood Rifle Club was formed in 1906 I joined it, and in a month we had over 500 members. From that time the club—whose practices were held at the Normal Powder Company's range, in Reuter's Lane, Hendon—increased until it became one of the largest rifle clubs in the kingdom. As soon as news of the sudden invasion reached us, we all reported ourselves at headquarters, and out of four thousand of us there were only thirty-three absentees, all the latter being too far from London to return. We were formed into small parties, and, taking our rifles and ammunition, we donned our distinctive khaki tunics and peaked caps, and each company made its way into Essex independently, in order to assist the Legion of Frontiersmen and the Free-shooters to harass the Germans.

"Three days after the enemy's landing, I found myself, with seventeen of my comrades, at a village called Dedham, close to the Stour, where we opened our campaign by lying in ambush and picking off a number of German sentries. It was exciting and risky work, especially when, under cover of darkness, we crept up to the enemy's outposts and attacked and harassed them. Assisted by a number of the Frontiersmen, we scoured the country across to Sudbury, and in that hot, exciting week that followed dozens of the enemy fell to our guns. We snatched sleep where we could, concealing ourselves in thickets and begging food from the cottagers, all of whom gave us whatever they could spare. One morning, when just outside Wormingford village, we were surprised by a party of

Germans. Whereupon we retired to a barn, and held it strongly for an hour until the enemy were forced to retire, leaving ten of their number dead and eight wounded. Ours was a very narrow escape, and had not the enemy been compelled to fight in the open, we should certainly have been overwhelmed and exterminated. We were an irregular force, therefore the Germans would give us no quarter. We carried our lives in our hands always.

"War brings with it strange companions. Many queer, adventurous spirits fought beside us in those breathless days of fire and blood, when Maldon was attacked by the Colchester garrison, and our gallant troops were forced back after the battle of Purleigh. Each day that went past brought out larger numbers of free-shooters from London, while the full force of the patriotic Legion of Frontiersmen had now concentrated until the whole country west of the line from Chelmsford to Saffron Walden seemed swarming with us, and we must have given the enemy great trouble everywhere. The day following the battle of Royston I had the most narrow escape. Lying in ambush with eight other men, all members of the Rifle Club, in College Wood, not far from Buntingford, I was asleep, being utterly worn out, when we were suddenly discovered by a large party of Uhlans. Two of my comrades were shot dead ere they could fire, while five others, including one of my best friends, Tom Martin, a clerk in the National Provincial Bank, who had started with me from Hendon, were taken prisoners. I managed to dodge the two big Uhlans who endeavoured to seize me, and into the face of one I fired my revolver, blowing half his bearded face away. In a moment a German bullet whistled past me; then another and another; but by marvellous good luck I was not hit, and managed to escape into the denser part of the wood, where I climbed a high tree, hiding among the branches, while the Germans below sought in vain for me. Those moments seemed hours. I could hear my own heart beat. I knew that they might easily discover me, for the foliage was not very thick. Indeed, twice one of the search parties passed right beneath me. Of my other comrade who had fled I had seen nothing. For three hours I remained concealed there. Once I heard loud shouts and then sounds of shots close by, and wondered whether any of our comrades, whom I knew were in the vicinity, had discovered the Germans. Then at last, just after sundown, I descended and carefully made my way out. For a long time I wandered about until the dusk was deepening into night, unable to discover my whereabouts. At last I found myself on the outskirts of the wood, but hardly had I gone a hundred yards in the open ere my eyes met a sight that froze my blood. Upon trees in close proximity to each other were hanging the dead bodies of my five comrades, including poor Tom Martin. They presented a grim, ghastly spectacle. The Uhlans had strung them to trees, and afterwards riddled them with bullets!

"Gradually, we were driven back upon London. Desperately we fought, each one of us, and the personal risk of every member of our club, of any other of the rifle clubs, and of the Frontiersmen, for the matter of that, was very great. We were insufficient in numbers. Had we been more numerous, I maintain that we could have so harassed the enemy that we could have held him in check for many months. With the few thousands of men we have we made it extremely uncomfortable for Von Kronhelm and his forces. Had our number been greater we could have operated more in unison with the British regular arms, and formed a line of defence around London so complete that it could never have been broken. As it was, however, when driven in, we were compelled to take a stand in manning the forts and entrenchments of the London lines, I finding myself in a hastily constructed trench not far from Enfield. While engaged there with the enemy, a bullet took away the little finger of my left hand, causing me excruciating pain, but it fortunately did not place me hors-de-combat. Standing beside me was a costermonger from Leman Street, Whitechapel, who had once been in the Militia, while next him was a country squire from Hampshire, who was a good shot at grouse, but who had never before handled a military rifle. In that narrow trench in which we stood beneath the rain of German bullets we were of a verity a strange, incongruous crowd, dirty, unkempt, unshaven, more than one of us wearing hastily applied bandages upon places where we had received injury. I had never faced death like that before, and I tell you it was a weird and strange experience. Every man among us knit his brows, loaded and fired, without speaking a word, except, perhaps, to exclaim a curse upon those who threatened to overwhelm us and capture our capital.

"At last, though we fought valiantly—three men beside me having fallen dead through injudiciously showing themselves above the earthworks—we were compelled to evacuate our position. Then followed a terrible guerilla warfare as, driven in across by Southgate to Finchley, we fell back south upon London itself. The enemy, victorious, were following upon the heels of our routed army, and it was seen that our last stand must be made at the barricades, which, we heard, had in our absence been erected in all the main roads leading in from the Northern Heights.

"On Hampstead Heath I found about a dozen or so of my comrades, whom I had not seen since I had left Hendon, and heard from them that they had been operating in Norfolk against the German Guards, who had landed at King's Lynn. With them I went through Hampstead and down Haverstock Hill to the great barricade that had been erected across that thoroughfare and Prince of Wales Road. It was a huge, ugly structure, built of every conceivable article—overturned tramcars, furniture, paving stones, pianos, wardrobes, scaffold boards, in fact everything and anything that came handiest—while intertwined everywhere were hundreds of yards of barbed wire. A small space had been left at the junction of the two roads in order to allow people to enter, while on the top a big Union Jack waved in the light breeze. In all the neighbouring houses I saw men with rifles, while from one house pointed the menacing muzzle of a Maxim, commanding the greater part of Haverstock Hill. There seemed also to be other barricades in the smaller roads in the vicinity. But the one at which I had been stationed was certainly a most formidable obstacle. All sorts and conditions of men manned it. Women, too, were there, fierce-eyed, towsled-haired women, who in their fury seemed to have become half savage. Men shouted themselves hoarse, encouraging the armed citizens to fight till death. But from the determined look upon their faces no incentive was needed. They meant, every one of them, to bear their part bravely, when the moment came.

"'We've been here three whole days awaiting the enemy,' one man said to me, a dark-haired, bearded City man in a serge suit, who carried his rifle slung upon his shoulder.

"'They'll be 'ere soon enough now, cockie,' remarked a Londoner of the lower class from Notting Dale. 'There'll be fightin' 'ere before long, depend on't. This is more excitin' sport than Kempton Park, ain't it—eh?'

"That man was right, for a few hours later, when Von Kronhelm appeared upon Hampstead Heath and launched his infantry upon London, our barricade became a perfect hell. I was on the roof of a house close by, lying full length behind a sheltering chimney-stack, and firing upon the advancing troops for all I was worth. From every window in the vicinity we poured forth a veritable rain of death upon the Germans, while our Maxim spat fire incessantly, and the men at the barricade kept up a splendid fusillade. Ere long Haverstock Hill became

County of London.

Looting, Housebreaking, and Other Offences.

Take Notice.

(1) That any person, whether soldier or civilian, who enters any premises whatsoever for the purposes of loot; or is found with loot in his possession; or who commits any theft within the meaning of the Act; or is guilty of theft from the person, or robbery, with or without violence; or wilfully damages property; or compels by threats any person to disclose the whereabouts of valuables, or who demands money by menaces; or enters upon any private premises, viz. house, shop, warehouse, office, or factory, without just or reasonable cause, will be at once arrested and tried by military court-martial, and be liable to penal servitude for a period not to exceed twenty years.

(2) That from this date all magistrates at the Metropolitan Police Courts will be superseded by military officers empowered to deal and adjudicate upon all offences in contravention to law.

(3) That the chief Military Court-martial is established at the Metropolitan Police Court at Bow Street.

Francis Bamford, General,
Military Governor of London.

Governor's Headquarters,
New Scotland Yard, S.W.,
September 19th, 1910.

The Above Proclamation Was Posted All Over The Metropolis On The Day Prior To The Bombardment.

a perfect inferno. Perched up where I was, I commanded a wide view of all that was in progress. Again and again the Germans were launched to the assault, but such a withering fire did we keep up that we held them constantly in check. Our Maxim served us admirably, for ever and anon it cut a lane in the great wall of advancing troops, until the whole roadway was covered with dead and maimed Germans. To my own gun many fell, as to those of my valiant comrades, for every one of us had sworn that the enemy should never enter London if we could prevent it.

"I saw a woman with her hair dishevelled deliberately mount to the top of the barricade and wave a small Union Jack; but next instant she paid for her folly with her life, and fell back dead upon the roadway below. If the enemy lost heavily, we did not altogether escape. At the barricade and in the houses in the immediate vicinity there were a number of dead and a quantity of wounded, the latter being carried away and tended to by a number of devoted ladies from Fitzjohn's Avenue, and the more select thoroughfares in the neighbourhood. Local surgeons were also there, working unceasingly. For fully an hour the frightful conflict continued. The Germans were dogged in their perseverance, while we were equally active in our desperate resistance. The conflict was awful. The scenes in the streets below me now were beyond description. In High Street, Hampstead, a number of shops had been set on fire and were burning; while above the din, the shouts and the crackle of the rifles, there was now and then heard the deep boom of field guns away in the distance.

"We had received information that Von Kronhelm himself was quite near us, up at Jack Straw's Castle, and more than one of us only wished he would show himself in Haverstock Hill, and thus allow us a chance of taking a pot-shot at him.

"Suddenly the enemy retreated back up Roslyn Hill, and we cheered loudly at what we thought was our victory. Alas! our triumph was not of long duration. I had descended from my position on the roof, and was walking at rear of the barricade, where the pavement and roadway were slippery with blood, when of a sudden the big guns, which it seemed had now been planted on Hampstead Heath, gave tongue, and a shot passed high above us far south into London. In a moment a dozen other guns roared, and within ten minutes we found ourselves beneath a perfect hail of high explosive projectiles, though being so near the guns we were comparatively safe. Most of us sought shelter in the neighbouring houses. No enemy was in sight, for they had now gathered up their wounded and retired back up to Hampstead. Their dead they left scattered over the roadway, a grim, awful sight on that bright, sunny morning.

"'They're surely not going to bombard a defenceless city?' cried a man to me—a man whom I recognised as a neighbour of mine at Hendon. 'It's against all the rules of war.'

"'They are bombarding London because of our defence,' I said, and scarcely were those words out of my mouth when there was a bright red flash, a loud report, and the whole front of a neighbouring house was torn out into the roadway, while my friend and myself reeled by force of the terrific explosion. Two men standing near us had been blown to atoms.

"Some of the women about us now became panic-stricken. But the men were mostly cool and determined, standing within the shelter walls of the houses, down areas, or in coal cellars beneath the street. Thus for over three hours we waited under fire, not knowing from one moment to another whether a shell might not fall among us.

"Suddenly our fears were increased, when, soon after four o'clock, the Germans again appeared in Haverstock Hill, this time with artillery, which, notwithstanding the heavy fire we instantly directed upon them, they established in such a position as to completely command our hastily-constructed defences. The fire from Hampstead Heath was slackening when suddenly one of those guns before us on Haverstock Hill sent a shell right into the centre of our barricade. The explosion was awful. The whole front of the house in which I was fell out into the roadway, while a dozen heroic men were blown out of all recognition, and a great breach made in the obstruction. Another shell, another and another, struck in our midst, utterly disorganising our defence, and each time making great breaches in our huge barricade. Neither Maxim nor rifle was of any use against those awful shells.

"I stood in the wrecked room covered with dust and blood, wondering what the end was to be. To fire my rifle in that moment was useless. Not only did the German artillery train their guns upon the barricade, but on the houses which we had placed in a state of defence. They pounded away at them, and in a few minutes had reduced several to ruins, burying in the débris the gallant Londoners defending them. The house upon the roof of which I had, earlier in the day, taken up my position, was struck by two shells in rapid succession, and simply demolished, over forty brave men losing their lives in the terrible catastrophe.

"Again the enemy, after wrecking our defences, retired smartly up the hill as the terrible bombardment of London ceased. Our losses in the shelling of the barricade had been terrible. The roadway behind us was strewn with dead and dying, and with others I helped to bandage the wounded and remove them to private houses in the Adelaide and King Henry's Roads, where the doctors were attending to their injuries. In Haverstock Hill lay the bodies of many women, more than one with a revolver still grasped in her stiffened hand. Ah! the scenes at that barricade defy description. They were awful. The pavements were like those of slaughter-houses and the whole road to beyond the Adelaide had been utterly wrecked, there being not a single house intact.

"And yet we rallied. Reinforcements came up from the direction of Regent's Park—a great, unorganised crowd of armed men and women, doubly enraged by the cruel bombardment and the burning of their homes. With these reinforcements we resolved to still hold the débris of our barricade—to still dispute the advance of the invader, knowing that one division must certainly come down that road. So we reorganised our force and waited—waited while the sun sank with its crimson afterglow and darkness crept on, watching the red fires of London reflected upon the night sky, and wondering each one of us what was to be our fate.

"For hours we waited there, until the Kaiser's legions came upon us, sweeping down Roslyn Hill to where we were still making a last stand. Though the street lamps were unlit, we saw them advancing by the angry glare of the fires of London, while we, too, were full in the light, and a mark for them. They fired upon us, and we returned their fusillade. We stood man to man, concealed behind the débris wherever we could get shelter from the rain of lead they poured upon us. They advanced by rushes, taking our position by storm. I was in the roadway, concealed behind an overturned tramcar, into the woodwork of which bullets were constantly imbedding themselves. The man next me fell backward—dead, without a word. But I kept on, well knowing that in the end we must give way. Those well-equipped hordes of the Kaiser I saw before me were, I knew, the conquerors of London. Yet we fought on valiantly for King and country—fought even when we came hand to hand. I shot a standard-bearer dead, but in an instant another took his place. For a second the German standard was trampled in the dust, but next moment it was aloft again, amid the ringing cheers of the conquerors. Again I fired, again, and yet again, as fast as I could reload, when of a sudden I knew that we were defeated, for our fire had slackened, and the Germans ran in past me. I turned, and as I did so I faced a big, burly fellow with a revolver. I put my hand to my own, but ere I could get it out a light flashed full in my face, and then I knew no more. When I recovered consciousness I found myself in the North-West London Hospital, in Kentish Town Road, with my head bandaged, and a nurse looking gravely into my face.

"And that is very briefly my story of how I fared during the terrible siege of London. I could tell you of many and many horrible scenes, of ruthless loss of life, and of women and children the innocent victims of those bloody engagements. But why should I? The horrors of the war are surely known to you, alas, only too well—far too well."

ANOTHER NARRATIVE OF GREAT INTEREST as showing the aspect of London immediately following its occupation by the Germans was that of a middle-aged linotype operator named James Jellicoe, employed on the *Weekly Dispatch*, who made the following statement to a reporter of the *Evening News*. It was published in the last edition of that journal prior to the suppression of the entire London Press by Von Kronhelm. He said:

"When the barricades in North London had been stormed by the Germans, and they had fought their way down to Oxford Street and Holborn, I chanced to be in Farringdon Street. Right through the bombardment during the whole afternoon we compositors on the *Mail*, the *Evening News*, and the *Dispatch* were compelled to work, and it had been a most exciting time, I can tell you. We didn't know from one moment to another when a shell might fall through the roof among us. Two or three places in Whitefriars were struck, and *Answers'* office in Tudor Street had been burned out. I had left work at eleven and gone to meet my boy Frank, who is on the *Star* in Stonecutter Street, intending to take him home to Kennington Park Road, where I live, when I first caught sight of the Germans. They were passing over the Viaduct, marching towards the City, while some of them ran down the steps into the Farringdon Road, ranging themselves along beneath the Viaduct as guards, in order to protect it, I suppose. They seemed a tall, sturdy, well-equipped body of men, and entirely surprised me, as they did the other people about me, who now saw them for the first time. I had been setting up 'copy' about the enemy for the past ten days or so, but had never imagined them to be such a sturdy race as they really were. There was no disorder among them. They obeyed the German words of command just like machines, while up above them marched battalion after battalion of infantry, and troop after troop of clattering cavalry, away to Newgate Street and the City.

"I heard it said that the Lord Mayor had already been taken a prisoner, and that the streets of the City proper were swarming with Germans. A quarter of an hour later I called for my boy, and together we made our way back along New Bridge Street to Blackfriars Bridge, when, to my amazement, I found such a great press of people flying south that many helpless women and children were being crushed to death. There was a frightful scene, illuminated by the red glare of the flames devouring St. Paul's Station. The railway bridge was thus cut off, otherwise it might have considerably relieved the frantic traffic. After half a dozen futile attempts to get across—for it seemed that there were two human tides meeting there, persons desirous of re-entering London after the bombardment, and those flying in terror from the enemy—I resolved to abandon it. Therefore, with my boy Frank, I walked along the Embankment until I got close to Waterloo Bridge, when, as I approached the great single arch that spans the roadway, I noticed a boat containing three men shoot out into the river from beneath the wall, close to where we were walking. It slipped silently beneath the shadow of the second arch, where there was some scaffolding, the fine old bridge being under repair.

"The bridge above was just as crowded as that at Blackfriars, the throng struggling both ways, meeting and fighting among themselves for the mastery. In those frantic efforts to cross the river, men and women had their clothes literally torn from their backs. The men were demons in that hour of terror; the women became veritable furies. On the Embankment where I stood in the shadow, however, there were few persons. The great fires in the Strand threw their reflection upon the surface of the water, but the Savoy, Somerset House, and the Cecil also threw great black shadows. The mysterious movements of the three men beneath the bridge attracted me. They had rowed so suddenly out just as we passed that they startled me, and now my curiosity became aroused. Concealed in the deep shadow I leaned over the parapet, and watching saw them make fast the boat to the scaffold platform on a level with the water, and then one man, clinging to the ladder, clambered up into the centre of the arch beneath the roadway. I could not distinctly see what he was doing, for he was hidden among the scaffolding and in the darkness.

"Presently a second man from the boat swung himself upon the ladder and ascended to his companion on the platform above. I could distinguish them standing together, apparently in consultation. Close to me was the pier of the Thames Police, and both of us slipped down there, but found nobody in charge. The police, Metropolitan, City, and Thames, were all engaged in the streets on that memorable night. Nevertheless, the trio beneath the bridge were acting suspiciously. What could we do? German secret agents had committed many outrages during the past ten days, more especially in blowing up bridges and wrecking public buildings with bombs, in order to disorganise any attempt at resistance, and strike terror into the hearts of Londoners. A bomb had been exploded on the terrace of the House of Commons two days before, causing great havoc, while the entrance hall of the Admiralty had also been wrecked. Penge tunnel had, by explosives, been rendered impassable, and an attempt in the tunnel at Merstham had very nearly been successful. Were these suspicious men engaged in the dastardly act of blowing up Waterloo Bridge?

"It suddenly struck me that it might be part of Von Kronhelm's scheme to blow up certain of the bridges in order to prevent those who had fled south from returning and harassing his troops, or else he wished to keep the inhabitants remaining north of the Thames, and prevent them from escaping. As I stood upon the police pier I saw the two men high upon the scaffold motion to the third man, still in the boat, when, after a few moments the last-named individual left the boat, carrying something very carefully, an object looking like a long iron cylinder, and slowly made his way up the perpendicular ladder to where the pair were standing right beneath the crown of the huge arch.

"Then I knew that they were Germans, and realised their foul intention. A few feet above them hundreds were fighting and struggling, all unconscious of that frightful explosive they were affixing to the arch. What could I do? To warn the crowd above was impossible. I was far below, and my voice would not be heard above the din.

"'What are those fellows doing, do you think, father?' inquired my boy, with curiosity.

"'Doing?' I cried. 'Why, they're going to blow up the bridge! And we must save it. But how?'

"I looked around, but there was unfortunately no one in the immediate vicinity. I had no weapon, but the fellows were no doubt armed and desperate. Into the dark police office I peered, but could see nothing. Then suddenly an idea occurred to me. If I raised the alarm at that moment, they would certainly escape. Both Frank and I could row, therefore I sprang into the police boat at the pier, unmoored her, and urged my son to take an oar with me. In less time than it takes to relate we had pulled across into the shadow of the big arch, and were alongside the empty boat of the conspirators.

"'Row away for your life!' I cried to Frank, as I sprang into the other boat. Then taking out my knife I cut her adrift in an instant and pulled out hard with the tide towards Cleopatra's Needle, while Frank, grasping my intention, shot away towards the Surrey bank. Scarce had I taken out my knife to sever the cord, however, than the three men above noticed me and shouted down in broken English. Indeed, as I pulled off there was the sharp crack of a revolver above me, and I think I narrowly escaped being winged. Nevertheless, I had caught the three blackguards in a trap. The explosive had already been fixed to the crown of the arch, but if they lit the fuse they must themselves be blown to atoms.

"I could hear their shouts and curses from where I rested upon my oars, undecided how to act. If I could only have found at that moment a couple of those brave 'Frontiersmen' or 'Britons,' or members of rifle clubs, who had been such trouble to the enemy out in Essex! There were hundreds upon hundreds of them in London, but they were in the streets still harassing the Germans wherever they could. I rested on my oars in full view of the spies, but beyond revolver range, mounting guard upon them, as it were. They might, after all, decide to carry out their evil design, for if they were good swimmers they might ignite the fuse and then dive into the water, trusting to luck to get to the steps around Cleopatra's Needle. Would they dare do this?

"They kept shouting to me, waving their hands excitedly; but I could not distinguish what they said, so great was the din on the bridge above. Frank had disappeared. Whither he had gone I knew not. He had, however, seen the revolver fired at me, and recognising what was taking place would, I felt certain, seek assistance. One of the men descending the ladder to the water, shouted again to me, waving his hand frantically and pointing upward. From this I concluded that he intended to convey that the time-fuse was already ignited and they were begging for their lives to be saved. Such men are always cowards at the supreme moment when they must face death. I saw the fellow's pale, black-bearded face in the shadow, and an evil, murderous countenance it was, I assure you. But to his shouts, his threats, his frantic appeals I made no response. I had caught all three of them, and paused there triumphant. Would

Frank ever return? Suddenly, however, I saw a boat in the full light out in the centre of the river, crossing in my direction, and hailed it frantically. The answering shout was my boy's, and as he drew nearer I saw that with him were four men armed with rifles. They were evidently four Freeshooters who had been in the roadway above to hold the bridge against the enemy's advance!

"With swift strokes of the oars Frank brought the police boat up alongside mine, and in a few brief sentences I explained the situation and pointed to the three conspirators.

"'Let's shoot them from where we are!' urged one of the men, who wore the little bronze badge of a Frontiersman, and without further word he raised his rifle and let fly at the man clinging to the ladder. The first shot went wide, but the second hit, for with a cry the fellow released his hold and fell back into the dark tide, his lifeless body being carried in our direction.

"The other three men in the boat, members of the Southfields (Putney) Rifle Club, opened a hail of fire upon the pair hidden in the scaffolding above. It was a dangerous proceeding, for had a stray bullet struck that case full of explosives, we should have been all blown to atoms in an instant. Several times all four emptied their magazines into that semicircular opening, but to no effect. The fusilade from the river quickly attracted the attention of those above, to whom the affair was a complete mystery. One rifleman upon the bridge, thinking we were the enemy, actually opened fire upon us; but we shouted who we were, and that spies were concealed below, whereupon he at once desisted.

"A dozen times our party fired, when at last one man's dark body fell heavily into the stream with a loud splash; and about a minute later the third fell backwards, and the rolling river closed over him. All three had thus met with their well-merited deserts.

"'I wonder if they've lit the fuse?' suggested one Frontiersman. 'Let's go nearer.'

"We both rowed forward beneath the arch, when, to our horror, we all saw straight above us, right under the crown, a faint red glow. A fuse was burning there!

"'Quick!' cried one of the sharpshooters. 'There's not an instant to spare. Land me at the ladder, and then row away for your lives. I'll go and put it out if there's yet time.'

"In a moment Frank had turned the bow of the boat, and the gallant fellow had run nimbly up the ladder as he sheered off again. We saw him up upon the scaffolding. We watched him struggling to get the iron cylinder free from the wire with which it was bound against the stone. He tugged and tugged, but in vain. At any instant the thing might explode and cause the death of hundreds, including ourselves. At last, however, something suddenly fell with a big splash into the stream. Then we sent up a ringing cheer.

"Waterloo Bridge was saved!

"People on the bridge above shouted down to us, asking what we were doing, but we were too occupied to reply, and as the man who had so gallantly risked his life to save the grand old bridge from destruction regained the boat we pulled away back to the police pier. Hardly had we got ashore when we distinctly saw a bright red flash beneath the Hungerford railway bridge, followed by a terrific explosion, as part of the massive iron structure fell into the river, a tangled mass of girders. All of us chanced to have our faces turned towards Charing Cross at that moment, and so great was the explosion that we distinctly felt the concussion. The dastardly work was, like the attempt we had just foiled, that of German spies, acting under orders to cause a series of explosions at the time of the entry of the troops into London, thus to increase the terror in the hearts of the populace. But instead of terrifying them it only irritated them. Such wanton destruction was both unpardonable and inconceivable, for it seemed most probable that the Germans would now require the South-Eastern Railway for strategic purposes. And yet their spies had destroyed the bridge.

"With the men who had shot the three Germans and my lad Frank I ascended to Waterloo Bridge by the steps from the Embankment, and there we fought our way through the entrance of the huge barricade that had been hastily erected. The riflemen who had so readily responded to Frank's alarm explained to us that they and their companions, aided by a thousand armed civilians of all kinds, intended to hold the bridge in case the enemy attempted to come southward upon the Surrey side. They told us also that all the bridges were being similarly held by those who had survived the terrible onslaught upon the barricades in the northern suburbs. The Germans were already in the City, the Lord Mayor was a prisoner, and the German flag was flying in the smoke above the War Office, upon the National Gallery, and other buildings. Of all this we were aware, and from the aspect of those fierce, determined-looking men around us we knew that if the enemy's hordes attempted to storm the bridges they would meet with a decidedly warm reception.

"Behind the bridge the multitude pressed on both ways, so that we were stopped close behind the barricade, where I found myself held tightly beside a neat-looking little Maxim, manned by four men in different military uniforms—evidently survivors from the disaster at Epping or at Enfield. This was not the only machine gun, for there were, I saw, four others, so placed that they commanded the whole of Wellington Street, the entrances to the Strand and up to Bow Street. The great crowd in the open space before Somerset House were struggling to get upon the bridge; but news having been brought of bodies of the enemy moving along the Strand from Trafalgar Square, the narrow entrance was quickly blocked up by paving-stones and iron railings, torn up from before some houses in the vicinity.

"We had not long to wait. The people left in Wellington Street, finding their retreat cut off, turned back into the Strand or descended the steps to the Embankment, and so had nearly all dispersed, when, of a sudden, a large body of the enemy's infantry swept round from the Strand, and came full upon the barricade. Next second our Maxims spat their deadly fire with a loud rattle and din, and about me on every hand men were shooting. I waited to see the awful effect of our rain of lead upon the Germans. Hundreds dropped, but hundreds still seemed to take their place. I saw them place a field-gun in position at the corner of the Strand, and then I recognised their intention to shell us. So, being unarmed and a non-combatant, I fled with my son towards my own home in the Kennington Park Road. I had not, however, got across the bridge before shells began to explode against the barricade, blowing it and several of our gallant men to atoms. Once behind I glanced, and saw too plainly that the attempt to hold the bridge was utterly hopeless. There were not sufficient riflemen. Then we both ran on—to save our lives. And you know the rest—ruin, disaster, and death reigned in London that night. Our men fought for their lives and homes, but the Germans, angered at our resistance, gave no quarter to those not in uniform. Ah! the slaughter was awful."

VIII

Germans Sacking the Banks

D ay dawned dismally and wet on September the 21st.
Over London the sky was still obscured by the smoke-pall,
though as the night passed many of the raging fires had spent themselves.

Trafalgar Square was filled with troops, who had piled arms and
were standing at their ease. The men were laughing and smoking,
enjoying a rest after the last forward movement and the street fighting
of that night of horrors.

The losses on both sides during the past three days had been enormous;
of the number of London citizens killed and wounded it was impossible
to calculate. There had, in the northern suburbs, been wholesale butchery
everywhere, so gallantly had the barricades been defended.

Great camps had now been formed in Hyde Park, in the Green Park
between Constitution Hill and Piccadilly, and in St. James's Park. The
Magdeburg Fusiliers were being formed up on the Horse Guards Parade,
and from the flagstaff there now fluttered the ensign of the commander
of an army corps in place of the British flag. A large number of Uhlans
and Cuirassiers were encamped at the west end of the Park, opposite
Buckingham Palace, and both the Wellington Barracks and the Cavalry
Barracks at Knightsbridge were occupied by Germans.

Many officers were already billeted in the Savoy, the Cecil, the Carlton,
the Grand, and Victoria hotels, while the British Museum, the National
Gallery, the South Kensington Museum, the Tower, and a number of
other collections of pictures and antiques were all guarded strongly by
German sentries. The enemy had thus seized our national treasures.

London awoke to find herself a German city.

In the streets lounging groups of travel-worn sons of the Fatherland
were everywhere, and German was heard on every hand. Every ounce
of foodstuff was being rapidly commandeered by hundreds of foraging
parties, who went to each grocer's, baker's, or provision shop in the
various districts, seized all they could find, valued it, and gave official
receipts for it.

The price of food in London that morning was absolutely prohibitive,
as much as two shillings being asked for a twopenny loaf. The Germans

had, it was afterwards discovered, been all the time, since the Sunday when they landed, running over large cargoes of supplies of all sorts to the Essex, Lincolnshire, and Norfolk coasts, where they had established huge supply bases, well knowing that there was not sufficient food in the country to feed their armed hordes in addition to the population.

Shops in Tottenham Court Road, Holborn, Edgeware Road, Oxford Street, Camden Road, and Harrow Road were systematically visited by the foraging parties, who commenced their work at dawn. Those places that were closed and their owners absent were at once broken open, and everything seized and carted to either Hyde Park or St. James's Park, for though Londoners might starve, the Kaiser's troops intended to be fed.

In some cases a patriotic shopkeeper attempted to resist. Indeed, in more than one case a tradesman wilfully set his shop on fire rather than its contents should fall into the enemy's hands. In other cases the tradesmen who received the official German receipts burned them in contempt before the officer's eyes.

The guidance of these foraging parties was, in very many cases, in the hands of Germans in civilian clothes, and it was now seen how complete and helpful the enemy's system of espionage had been in London. Most of these men were Germans who, having served in the army, had come over to England and obtained employment as waiters, clerks, bakers, hairdressers, and private servants, and being bound by their oath to the Fatherland had served their country as spies. Each man, when obeying the Imperial command to join the German arms, had placed in the lapel of his coat a button of a peculiar shape, with which he had long ago been provided, and by which he was instantly recognised as a loyal subject of the Kaiser.

This huge body of German solders, who for years had passed in England as civilians, was, of course, of enormous use to Von Kronhelm, for they acted as guides not only on the march and during the entry to London, but materially assisted in the victorious advance in the Midlands. Indeed, the Germans had for years kept a civilian army in England, and yet we had, ostrich-like, buried our heads in the sand and refused to turn our eyes to the grave peril that had for so long threatened.

Systematically, the Germans were visiting every shop and warehouse in the shopping districts, and seizing everything eatable they could discover. The enemy were taking the food from the mouths of the poor in East and South London, and as they went southward across the river, so the populace retired, leaving their homes at the mercy of the ruthless invader.

Upon all the bridges across the Thames stood German guards, and none were allowed to cross either way without permits.

Soon after dawn Von Kronhelm and his staff rode down Haverstock Hill with a large body of cavalry, and made his formal entry into London, first having an interview with the Lord Mayor, and an hour afterwards establishing his headquarters at the new War Office in Whitehall, over which he hoisted his special flag as Commander-in-Chief. It was found that, though a good deal of damage had been done externally to the building, the interior had practically escaped, save one or two rooms. Therefore, the Field-Marshal installed himself in the private room of the War Minister, and telegraphic and telephonic communication was quickly established, while a wireless telegraph apparatus was placed upon the ruined summit of Big Ben for the purpose of communicating with Germany, in case the cables were interrupted by being cut at sea.

The day after the landing a similar apparatus had been erected on the Monument at Yarmouth, and it had been daily in communication with the one at Bremen. The Germans left nothing to chance. They were always prepared for every emergency.

The clubs in Pall Mall were now being used by German officers, who lounged in easy-chairs, smoking and taking their ease, German soldiers being on guard outside. North of the Thames seemed practically deserted, save for the invaders, who swarmed everywhere. South of the Thames the cowed and terrified populace were asking what the end was to be. What was the Government doing? It had fled to Bristol and left London to its fate, they complained.

What the German demands were was not known until midday, when the *Evening News* published an interview with Sir Claude Harrison, the Lord Mayor, which gave authentic details of them.

They were as follows:—

1. *Indemnity of £300,000,000, paid in ten annual instalments.*
2. *Until this indemnity is paid in full, German troops to occupy Edinburgh, Rosyth, Chatham, Dover, Portsmouth, Devonport, Pembroke, Yarmouth, Hull.*
3. *Cession to Germany of the Shetlands, Orkneys, Bantry Bay, Malta, Gibraltar, and Tasmania.*

4. *India, north of a line drawn from Calcutta to Baroda, to be ceded to Russia.*
5. *The independence of Ireland to be recognised.*

Of the claim of £300,000,000, fifty millions was demanded from London, the sum in question to be paid within twelve hours.

The Lord Mayor had, it appeared, sent his secretary to the Prime Minister at Bristol bearing the original document in the handwriting of Von Kronhelm. The Prime Minister had acknowledged its receipt by telegraph both to the Lord Mayor and to the German Field-Marshal, but there the matter had ended.

The twelve hours' grace was nearly up, and the German Commander, seated in Whitehall, had received no reply.

In the corner of the large, pleasant, well-carpeted room sat a German telegraph engineer with a portable instrument, in direct communication with the Emperor's private cabinet at Potsdam, and over that wire, messages were continually passing and repassing.

The grizzled old soldier paced the room impatiently. His Emperor had only an hour ago sent him a message of warm congratulation, and had privately informed him of the high honours he intended to bestow upon him. The German Eagle was victorious, and London—the great, unconquerable London—lay crushed, torn, and broken.

The marble clock upon the mantelshelf chimed eleven upon its silvery bells, causing Von Kronhelm to turn from the window to glance at his own watch.

"Tell His Majesty that it is eleven o'clock, and that there is no reply to hand," he said sharply in German to the man in uniform seated at the table in the corner.

The instrument clicked rapidly, and a silence followed.

The German Commander waited anxiously. He stood bending slightly over the green tape in order to read the Imperial order the instant it flashed from beneath the sea.

Five minutes—ten minutes passed. The shouting of military commands in German came up from Whitehall below. Nothing else broke the quiet.

Von Kronhelm, his face more furrowed and more serious, again paced the carpet.

Suddenly the little instrument whirred and clicked as its thin green tape rolled out.

In an instant the Generalissimo of the Kaiser's army sprang to the telegraphist's side, and read the Imperial command.

For a moment he held the piece of tape between his fingers, then crushed it in his hand and stood motionless.

He had received orders which, though against his desire, he was compelled to obey.

Summoning several members of his staff who had installed themselves in other comfortable rooms in the vicinity, he held a long consultation with them.

In the meantime telegraphic despatches were received from Sheffield, Manchester, Birmingham, and other German headquarters, all telling the same story—the complete investment and occupation of the big cities and the pacification of the inhabitants.

One hour's grace was, however, allowed to London—till noon.

Then orders were issued, bugles rang out across the parks, and in the main thoroughfares, where arms were piled, causing the troops to fall in, and within a quarter of an hour large bodies of infantry and engineers were moving along the Strand, in the direction of the City.

At first the reason of all this was a mystery, but very shortly it was realised what was intended when a detachment of the 5th Hanover Regiment advanced to the gate of the Bank of England opposite the Exchange, and, after some difficulty, broke it open and entered, followed by some engineers of Von Mirbach's Division. The building was very soon occupied, and, under the direction of General von Klepper himself, an attempt was made to open the strong-rooms, wherein was stored that vast hoard of England's wealth. What actually occurred at that spot can only be imagined, as the commander of the IVth Army Corps and one or two officers and men were the only persons present. It is surmised, however, that the strength of the vaults was far greater than they had imagined, and that, though they worked for hours, all was in vain.

While this was in progress, however, parties of engineers were making organised raids upon the banks in Lombard Street, Lothbury, Moorgate Street, and Broad Street, as well as upon branch banks in Oxford Street, the Strand, and other places in the West End.

At one bank on the left-hand side of Lombard Street, dynamite being used to force the strong-room, the first bullion was seized, while at nearly all the banks sooner or later the vaults were opened, and great bags and boxes of gold coin were taken out and conveyed in carefully-guarded carts to the Bank of England, now in the possession of Germany.

In some banks—those of more modern construction—the greatest resistance was offered by the huge steel doors and concrete and steel walls and other devices for security. But nothing could, alas! resist the high explosives used, and in the end breaches were made, in all cases, and wealth uncounted and untold extracted and conveyed to Threadneedle Street for safe keeping.

Engineers and infantry handled those heavy boxes and those big bundles of securities gleefully, officers carefully counting each box or bag or packet as it was taken out to be carted or carried away by hand.

German soldiers under guard struggled along Lothbury beneath great burdens of gold, and carts, requisitioned out of the East End, rumbled heavily all the afternoon, escorted by soldiers. Hammersmith, Camberwell, Hampstead, and Willesden yielded up their quota of the great wealth of London; but though soon after four o'clock a breach was made in the strong-rooms of the Bank of England by means of explosives, nothing in the vaults was touched. The Germans simply entered there and formally took possession.

The coin collected from other banks was carefully kept, each separate from another, and placed in various rooms under strong guards, for it seemed to be the intention of Germany simply to hold London's wealth as security.

That afternoon very few banks—except the German ones—escaped notice. Of course, there were a few small branches in the suburbs which remained unvisited, yet by six o'clock Von Kronhelm was in possession of enormous quantities of gold.

In one or two quarters there had been opposition on the part of the armed guards established by the banks at the first news of the invasion. But any such resistance had, of course, been futile, and the man who had dared to fire upon the German soldiers had in every case been shot down.

Thus, when darkness fell, Von Kronhelm, from the corner of his room in the War Office, was able to report to his Imperial Master that not only had he occupied London, but that, receiving no reply to his demand for indemnity, he had sacked it and taken possession not only of the Bank of England, but of the cash deposits in most of the other banks in the metropolis.

That night the evening papers described the wild happenings of the afternoon, and London saw herself not only shattered but ruined.

The frightened populace across the river stood breathless.

What was now to happen?

Though London lay crushed and occupied by the enemy, though the Lord Mayor was a prisoner of war and the banks in the hands of the Germans, though the metropolis had been wrecked and more than half its inhabitants had fled southward and westward into the country, yet the enemy received no reply to their demand for an indemnity and the cession of British territory.

Von Kronhelm, ignorant of what had occurred in the House of Commons at Bristol, sat in Whitehall and wondered. He knew well that the English were no fools, and their silence, therefore, caused him considerable uneasiness. He had lost in the various engagements over 50,000 men, yet nearly 200,000 still remained. His army of invasion was a no mean responsibility, especially when at any moment the British might regain command of the sea. His supplies and reinforcements would then be at once cut off. It was impossible for him to live upon the country, and his food bases in Suffolk and Essex were not sufficiently extensive to enable him to make a prolonged campaign. Indeed, the whole scheme of operations which had been so long discussed and perfected in secret in Berlin was more of the nature of a raid than a prolonged siege.

The German Field-Marshal sat alone and reflected. Had he been aware of the true state of affairs he would certainly have had considerable cause for alarm. True, though Lord Byfield had made such a magnificent stand, considering the weakness of the force at his disposal, and London was occupied, yet England, even now, was not conquered.

No news had leaked out from Bristol. Indeed, Parliament had taken every precaution that its deliberations were in secret.

The truth, however, may be briefly related. On the previous day the House had met at noon in the Colston Hall—a memorable sitting, indeed. The Secretary of State for War had, after prayers, risen in the hall and read an official despatch he had just received from Lord Byfield, giving the news of the last stand made by the British north of Enfield, and the utter hopelessness of the situation.

It was received by the assembled House in ominous silence.

During the past week through that great hall the Minister's deep voice, shaken by emotion, had been daily heard as he was compelled to report defeat after defeat of the British arms. Both sides of the House had, after the first few days, been forced to recognise Germany's superiority in numbers, in training, in organisation—in fact, in everything appertaining to military power. Von Kronhelm's strategy had been perfect. He knew

CITY OF LONDON.

CITIZENS OF LONDON.

WE, the GENERAL COMMANDING the German Imperial Army occupying London, give notice that:

(1) THE STATE OF WAR AND OF SIEGE continues to exist, and all categories of crime, more especially the contravention of all orders already issued, will be judged by Councils of War, and punished in conformity with martial law.

(2) THE INHABITANTS OF LONDON and its suburbs are ordered to instantly deliver up all arms and ammunition of whatever kind they possess. The term arms includes firearms, sabres, swords, daggers, revolvers, and sword-canes. Landlords and occupiers of houses are charged to see that this order is carried out, but in the case of their absence the municipal authorities and officials of the London County Council are charged to make domiciliary visits, minute and searching, being accompanied by a military guard.

(3) ALL NEWSPAPERS, JOURNALS, GAZETTES, AND PROCLAMATIONS, of whatever description, are hereby prohibited, and until further notice nothing further must be printed, except documents issued publicly by the military commander.

(4) ANY PRIVATE PERSON OR PERSONS taking arms against the German troops after this notice will be EXECUTED.

(5) ON THE CONTRARY, the Imperial German troops will respect private property, and no requisition will be allowed to be made unless it bears the authorisation of the Commander-in-Chief.

(6) ALL PUBLIC PLACES are to be closed at 8 P.M. All persons found in the streets of London after 8 P.M. will be arrested by the patrols. There is no exception to this rule except in the case of German Officers, and also in the case of doctors visiting their

patients. Municipal officials will also be allowed out, providing they obtain a permit from the German headquarters.

(7) Municipal Authorities Must provide for the lighting of the streets. In cases where this is impossible, each householder must hang a lantern outside his house from nightfall until 8 A.M.

(8) After To-morrow morning, at 10 o'clock, the women and children of the population of London will be allowed to pass without hindrance.

(9) Municipal Authorities Must, with as little delay as possible, provide accommodation for the German troops in private dwellings, in fire-stations, barracks, hotels, and houses that are still habitable.

Von Kronhelm,
Commander-in-Chief.

German Military Headquarters,
Whitehall, London, *September 21, 1910*.

Von Kronhelm's Proclamation to the Citizens of London.

more of Eastern England than the British Commander himself, and his marvellous system of spies and advance agents—Germans who had lived for years in England—had assisted him forward, until he had now occupied London, the city always declared to be impregnable.

Through the whole of September 20 the Minister constantly received despatches from the British Field-Marshal and from London itself, yet each telegram communicated to the House seemed more hopeless than its predecessor.

The debate, however, proceeded through the afternoon. The Opposition were bitterly attacking the Government and the Blue Water School for its gross negligence in the past, and demanding to know the whereabouts of the remnant of the British Navy. The First Lord of the Admiralty flatly refused to make any statement. The whereabouts of our Navy at that moment was, he said, a secret which must, at all hazards, be withheld from our enemy. The Admiralty were not asleep, as the country believed, but were fully alive to the seriousness of the crisis. He urged the House to remain patient, saying that as soon as he dared make a clear statement, he would do so.

This was greeted by loud jeers from the Opposition, from whose benches, members, one after another, rose, and, using hard epithets, blamed the Government for the terrible disaster. The cutting down of our defences, the meagre naval programmes, the discouragement of the Volunteers and of recruiting, and the disregard of Lord Roberts' scheme in 1906 for universal military training, were, they declared, responsible for what had occurred. The Government had been culpably negligent, and Mr. Haldane's scheme had been all insufficient. Indeed, it had been nothing short of criminal to mislead the Empire into a false sense of security which did not exist.

For the past three years Germany, while sapping our industries, had sent her spies into our midst, and laughed at us for our foolish insular superiority. She had turned her attention from France to ourselves, notwithstanding the *entente cordiale*. She remembered how the much-talked-of Franco-Russian alliance had fallen to pieces, and relied upon a similar outcome of the friendship between France and Great Britain.

The aspect of the House, too, was strange; the Speaker in his robes looked out of place in his big uncomfortable chair, and members sat on cane-bottomed chairs instead of their comfortable benches at Westminster. As far as possible the usual arrangement of the House was adhered to, except that the Press were now excluded, official reports being furnished to them at midnight.

The clerks' table was a large plain one of stained wood, but upon it was the usual array of despatch-boxes, while the Serjeant-at-Arms, in his picturesque dress, was still one of the most prominent figures. The lack of committee rooms, of an adequate lobby, and of a refreshment department caused much inconvenience, though a temporary post and telegraph office had been established within the building, and a separate line connected the Prime Minister's room with Downing Street.

If the Government were denounced in unmeasured terms, its defence was equally vigorous. Thus, through that never-to-be-forgotten afternoon the sitting continued past the dinner hour on to late in the evening.

Time after time the despatches from London were placed in the hands of the War Minister, but, contrary to the expectation of the House, he vouchsafed no further statement. It was noticed that just before ten o'clock he consulted in an earnest undertone with the Prime Minister, the First Lord of the Admiralty, and the Home Secretary, and that a quarter of an hour later all four went out and were closeted in one of the smaller rooms with other members of the Cabinet for nearly half an hour.

Then the Secretary of State for War re-entered the House and resumed his seat in silence.

A few minutes afterwards, Mr. Thomas Askern, member for one of the metropolitan boroughs, and a well-known newspaper proprietor, who had himself received several private despatches, rose and received leave to put a question to the War Minister.

"I would like to ask the Right Honourable the Secretary of State for War," he said, "whether it is not a fact that soon after noon to-day the enemy, having moved his heavy artillery to certain positions commanding North London, and finding the capital strongly barricaded, proceeded to bombard it? Whether that bombardment, according to the latest despatches, is not still continuing at this moment; whether it is not a fact that enormous damage has already been done to many of the principal buildings of the metropolis, including the Government Offices at Whitehall, and whether great loss of life has not been occasioned?"

The question produced the utmost sensation. The House during the whole afternoon had been in breathless anxiety as to what was actually happening in London; but the Government held the telegraphs and telephone, and the only private despatches that had come to Bristol were the two received by some roundabout route known only to the ingenious journalists who had despatched them. Indeed, the despatches had been conveyed the greater portion of the way by motor-car.

A complete silence fell. Every face was turned towards the War Minister, who, seated with outstretched legs, was holding in his hand a fresh despatch he had just received.

He rose, and, in his deep bass voice, said—

"In reply to the honourable member for South-East Brixton, the statement he makes appears, from information which has just reached me, to be correct. The Germans are, unfortunately, bombarding London. Von Kronhelm, it is reported, is at Hampstead, and the zone of the enemy's artillery reaches, in some cases, as far south as the Thames itself. It is true, as the honourable member asserts, an enormous amount of damage has already been done to various buildings, and there has undoubtedly been great loss of life. My latest information is that the non-combatant inhabitants—old persons, women, and children—are in flight across the Thames, and that the barricades in the principal roads leading in from the north are held strongly by the armed populace, driven back into London."

He sat down without further word.

A tall, thin, white-moustached man rose at that moment from the Opposition side of the House. Colonel Farquhar, late of the Royal Marines, was a well-known military critic, and represented West Bude.

"And this," he said, "is the only hope of England! The defence of London by an armed mob, pitted against the most perfectly equipped and armed force in the world! Londoners are patriotic, I grant. They will die fighting for their homes, as every Englishman will when the moment comes; yet, what can we hope, when patriotism is ranged against modern military science? There surely is patriotism in the savage negro races of Central Africa, a love of country perhaps as deep as in the white man's heart; yet a little strategy, a few Maxims, and all defence is quickly at an end. And so it must inevitably be with London. I contend, Mr. Speaker," he went on, "that by the ill-advised action of the Government from the first hour of their coming into power, we now find ourselves conquered. It only remains for them now to make terms of peace as honourable to themselves as the unfortunate circumstances will admit. Let the country itself judge their actions in the light of events of to-day, and let the blood of the poor murdered women and children of London be upon their heads. (Shame.) To resist further is useless. Our military organisation is in chaos, our miserably weak army is defeated, and in flight. I declare to this House that we should sue at this very moment for peace—a dishonourable peace though it be; but the bitter truth is too plain—England is conquered!"

As he sat down amid the "hear, hears" and loud applause of the Opposition there rose a keen-faced, dark-haired, clean-shaven man of thirty-seven or so. He was Gerald Graham, younger son of an aristocratic house, the Yorkshire Grahams, who sat for North-East Rutland. He was a man of brilliant attainments at Oxford, a splendid orator, a distinguished writer and traveller, whose keen brown eye, lithe upright figure, quick activity, and smart appearance rendered him a born leader of men. For the past five years he had been marked out as a "coming man."

As a soldier he had seen hard service in the Boer War, being mentioned twice in despatches; as an explorer he had led a party through the heart of the Congo and fought his way back to civilisation through an unexplored land with valiant bravery that had saved the lives of his companions. He was a man who never sought notoriety. He hated to be lionised in society, refused the shoals of cards of invitation which poured in upon him, and stuck to his Parliamentary duties, and keeping faith with his constituents to the very letter.

As he stood up silent for a moment, gazing around him fearlessly, he presented a striking figure, and in his navy serge suit he possessed the unmistakable cut of the smart, well-groomed Englishman who was also a man of note.

The House always listened to him, for he never spoke without he had something of importance to say. And the instant he was up a silence fell.

"Mr. Speaker," he said, in a clear, ringing voice, "I entirely disagree with my honourable friend the member for West Bude. England is not conquered! She is not beaten!"

The great hall rang with loud and vociferous cheers from both sides of the House. Then, when quiet was restored by the Speaker's stentorian "Order-r-r! Order!" he continued—

"London may be invested and bombarded. She may even be sacked, but Englishmen will still fight for their homes, and fight valiantly. If we have a demand for indemnity, let us refuse to pay it. Let us civilians— let the civilians in every corner of England—arm themselves and unite to drive out the invader! (Loud cheers.) I contend, Mr. Speaker, that there are millions of able-bodied men in this country who, if properly organised, will be able to gradually exterminate the enemy. Organisation is all that is required. Our vast population will rise against the Germans, and before the tide of popular indignation and desperate resistance the power of the invader must soon be swept away. Do not let us sit calmly here in security, and acknowledge that we are beaten. Remember, we have at this moment to uphold the ancient tradition of the British race, the honour of our forefathers, who have never been conquered. Shall we acknowledge ourselves conquered in this the twentieth century?"

"No!" rose from hundreds of voices, for the House was now carried away by young Graham's enthusiasm.

"Then let us organise!" he urged. "Let us fight on. Let every man who can use a sword or gun come forward, and we will commence hostilities against the Kaiser's forces that shall either result in their total extermination or in the power of England being extinguished. Englishmen will die hard. I myself will, with the consent of this House, head the movement, for I know that in the country we have millions

WILLIAM LE QUEUX

who will follow me and will be equally ready to die for our country if necessary. Let us withdraw this statement that we are conquered. The real, earnest fight is now to commence," he shouted, his voice ringing clearly through the hall. "Let us bear our part, each one of us. If we organise and unite, we shall drive the Kaiser's hordes into the sea. They shall sue us for peace, and be made to pay us an indemnity, instead of us paying one to them. I will lead!" he shouted; "who will follow me?"

In London the Lord Mayor's patriotic proclamations were now obliterated by a huge bill bearing the German Imperial arms, the text of which told its own grim tale. It is reproduced on next page, and at its side was printed a translation in German text.

In the meantime the news of the fall of London was being circulated by the Germans to every town throughout the kingdom, their despatches being embellished by lurid descriptions of the appalling losses inflicted upon the English. In Manchester, a great poster, headed by the German Imperial arms, was posted up on the Town Hall, the Exchange, and other places, in which Von Kronhelm announced the occupation of London; while in Leeds, Bradford, Stockport, and Sheffield, similarly worded official announcements were also posted. The Press in all towns occupied by the Germans had been suppressed, papers only appearing in order to publish the enemy's orders. Therefore, this official intelligence was circulated by proclamation, calculated to impress upon the inhabitants of the country how utterly powerless they were.

While Von Kronhelm sat in that large sombre room in the War Office, with his telegraph instrument to Potsdam ever ticking, and the wireless telegraphy constantly in operation, he wondered, and still wondered, why the English made no response to his demands. He was in London. He had carried out his Emperor's instructions to the letter, he had received the Imperial thanks, and he held all the gold coin he could discover in London as security. Yet, without some reply from the British Government, his position was an insecure one. Even his thousand and one spies who had served him so well ever since he had placed foot upon English soil could tell him nothing. The deliberations of the House of Commons at Bristol were a secret.

In Bristol the hot, fevered night had given place to a gloriously sunny morning, with a blue and cloudless sky. Above Leigh Woods the lark rose high in the sky, trilling his song, and the bells of Bristol rang out as merrily as they ever did, and above the Colston Hall still floated the Royal Standard—a sign that the House had not yet adjourned.

Notice and Advice.

To the Citizens of London.

I Address You Seriously.

We are neighbours, and in time of peace cordial relations have always existed between us. I therefore address you from my heart in the cause of humanity.

Germany is at war with England. We have been forced to penetrate into your country.

But each human life spared, and all property saved, we regard as in the interests of both religion and humanity.

We are at war, and both sides have fought a loyal fight.

Our desire is, however, to spare disarmed citizens and the inhabitants of all towns and villages.

We maintain a severe discipline, and we wish to have it known that punishment of the severest character will be inflicted upon any who are guilty of hostility to the Imperial German arms, either open or in secret.

To our regret any incitements, cruelties, or brutalities we must judge with equal severity.

I therefore call upon all local mayors, magistrates, clergy, and schoolmasters to urge upon the populace, and upon the heads of families, to urge upon those under their protection, and upon their domestics, to refrain from committing any act of hostility whatsoever against my soldiers.

All misery avoided is a good work in the eye of our Sovereign Judge, who sees all men.

I earnestly urge you to heed this advice, and I trust in you.

Take notice!

Von Kronhelm,
Commanding the Imperial German Army.

German Military Headquarters,
Whitehall, London, *September 20, 1910*.

While Von Kronhelm held London, Lord Byfield and the remnant of the British Army, who had suffered such defeat in Essex and north of London, had, four days later, retreated to Chichester and Salisbury, where reorganisation was in rapid progress. One division of the defeated troops had encamped at Horsham. The survivors of those who had fought the battle of Charnwood Forest, and had acted so gallantly in the defence of Birmingham, were now encamped on the Malvern Hills, while the defenders of Manchester were at Shrewsbury. Speaking roughly, therefore, our vanquished troops were massing at four points, in an endeavour to make a last attack upon the invader. The Commander-in-Chief, Lord Byfield, was near Salisbury, and at any hour he knew that the German legions might push westward from London to meet him and to complete the *coup*.

The League of Defenders formed by Gerald Graham and his friends was, however, working independently. The wealthier classes, who, driven out of London, were now living in cottages and tents in various parts of Berks, Wilts, and Hants, worked unceasingly on behalf of the League, while into Plymouth, Exmouth, Swanage, Bristol, and Southampton more than one ship had already managed to enter laden with arms and ammunition of all kinds, sent across by the agents of the League in France. The cargoes were of a very miscellaneous character, from modern Maxims to old-fashioned rifles that had seen service in the war of 1870. There were hundreds of modern rifles, sporting guns, revolvers, swords— in fact, every weapon imaginable, modern and old-fashioned. These were at once taken charge of by the local branches of the League, and to those men who presented their tickets of identification the arms were served out, and practice conducted in the open fields. Three shiploads of rifles were known to have been captured by German warships, one off Start Point, another a few miles outside Padstow, and a third within sight of the coastguard at Selsey Bill. Two other ships were blown up in the Channel by drifting mines. The running of arms across from France and Spain was a very risky proceeding; yet the British skipper is nothing if not patriotic, and every man who crossed the Channel on those dangerous errands took his life in his hand.

Into Liverpool, Whitehaven, and Milford weapons were also coming over from Ireland, even though several German cruisers, who had been up at Lamlash to cripple the Glasgow trade, had now come south, and were believed still to be in the Irish Sea.

IX

What was Happening at Sea

Our fleet, however, was not inactive. The Germans had mined the Straits of Dover, and one of the turbine Channel steamers had been sunk with great loss of life. They had bombarded Brighton, mined Portsmouth, and made a raid on the South Wales coal ports.

How these raiders were pursued is best described in the official history of the invasion, as follows:—

The Trevose wireless station signalled that the Germans were off Lundy about 2 P.M., steaming west with fourteen ships of all kinds, some moving very slowly. The *Lion* and *Kincardineshire* at once altered course to the north, so as to intercept them and draw across their line of retreat. At the same time they learnt that two British protected cruisers had arrived from Devonport off the Longships, and were holding the entrance to the English Channel, and moving slowly north behind them.

About 3.30 the wireless waves came in so strongly from the northeast that the captain of the *Lion*, who was in charge of the cruiser division, became certain of the proximity of the German force. The signals could not be interpreted, as they were tuned on a different system from the British. The Germans must have also felt the British signals, since about this time they divided, the three fast liners increasing speed and heading west, while the rest of the detachment steered north-west. The older German vessels were delayed some fifteen minutes by the work of destroying the four colliers, which they had carried off forcibly with them from Cardiff, and removing their crews. Delay at such a moment was most dangerous.

Soon after 3.45 P.M. the lookout on board the *Lion* reported from the masthead, smoke on the horizon right ahead. The *Lion's* head was set towards the smoke, which could be only faintly seen, and her speed was increased to twenty-one knots. The *Kincardineshire* altered course simultaneously—she was ten miles away on the port beam of the *Lion*, and in constant communication by wireless with the *Selkirk*, which was still farther out. Ten minutes later the *Selkirk* signalled that she saw smoke, and that with the ten destroyers accompanying her she was steering towards it. Her message added that the Irish Sea destroyers were in sight, coming in very fast from the north, nine strong, with intervals of two miles between each boat, still keeping their speed of thirty knots.

The cordon was now complete, and the whole force of twenty-two cruisers and torpedo craft turned in towards the spot where the enemy was located. At 4.5 the lookout on the *Lion* reported a second cloud of smoke on the horizon, rather more to starboard than the one first seen, which had been for some minutes steadily moving west. This second cloud was moving very slowly north-westwards.

The captain of the *Lion* determined to proceed with his own ship towards this second cloud, and directed the *Kincardineshire*, which was slightly the faster cruiser, to follow the movements of the first-seen smoke and support the *Selkirk* in attacking the ships from which it proceeded.

The enemy's fleet soon came into view several miles away. Three large steamers were racing off towards the Atlantic and the west; seven smaller ships were steaming slowly north-west. In the path of the three big liners were drawn up the *Selkirk* and the ten destroyers of the Devonport flotilla, formed in line abreast, with intervals of two miles between each vessel, so as to cover as wide an extent of sea as possible. The *Kincardineshire* was heading fast to support the *Selkirk* and attack the three large German ships. Farther to the north, but as yet invisible to the *Lion*, and right in the path of the squadron of old German ships, were nine destroyers of the Irish Sea flotilla, vessels each of 800 tons and thirty-three knots, also drawn up in line abreast, with intervals of two miles to cover a wide stretch of water.

The moment the Germans came into view the two protected cruisers at Land's End were called up by wireless telegraphy, and ordered to steam at nineteen knots towards the *Selkirk*. The two Devonport battleships, which had now reached Land's End, were warned of the presence of the enemy.

Sighting the ten Devonport destroyers and the *Selkirk* to the west of them, the three fast German liners, which were the *Deutschland*, *Kaiser Wilhelm II*, and *Kronprinz Wilhelm*, all three good for twenty-three knots in any weather, made a rush for the gap between the Devonport destroyers and the *Kincardineshire*. Perceiving their intention, the *Kincardineshire* turned to cut them off, and the ten destroyers and the *Selkirk* headed to engage them. In danger of all being brought to action and destroyed if they kept together, the German liners scattered at 4.15: the *Deutschland* steered south-east to pass between the *Kincardineshire* and the *Lion*; the *Kaiser Wilhelm* steered boldly for a destroyer which was closing in on her from the starboard bow; and the *Kronprinz Wilhelm* ran due north.

The *Deutschland*, racing along at a tremendous speed, passed between the *Kincardineshire* and the *Lion*. The *Lion* at long range put three 9.2-inch shells into her without stopping her; the *Kincardineshire* gave her a broadside from her 6-inch guns at about 5000 yards, and hit her several times. But the British fire did not bring her to, and she went off to the south-west at a great pace, going so fast that it was clear the armoured cruisers would stand little chance of overhauling her.

The *Kaiser Wilhelm* charged through the line of destroyers, receiving a heavy fire from the 6-inch weapons of the *Selkirk* and *Kincardineshire*, and in her turn pouring a rapid fire upon two of the Devonport destroyers, which attempted to torpedo her, and missed her at about 900 yards. The *Selkirk*, however, was close astern of her, and with her engines going twenty-three knots, which was just a fraction less than what the German engineers were doing, concentrated upon her a very heavy fire from all her 6-inch guns that would bear.

The fore-turret with its two 6-inch weapons in two minutes put twenty shells into the German stern. One of these projectiles must have hit the steering gear, for suddenly and unexpectedly the *Kaiser Wilhelm* came round on a wide circle, and as she wheeled, the broadside of the British cruiser came into action with a loud crash, and at 3000 yards rained 100-lb. and 12-lb. shells upon the liner. The beating of the pom-poms in the *Selkirk* could be heard above the roar of the cannonade; and seeing that the liner was now doomed, the British destroyers drew off a little.

Under the storm of shells the German crew could not get the steering gear in working order. The great ship was still turning round and round in a gigantic circle, when the *Lion* came into action with her two 9.2's and her broadside of eight 6-inch weapons. Round after round from these was poured into the German ship. The British gunners shot for the water-line, and got it repeatedly. At 4.40, after a twenty minutes' fight, the white flag went up on board the *Kaiser Wilhelm*, and it was seen that she was sinking. Her engines had stopped, she was on fire in twenty places, and her decks were covered with the dying and the dead. The first of the raiders was accounted for.

Meantime, the *Kronprinz Wilhelm* had with equal swiftness dashed north, receiving only a few shots from the *Selkirk*, as she passed her, 8000 yards away. The British armoured cruiser *Kincardineshire* followed in the German ship's wake ten miles astern and quite out of range. The German liner was seen by the ocean-going destroyers of the Irish Sea flotilla, which headed after her, and four of them going thirty knots easily drew ahead of her. To attack such a vessel with the torpedo was an undertaking which had no promise of success.

The British destroyer officers, however, were equal to the occasion. They employed skilful tactics to effect their object. The four big destroyers took station right ahead of the German ship and about 1500 yards away from her. In this direction none of her guns would bear. From this position they opened on her bows with their sternmost 13-pounders, seeking to damage the bow of the *Kronprinz Wilhelm*, breach the forward compartments, and so delay the ship. If she turned or yawed, her turn must give time for the *Kincardineshire* to get at her.

The gunners in the four destroyers shot magnificently. Their projectiles were small, but for fifteen minutes they made incessant hits upon the German ship's bow. At last their punishment had the desired effect upon her. Angry at the attack of these puny little antagonists, the German captain turned to bring his broadside to bear. As he did so, the destroyers quickened to thirty knots, and altered course. Though the German guns maintained a rapid fire upon them, they were going so fast that they escaped out of effective range without any serious damage, regained their station on their enemy's bow, and then reduced speed till they were within easy range for their little guns. But in the interval the *Kincardineshire* had perceptibly gained on the German ship, and was now within extreme range. About 5.50 P.M. she fired a shot from her fore-turret, and, as it passed over the German ship, opened a slow but precise fire from all her 6-inch guns that would bear at about 9000 yards range.

The small shells of the destroyers were beginning to have some effect. The fore-compartment of the *Kronprinz Wilhelm* was riddled, and water was pouring into it at such a pace that the pumps could not keep the inrush down. The trim of the ship altered slightly, and with this alteration of trim her speed fell by nearly a knot. The *Kincardineshire* began to gain visibly, and her fire to tell more and more. At 6.50 she was only 7000 yards off the German ship, and her 6-inch guns began to make many hits on the enemy's stern.

To increase his speed to the utmost the captain of the *Kincardineshire*

WILLIAM LE QUEUX

set all his spare hands at work to jettison coal, and flung overboard every bit of lumber. The spare water in his tanks shared the fate of his surplus fuel. At the same time the stokers in the engine-rooms were told that the ship was closing the enemy, and worked with a redoubled will. Large parties of bluejackets led by lieutenants were sent down to pass coal from the bunkers; in the engine-rooms the water was spouting from half a dozen hoses upon the bearings. The engineer-lieutenants, standing in a deluge of spray, kept the pointer of the stokehold telegraphs always at "more steam." Smoke poured from the funnels, for no one now cared about the niceties of naval war.

The ship seemed to bound forward, and with a satisfied smile the engineer-captain came down into the turmoil to tell his men that the cruiser was going twenty-four knots, her speed on her trials nearly six years before. Five minutes later the shock and heavy roar of firing from twenty guns told the men below that the broadside battery was coming into action, and that the race was won.

At 7.25 the *Kincardineshire* had closed the German ship within 5000 yards. About this time the *Kronprinz Wilhelm's* speed seemed markedly to decline, and the big armoured cruiser gained upon her rapidly, spouting shell from all her guns that would bear.

At 7.40 the British warship was only 3000 yards off, and slightly altered course to bring her enemy broader on the beam and get the broadside into battle. Five minutes later a succession of 6-inch hits from the British guns caused a great explosion in the German ship, and from under the base of her fourth funnel rose a dense cloud of steam, followed by the glow of fire through the gathering darkness.

A minute later the *Kronprinz Wilhelm* stopped, and the chase was over. She hoisted the white flag, while her captain opened her sea-valves, to send her to the bottom. But the British destroyers were too quick for him; a boarding party dashed on board from the *Camelopard*, and closed the Kingston valves before enough water had been taken into the double bottom to endanger the liner.

In this brief action between two very unequally matched ships, the Germans suffered very severely. They had fifty officers and men killed or wounded out of a crew of 500, while in the British cruiser and the destroyers only fifteen casualties were recorded. The *Kincardineshire* stood by her valuable prize to secure it and clear the vessel of the German crew. The *Kronprinz Wilhelm* was on fire in two places, and was badly damaged by the British shells. One of her boilers had exploded, and her fore-compartment was full of water. But she was duly taken into Milford next morning, to be repaired at Pembroke Dockyard, and hoist the British flag.

Meantime, the *Lion* had been attending to the other German vessels. After taking part in the destruction of the *Kaiser Wilhelm* she had turned north and chased them, aided by the *Selkirk*. Five of the ocean-going destroyers and the ten Devonport destroyers had already proceeded to keep them under observation and harry them to the utmost.

They were still going north-west, and had obtained about twenty-five miles' start of the two big British cruisers. But as they could only steam twelve or thirteen knots, while the British ships were good for twenty-one, they had little chance of escape, the less so as the 14,000-ton-protected cruiser *Terrific*, the flagship of the torpedo flotilla, was fast coming up at twenty knots from Kingstown, and at 6 P.M. had passed the Smalls, reporting herself by wireless telegraphy, and taking charge of the operations in virtue of the fact that she carried a rear-admiral's flag.

The approach of this new antagonist must have been known to the Germans by the indications which her wireless waves afforded. On the way she had received the news of a serious British defeat in the North Sea, and her Admiral was smarting to have some share in reversing that great calamity.

Before dusk she was in sight of the seven German ships, with their attendant British destroyers. The Germans once more scattered. The *Gefion*, which was the only really fast ship, made off towards the west, but was promptly headed off by the *Terrific* and driven back. The *Pfeil* headed boldly towards Milford, and as the batteries at that place were not yet manned, caused some moments of great anxiety to the British. Two of the fast ocean-going destroyers were ordered to run in between her and the port and to torpedo her if she attempted to make her way in through the narrow entrance. Observing their manœuvre, the German captain once more turned south. The other five German ships kept in line, and attemped to pass between the Smalls and the Welsh coast.

The *Terrific* had now closed the *Gefion* sufficiently to open fire with her 9.2's and 6-inch guns. The fight was so unequal that it could not be long protracted. With every disadvantage of speed, protection, and armament, the German cruiser was shattered by a few broadsides, and, in a sinking condition, surrendered just after dark.

The *Selkirk* and *Lion* passed her and fired a few shots at her just before she struck, but were ordered by the Rear-Admiral to attend to the other German ships. Five shots from the *Lion's* bow 9.2-inch gun settled the *Pfeil*, which beached herself in Freshwater Bay, where the crew blew up the ship, and were captured a few hours later. Thus four of the ten raiders were disposed of, and there now remained only five within reach of the British ships clearing the Bristol Channel.

It was 9 P.M. before the *Lion* and *Selkirk* had closed on the remnant of the German squadron which had raided the South Wales ports sufficiently to engage it. The five German ships had passed through the dangerous passage between the Smalls and the mainland without misadventure, and were slightly to the north-west of St. David's Head.

Right ahead of them were the British destroyers, ready to co-operate in the attack as soon as the big cruisers came up; abreast of the German line were the two large British armoured cruisers; well astern of them was the *Terrific*, heading to cut off their retreat. The German ships were formed up with the *Cormoran* at the head, and astern of her in line the *Sperber*, *Schwalbe*, *Meteor*, and *Falke*. None of these poor old vessels mounted anything larger than a 4-inch gun, and none of them could steam more than twelve knots. The only course remaining for them was to make some show of fight for the honour of the German flag, and to their credit be it said that they did this.

The task of the British cruisers was a simple one. It was to destroy the German vessels with their powerful ordnance, keeping at such a distance that the German projectiles could do them no serious damage. At 9.10 the fight began, and the *Lion* and *Selkirk* opened with their entire broadsides upon the *Cormoran* and *Falke*. The Germans gallantly replied to the two great cruisers, and for some minutes kept up a vigorous fire.

Then the *Cormoran* began to burn, and a few minutes later the *Falke* was seen to be sinking. The British ships turned all their guns upon the three remaining vessels. The *Meteor* blew up with a terrific crash, and went to the bottom; the *Sperber* and *Schwalbe* immediately after this hoisted the white flag and made their surrender. The battle, if it could be called a battle, was over before ten, and the officers and men of the British ships set to work to rescue their enemies. The British casualties were again trifling, and the German list a heavy one. Of the officers and men in the five German cruisers over a hundred were drowned, killed, or wounded.

Thus the British Navy had made a speedy end of the raiders in the Bristol Channel, and, owing to the vigorous initiative of the Devonport commander and the Rear-Admiral in charge of the torpedo flotilla, had practically wiped out a German squadron. Only the *Deutschland* had got away to sea, but the Portsmouth armoured cruisers had been instructed to proceed in search of her, co-operating with the cruisers of the Channel Fleet.

The Channel Cruiser Squadron during the afternoon of Sunday had been ordered to deflect its movement and steer for Queenstown, so as to get across the line of retreat of the German ships. Constant communication with it was maintained by the great long-distance naval wireless station at Devonport, one of the three such stations for which funds had been obtained with the utmost difficulty by the Admiralty from a reluctant Treasury. Its value at the present juncture was immense.

As night came down, Rear-Admiral Hunter, in command of the Channel Cruiser Squadron, was informed that a large German liner had escaped from the Bristol Channel. His most advanced ship was now in touch with Queenstown, and about sixty miles from the place. The rest of his force was spaced at intervals of ten miles between each ship, covering eighty miles of sea.

The two protected cruisers of the Devonport Reserve Squadron, *Andromache* and *Sirius*, ships of 11,000 tons and about nineteen knots sea speed, had taken station to the north of the Scillies, with one of the battleships of the Devonport Reserve supporting them. The other battleship was posted between the Scillies and the Longships. Off Land's End a powerful naval force was fast assembling, as ships and torpedo vessels came up one by one from Devonport as soon as they had mobilised.

Ten more destroyers arrived at four on Sunday afternoon, and were at once extended north; at 8 P.M. the two fast Portsmouth armoured cruisers *Southampton* and *Lincoln* arrived, and steamed northwards to prolong the cordon formed by the ships to the north of the Scillies, and a few minutes later a third ship of the "County" class, hastily mobilised, the *Cardigan*, arrived, and placed herself under Rear-Admiral Armitage, commanding the Devonport Reserve. She was stationed just to the south of the Scillies.

All the evening, wireless signals had been coming in from the Channel Cruiser Squadron, as it moved northwards far out at sea beyond the advanced guard about Land's End. At 8.50 P.M. a signal from it announced that a large liner was in sight moving south-west, and that Admiral Hunter's ships were in full chase of her. The British cruiser *Andromache*, off the Scillies, and the three ships of the "County" class off Land's End, were at once directed upon the point where Admiral Hunter's signals had reported the enemy. Thirteen British vessels thus were converging upon her, twelve of them good for twenty-three knots or more.

The captain of the *Deutschland*, after dashing through the British cordon off Lundy Island, stood for several hours westwards at twenty knots, intending at dusk to turn and pass wide of the Scillies, and hoping to escape the British under cover of darkness. He was under no illusions as to the danger which threatened him. From every quarter British wireless signals were coming in—from the west, south, and north—while to the east of him was the *cul-de-sac* of the Bristol Channel. All lights were screened on board his gigantic liner.

About 8 P.M. his lookouts reported a large ship rapidly moving north, ten miles away. He slightly altered course, hoping that he had escaped observation, and stood more to the south. Two minutes later the lookouts reported another very large ship with four funnels passing right across the line of his advance.

The strange ship, which was the British armoured cruiser *Iphigenia*, fired a gun and discharged two rockets in quick succession. Another half-minute and the beam of a searchlight from her rose skywards, signalling to her sister ships that here at last was the prey. Five other searchlight beams travelled swiftly over the water towards the *Deutschland* and caught the liner in their glare. Forthwith from south and north came the flashing of searchlights and the heavy boom of guns, and the whole nine cruisers of the Channel Squadron over their front of eighty miles began to move in upon the German vessel.

Her only chance was to make a dash through one of the wide gaps that parted each pair of British cruisers, and this was not a very hopeful course. The German captain had already recognised the British ships from their build, and knew that the two nearest were good for 23½ knots, and that they each carried four 12-inch and eight 9.2-inch guns. He steered between the *Iphigenia* and *Intrepid*, fearful if he turned back that he would be cut off by the British cruisers behind him in the Bristol Channel.

Observing his tactics, the two British ships closed up, steaming inwards till the gap narrowed to five miles. The *Deutschland* turned once more, and endeavoured to pass south of the *Iphigenia* and between her and the next vessel in the British line, the *Orion*; but her change of course enabled the *Iphigenia* to close her within 7000 yards and to open fire from the forward 12-inch barbette. Five shots were fired with both vessels racing their fastest, the *Deutschland* to escape and the *Iphigenia* to cut her off, and the fifth shell caught the German vessel right amidships, exploding with great violence. The starboard 9.2-inch barbette simultaneously hit her three times astern, just between her fourth funnel and the mainmast, but all these shells seemed to pass right through the ship. The *Deutschland* doubled yet again, to avoid the fire, but now found the *Orion* coming up astern.

The German vessel was going about twenty-four knots, but the *Orion* put two 12-inch shells into her from the fore-barbette before she passed out of practical range. Just then the *Sirius* came up from the east, and steering across the bows of the *Deutschland* at about 5000 yards fired in a couple of minutes about 120 6-inch shells at her, hitting her repeatedly.

The arrival of this new antagonist from the east compelled the German captain to alter course afresh and make one more bid for safety. The damage done to his ship by the British shells had been exceedingly serious; two fires had broken out amidships, and were gaining; one of the funnels was so riddled that the draught in the group of boilers which it served had fallen, and the speed of the ship had diminished by a full knot. The big British armoured cruisers, after being for a few minutes left astern, were fast gaining on her. Nevertheless she now stood towards them and endeavoured to pass between them.

The desperate effort was doomed to fail. The *Orion* and *Iphigenia* closed her, one on each beam, and opened fire with their tremendous broadsides. The end came quickly. Three 12-inch shells from the *Iphigenia* caught her amidships, low down on the hull near the waterline, and amidst a series of explosions her engines stopped and she began to sink. The injury done to her was too extensive to save her, and at 9.50 P.M. the sea closed over the last of the German raiders in that vicinity.

Those of the crew who survived were rescued by the *Orion*. Meantime the rest of the British cruisers had set to work to scout in the entrance to the Channel in order to capture the German ships which had appeared off Portsmouth. No trace, however, could be discovered of them, and at dawn on Monday the British Admiral reported that the Channel was thoroughly cleared. The *Sirius* and *Andromache* were then instructed to proceed to the west coast of Ireland, off which three German liners had appeared, damaged the Atlantic cables at Valentia, and captured a British steamer in sight of Cape Clear.

After the hard work in the Channel, most of the cruisers needed coal. Detachments of the Fleet put into Falmouth, Portland, Milford, and Queenstown to fill their bunkers. Two of the "County" cruisers were sent north to watch off Cape Wrath for the approach of any German force from Lerwick. Two more of the same class were sent up the Channel and took station between Dungeness and Boulogne. Monday and Tuesday were quiet days from the naval point of view, as there was great delay in the coaling, owing to the damage done by the Germans in South Wales.

For military reasons, the Admiralty, which had now at last been freed from hampering civilian control and granted a free hand, issued orders on the Sunday night that all news of the British successes should be suppressed. It was publicly given out in London that the raiders had escaped after a sharp action in the Channel, and that only one of them had been captured. The officers and men in the British ships engaged most loyally observed secrecy, and the large number of prisoners were sent north to the Isle of Man, control of which island and the telegraph cables leading to it the Admiralty had now taken over.

It was strange and tragi-comic that, though the German ships which had made the raid were lying at the bottom of the sea or in British hands, the public furiously attacked the Navy for its failure to destroy them or prevent their attacks. The news had come during the afternoon of Sunday that heavy and continuous firing had been heard off the South Wales coast. From Newquay, reports had been telegraphed to much the same effect, of heavy gusts of cannonading during the afternoon and evening far out to sea, and had raised men's hopes and expectations.

No one was allowed to telegraph from Milford the news that a great German liner had arrived there under a British prize crew. The Press messages were accepted at the post-office and were quietly popped into the waste-paper basket by a lieutenant, who, with a file of marines, had been installed there to act as censor. The towns of Pembroke and Milford were placed under martial law by special proclamation, and on Sunday night a British general order appeared stating that any person found sending military or naval news would be shot by drum-head court-martial.

On Monday similar proclamations were posted up in Portsmouth, Devonport, and Chatham, and caused quite a scurry of correspondents from these towns. The Government and the Admiralty were most furiously attacked for this interference with liberty, and, but for the terrible series of defeats and the rapid progress of the German invasion, the Government would probably have thrown the Admiralty over and surrendered to the cries of the mob.

Most violent were the attacks upon the Admiralty for its foolish and unwise reductions in the Navy, for selling old ships which might in this emergency have done good service, for its failure to station torpedo craft along the east coast, and to instal wireless telegraph stations there. These attacks had reason behind them, and they greatly weakened the hand of the Admiralty at a dangerous moment. Fortunately, however, the young officers of the Navy had been taught fearlessness of all consequences, and they carried out with an iron hand the regulations which were essential for success in regaining the command of the sea.

Nor were the Germans even on the east coast, where they were as yet left undisturbed, to have matters all their own way. Their cruisers, indeed, were stationed right up the coast, maintaining an effective blockade and transmitting wireless signals. At Lerwick was a considerable squadron; off Wick was the *Kaiserin Augusta*; off Aberdeen, the *Hansa*; off Newcastle, the *Vineta*; off Hull, the *Freya*; and farther south the whole massed force of the German Navy. They levied ransoms, intercepted shipping, and did what they liked beyond the range of the few coast batteries.

But in the Straits of Dover they had one very serious misadventure. People on the cliffs of Dover on Tuesday morning, watching that stretch of water, which was now empty of all shipping but for the German torpedo vessels incessantly on the patrol, and but for the outlines of large German cruisers on the northern horizon, were certain that they saw one of the big German cruisers strike a mine.

There was a great cloud of smoke, and a heavy boom came over the sea; then a big four-funnelled vessel was seen to be steering for the French coast with a very marked list. On the Wednesday it was known that the German armoured cruiser *Scharnhorst* had struck one of the German mines adrift in the Straits of Dover, and had sustained such serious injury that she had been compelled to make for Dunkirk in a sinking condition.

There she was immediately interned by the French authorities, and when the German Government remonstrated, the French Ministry pointed out that a precisely similar course had been taken by Germany at Kiaochau, during the Far Eastern war, with the Russian battleship *Tzarevitch*.

Very late on Monday night the battleships of the Channel Fleet passed the Lizard, having received orders to proceed up Channel and join the great fleet assembling at Portland. Already there were concentrated at that point eleven battleships of the Devonport and Portsmouth reserve squadrons, seven armoured cruisers, and fifty torpedo vessels of all kinds. At Chatham, where the activity shown had not been what was expected of the British Navy, the Commander-in-Chief had been removed on Monday morning and replaced, and a fresh officer had also been appointed to the command of the reserve squadron.

The policy enjoined on him was, however, a waiting one; the vessels at Chatham, being exposed, if they ventured out, to attack by the whole force of the Germans, were to remain behind the guns of the forts, or such guns as had not been sold off by the War Office and the British Government in the general anxiety to effect retrenchments. The entire naval force was mobilised, though the mobilisation was not as yet quite complete.

On Tuesday night the British Admiralty had available the following ships:—

At Portland—

Eleven battleships of the Channel Fleet.
Eleven battleships of the Reserve.
Seven armoured cruisers.
Twelve ocean-going destroyers.
Twelve coastal destroyers.
Ten submarines.
Twenty older destroyers.
Ten protected cruisers.

Off Dungeness—

Two armoured cruisers.
Ten submarines.
Four sea-going destroyers.
Ten older destroyers.
Twelve coastal destroyers.

West Coast Of Ireland—

Two large protected cruisers.

Milford Haven—

Nine armoured cruisers of the Channel Cruiser Squadron.
Eight ocean-going destroyers.

Land's End—

One large protected cruiser.
Ten older destroyers.

Cape Wrath—

Two armoured cruisers.
Ten older destroyers.
Twelve ocean-going destroyers.

And at various points along the south coast twelve coastal destroyers and a dozen old protected cruisers. The Chatham ships were not included in this force, and mustered eight battleships, four armoured cruisers, twelve coastal destroyers, twenty older destroyers, and twenty submarines, besides a number of smaller and older cruisers of doubtful value.

On Tuesday evening the Admiralty ordered the Channel Armoured Cruiser Squadron to put to sea from Milford, proceed north round the coast of Scotland, picking up on its way the two armoured cruisers and torpedo flotilla off Cape Wrath, which had taken up their position at Loch Eriboll, and then to attack the German detachment at Lerwick, and clear the northern entrance to the North Sea. A large number of colliers were to accompany or follow the fleet, which was strictly ordered not to risk an engagement with the main German forces, but to retire if they appeared, falling back on the Irish Sea.

The squadron at 6 P.M. that night, with bunkers full, weighed anchor and proceeded at 18 knots. It passed rapidly up the west coast of Scotland without communicating with the shore, and shortly before midnight on Wednesday joined the Loch Eriboll detachment, which was waiting its arrival, ready to proceed with it. At Loch Eriboll it refilled its bunkers from four colliers that had been sent in advance, and soon after daybreak on Thursday steamed out from that remote Scottish haven for the scene of action, leaving four destroyers to watch the harbour. Two more colliers arrived as it left.

One of the armoured cruisers and eight ocean-going destroyers were instructed to wait till the afternoon, and then move towards the Pentland Firth. Six of the older destroyers were to follow them, and hold the waters of the Firth if the Germans were not in any great force. The other ten armoured cruisers, with four ocean-going destroyers, would make a wide sweep at full speed round the north of the Orkneys, so as to cut off any German vessels in the Pentland Firth. Strict orders were given that if the German battleships or armoured cruisers in any force were encountered a prompt retreat must be beaten, and that until the approach of the British Fleet had been detected by the enemy, wireless signalling was not to be used.

The great expanse of ocean was troubled only by a heavy swell as the ten cruisers passed away from sight of land to the north-east. At 10 A.M. they passed to the north of Westray; at noon they rounded North Ronaldshay. Up to this point not a vessel had been seen, whether foe or friend or neutral. Now they steered south, keeping well out so as to come in upon the Orkneys, where the Germans were believed to have landed men, from the east. They were a little to the south of Fair Island when a large destroyer was seen running away fast to the north.

Two of the four ocean-going destroyers with the cruisers at once started in pursuit, and the armoured cruiser *Lincoln* followed in support. The rest of the British squadron continued towards the Pentland Skerries, and as it moved, felt the wireless signals of a strange force. Five minutes later a steamer was made out to the south, and, when the British cruisers neared her, was seen to be the *Bremen*, or one of her class. She fired guns, and stood away to the east.

The *Orion* at once gave chase to her, while the other eight British cruisers now divided, two making a wide sweep south for Wick, to look for the German cruiser reported off that place, and the remaining six steering for the Pentland Firth, in which, according to local reports, the German torpedo craft were constantly cruising. The *Orion* was soon lost to view as she went off fast to the east after the German ship.

Three hours after passing North Ronaldshay the six cruisers and their two destroyers drew in towards the Pentland Skerries from the east. The sound of shots from the Firth and from behind Stroma told that the co-operating division of the fleet was already at work. And presently through the Firth came racing, at top speed, two German torpedo boats, with eight British destroyers firing furiously at them, astern of them.

The chase was over in a minute. Finding themselves surrounded and their escape cut off, with the much faster British destroyers astern of them and the Armoured Cruiser Squadron ahead of them, the two German boats turned and ran ashore close under John o' Groats House, where their crews blew them up and surrendered.

The Firth was cleared, and the co-operating squadron joined hands with the main force. A fresh detachment of two cruisers was sent off to steam direct for Aberdeen, and attack the German cruiser off that place, in case she had not already retired. If she had gone, the two cruisers were to move direct on Lerwick. But the arrival, two hours later, of the two cruisers which had been sent to look after the German ship at Wick, with the news that she had hurriedly left about the time when the *Bremen* was sighted, no doubt alarmed by the *Bremen's* wireless signals, suggested that there was little chance of catching the enemy at Aberdeen.

The seven armoured cruisers and the ten big destroyers now steamed well out into the North Sea, going full speed to get upon the German line of retreat from Lerwick, before moving up along it on the Shetlands. For six hours they kept generally eastwards, and at 10 P.M. were extended over a front of about 100 miles, with six miles' interval between each cruiser and destroyer. Two of the very fastest turbine destroyers, which could do 30 knots at sea, formed the north-eastern extremity of the line, to the east of the Bressay Bank.

These skilful tactics were rewarded with a measure of success. The wireless signals of the *Bremen* had alarmed the German squadron at Lerwick, about 1 P.M. on Thursday. Its division of fast cruisers put to sea without a moment's delay. The older cruisers, *Irene* and *Grief*, however, were coaling, and were delayed two hours in getting to sea, while the two gun-boats *Eber* and *Panther* had not got steam up, and had to be left to co-operate with the garrison.

Two torpedo boats were also detached for the purpose of assisting the German land force, which had thrown up two batteries and mounted two 5-in. howitzers and two 4-in. guns to protect the mine-fields laid in the entrances to the harbour. The Germans knew every point and feature in the island group, as the British Admiralty had permitted them to use it for their manœuvres in 1904.

Of the German torpedo flotilla, one large destroyer had been cruising off the Orkneys, and had been seen and chased without success by the British Fleet. Two torpedo boats in the Pentland Firth had already been accounted for. Four large destroyers were lying with steam up at Lerwick, and put to sea with the fast German cruisers. Seven other destroyers, boats of 750 tons, were engaged in patrolling the waters eastwards from the Shetlands to the Norway coast, and were speedily warned.

The faster German vessels successfully escaped round the front of the British cordon of cruisers and destroyers. The *Irene* and *Grief* were less fortunate. They were sighted soon after 10 P.M., steaming due east, and were easily overtaken and destroyed with little more than a show of resistance. The British vessels which were innermost in the long line were near Lerwick a couple of hours later, and sent in three ocean-going destroyers to watch the port, waiting till daylight before attacking it.

During the night the *Orion* communicated by wireless signals the news that, after a long chase, she had overtaken and sunk the *Bremen*, which had made a gallant fight against overwhelming odds. The *Lincoln*, with her two destroyers, rejoined the fleet, reporting that the German destroyer which they had pursued had got away. A British destroyer was sent south to Fair Island to watch the channel between the Orkneys and Shetlands. Another destroyer was sent off to Loch Eriboll to bring up the rest of the older British destroyers and the colliers to Kirkwall, where the British vessels intended to establish an advanced base. The news of the successes gained was at once communicated to the Admiralty by cipher message.

On Friday at daybreak one of the British ocean-going destroyers steamed into Lerwick under the white flag, with a demand from Rear-Admiral Hunter for the immediate surrender of the place. Failing surrender, the communication informed the German commandant that the British ships would shell the town, and would exact exemplary punishment from the German force. The commander of the destroyer was instructed, if the German commandant showed a bold front, to call upon him to clear the town of civilians and permit the British inhabitants to withdraw.

The British destroyer which took in this communication was not permitted to approach the mine-field. One of the German torpedo boats came out and received the letter. If the demand for the surrender was acceded to the German commandant was instructed to hoist a white flag within twenty minutes.

The officers of the destroyer could see that four large merchant steamers and some warships were inside Bressay Sound. Small guns could be made out on Fort Charlotte and the Wart of Bressay, and two heavy weapons in position near Lerwick behind newly-raised earthworks.

The British note stated that operations would be at once commenced against the town, but the Admiral gave his ships orders not as yet to train their weapons on it, hoping to escape the cruel necessity of shelling a British seaport. At the expiration of twenty minutes the German flag still flew over the German works, and it became clear that the enemy did not intend to surrender. Signals were therefore made in the international code that a respite of three and a half hours would be allowed for the civilians, women and children, to quit Lerwick, but that the British warships would forthwith attack the German positions away from the harbour.

Four of the smaller destroyers pushed carefully in under Hildesay, searching and sweeping for mines. They were fired upon from the shore, and replied with their 12-pounders, shelling the German works vigorously, but carefully avoiding the town. Apparently the Germans had not mined the waters to the west of the long and narrow peninsula upon which Lerwick stands. Mines were seen at both ends of Bressay Sound, but Deal's Voe seemed to be clear.

At noon the *Iphigenia* steamed inside Hildesay to shell the town and works from the west. The *Orion* closed in cautiously from the north-east upon Deal's Voe. The other armoured cruisers took up a position about 8000 yards from Lerwick, to the south of the southern entrance to Bressay Sound. The destroyers were close at hand, and one of the large cruisers was stationed to the south-east to give timely notice in case any German naval force should appear.

At 12.5 the first shot was fired by the *Iphigenia*, which trained her two forward 12-in. guns upon Fort Charlotte and fired them in succession. Both hit the target, and the two huge shells demolished the fort, putting the small German guns there out of action, and killing or wounding their gunners. Simultaneously the other cruisers had opened upon Lerwick and the German works on the Wart of Bressay, firing their 12-in. and 9.2-in. guns slowly, with extreme accuracy and prodigious effect. A few shots silenced the four heavy German guns.

The *Orion* did magnificent shooting with her 9.2's, which she chiefly used; these big guns tore down the German earthworks, and set the town on fire. The cruisers to the south directed several shells upon the German ships in the Sound, and sank one of the big steamers, setting another on fire, and badly damaging the gunboats *Eber* and *Panther*. Both the German torpedo boats were hit and damaged.

The German force was in a difficulty—indeed, a desperate position. Seemingly, the German Admiralty had not calculated upon such a rapid move of the British cruisers by the Irish Sea northward, but had rather expected them to come up the North Sea. Reports that a movement up the North Sea was intended had reached Berlin from the German secret agents in London late on Tuesday night, with the result that the German Fleet had concentrated off the Suffolk coast.

The troops at Lerwick had not had time to fortify the position or to construct bomb-proofs and shelters. If the bulk of the garrison withdrew from the town, the British ships might land parties of Marines and seize it; if the Germans remained, they must face a terrific fire, which did great execution, and this though a good many of the British shells failed to explode.

From time to time the British destroyers came in closer than the large ships, and, now that the German artillery was silenced, shelled the town and any troops that they saw with their 12-pounders and 3-pounders. They were also getting to work in the Sound to clear away the mines, exploding heavy charges in the minefield, and sweeping for mines under the guns of the big ships.

They made so much progress that late in the afternoon the *Warspite* was able to steam in to 4500 yards, at which range her 9.2-in. guns speedily completed the destruction of the war-vessels and shipping in the harbour. She was also able to fire with deadly effect upon the German earthworks. Her shells exploded a magazine of ammunition and set fire to a large depôt of food, consisting of boxes which had been hastily landed, and were lying ashore covered with tarpaulins.

Her smaller guns at this short range were most effective; the 3-pounders played on the German works on the Wart of Bressay, and drove the remnant of the force holding them to flight. But as the troops endeavoured to make their escape they were caught by the fire of two of the destroyers, which turned their 12-pounders and rained shells upon them.

At dusk the British cruisers to the east of Lerwick drew off, to avoid any mines that might have got adrift. The *Iphigenia* remained to the west of the town, and fired several shots during the night, while the British destroyers were most active, firing their small guns whenever they saw any sign of movement.

Early next day the attack was about to recommence, when the German colonel in command hoisted the white flag, and made his surrender. Owing to the destruction of his food depôt and the explosion of his magazine he was short both of ammunition and food. Thus, after a brief spell of German rule—for the place had been solemnly annexed to the German Empire by proclamation—the British took possession of a ruined town and captured a considerable German force, numbering about 1100 men.

While the British cruisers were busy recovering control of the Shetlands, the Atlantic Fleet, four battleships strong, had arrived at Portland, and joined the imposing fleet which was assembling at that splendid harbour. The Mediterranean Fleet, four battleships strong, was following in its wake, detaching its two armoured cruisers for work off Gibraltar and the entrance to the Mediterranean, where German commerce-destroyers were reported to be busy.

The British Admiralty had decided to evacuate the Mediterranean and leave Egypt to its fate. Orders were given to block the Suez Canal, and though this act was an obvious infraction of international law, it elicited only mild protests from the Powers, which anxiously hoped for a British victory in the war. The protests were formal, and it was intimated that there was no intention of supporting them by force, provided the British Government would defray the loss caused by its action to neutral shipping.

A conflict between the military and civil authorities occurred on the Saturday following the outbreak of war. The Admiralty up to this point had succeeded in throwing a veil of silence over the British movements, and not even the striking successes of the British Fleet were generally known. But Ministers, and the First Lord of the Admiralty in particular, fearing for their own lives, and appalled by the furious outcry against themselves, on Saturday insisted upon issuing an official notice to the effect that the German Fleet which had raided South Wales had been completely annihilated, and Lerwick recaptured by the British Navy. Hundreds of German prisoners, added the proclamation, had been made.

To such a degree had the public lost faith in the Government, that the news was received with scepticism. The official Press in Germany ridiculed the intelligence, though the German Government must have been aware of its truth. It was only with extreme difficulty that the civilian members of the Government were prevented from publishing the exact strength of the British naval force available for operations against the Germans, but a threat by the Sea Lords to take matters into their own hands and appeal to the nation, prevented such a crowning act of folly.

Four armoured cruisers of the "County" class, exceedingly fast ships, had been pushed up behind the Channel cruisers, with instructions to carry on the work of harassing the Germans while the Channel cruisers coaled. The new cruiser detachment was to join the two ships of the "County" class already at Kirkwall, move cautiously south, with six ocean-going destroyers and six of the older destroyers, along the Scotch coast, establish its base at Aberdeen or Rosyth, and raid the German line of communications.

It was to be known as the Northern Squadron, and was placed under the orders of Rear-Admiral Jeffries, an able and enterprising officer. In case the Germans moved against it in force, it was to retire northwards, but its commander was given to understand that on September 17 the main British Fleet would advance from the north and south into the North Sea and deliver its attack upon the massed force of the German Navy.

Meanwhile, in preparation for the great movement, assiduous drill and target practice proceeded in the neighbourhood of Portland. The British battleships daily put to sea to fire and execute evolutions. The most serious difficulty, however, was to provide the ample supplies of ammunition needed, now that the Germans were in possession of so much of England, that the railway service was disorganised, and that an enormous consumption of cordite by the British land forces was taking place. The coal question was also serious, as the South Wales miners had struck for higher wages, and had only been induced to return to their work by the promise of great concessions. The officers and men of the Navy could not but be painfully struck by the strange want of zeal and national spirit in this great emergency shown by the British people.

On the 11th two of the "County" cruisers steamed south from Dingwall to replace the two ships which had, earlier in the operations against the Shetlands, been despatched to Aberdeen, and which were now to rejoin the Channel cruisers and concentrate in the Dornoch Firth. They reported that the German cruiser off Aberdeen had made good her escape, and that they had scouted so far south as the entrance of the Forth without discovering any trace of German vessels.

On the 12th the four other cruisers of the "County" class and the destroyers reached Aberdeen early in the morning, and the Rear-Admiral set to work with zeal and energy to disturb and harass his enemy to the utmost. The *Southampton* and *Kincardine*, two of the fast cruisers, with two ocean-going destroyers, were instructed to steam direct for the German coast, and sink any vessel that they sighted. The *Selkirk* and *Lincoln*, with the rest of the destroyers, under his own orders, would clear the Forth entrance and move cautiously southward towards Newcastle, if no enemy were encountered. Yet another pair of cruisers, the *Cardigan* and *Montrose*, were to steam for the Dutch coast and there destroy German vessels and transports. Two of the older protected cruisers were brought to link up the advanced detachments by wireless telegraphy with the Forth, when the Germans were forced away from that point.

About noon the Rear-Admiral, with his cruisers, appeared off the Forth, and learnt that for three days no German vessels had been reported off the coast, but that the entrance to the estuary was believed to have been mined afresh by the Germans and was exceedingly unsafe. The armoured cruiser *Impérieuse*, which had been damaged in the battle of North Berwick, had now been sufficiently repaired to take the sea again. She had coaled and received ammunition, and was at once ordered to join the Northern Squadron.

The armoured cruisers *Olympia* and *Aurora*, and the battleship *Resistance*, which had been badly damaged in the torpedo attack that opened the war, were also nearly ready for service, and could be counted on for work in forty-eight hours. It had been supposed at the time that they were permanently injured, but hundreds of skilled Glasgow artisans had been brought over by train and set to work upon them, and with such energy had they laboured that the damage had been almost made good. For security against any German attack, the ships lay with booms surrounding them behind a great mine-field, which had been placed by the naval authorities.

The Rear-Admiral in command of the Northern Fleet ordered a passage through the German minefield to be cleared without delay, and the repaired ships to remain for the time being to guard the port, as their speed was not such as to enable them to run if the enemy appeared in force. Taking with him the *Impérieuse*, he moved down the coast towards Newcastle, steaming at 15 knots. At 8 p.m. he passed the mouth of the Tyne, and sighted the *Southampton*, one of the two cruisers which he had despatched to menace the German coast; they had chased and sunk a large German collier, apparently proceeding to Lerwick, and quite unaware of the sudden turn which the naval war had taken.

The *Southampton* had returned to report the fact that she had sighted three German destroyers, which went off very fast to the south, one now having rejoined the flag. The four British armoured cruisers—*Southampton*, *Selkirk*, *Lincoln*, and *Impérieuse*—extended in open order, with the four ocean-going destroyers in advance and the six older destroyers inshore, on the lookout for Germans.

In this order the Admiral moved, with all lights out, towards the German line of communications. Steering wide of Flamborough Head, and clearing the sandbanks off the Wash, he passed down what was now an enemy's coast, carefully refraining from using his ships' long-distance wireless instruments, which might have given the alarm.

At about 1 A.M. of the 13th the *Southampton* sighted a large steamer proceeding slowly eastwards. She gave chase forthwith, and in fifteen minutes was alongside the stranger. The vessel proved to be a German transport returning from Hull empty. A small prize-crew was placed on board, the German seamen were transhipped to the British cruiser, and the vessel was sent back to Newcastle under escort of one of the older destroyers.

At 3.30 A.M. the flagship *Selkirk* sighted another large steamer proceeding west, towards the Wash. Chase was instantly given to her, and in ten minutes the fast cruiser, running 21 knots, was within easy range. As the steamer did not obey the order to stop, even when shotted guns were fired over her bow, the *Selkirk* poured a broadside into her at 3000 yards. This brought her to, and two ocean-going destroyers were sent to overhaul her, while the *Lincoln* and *Southampton* steamed in towards her, with guns laid upon her to prevent any tricks.

A few minutes later the destroyers signalled that the vessel was laden with German troops, reserve stores, ammunition, and supplies of all kinds. It would have been awkward to sink her and tranship the men, and remembering the humanity which the Germans had displayed in the battles at the opening of the war, the Admiral ordered the *Impérieuse* to escort her to Newcastle, with instructions to sink her if she offered any resistance. A lieutenant and ten men were put on board her, to keep an eye on her crew and see that they obeyed the injunctions of the *Impérieuse*, which followed 300 yards astern with her 9.2-in. guns trained menacingly upon the transport.

Scarcely had possession been taken of this vessel, which proved to be the 10,000-ton Hamburg-American cargo-vessel *Bulgaria*, when two more ships were sighted, and the sound of alarm guns hurriedly firing was heard from the *Leman* lightship. To silence the lightship, which was known to be in German hands, a fast destroyer was despatched with orders to torpedo it and destroy it.

As the enemy had undoubtedly taken the alarm, and might be expected any minute to put in an appearance, the British cruisers made ready to retire. The destroyers were sent off to the north; the three remaining armoured cruisers hovered waiting for the Germans to show, as they intended to draw them off towards the north-east, and thus take them away from the *Bulgaria* and her escort.

At 4.20 A.M. a big ship, evidently an armoured cruiser, accompanied by two or three destroyers, was seen approaching from the direction of Hull. Simultaneously wireless waves came in strong from the south, and from that quarter there came into sight another big armoured cruiser, accompanied by at least six destroyers and two smaller cruisers. They were the scouts of the German Fleet, and before them ran at 30 knots the British destroyer which had been charged with the destruction of the *Leman* lightship, and which had accomplished her task only two or three minutes before the Germans appeared from the south.

Noting that his enemy was in no great strength, and feeling minded to deal him a blow, if possible, the British Admiral now fell back north-eastward, without increasing speed sufficiently to draw away from the Germans. His ships, of the "County" class, with their weak 6-in. batteries, were no match for the German cruisers, but if he could entice the Germans within reach of the armoured vessels at Rosyth it would be another matter. Moreover, at any moment his detached armoured cruisers might rejoin the fleet.

Both forces were keeping well together, the Germans not steaming more than 20 knots, so as not to draw away from their smaller cruisers, while the British cruisers and destroyers made their pace with perfect ease, and for hours maintained an interval of eight miles from the enemy.

After two hours' chase the British Admiral altered course slightly, and began to edge away to the north-east. The Germans followed, and at five in the afternoon of the 13th both squadrons were abreast of St. Abbs Head, far out to sea. About this time another German cruiser was noted, following to the support of the German vessels, and simultaneously the British Admiral opened up wireless communication with the powerful armoured ships at Rosyth.

X

SITUATION SOUTH OF THE THAMES

The enemy on land had operated rapidly and decisively upon a prearranged scheme that was perfect in every detail.

By September 24th, three weeks after the first landing, England had, alas! learnt a bitter lesson by the shells showered down upon her open towns if they made a show of resistance. She had been taught it by her burning villages, scientifically fired with petrol, for having harboured Frontiersmen or Free-shooters, whom the German Staff did not choose to acknowledge as belligerents, by the great sacrifice of lives of innocent children and women, by war contributions, crushing requisitions, and the ruin and desolation that had marked every bivouac of the invading army. And now, while the Germans stood triumphant in London north of the Thames, South London was still held by the desperate populace, aided by many infantry and artillery, who, after their last stand on the northern heights, had made a detour to the south by crossing the river at Richmond Bridge and coming up to the Surrey shore by way of Wandsworth. By their aid the barricades were properly reconstructed with paving-stones, sacks of sand and sawdust, rolls of carpet, linoleum and linen—in fact, anything and everything that would stop bullets.

The assault at Waterloo Bridge on the night of the enemy's occupation had in the end proved disastrous to the Germans, for, once within, they found themselves surrounded by a huge armed mob in the Waterloo Road and in the vicinity of the South-Western terminus; notwithstanding their desperate defence, they were exterminated to a man, until the gutters beneath the railway bridges ran with blood. Meanwhile the breach in the barricade was repaired, and two guns and ammunition captured from the enemy mounted in defence. There was a similar incident on Vauxhall Bridge, the populace being victorious, and now the Germans were offering no further opposition, as they had quite sufficient to occupy them on the Middlesex side.

The division of Lord Byfield's army which had gone south to Horsham had moved north, and on the 24th were holding the country across from Epsom to Kingston-on-Thames, while patrols and motorists were out from Ewell, through Cheam, Sutton, Carshalton, Croydon, and Upper Norwood, to the high ground at the Crystal Palace. From Kingston to the Tower Bridge all approaches across the Thames were barricaded and held by desperate mobs, aided by artillerymen.

In those early days after the occupation, military order had apparently disappeared in London, as far as the British were concerned. General Sir Francis Bamford had, on the proclamation of martial law in London, been appointed military governor, and had, on the advance of the Germans, retired to the Crystal Palace, where he had now established his headquarters in the palace itself, with a wireless telegraph apparatus placed upon the top of the left-hand tower, by means of which he was in constant communication with Lord Byfield at Windsor, where the apparatus had been hoisted upon the flagstaff of the Round Tower.

The military tribunals established by the Proclamation of the 14th still existed in the police courts of South London, but those north of the Thames had already been replaced by German officers, and the British officers went across the bridges into the British lines. Von Kronhelm's clever tactics, by which he had established an advisory board of British officials to assist in the government of London, seemed to have had the desired effect of reassurance in the case of London north of the Thames. But south of the river the vast population in that huge area from Gravesend, through Dartford, Bexley, Bromley, Croydon, Merton, Wimbledon, and Kingston, lived still at the highest tension, while the defenders at the bridges and along the river-front kept up unceasing vigilance night and day, never knowing at what spot the Germans might throw across their pontoons. In peace time the enemy had for years practised the pontooning of the Rhine and the Elbe; therefore, they knew it to be an easy matter to cross the narrower reaches of the Thames if they so desired.

On the 24th the rumour became current, too, that during the night German wagons had moved large quantities of specie from the Bank of England out to their base at Southminster; but, though it was most probable, the news was not confirmed. On this date the position as regards London, briefly reviewed, was as follows:—

London north of the Thames, eastward to the sea, and the whole of the country east of a line drawn from the metropolis to Birmingham, was in the hands of the Germans. The enemy's Guard Corps, under the Duke of Mannheim, who had landed at King's Lynn, had established their headquarters at Hampstead, and held North London, with a big encampment in Regent's Park. The Xth Corps, under Von Wilberg, from Yarmouth, were holding the City proper; the IXth Corps, from

Lowestoft, were occupying the outskirts of East London, and keeping the lines of communication with Southminster; the IVth Corps, from Weybourne, under Von Kleppen, were in Hyde Park, and held Western London; while the Saxons had been pushed out from Shepperton through Staines to Colnbrook, as a safeguard from attack by Lord Byfield's force, so rapidly being reorganised at Windsor. The remnants of the beaten army had gone to Chichester and Salisbury, but were now coming rapidly north, as the British Commander-in-Chief, had, it appeared, decided to give battle again, aided by the infuriated populace of Southern London.

At no spot south of the Thames, except perhaps the reconnoitring parties who crossed at Egham, Thorpe, and Weybridge, and recrossed each night, were there any Germans. The ground was so vast and the population so great, that Von Kronhelm feared to spread out his troops over too great an area. The Saxons had orders simply to keep Lord Byfield in check, and see that he did not cross the river. Thus it became for the time a drawn game. The Germans held the north of the Thames, while the British were continually threatening and making demonstrations from the south.

So great, however, was the population now assembled in South London that food was rising to absolutely famine prices. The estuary of the river had been so thickly mined by the Germans that no ships bearing food dared to come up. The Straits of Dover and the Solent were still dangerous on account of the floating mines, and it was only at places such as Brighton, Eastbourne, Hastings, and Folkestone that supplies could be landed at that moment. Trucks full of flour, coffee, rice, brandy, canned meats, boots, uniforms, arms, were daily run up to Deptford, Herne Hill, Croydon, and Wimbledon, but such supplies were very meagre for the millions now crowded along the river front, full of enthusiasm still to defy the enemy. At the first news of the invasion all the coal and coke in London had been expressly reserved for public purposes, small quantities only being issued to printing establishments and other branches of public necessity; but to private individuals they were rigorously denied. Wood, however, was sold without restriction, and a number of barges, old steamers of the County Council, and such-like craft were broken up for fuel.

THROUGH THE PAST TEN DAYS the darkness, gloom, and ever-deepening hunger had increased, and though London retained the same spirit with which it had received the news of the audacious invasion, that portion south of the Thames was starving. Between the 20th and 24th September the price of every article of food rose enormously. On the 24th Ostend rabbits were sold in the Walworth Road for a sovereign each, and a hare cost double. An apple cost 1s. 6d., a partridge 15s., a fresh egg 2s., while bacon was 6s. 6d. a pound, and butter £1 per pound. Shops in the Old Kent Road, Camberwell, Brixton, Kennington, Walworth, Waterloo, and London Roads, which had hitherto been perhaps the cheapest places in which to buy provisions in the whole of London, were now prohibitive in their prices to the poor, though ladies habitually living in the West End and driven there through force of circumstances readily paid the exorbitant charges demanded. Indeed, there was often a fight in those shops for a rabbit, a ham, or a tin of pressed beef, one person bidding against another for its possession. Tallow was often being used for the purposes of cookery, and is said to have answered well.

If South London was in such a state of starvation, even though small quantities of food were daily coming in, Von Kronhelm's position must have been one of extreme gravity when it is remembered that his food supply was now cut off. It was calculated that each of his five army corps operating upon London consumed in the space of twenty-four hours 18,000 loaves weighing 3 lb. each, 120 cwt. of rice or pearl barley, seventy oxen or 120 cwt. of bacon, 18 cwt. of salt, 30 cwt. of coffee, 12 cwt. of oats, 3 cwt. of hay, 3500 quarts of spirits and beer, with 60 cwt. of tobacco, 1,100,000 ordinary cigars, and 50,000 officers' cigars for every ten days.

And yet all was provided for at Southminster, Grimsby, King's Lynn, Norwich, and Goole. Huge food bases had been rapidly established from the first day of the invasion. The German Army, whatever might be said of it, was a splendid military machine, and we had been in every way incapable of coping with it. Yet it was impossible not to admire the courage and patriotism of the men under Byfield, Hibbard, and Woolmer in making the attempt, though from the first the game had been known to be hopeless.

West of London the members of the Hendon and other rifle clubs, together with a big body of Frontiersmen and other free-shooters, were continually harassing the Saxon advanced posts between Shepperton and Colnbrook, towards Uxbridge. On the 24th a body of 1,500 riflemen and Frontiersmen attacked a company of Saxon Pioneers close to where the Great Western Railway crosses the River Crane, north of Cranford. The Germans, being outnumbered, were obliged to withdraw to Hayes with a loss of twenty killed and a large force of wounded. Shortly afterwards, on the following day, the Pioneers, having been reinforced, retraced their steps in order to clear the districts on the Crane of our irregular forces; and they announced that if, as reported, the people of Cranford and Southall had taken part in the attack, both places would be burned.

That same night the railway bridges over the Crane and the Grand Junction Canal in the vicinity were blown up by the Frontiersmen. The fifty Saxons guarding each bridge were surprised by the British sharpshooters, and numbers of them shot. Three hours later, however, Cranford, Southall, and Hayes were burned with petrol, and it was stated by Colonel Meyer, of the Saxons, that this was to be the punishment of any place where railways were destroyed. Such was the system of terrorism by which the enemy hoped to terminate the struggle. Such proceedings— and this was but one of a dozen others in various outlying spots beyond the Metropolitan area—did not produce the effect of shortening the duration of hostilities. On the contrary, they only served to prolong the deadly contest by exciting a wild desire for revenge in many who might otherwise have been disposed towards an amicable settlement.

With the dawn of the 25th September, a grey day with fine drizzling rain in London, the situation seemed still more hopeless. The rain, however, did not by any means damp the ardour of the defenders at the bridges. They sang patriotic songs, while barrel-organs and bands played about them night and day. Though hungry, their spirits never flagged. The newspapers printed across the river were brought over in small boats from the Surrey side, and eagerly seized and read by anxious thousands. The lists of British casualties were being published, and the populace were one and all anxious for news of missing friends.

The chief item of news that morning, however, was a telegram from the Emperor William, in which he acknowledged the signal services rendered by Field-Marshal Von Kronhelm and his army. He had sent one hundred and fifty Orders of the Iron Cross for distribution among officers who had distinguished themselves, accompanied by the following telegraphic despatch, which every paper in London was ordered to print:—

The wharves and embankments of the Surrey shore of the Thames, from Erith to Kingston, were being patrolled day and night by armed

THE TELEGRAM SENT BY THE GERMAN EMPEROR TO
FIELD-MARSHAL VON KRONHELM.

men. Any boat crossing the river was at once challenged, and not allowed to approach unless under a flag of truce, or it was ascertained that its occupants were non-belligerents. Everywhere the greatest precaution was being taken against spies, and on the two or three occasions when the Germans had reconnoitered by means of balloons, sharpshooters had constantly fired at them.

As may well be imagined, spy-mania was now rife in every quarter in South London, and any man bearing a foreign name, no matter of what nationality, or known to be a foreigner, was at once suspected, and often openly insulted, even though he might be a naturalised Englishman. It was very unsafe for any foreigner now to go abroad. One deplorable incident occurred that afternoon. A German baker, occupying a shop in Newington Butts, and who had lived in England twenty-five years and become a naturalised British subject, was walking along the Kennington Road with his wife, having come forth in curiosity to see what was in progress, when he was met by a man with whom he had had some business quarrel. The man in question, as he passed, cried out to the crowd that he was a German. "He's one of Von Kronhelm's spies!" he shouted.

At the word "spy" the crowd all turned. They saw the unfortunate man had turned pale at this charge, which was tantamount to a sentence of death, and believed him to be guilty. Some wild and irrepressible men set up a loud cry of "Spy! Spy! Down with him! Down with the traitor!" and ere the unfortunate baker was aware of it he was seized by a hundred hands, and lynched.

More than once real spies were discovered, and short shrift was meted out to them; but in several instances it is feared that gross mistakes were made, and men accused as spies out of venomous personal spite. There is little doubt that under cover of night a number of Von Kronhelm's English-speaking agents were able to cross the river in boats and return on the following night, for it was apparent by the tone of the newspapers that the German generalissimo was fully aware of what was in progress south of the river.

To keep a perfect watch upon a river-front of so many miles against watermen who knew every landing-place and every point of concealment, was utterly impossible. The defenders, brave men all, did their best, and they killed at sight every spy they captured; but it was certain that the enemy had established a pretty complete system of intelligence from the camp of the defiant Londoners.

At the barricades was a quiet, calm enthusiasm. Now that it was seen that the enemy had no immediate intention of storming the defences at the bridges, those manning them rested, smoked, and, though ever vigilant, discussed the situation. Beneath every bridge men of the Royal Engineers had effected certain works which placed them in readiness for instant destruction. The explosives were there, and only by the pressing of the button the officer in command of any bridge could blow it into the air, or render it unsafe for the enemy to venture upon.

The great League of Defenders was in course of rapid formation. Its proclamations were upon every wall. When the time was ripe, London would rise. The day of revenge was fast approaching.

London, north of the Thames, though shattered and wrecked, began, by slow degrees, to grow more calm.

One half of the populace seemed to have accepted the inevitable; the other half being still terrified and appalled at the havoc wrought on every hand. In the case of Paris, forty years before, when the Germans had bombarded the city, their shells had done but little damage. In those days neither guns nor ammunition were at such perfection as they now were, the enemy's high-power explosives accounting for the fearful destruction caused.

A very curious fact about the bombardment must here be noted. Londoners, though terrified beyond measure when the shells began to fall among them and explode, grew, in the space of a couple of hours, to be quite callous, and seemed to regard the cannonade in the light of a pyrotechnical display. They climbed to every point of vantage, and regarded the continuous flashes and explosions with the same open-mouthed wonder as they would exhibit at the Crystal Palace on a firework night.

The City proper was still held by the Xth Corps under General von Wilburg, who had placed a strong cordon around it, no unauthorised person being allowed to enter or leave. In some of the main roads in Islington, Hoxton, Whitechapel, Clapton, and Kingsland, a few shops that had not been seized by the Germans had courageously opened their doors. Provision shops, bakers, greengrocers, dairies, and butchers were, however, for the most part closed, for in the Central Markets there was neither meat nor vegetables, every ounce of food having been commandeered by German foraging parties.

As far as possible, however, the enemy were, with the aid of the English Advisory Board, endeavouring to calm the popular excitement and encourage trade in other branches. At certain points such as at Aldgate, at Oxford Circus, at Hyde Park Corner, in Vincent Square, Westminster, at St. James's Park near Queen Anne's Gate, and in front of Hackney Church, the German soldiers distributed soup once a day to all comers, Von Kronhelm being careful to pretend a parental regard for the metropolis he had occupied.

The population north of the Thames was not, however, more than one quarter what it usually was, for most of the inhabitants had fled across the bridges during the bombardment, and there remained on the Surrey side in defiance of the invader.

Night and day the barricade-builders were working at the bridges in order to make each defence a veritable redoubt. They did not intend that the disasters of the northern suburbs—where the bullets had cut through the overturned carts and household furniture as through butter—should be repeated. Therefore at each bridge, behind the first hastily-constructed defence, there were being thrown up huge walls of sacks filled with earth, and in some places where more earth was obtainable earthworks themselves with embrasures. Waterloo, Blackfriars, Southwark, London, and Cannon Street bridges were all defended by enormous earthworks, and by explosives already placed for instant use if necessary. Hungerford Bridge had, of course, been destroyed by the Germans themselves, huge iron girders having fallen into the river; but Vauxhall, Lambeth, Battersea, Hammersmith, and Kew and other bridges were equally strongly defended as those nearer the centre of London. Many other barricades had been constructed at various points in South London, such as across the Bridge End Road, Wandsworth, several across the converging roads at St. George's Circus, and again at the Elephant and Castle, in Bankside, in Tooley Street, where it joins Bermondsey Street, at the approach to the Tower Bridge, in Waterloo Road at its junction with Lower Marsh, across the Westminster Bridge and Kennington Roads, across the Lambeth Road where it joins the Kennington Road, at the junction of Upper Kennington Lane with Harleyford Road, in Victoria Road at the approach to Chelsea Bridge, and in a hundred other smaller thoroughfares. Most of these barricades were being built for the protection of certain districts rather than for the general strategic defence of South London. In fact, most of the larger open spaces were barricaded, and points of entrance carefully blocked. In some places exposed barricades were connected with one another by a covered way, the neighbouring houses being crenellated and their windows protected with coal sacks filled with earth. Cannon now being brought in by Artillery from the south were being mounted everywhere, and as each hour went by the position of South London became strengthened by both men and guns.

XI

Defences of South London

Preparations were being continued night and day to place the working-class districts in Southwark and Lambeth in a state of strong defence, and the constant meetings convened in public halls and chapels by the newly-formed League of Defenders incited the people to their work. Everybody lent a willing hand, rich and poor alike. People who had hitherto lived in comfort in Regent's Park, Hampstead, or one or other of the better-class northern suburbs, now found themselves herded among all sorts and conditions of men and women, and living as best they could in those dull, drab streets of Lambeth, Walworth, Battersea, and Kennington. It was, indeed, a strange experience for them. In the sudden flight from the north parents had become separated from their children and husbands from their wives, so that in many cases haggard and forlorn mothers were in frantic search of their little ones, fearing that they might have already died of starvation or been trampled under foot by the panic-stricken multitudes. The dense population of South London had already been trebled. They were penned in by the barricades in many instances, for each district seemed to be now placing itself in a state of defence, independent of any other.

Kennington, for instance, was practically surrounded by barricades, tons upon tons of earth being dug from the "Oval" and the "Park." Besides the barricades in Harleyford Road and Kennington Lane, all the streets converging on the "Oval" were blocked up, a huge defence arm just being completed across the junction of Kennington and Kennington Park roads, and all the streets running into the latter thoroughfare from that point to the big obstruction at the "Elephant" were blocked by paving stones, bags of sand, barrels of cement, bricks, and such-like odds and ends impervious to bullets. In addition to this, there was a double fortification in Lambeth Road—a veritable redoubt—as well as the barricade at Lambeth Bridge, while all the roads leading from Kennington into the Lambeth Road, such as St. George's Road, Kennington Road, High Street, and the rest, had been rendered impassable and the neighbouring houses placed in a state of defence. Thus the whole district of Kennington became therefore a fortress in itself.

This was only a typical instance of the scientific methods of defence now resorted to. Mistakes made in North London were not now repeated. Day and night every able-bodied man, and woman too, worked on with increasing zeal and patriotism. The defences in Haverstock Hill, Holloway Road, and Edgware Road, which had been composed of overturned tramcars, motor 'buses, household furniture, etc., had been riddled by the enemy's bullets. The lesson had been heeded, and now earth, sand, tiles, paving stones, and bricks were very largely used.

From nearly all the principal thoroughfares south of the river, the paving-stones were being rapidly torn up by great gangs of men, and whenever the artillery brought up a fresh Maxim or field-gun the wildest demonstrations were made. The clergy held special services in churches and chapels, and prayer-meetings for the emancipation of London were held twice daily in the Metropolitan Tabernacle at Newington. In Kennington Park, Camberwell Green, the Oval, Vauxhall Park, Lambeth Palace Gardens, Camberwell Park, Peckham Rye, and Southwark Park a division of Lord Byfield's army was encamped. They held the Waterloo terminus of the South-Western Railway strongly, the Chatham Railway from the Borough Road Station—now the terminus—the South-Eastern from Bricklayers' Arms, which had been converted into another terminus, as well as the Brighton line, both at Battersea Park and York Road.

The lines destroyed by the enemy's spies in the early moments of the invasion had long ago been repaired, and up to the present railway and telegraphic communication south and west remained uninterrupted. The *Daily Mail* had managed to transfer some of its staff to the offices of a certain printer's in Southwark, and there, under difficulties, published several editions daily despite the German censorship. While northern London was without any news except that supplied from German sources, South London was still open to the world, the cables from the south coast being, as yet, in the hands of the British, and the telegraphs intact to Bristol and to all places in the West.

Thus, during those stifling and exciting days following the occupation, while London was preparing for its great uprising, the *South London Daily Mirror*, though a queer, unusual-looking sheet, still continued to appear, and was read with avidity by the gallant men at the barricades.

Contrary to expectation, Von Kronhelm was leaving South London severely alone. He was, no doubt, wise. Full well he knew that his men, once within those narrow, tortuous streets beyond the river, would have no opportunity to manœuvre, and would, as in the case of the assault of Waterloo Bridge, be slaughtered to a man. His spies reported that each hour that passed rendered the populace the stronger, yet he did nothing, devoting his whole time, energy, and attention to matters in that half of London he was now occupying.

Everywhere the walls of South London were placarded with manifestoes of the League of Defenders. Day after day fresh posters appeared, urging patience and courage, and reporting upon the progress of the League. The name of Graham was now upon everyone's lips. He had, it seemed, arisen as saviour of our beloved country. Every word of his inspired enthusiasm, and this was well illustrated at the mass meeting on Peckham Rye, when, beneath the huge flag of St. George, the white banner with the red cross,—the ancient standard of England,—which the League had adopted as theirs, he made a brilliant and impassioned appeal to every Londoner and every Englishman.

Report had it that the Germans had set a price upon his head, and that he was pursued everywhere by German spies—mercenaries who would kill him in secret if they could. Therefore he was compelled to go about with an armed police guard, who arrested any suspected person in his vicinity. The Government, who had at first laughed Graham's enthusiasm to scorn, now believed in him. Even Lord Byfield, after a long council, declared that his efforts to inspire enthusiasm had been amazingly successful, and it was now well known that the "Defenders" and the Army had agreed to act in unison towards one common end— the emancipation of England from the German thraldom.

Some men of the Osnabrück Regiment, holding Canning Town and Limehouse, managed one night, by strategy, to force their way through the Blackwall Tunnel and break down its defence on the Surrey side in an attempt to blow up the South Metropolitan Gas Works close by.

The men holding the tunnel were completely overwhelmed by the numbers that pressed on, and were compelled to fall back, twenty of their number being killed. The assault was a victorious one, and it was seen that the enemy were pouring out, when, of a sudden, there was a dull, heavy roar, followed by wild shouts and terrified screams, as there rose from the centre of the river a great column of water, and next instant the tunnel was flooded, hundreds of the enemy being drowned like rats in a hole.

The men of the Royal Engineers had, on the very day previous, made preparations for destroying the tunnel if necessary, and had done so ere the Germans were aware of their intention. The exact loss of life is unknown, but it is estimated that over 400 men must have perished in that single instant, while those who had made the sudden dash towards the Gas Works were all taken prisoners, and their explosives confiscated.

The evident intention of the enemy being thus seen, General Sir Francis Bamford from his headquarters at the Crystal Palace gave orders for the tunnels at Rotherhithe and that across Greenwich Reach, as well as the several "tube" tunnels and subways, to be destroyed, a work which was executed without delay, and was witnessed by thousands, who watched for the great disturbances and upheavals in the bed of the river.

In the Old Kent Road the bridge over the canal, as well as the bridges in Wells Street, Sumner Road, Glengall Road, and Canterbury Road, were all prepared for demolition in case of necessity, the canal from the Camberwell Road to the Surrey Docks forming a moat behind which the defenders might, if necessary, retire. Clapham Common and Brockwell Park were covered with tents, for General Bamford's force, consisting mostly of auxiliaries, were daily awaiting reinforcements.

Lord Byfield, now at Windsor, was in constant communication by wireless telegraphy with the London headquarters at the Crystal Palace, as well as with Hibbard on the Malvern Hills and Woolmer at Shrewsbury. To General Bamford at Sydenham came constant news of the rapid spread of the national movement of defiance, and Lord Byfield, as was afterwards known, urged the London commander to remain patient, and invite no attack until the League were strong enough to act upon the offensive.

Affairs of outposts were, of course, constantly recurring along the river bank between Windsor and Egham, and the British free-shooters and Frontiersmen were ever harassing the Saxons.

Very soon Von Kronhelm became aware of Lord Byfield's intentions, but his weakness was apparent when he made no counter-move. The fact was that the various great cities he now held required all his attention and all his troops. From Manchester, from Birmingham, from Leeds, Bradford, Sheffield, and Hull came similar replies. Any withdrawal of troops from either city would be the signal for a general rising of the inhabitants. Therefore, having gained possession, he could only now sit tight and watch.

From all over Middlesex, and more especially from the London area, came sensational reports of the drastic measures adopted by the Germans to repress any sign of revolt. In secret, the agents of the

League of Defenders were at work going from house to house, enrolling men, arranging for secret meeting-places, and explaining in confidence the programme as put forward by the Bristol committee. Now and then, however, these agents were betrayed, and their betrayal was in every case followed by a court-martial at Bow Street, death outside in the yard of the police station, and the publication in the papers of their names, their offence, and the hour of the execution.

Yet, undaunted and defiantly, the giant organisation grew as no other society had ever grown, and its agents and members quickly developed into fearless patriots. It being reported that the Saxons were facing Lord Byfield with the Thames between them, the people of West London began in frantic haste to construct barricades. The building of obstructions had, indeed, now become a mania north of the river as well as the south. The people, fearing that there was to be more fighting in the streets of London, began to build huge defences all across West London. The chief were across King Street, Hammersmith, where it joins Goldhawk Road, across the junction of Goldhawk and Uxbridge Roads, in Harrow Road where it joins Admiral Road, and Willesden Lane, close to the Paddington Cemetery, and the Latimer Road opposite St. Quintin Park Station. All the side streets leading into the Goldhawk Road, Latimer Road, and Ladbroke Grove Road, were also blocked up, and hundreds of houses placed in a state of strong defence.

With all this Von Kronhelm did not interfere. The building of such obstructions acted as a safety-valve to the excited populace, therefore he rather encouraged than discountenanced it. The barricades might, he thought, be of service to his army if Lord Byfield really risked an attack upon London from that direction.

Crafty and cunning though he was, he was entirely unaware that those barricades were being constructed at the secret orders of the League of Defenders, and he never dreamed that they had actually been instigated by the British Commander-in-chief himself.

Thus the Day of Reckoning hourly approached, and London, though crushed and starving, waited in patient vigilance.

At Enfield Chase was a great camp of British prisoners in the hands of the Germans, amounting to several thousands. Contrary to report, both officers and men were fairly well treated by the Germans, though with his limited supplies Von Kronhelm was already beginning to contemplate releasing them. Many of the higher grade officers who had fallen into the hands of the enemy, together with the Lord Mayor of London, the Mayors of Hull, Goole, Lincoln, Norwich, Ipswich, and the Lord Mayors of Manchester and Birmingham, had been sent across to Germany, where, according to their own reports, they were being detained in Hamburg and treated with every consideration. Nevertheless, all this greatly incensed Englishmen. Lord Byfield, with Hibbard and Woolmer, was leaving no stone unturned in order to reform our shattered Army, and again oppose the invaders. All three gallant officers had been to Bristol, where they held long consultation with the members of the Cabinet, with the result that the Government still refused to entertain any idea of paying the indemnity. The Admiralty were confident now that the command of the sea had been regained, and in Parliament itself a little confidence was also restored.

Yet we had to face the hard facts that nearly two hundred thousand Germans were upon British soil, and that London was held by them. Already parties of German commissioners had visited the National Gallery, the Wallace Collection, the Tate Gallery, and the British and South Kensington Museums, deciding upon and placing aside certain art treasures and priceless antiques ready for shipment to Germany. The Raphaels, the Titians, the Rubenses, the Fra Angelicos, the Velasquezes, the Elgin Marbles, the best of the Egyptian, Assyrian, and Roman antiques, the Rosetta Stone, the early Biblical and classical manuscripts, the historic charters of England, and suchlike treasures which could never be replaced, were all catalogued and prepared for removal. The people of London knew this; for though there had been no newspapers, information ran rapidly from mouth to mouth. German sentries guarded our world-famous collections, which were now indeed entirely in the enemy's hands, and which the Kaiser intended should enrich the German galleries and museums.

One vessel flying the British flag had left the Thames laden with spoil, in an endeavour to reach Hamburg, but off Harwich she had been sighted and overhauled by a British cruiser, with the result that she had been steered to Dover. Therefore our cruisers and destroyers, having thus obtained knowledge of the enemy's intentions, were keeping a sharp lookout along the coast for any vessels attempting to leave for German ports.

Accounts of fierce engagements in the Channel between British and German ships went the rounds, but all were vague and unconvincing. The only solid facts were that the Germans held the great cities of England, and that the millions of Great Britain were slowly but surely preparing to rise in an attempt to burst asunder the fetters that now held them.

Government, Army, Navy, and Parliament had all proved rotten reeds. It was now every man for himself—to free himself and his loved ones—or to die in the attempt.

Through the south and west of England, Graham's clear, manly voice was raised everywhere, and the whole population were now fast assembling beneath the banner of the Defenders, in readiness to bear their part in the most bloody and desperate encounter of the whole war—a fierce guerilla warfare, in which the Germans were to receive no quarter. The firm resolve now was to exterminate them.

The swift and secret death being meted out to the German sentries, or, in fact, to any German caught alone in a side street, having been reported to Von Kronhelm, he issued another of his now famous proclamations, which was posted upon half the hoardings in London, but the populace at once amused themselves by tearing it down wherever it was discovered. Von Kronhelm was the arch-enemy of London, and it is believed that there were at that moment no fewer than five separate conspiracies to encompass his death. Londoners detested the Germans, but with a hatred twenty times the more intense did they regard those men who, having engaged in commercial pursuits in England, had joined the colours and were now acting as spies in the service of the enemy.

Hundreds of extraordinary tales were told of Germans who, for years, had been regarded as inoffensive toilers in London, and yet who were now proved by their actions to be spies. It was declared, and was no doubt a fact, that without the great army of advance-agents— every man among them having been a soldier—Germany would never have effected the rapid coup she had done. The whole thing had been carefully thought out, and this invasion was the culmination of years of careful thought and most minute study.

XII

Daily Life of the Beleaguered

They were dark days in London—days of terror, starvation—death. Behind the barricades south of the Thames it was vaguely known that our Admiralty—whose chief offices had been removed to Portsmouth before the entry of the enemy into London—were keenly alive to the critical position. Reports of the capture of a number of German liners in the Atlantic, and of several ships laden with provisions, attempting to cross the North Sea were spread from mouth to mouth, but so severe was the censorship upon the Press that no word of such affairs was printed.

The *London Gazette*, that journal which in ordinary circumstances the public never sees, was published each evening at six o'clock, but, alas, in German. It contained Von Kronhelm's official orders to his army, and the various proclamations regarding the government of London. The *Daily Mail*, as the paper with the largest circulation, was also taken over as the German official organ.

At the head of each newspaper office in and about Fleet Street was a German officer, whose duty was to read the proofs of everything before it appeared. He installed himself in the editorial chair, and the members of the staff all attempted to puzzle him and his assistants by the use of London slang. Sometimes this was passed by the officer in question, who did not wish to betray his ignorance, but more often it was promptly crossed out. Thus the papers were frequently ridiculous in their opinions and reports.

The drawn game continued.

On one side of the Thames the Germans held complete possession, while on the other the people of London were defiant behind their barricaded bridges. West London was occupied in building barricades in all quarters to prevent any further entry into London, while Von Kronhelm, with his inborn cunning, was allowing the work to proceed. In this, however, the German Commander-in-Chief did not display his usual caution, as will be seen in later chapters of this history.

Once it was rumoured that the enemy intended to besiege the barricades at the bridges by bringing their field howitzers into play, but very soon it became apparent that Von Kronhelm, with discreet forbearance, feared to excite further the London populace.

The fact that the Lord Mayor had been deported had rendered them irritable and viciously antagonistic, while the terms of the indemnity demanded, now known everywhere—as they had been published in papers at Brighton, Southampton, Bristol, and other places—had aroused within the hearts of Londoners a firm resolve to hold their own at no matter what cost.

Beyond all this remained the knowledge of Gerald Graham's movement—that gigantic association, the League of Defenders, which had for its object the freeing of England from the grip of the now detested eagle of Germany.

Daily the League issued its bulletins, notices, manifestoes, and proclamations, all of which were circulated throughout South London. South Coast resorts were now crowded to excess by fugitive Londoners, as well as towns inland. Accommodation for them all was, of course, impossible, but everywhere were encampments over the Kentish hop fields and the Sussex pastures.

Some further idea of life in South London at this time may be obtained from the personal narrative of Joseph Cane, a tram driver, in the employ of the London County Council, living at Creek Road, Battersea. His story, written by himself, and subsequently published in the *Daily Express*, was as follows:—

"Five days have passed since the Germans bombarded us. I have been out of work since the seventh, when the Council suspended greater part of the tramway service, my line from Westminster Bridge included. I have a wife and four children dependent upon me, and, unfortunately, all of them are starving. We are waiting. The Defenders still urge us to wait. But this waiting is very wearisome. For nineteen days have I wandered about London in idleness. I have mixed with the crowds in the West End; I have listened to the orators in the parks; I helped to build the big barricade in the Caledonian Road; I watched the bombardment from the waterside at Wandsworth, and I saw, on the following day, German soldiers across on West Wharf.

"Since that day we South Londoners have barricaded ourselves so strongly that it will, I am certain, take Von Kronhelm all his time to turn us out. Our defences are abundant and strong. Not only are there huge barricades everywhere, but hundreds of houses and buildings have been put in a state of defence, especially the positions commanding the main thoroughfares leading to the bridges. As a member of the League of Defenders, I have been served with a gun, and practise daily with thousands of others upon the new range in Battersea Park. My post, however, is at the barricade across Tarn's Corner and Newington Causeway, opposite the Elephant and Castle.

"Every road to the bridges at that converging point is blocked. The entrances to St. George's Road, London Road, Walworth Road, and Newington Butts are all strongly barricaded, the great obstructions reaching up to the second storey windows. The New Kent Road remains open, as there is a barricade at the end of Great Dover Street. The houses all round are also fortified. From Tarn's, quantities of goods, such as bales of calico, flannel, and dress materials, have been seized and utilised in our barriers. I assisted to construct the enormous wall of miscellaneous objects, and in its building we were directed by a number of Royal Engineers. Our object is to repel the invader should he succeed in breaking down the barrier at London Bridge.

"All is in readiness, as far as we are concerned. Seven maxims are mounted on our defence, while inside Tarn's are hundreds of Frontiersmen, sharpshooters, members of rifle clubs, and other men who can shoot. Yesterday some artillery men arrived with five field guns, and upon our barricade one has been mounted. The men say they have come across from Windsor, and that other batteries of artillery are on their way to strengthen us. Therefore, old Von Kronhelm, notwithstanding all his orders and daily proclamations about this and about that, has us Cockneys to deal with yet. And he'll find the Elephant and Castle a tough nut to crack. Hundreds of the men in our tram service are at the barricades. We never thought, a month ago, when we used to drive up and down from the bridges, that we'd so soon all of us become soldiers. Life, however, is full of ups and downs. But nowadays London doesn't somehow seem like London. There is no traffic, and the side streets all seem as silent as the grave. The main thoroughfares, such as the Walworth, Old Kent, Kennington Park, Clapham, and Wandsworth Roads, are crowded night and day by anxious, hungry people, eager for the revenge which is declared by the Defenders to be at hand. How soon it comes no one cares. There is still hope in Walworth and Kennington, and though our stomachs may be empty we have sworn not to capitulate.

"Food is on its way to us, so it is said. We have regained command of the sea, therefore the ports are reopened, and in a day or two food will no longer be scarce.

"I saw this morning a poster issued by the League of Defenders, the *Daily Bulletin*, it is called, declaring that relief is at hand. I hope it is, for the sake of my distracted wife and family. The County Council have been very good to us, but as money won't buy anything, what is the good of it? The supply is growing daily more limited. Half a crown was paid yesterday by a man I know for a small loaf of bread at a shop in the Wandsworth Road.

"Our daily life at the barricade is monotonous and very wearying. Now that the defences are complete and there is nothing to do, everyone is anxious to have a brush with the enemy, and longing that he may make an attack upon us. As newspapers are very difficult to get within the barricades, several new ones have sprung up in South London, most of them queer, ill-printed sheets, but very interesting on account of the news they give.

"The one most in favour is called *The South London Mirror*. I think it is in connection with the *Daily Mail*. It now and then gives photographs, like the *Daily Mirror*. Yesterday it gave a good one of the barricade where I am stationed. The neighbourhood of the Elephant presents an unusual picture, for everywhere men are scrambling over the roofs, and windows of the houses are being half-covered with sheet iron, while here and there is seen protruding the muzzle of a Maxim.

"I hear on the best authority that explosives are already in position under all the bridges, ready to blow them up at any moment. Yesterday I went along to Southwark Bridge to see the defences there. They are really splendid. Before they can be taken by assault the loss of life must be appalling to the enemy. There are mines laid in front by which the Germans could be blown to atoms. Certainly our first line of defence is at least a reliable one. Now that Londoners have taken the law into their own hands, we may perhaps hope for some success. Our Army, our Navy, our War Office, our Admiralty, have proved themselves utterly incompetent.

"By day and by night we guard our barricades. The life is an idle one, now that there is no further work to do. Imagine a huge wall erected right across the road from Tarn's front to the public-house opposite, an obstruction composed of every conceivable object that might resist the German bullets, and with loopholes here and there to admit of our fire. Everything, from paving-stones torn up from the footpath to iron coal-scuttles, has been used in its construction, together with thousands of yards of barbed wire. Roughly, I believe that fully a thousand men are holding my own particular defence, every one of them members of this new League, which, encouraged and aided by Government, is making such rapid progress in every direction. Every man who stands shoulder to shoulder with me has sworn allegiance to King and Country, and will fight and die in the defence of the city he loves. During the past four days I have only been home once. Alas! my clean little home is now one of suffering and desolation. I cannot bear to hear the children cry for bread, so I now remain at my post, bearing my own humble part in the defence of London. The wife bears up in patience, as so many thousands of the good wives of humble folk are now doing. She is pale-faced and dark-eyed, for privation is fast telling upon her. Yet she uttered no word of complaint. She only asked me simply when this cruel war would end.

"When? Ay, when?

"It will end when we have driven the Germans back into the sea— when we have had blood for blood—when we have avenged the lives of those innocent Englishmen and Englishwomen who have been killed in Suffolk, Norfolk, Essex, and Yorkshire. Then the war will end—with victory for our dear old England.

"Of tobacco and drink there is still an abundance. Of the latter, alas, we see examples of its abuse every day. Men and women, deprived of food in many cases, have recourse to drink, with terrible effect. In every quarter, as one walks through South London, one sees riotous drunkenness, and often a lawlessness, which, if not put down by the people themselves, would quickly assume alarming proportions. There are no police now; but the Defenders act the part of officers of the law, and repress any acts of violence or riotous behaviour.

"A certain section of the public are, of course, in favour of stopping the war at all costs, and towards that end are continually holding meetings, and have even gone the length of burning the barricade outside the police station in Kennington Road. This shameful act was committed last night, and one of its perpetrators was, I hear, caught and promptly lynched by the infuriated mob. The barricade is now in rapid process of re-building. On every hand, horses—or the few that now remain in South London—are being killed and used as food. Even such meat as that is at a price almost prohibitive. This afternoon a company of military telegraph engineers came to our barricade, and established telephonic communication between us and the similar obstructions at London Bridge, and on our right in Great Dover Street. From one hour to another we never know when Von Kronhelm may give the order to attack the bridges, therefore through the whole twenty-four hours we have to be alert and watchful, even though we may smoke and gossip around our stacks of piled arms. When the conflict comes it will be a long and bloody one, that is certain. Not a man in South London will shirk his duty to the Empire. The future, whether England shall still remain Mistress of the World, lies with us. It is that important all-present fact that the League of Defenders is impressing upon us from all the hoardings, and it is also the fact which stimulates each one of us to bear our part in the defence of our homes and our loved ones.

"Germany shall yet rue the day when she launched her legions upon us."

Life in London north of the Thames at that moment was more exciting than that within the fortress of South London. In the latter, everyone was waiting in hunger and patience the march of events, while north of the river the ever-present Germans in foraging parties were a constant source of annoyance and anger.

All roads leading into London from the west, right across from Hammersmith Bridge nearly to the Welsh Harp, were now heavily barricaded. More than once Von Kronhelm was inclined to forbid this, but the real fact was that he was pleased to allow the people some vent for their outraged feelings. Londoners declared that they would allow no more Germans to enter, and for that reason they were blocking the roads.

Had it not been for the fact that the bulk of London's millions had been driven south of the Thames by the bombardment and subsequent street fighting, Von Kronhelm, with his men now seriously reduced, would have found himself in a very queer position.

As it was, London was, for him, a hornets' nest.

The disposition of his troops was as follows: Along the northern heights of London was spread Frölich's cavalry division. The IXth Corps from Essex, who were still practically fresh, were guarding the lines of communication to Southminster and Harwich; the Xth Corps were occupying the City proper, the IVth Corps were encamped in Hyde Park and held West London, the Garde Corps were holding the Regent's Park neighbourhood, while the Saxons were outside London at Staines. From this latter quarter constant brushes with the British and with bodies of auxiliaries were being reported, and Staines Bridge had at last been blown up by the Germans.

Notwithstanding all Von Kronhelm's cunning and diplomacy, London was nevertheless a city of growing unrest. Union Jacks still flew, though the Germans were on the alert everywhere, and the *Daily Bulletin* of the Defenders, encouraging the people of London to hold out, made its appearance upon hoardings and walls in every quarter. Many homeless people were living in the ruins of houses, but, alas, hardly living, such was the acute state of affairs. Daily the enemy distributed soup, but only in meagre quantities, for, truth to tell, the portion of the Metropolis under German rule was quite as badly off for food as the huge fortress across the Thames.

"Courage" was everywhere the Londoners' watchword. A band of adventurous spirits, having captured a small party of German engineers in Pentonville Road as they were about to demolish some unsafe houses with explosives, seized the latter, and got safely away. The next day, the 26th, with great daring they made an attempt to blow up Von Kronhelm's apartments in the new War Office.

The manner in which it was accomplished, it appears, was by two of the number obtaining German infantry uniforms—exactly how it is not stated, but probably from dead soldiers—of the regiment who were mounting guard in Whitehall. Thus disguised, they were enabled to pass the sentries, obtain access to the long corridor leading past the big room of the Commander-in-Chief, and there place the explosive already prepared in the form of a bomb fired by clockwork, just beside the door. They ran for their lives, and just succeeded in escaping when there was a terrific explosion, and the whole front behind those columns of the façade on the principal floor was blown, with its furniture, etc., out into Whitehall.

Four German clerks and a secretary were killed; but Von Kronhelm himself, who was believed to have been at work there, had, half an hour before, gone across the road to the Horse Guards.

The sensation caused among Londoners was enormous, for it was at first rumoured that Von Kronhelm had really been killed. Upon this there were wild demonstrations on the part of the more lawless section of the public, a section which was indeed increasing hourly. Even quiet, respectable citizens found their blood boiling when they gazed upon their wrecked homes and realised that their fortunes were ruined.

The explosion at Whitehall resulted in a most vigorous inquiry. The German Field-Marshal's headquarters were removed to another portion of the building, and within an hour of the outrage the telegraph instrument—which had been blown to atoms—was replaced by another, and communication with Berlin re-established.

Most rigorous measures were now ordered to be taken for the preservation of law and order. That evening still another of those famous proclamations made its appearance, in which the regulations were repeated, and it was also ordered that in consequence of the outrage any person found in the possession of arms or of explosives was liable to be shot at sight and without any form of trial.

The vagabond part of London was, however, to the fore in giving the Germans all the trouble they could. As the soldiers patrolled the streets they were closely scanned, pointed at, hooted, and assailed with slang that they could not understand. Often the people, in order to show their antagonism, would post themselves in great numbers across a street, say, in Piccadilly, Oxford Street, or the Strand, and refuse to move, so that the troops, to avoid a collision, were obliged to go round by the side streets, amid the loud jeers of the populace.

Whenever a German flag was discovered, a piece of crape was tied to it, or it received some form of insult. The Germans went about with self-possession, even with bravado. In twos or threes they walked together, and seemed as safe as though they were in large numbers. Sometimes a mob of boys would follow, hooting, ridiculing them, and calling them by opprobrious epithets. Occasionally men and women formed around them in groups and engaged in conversation, while everywhere during that first week of the occupation the soldiers of the Kaiser were objects of great curiosity on the part of the alien rabble of the East End.

Hundreds upon hundreds of German workers from Whitechapel fraternised with the enemy, but woe betide them when the angry bands of Londoners watched and caught them alone afterwards. In dozens of cases they paid for their friendliness with the enemy with their lives.

From the confident tone of the Berlin Press, coupled with the actions of Von Kronhelm, it was quite plain to all the world that the German Emperor was now determined to take the utmost advantage of his success, and, having England in his power, to make her drink the cup of adversity to the very dregs.

Many a ghastly tale was now reaching London from West Middlesex. A party of eleven Frontiersmen, captured by the Saxons five miles north of Staines, were obliged to dig their own graves, and were then shot as they stood before them. Another terrible incident reported by a reliable war correspondent was that, as punishment for an attack on a requisitioning party, the entire town of Feltham had been put to the sword, even the children. Eighty houses were also burnt down. At Bedfont, too, a whole row of houses had been burned, and a dozen men and women massacred, because of a shot fired at a German patrol.

The German Army might possess many excellent qualities, but chivalry was certainly not among them. War with them was a business. When London fell there was no sentimental pity for it, but as much was to be made out of it as possible.

This was apparent everywhere in London. As soon as a German was quartered in a room his methods were piratical. The enemy looted everywhere, notwithstanding Von Kronhelm's orders.

Gradually to the abyss of degradation was our country thus being brought. Where would it end?

England's down-trodden millions were awaiting in starvation and patience the dawn of the Day of Revenge.

It now became known that the Secretary of State for Foreign Affairs had sent to the British diplomatic agents abroad (with a view to its ultimate submittal to the various European Cabinets) a protest of the British Government against the bombardment of London.

XIII

Revolts in Shoreditch and Islington

On the night of the 27th September, a very serious conflict, entailing much loss of life on both the London civilian and German side, occurred at the point where Kingsland Road joins Old Street, Hackney Road, and High Street. Across both Hackney and Kingsland Roads the barricades built before the bombardment still remained in a half-ruined state, any attempt at clearing them away being repulsed by the angry inhabitants. Dalston, Kingsland, Bethnal Green, and Shoreditch were notably antagonistic to the invaders, and several sharp encounters had taken place. Indeed, those districts were discovered by the enemy to be very unsafe.

The conflict in question, however, commenced at the corner of Old Street at about 9.30 in the evening, by three German tailors from Cambridge Road being insulted by two men, English labourers. The tailors appealed in German to four Westphalian infantrymen who chanced to be passing, and who subsequently fired and killed one of the Englishmen. This was the signal for a local uprising. The alarm given, hundreds of men and women rushed from their houses, many of them armed with rifles and knives, and, taking cover behind the ruined barricades, opened fire upon a body of fifty Germans, who very quickly ran up. The fire was returned, when from the neighbouring houses a perfect hail of lead was suddenly rained upon the Germans, who were then forced to retire down High Street towards Liverpool Street Station, leaving many dead in the roadway.

Very quickly news was sent over the telephone, which the Germans had now established in many quarters of London, and large reinforcements were soon upon the scene. The men of Shoreditch had, however, obtained two Maxim guns, which had been secreted ever since the entry of the Germans into the Metropolis, and as the enemy endeavoured to storm their position they swept the street with a deadly fire. Quickly the situation became desperate, but the fight lasted over an hour. The sound of firing brought hundreds upon hundreds of Londoners upon the scene. All these took arms against the Germans, who, after many fruitless attempts to storm the defences, and being fired upon from every side, were compelled to fall back again.

They were followed along High Street into Bethnal Green Road, up Great Eastern Street into Hoxton Square and Pitfield Street, and there cut up, being given no quarter at the hands of the furious populace. In those narrow thoroughfares they were powerless, and were therefore simply exterminated, until the streets ran with blood.

The victory for the men of Shoreditch was complete, over three hundred and fifty Germans being killed, while our losses were only about fifty.

The conflict was at once reported to Von Kronhelm, and the very fact that he did not send exemplary punishment into that quarter was quite sufficient to show that he feared to arouse further the hornets' nest in which he was living, and more especially that portion of the populace north of the City.

News of the attack, quickly spreading, inspired courage in every other part of the oppressed Metropolis.

The successful uprising against the Germans in Shoreditch incited Londoners to rebel, and in various other parts of the Metropolis, especially in Westbourne Grove, in Notting Hill, in Marylebone Road, and in Kingsland, there occurred outbreaks of a more or less serious nature.

Between invaders and defenders there was now constant warfare. Von Kronhelm had found to his cost that London was not to be so easily cowed, after all, notwithstanding his dastardly bombardment. The size and population of the Metropolis had not been sufficiently calculated upon. It was as a country in itself, while the intricacies of its by-ways formed a refuge for the conspirators, who were gradually completing their preparations to rise *en masse* and strike down the Germans wherever found. In the open country his great army could march, manœuvre, and use strategy, but here in the maze of narrow London streets it was impossible to know in one thoroughfare what was taking place in the next.

Supplies, too, were now running very short. The distress among our vanquished populace was most severe; while Von Kronhelm's own army was put on meagre rations. The increasing price of food and consequent starvation had not served to improve the relations between the invaders and the citizens of London, who, though they were assured by various proclamations that they would be happier and more prosperous under

German rule, now discovered that they were being slowly starved to death.

Their only hope, therefore, was in the efforts of that now gigantic organisation, the League of Defenders.

A revolt occurred in Pentonville Road, opposite King's Cross Underground Station, which ended in a fierce and terrible fray. A company of the Bremen Infantry Regiment No. 75, belonging to the IXth Corps, were marching from the City Road towards Regent's Park, when several shots were fired at them from windows of shops almost opposite the station. Five Germans fell dead, including one lieutenant, a very gorgeous person who wore a monocle. Another volley rang out before the infantrymen could realise what was happening, and then it was seen that the half-ruined shops had been placed in such a state of defence as to constitute a veritable fortress.

The fire was returned, but a few moments later a Maxim spat its deadly fire from a small hole in a wall, and a couple of dozen of the enemy fell upon the granite setts of the thoroughfare. The rattle of musketry quickly brought forth the whole of that populous neighbourhood—or all, indeed, that remained of them—the working-class district between Pentonville Road and Copenhagen Street. Notwithstanding the wreck of London, many of the poorer classes still clung to their own districts, and did not migrate with the middle and upper classes across the Thames.

Quickly the fight became general. The men of Bremen endeavoured to take the place by assault, but found that it was impossible. The strength of the defences was amazing, and showed only too plainly that Londoners were in secret preparing for the great uprising that was being planned. In such a position were the houses held by the Londoners, that their fire commanded both the Pentonville and King's Cross Roads; but very soon the Germans were reinforced by another company of the same regiment, and these being attacked in the rear from Rodney Street, Cumming Street, Weston Street, York Street, Winchester Street, and other narrow turnings leading into the Pentonville Road, the fighting quickly became general.

The populace came forth in swarms, men and women, armed with any weapon or article upon which they could lay their hands, and all fired with the same desire.

And in many instances they succeeded, be it said. Hundreds of men who came forth were armed with rifles which had been carefully secreted on the entry of the enemy into the metropolis. The greater part of those men, indeed, had fought at the barricades in North London, and had subsequently taken part in the street fighting as the enemy advanced. Some of the arms had come from the League of Defenders, smuggled into the metropolis nobody exactly knew how. All that was known was that at the various secret headquarters of the League, rifles, revolvers, and ammunition were forthcoming, the majority of them being of foreign make, and some of them of a pattern almost obsolete.

Up and down the King's Cross, Pentonville, and Caledonian Roads the crowd swayed and fought. The Germans against that overwhelming mass of angry civilians seemed powerless. Small bodies of the troops were cornered in the narrow by-streets, and then given no quarter. Brave-hearted Londoners, though they knew well what dire punishment they must inevitably draw upon themselves, had taken the law into their own hands, and were shooting or stabbing every German who fell into their hands.

The scene of carnage in that hour of fighting was awful. The *Daily Chronicle* described it as one of the most fiercely-contested encounters in the whole history of the siege. Shoreditch had given courage to King's Cross, for, unknown to Von Kronhelm, houses in all quarters were being put in a state of defence, their position being carefully chosen by those directing the secret operations of the League of Defenders.

For over an hour the houses in question gallantly held out, sweeping the streets constantly with their Maxim. Presently, however, on further reinforcements arriving, the German colonel directed his men to enter the houses opposite. In an instant a door was broken in, and presently glass came tumbling down as muzzles of rifles were poked through the panes, and soon sharp crackling showed that the Germans had settled down to their work. The movements of the enemy throughout were characterised by their coolness and military common sense. They did the work before them in a quiet, business-like way, not shirking risk when it was necessary, but, on the other hand, not needlessly exposing themselves for the sake of swagger.

The defence of the Londoners was most obstinate. In the streets, Londoners attacked the enemy with utter disregard for the risks they ran. Women, among them many young girls, joined in the fray, armed with pistols and knives.

After a while a great body of reinforcements appeared in the Euston Road, having been sent hurriedly along from Regent's Park. Then the option was given to those occupying the fortified house to surrender, the colonel promising to spare their lives. The Londoners peremptorily refused. Everywhere the fighting became more desperate, and spread all through the streets leading out of St. Pancras, York, and Caledonian Roads, until the whole of that great neighbourhood became the scene of a fierce conflict, in which both sides lost heavily. Right across Islington the street fighting spread, and many were the fatal traps set for the unwary German who found himself cut off in that maze of narrow streets between York Road and the Angel. The enemy, on the other hand, were shooting down women and girls as well as the men, even the non-combatants—those who came out of their houses to ascertain what was going on—being promptly fired at and killed.

In the midst of all this somebody ignited some petrol in a house a few doors from the chapel in Pentonville Road, and in a few moments the whole row of buildings were blazing furiously, belching forth black smoke and adding to the terror and confusion of those exciting moments. Even that large body of Germans now upon the scene were experiencing great difficulty in defending themselves. A perfect rain of bullets seemed directed upon them on every hand, and to-day's experience certainly proves that Londoners are patriotic and brave, and in their own districts they possess a superiority over the trained troops of the Kaiser.

At length, after a most sanguinary struggle, the Londoners' position was carried, the houses were entered, and twenty-two brave patriots, mostly of the working class, taken prisoners. The populace now realising that the Germans had, after all, overpowered their comrades in their fortress, fell back; but being pursued northward towards the railway line between Highbury and Barnsbury Stations, many of them were despatched on the spot.

What followed was indeed terrible. The anger of the Germans now became uncontrollable. Having in view Von Kronhelm's proclamation,— which sentenced to death all who, not being in uniform, fired upon German troops,—they decided to teach the unfortunate populace a lesson. As a matter of fact, they feared that such revolts might be repeated in other quarters.

So they seized dozens of prisoners, men and women, and shot them down. Many of these summary executions took place against the wall of the St. Pancras Station at the corner of Euston Road. Men and women were pitilessly sent to death. Wives, daughters, fathers, sons were ranged up against that wall, and, at signal from the colonel, fell forward with German bullets through them.

Of the men who had so gallantly held the fortified house, not a single one escaped. Strings of men and women were hurried to their doom in one day, for the troops were savage with the lust of blood, and Von Kronhelm, though he was aware of it by telephone, lifted not a finger to stop those arbitrary executions.

But enough of such details. Suffice it to say that the stones of Islington were stained with the blood of innocent Londoners, and that those who survived took a fierce vow of vengeance. Von Kronhelm's legions had the upper hand for the moment, yet the conflict and its bloody sequel had the effect of arousing the fiercest anger within the heart of every Briton in the metropolis.

What was in store for us none could tell. We were conquered, oppressed, starved; yet hope was still within us. The League of Defenders were not idle, while South London was hourly completing her strength.

When the day dawned for the great revenge—as it would ere long—then every man and woman in London would rise simultaneously, and the arrogant Germans would cry for quarter that certainly would never be given them.

It seems that after quelling the revolt at King's Cross wholesale arrests were made in Islington. The guilt or innocence of the prisoners did not seem to matter, Von Kronhelm dealing out to them exemplary and summary punishment. In all cases the charges were doubtful, and in many cases the innocent have, alas! paid the penalty with their lives.

Terror reigns in London. One newspaper correspondent—whose account is published this morning in South London, having been sent across the Thames by carrier pigeon, many of which were now being employed by the newspapers—had an opportunity of witnessing the wholesale executions which took place yesterday afternoon outside Dorchester House, where Von Kleppen has established his quarters. Von Kleppen seems to be the most pitiless of the superior officers. The prisoners, ranged up for inspection in front of the big mansion, were mostly men from Islington, all of whom knew only too well the fate in store for them. Walking slowly along and eyeing the ranks of these unfortunate wretches, the German General stopped here and there, tapping a man on the shoulder or beckoning him out of the rear ranks. In most cases, without further word, the individual thus selected was marched into the Park at Stanhope Gate, where a small supplementary column was soon formed.

Those chosen knew that their last hour had come. Some clasped their hands and fell upon their knees, imploring pity, while others remained silent and stubborn patriots. One man, his face covered with blood and his arm broken, sat down and howled in anguish, and others wept in silence. Some women—wives and daughters of the condemned men—tried to get within the Park to bid them adieu and to urge courage, but the soldiers beat them back with their rifles. Some of the men laughed defiantly, others met death with a stony stare. The eye-witness saw the newly-dug pit that served as common grave, and he stood by and saw them shot and their corpses afterwards flung into it.

One young fair-haired woman, condemned by Von Kleppen, rushed forward to that officer, threw herself upon her knees, implored mercy, and protested her innocence wildly. But the officer, callous and pitiless, simply motioned to a couple of soldiers to take her within the Park, where she shared the same fate as the men.

How long will this awful state of affairs last? We must die, or conquer. London is in the hands of a legion of assassins—Bavarians, Saxons, Würtembergers, Hessians, Badeners—all now bent upon prolonging the reign of terror, and thus preventing the uprising that they know is, sooner or later, inevitable.

Terrible accounts are reaching us of how the Germans are treating their prisoners on Hounslow Heath, at Enfield, and other places; of the awful sufferings of the poor unfortunate fellows, of hunger, of thirst, and of inhuman disregard for either their comfort or their lives.

At present we are powerless, hemmed in by our barricades. Behind us, upon Sydenham Hill, General Bamford is in a strong position, and his great batteries are already defending any attack upon London from the south. From the terrace in front of the Crystal Palace his guns can sweep the whole range of southern suburbs. Through Dulwich, Herne Hill, Champion Hill, and Denmark Hill are riding British cavalry, all of whom show evident traces of the hard and fierce campaign. We see from Sydenham constant messages being heliographed, for General Bamford and Lord Byfield are in hourly communication by wireless telegraphy or by other means.

What is transpiring at Windsor is not known, save that every night there are affairs of outposts with the Saxons, who on several occasions have attempted to cross the river by pontoons, and have on each occasion been driven back.

It was reported to Parliament at its sitting at Bristol yesterday that the Cabinet had refused to entertain any idea of paying the indemnity demanded by Germany, and that their reply to Von Kronhelm is one of open defiance. The brief summary of the speeches published shows that the Government are hopeful, notwithstanding the present black outlook. They believe that when the hour comes for the revenge, London will rise as a man, and that Socialists, Nonconformists, Labour agitators, Anarchists, and demagogues will unite with us in one great national, patriotic effort to exterminate our conquerors as we would exterminate vermin.

Mr. Gerald Graham has made another great speech in the House, in which he reported the progress of the League of Defenders and its widespread ramifications. He told the Government that there were over seven millions of able-bodied men in the country ready to revolt the instant the word went forth. That there would be terrible bloodshed he warned them, but that the British would eventually prove the victors he was assured. He gave no details of the organisation, for to a great measure it was a secret one, and Von Kronhelm was already taking active steps to combat its intentions; but he declared that there was still a strong spirit of patriotism in the country, and explained how sturdy Scots were daily making their way south, and how men from Wales were already massing in Oxford.

The speech was received on both sides of the House with ringing cheers, when, in conclusion, he promised them that, within a few days, the fiat would go forth, and the enemy would find himself crushed and powerless.

"South London," he declared, "is our stronghold, our fortress. To-day it is impregnable, defended by a million British patriots, and I defy Von Kronhelm—indeed, I dare him to attack it!"

Von Kronhelm was, of course, well aware of the formation of the Defenders, but treated the League with contempt. If there was any attempt at a rising, he would shoot down the people like dogs. He declared this openly and publicly, and he also issued a warning to the English people in the German official *Gazette*, a daily periodical printed in one of the newspaper offices in Fleet Street in both German and English.

The German Commander fully believed that England was crushed; yet, as the days went on, he was puzzled that he received no response to his demand for indemnity. Twice he had sent special despatch-bearers to Bristol, but on both occasions the result was the same. There was no reply.

Diplomatic representations had been made in Berlin through the Russian Ambassador, who was now in charge of British interests

COPY OF THE "DAILY BULLETIN" OF THE LEAGUE OF DEFENDERS.

in Germany, but all to no purpose. Our Foreign Minister simply acknowledged receipt of the various despatches. On the Continent the keenest interest was manifested at what was apparently a deadlock. The

British had, it was known, regained command of the sea. Von Kronhelm's supplies were already cut off. The cables in direct communication between England and Germany had been severed, and the Continental Press, especially the Paris journals, gleefully recounted how two large Hamburg-American liners attempting to reach Hamburg by passing north of Scotland had been captured by British cruisers.

In the Channel, too, a number of German vessels had been seized, and one that showed fight off the North Foreland was fired upon and sunk. The public at home, however, were more interested in supremacy on land. It was all very well to have command of the sea, they argued, but it did not appear to alleviate perceptibly the hunger and privations on land. The Germans occupied London, and while they did so all freedom in England was at an end.

A great poster headed "Englishmen," here reproduced, was seen everywhere. The whole country was flooded with it, and thousands upon thousands of heroic Britons, from the poorest to the wealthiest, clamoured to enrol themselves. The movement was an absolutely national one in every sense of the word. The name of Gerald Graham, the new champion of England's power, was upon everyone's tongue. Daily he spoke in the various towns in the west of England, in Plymouth, Taunton, Cardiff, Portsmouth, and Southampton, and, assisted by the influential committee, among whom were many brilliant speakers and men whose names were as household words, he aroused the country to the highest pitch of hatred against the enemy. The defenders, as they drilled in various centres through the whole of the west of England, were a strange and incongruous body. Grey-bearded Army pensioners ranged side by side with keen, enthusiastic youths, advised them and gave them the benefit of their expert knowledge. Volunteer officers in many cases assumed command, together with retired drill sergeants. The digging of trenches and the making of fortifications were assigned to navvies, bricklayers, platelayers, and agricultural labourers, large bodies of whom were under railway gangers, and were ready to perform any excavation work.

The Maxims and other machine guns were mostly manned by Volunteer artillery; but instruction in the working of the Maxim was given to select classes in Plymouth, Bristol, Portsmouth, and Cardiff. Time was of utmost value, therefore the drilling was pushed forward day and night. It was known that Von Kronhelm was already watchful of the movements of the League, and was aware daily of its growth. Whether its gigantic proportions would place him upon his guard was, however, quite uncertain.

Englishmen!

Your Homes are Desecrated!
Your Children are Starving!
Your Loved Ones are Dead!

Will You Remain In Cowardly Inactivity?

The German Eagle flies over London. Hull, Newcastle, and Birmingham are in ruins. Manchester is a German City. Norfolk, Essex, and Suffolk form a German colony.

The Kaiser's troops have brought death, ruin, and starvation upon you.

Will You Become Germans?

No!

Join The Defenders and fight for England. You have England's Millions beside you.

Let Us Rise!

Let us drive back the Kaiser's men.

Let us shoot them at sight.

Let us exterminate every single man who has desecrated English soil.

Join the New League of Defenders.

Fight for your homes. Fight for your wives. Fight for England.

Fight For Your King!

The National League of Defenders' Head Offices, Bristol, September 21st, 1910.

A Copy of the Manifesto of the League of Defenders Issued on 21st September 1910.

In London, with the greatest secrecy, the defenders were banding together. In face of the German proclamation posted upon the walls, Londoners were holding meetings in secret and enrolling themselves. Such meetings had, perforce, to be held in unsuspected places, otherwise all those present would be arrested and tried for conspiracy by martial law. Many of the smaller chapels in the suburbs, schoolrooms, mission halls, and such-like buildings were used as meeting-places; but the actual local headquarters of the League were kept a profound secret except to the initiated.

German spies were everywhere. In one case at a house in Tottenham Court Road, where a branch of the League was discovered, no fewer than twenty-seven persons were arrested, three of whom were on the following day shot on the Horse Guards' Parade as warning to others who might seek to incite the spirit of revolt against German rule.

Nevertheless, though there were many arrests, and though every branch of the Defenders was crushed vigorously and stamped out wherever found, the movement proceeded apace, and in no city did it make greater headway, nor were the populace more eager to join, than in our dear old London.

Though the German Eagle flew in Whitehall and from the summit of St. Stephen's Tower, and though the heavy tramp of German sentries echoed in Trafalgar Square, in the quiet, trafficless streets in the vicinity, England was not yet vanquished.

The valiant men of London were still determined to sell their liberty dearly, and to lay down their lives for the freedom of their country and honour of their King.

BOOK III
THE REVENGE

I

A BLOW FOR FREEDOM

'DAILY MAIL' OFFICE, *Oct. 1st*, 2 P.M.
"Three days have passed since the revolt at King's Cross, and each day, both on the Horse Guards' Parade and in the Park, opposite Dorchester House, there have been summary executions. Von Kronhelm is in evident fear of the excited London populace, and is endeavouring to cow them by his plain-spoken and threatening proclamations, and by these wholesale executions of any person found with arms in his or her possession. But the word of command does not abolish the responsibility of conscience, and we are now awaiting breathlessly for the word to strike the blow in revenge.

"The other newspapers are reappearing, but all that is printed each morning is first subjected to a rigorous censorship, and nothing is allowed to be printed before it is passed and initialled by the two gold-spectacled censors who sit and smoke their pipes in an office to themselves. Below, we have German sentries on guard, for our journal is one of the official organs of Von Kronhelm, and what now appears in it is surely sufficient to cause our blood to boil.

"To-day, there are everywhere signs of rapidly-increasing unrest. Londoners are starving, and are now refusing to remain patient any longer. The *Daily Bulletin* of the League of Defenders, though the posting of it is punishable by imprisonment, and it is everywhere torn down where discovered by the Germans, still gives daily brief news of what is in progress, and still urges the people to wait in patience for 'the action of the Government,' as it is sarcastically put.

"Soon after eleven o'clock this morning a sudden and clearly premeditated attack was made upon a body of the Bremen infantry who were passing along Oxford Street from Holborn to the Marble Arch. The soldiers were suddenly fired upon from windows of a row of shops between Newman Street and Rathbone Place, and before they could halt and return the fire they found themselves surrounded by a great armed rabble, who were emerging from all the streets leading into Oxford Street on either side.

"While the Germans were manœuvring, some unknown hand launched from a window a bomb into the centre of them. Next second there was a red flash, a loud report, and twenty-five of the enemy were blown to atoms. For a few moments the soldiers were demoralised, but orders were shouted loudly by their officers, and they began a most vigorous defence. In a few seconds the fight was as fierce as that at King's Cross; for out of every street in that working-class district lying between the Tottenham Court Road and Great Portland Street on the north, and out of Soho on the south, poured thousands upon thousands of fierce Londoners, all bent upon doing their utmost to kill their oppressors. From almost every window along Oxford Street a rain of lead was now being poured upon the troops, who vainly strove to keep their ground. Gradually, however, they were, by slow degrees, forced back into the narrow side-turnings up Newman Street, and Rathbone Place into Mortimer Street, Foley Street, Goodge Street, and Charlotte Street; and there they were slaughtered almost to a man.

"Two officers were captured by the armed mob in Tottenham Street, and after being beaten were stood up and shot in cold blood as vengeance for those shot during the past three days at Von Kleppen's orders at Dorchester House.

"The fierce fight lasted quite an hour; and though reinforcements were sent for, yet, curiously enough, none arrived.

"The great mob, however, were well aware that very soon the iron hand of Germany would fall heavily upon them; therefore, in frantic haste they began soon after noon to build barricades, and block up the narrow streets in every direction. At the end of Rathbone Place, Newman Street, Berners Street, Wells Street, and Great Titchfield Street huge obstructions soon appeared, while on the east all by-streets leading into Tottenham Court Road were blocked up, and the same on the west in Great Portland Street, and on the north where the district was flanked by the Euston Road. So that by two o'clock the populous neighbourhood bounded by the four great thoroughfares was rendered a fortress in itself.

"Within that area were thousands of armed men and women from Soho, Bloomsbury, Marylebone, and even from Camden Town. There they remained in defiance of Von Kronhelm's newest proclamation, which stared one in the face from every wall."

'DAILY TELEGRAPH' OFFICE, FLEET STREET,
Oct. 1st, 2 P.M.

"The enemy were unaware of the grave significance of the position of affairs, because Londoners betrayed no outward sign of the truth. Now, however, nearly every man and woman wore pinned upon their breasts a small piece of silk about two inches square, printed as a miniature Union Jack—the badge adopted by the League of Defenders. Though Von Kronhelm was unaware of it, Lord Byfield, in council with Greatorex and Bamford, had decided that, in order to demoralise the enemy and give him plenty of work to do, a number of local uprisings should take place north of the Thames. These would occupy Von Kronhelm, who would experience great difficulty in quelling them, and would no doubt eventually recall the Saxons from West Middlesex to assist. If the latter retired upon London they would find the barricades held by Londoners in their rear and Lord Byfield in their front, and be thus caught between two fires.

"In each district of London there is a chief of the Defenders, and to each chief these orders had been conveyed in strictest confidence. Therefore, to-day, while the outbreak occurred in Oxford Street, there were fully a dozen others in various parts of the metropolis, each of a more or less serious character. Every district has already prepared its own secret defences, its fortified houses, and its barricades in hidden by-ways. Besides the quantities of arms smuggled into London, every dead German has had his rifle, pistol, and ammunition stolen from him. Hundreds of the enemy have been surreptitiously killed for that very reason. Lawlessness is everywhere. Government and Army has failed them, and Londoners are now taking the law into their own hands.

"In King Street, Hammersmith; in Notting Dale, in Forest Road, Dalston; in Wick Road, Hackney; in Commercial Road East, near Stepney Station; and in Prince of Wales Road, Kentish Town, the League of Defenders this morning—at about the same hour—first made their organisation public by displaying our national emblem, together with the white flags, with the scarlet St. George's Cross, the ancient battle-flag of England.

"For that reason, then, no reinforcements were sent to Oxford Street. Von Kronhelm was far too busy in other quarters. In Kentish Town, it is reported, the Germans gained a complete and decisive victory, for the people had not barricaded themselves strongly; besides, there were large reinforcements of Germans ready in Regent's Park, and these came upon the scene before the Defenders were sufficiently prepared. The flag was captured from the barricade in Prince of Wales Road, and the men of Kentish Town lost over four hundred killed and wounded.

"At Stepney the result was the reverse. The enemy, believing it to be a mere local disturbance and easily quelled, sent but a small body of men to suppress it. But very quickly, in the intricate by-streets off Commercial Road, these were wiped out, not one single man surviving. A second and a third body were sent, but so fiercely was the ground contested that they were at length compelled to fall back and leave the men of Stepney masters of their own district. In Hammersmith and in Notting Dale the enemy also lost heavily, though in Hackney they were successful after two hours' hard fighting.

"Everyone declares that this secret order issued by the League means that England is again prepared to give battle, and that London is commencing by her strategic movement of local rebellions. The gravity of the situation cannot now, for one moment, be concealed. London north of the Thames is destined to be the scene of the fiercest and most bloody warfare ever known in the history of the civilised world. The Germans will, of course, fight for their lives, while we shall fight for our homes and for our liberty. But right is on our side, and right will win.

"Reports from all over the metropolis tell the same tale. London is alert and impatient. At a word she will rise to a man, and then woe betide the invader! Surely Von Kronhelm's position is not a very enviable one. Our two censors in the office are smoking their pipes very gravely. Not a word of the street fighting is to be published, they say. They will write their own account of it before the paper goes to press!

"10 P.M.

"There has been a most frightful encounter at the Oxford Street and Tottenham Court Road barricades—a most stubborn resistance and gallant defence on the part of the men of Marylebone and Bloomsbury.

"From the lips of one of our correspondents who was within the barricades I have just learned the details. It appears that just about four o'clock General Von Wilberg sent from the City a large force of the 19th Division under Lieutenant-General Frankenfeld, and part of these, advancing through the squares of Bloomsbury into Gower Street, attacked the Defenders' position from the Tottenham Court Road, while others coming up Holborn and New Oxford Street entered Soho from Charing Cross Road and threw up counter barricades at the end of Dean Street, Wardour Street, Berwick, Poland, Argyll, and the other streets, all of which were opposite the defences of the populace. In Great Portland Street, too, they adopted a similar line, and without much ado the fight, commenced in a desultory fashion, soon became a veritable battle.

"Within the barricades was a dense body of armed and angry citizens, each with his little badge, and every single one of them was ready to fight to the death. There is no false patriotism now, no mere bravado. Men make declarations, and carry them out. The gallant Londoners, with their several Maxims, wrought havoc among the invaders, especially in the Tottenham Court Road, where hundreds were maimed or killed.

"In Oxford Street, the enemy being under cover of their counter-barricades, little damage could be done on either side. The wide, open, deserted thoroughfare was every moment swept by a hail of bullets, but no one was injured. On the Great Portland Street side the populace made a feint of giving way at the Mortimer Street barricade, and a body of the enemy rushed in, taking the obstruction by storm. But next moment they regretted it, for they were set upon by a thousand armed men and by wild-haired women, so that every man paid for his courage with his life. The women, seizing the weapons and ammunition of the dead Germans, now returned to the barricade to use them.

"The Mortimer Street defences were at once repaired, and it was resolved to relay the fatal trap at some other point. Indeed, it was repeated at the end of Percy Street, where about fifty more Germans, who thought themselves victorious, were set upon and at once exterminated.

"Until dusk the fight lasted. The Germans, finding their attack futile, began to hurl petrol bombs over the barricades, and these caused frightful destruction among our gallant men, several houses in the vicinity being set on fire. Fortunately, there was still water in the street hydrants, and two fire-engines had already been brought within the beleaguered area in case of necessity.

"At last, about seven o'clock, the enemy, having lost very heavily in attempting to take the well-chosen position by storm, brought down several light field guns from Regent's Park; and, placing them at their counter-barricades—where, by the way, they had lost many men in the earlier part of the conflict while piling up their shelters—suddenly opened fire with shell at the huge obstructions before them.

"At first they made but little impression upon the flagstones, etc., of which the barricades were mainly composed. But before long their bombardment began to tell; for slowly, here and there, exploding shells made great breaches in the defences that had been so heroically manned. More than once a high explosive shell burst right among the crowd of riflemen behind a barricade, sweeping dozens into eternity in a single instant. Against the fortified houses each side of the barricades the German artillery trained their guns, and very quickly reduced many of those buildings to ruins. The air now became thick with dust and smoke;

and mingled with the roar of artillery at such close quarters came the screams of the injured and the groans of the dying. The picture drawn by the eye-witness who described this was a truly appalling one. Gradually the Londoners were being overwhelmed, but they were selling their lives dearly, fully proving themselves worthy sons of grand old England.

"At last the fire from the Newman Street barricade of the Defenders was silenced, and ten minutes later, a rush being made across from Dean Street, it was taken by storm. Then ensued fierce and bloody hand-to-hand fighting right up to Cleveland Street, while almost at the same moment the enemy broke in from Great Portland Street.

"A scene followed that is impossible to describe. Through all those narrow, crooked streets the fighting became general, and on either side hundreds fell. The Defenders in places cornered the Germans, cut them off, and killed them. Though it was felt that now the barricades had been broken the day was lost, yet every man kept courage, and fought with all the strength left within him.

"For half an hour the Germans met with no success. On the contrary, they found themselves entrapped amid thousands of furious citizens, all wearing their silken badges, and all sworn to fight to the death.

"While the Defenders still struggled on, loud and ringing cheers were suddenly raised from Tottenham Court Road. The people from Clerkenwell, joined by those in Bloomsbury, had arrived to assist them. They had risen, and were attacking the Germans in the rear.

"Fighting was now general right across from Tottenham Court Road to Gray's Inn Road, and by nine o'clock, though Von Wilberg sent reinforcements, a victory was gained by the Defenders. Over two thousand Germans are lying dead and wounded about the streets and squares of Bloomsbury and Marylebone. The League had struck its first blow for Freedom.

"What will the morrow bring us? Dire punishment—or desperate victory?"

'DAILY MAIL' OFFICE, *Oct. 4*, 6 P.M.

"The final struggle for the possession of London is about to commence.

"The metropolis is in a ferment of excitement. Through all last night there were desultory conflicts between the soldiers and the people, in which many lives have, alas! been sacrificed.

"Von Wilberg still holds the City proper, with the Mansion House as his headquarters. Within the area already shown upon the map there are no English, all the inhabitants having been long ago expelled. The great wealth of London is in German hands, it is true, but it is Dead Sea fruit. They are unable either to make use of it or to deport it to Germany. Much has been taken away to the base at Southminster and other bases in Essex, but the greater part of the bullion still remains in the Bank of England.

"Here, in Whitefriars, the most exciting stories have been reaching us during the last twenty-four hours, none of which, however, have passed the censor. For that reason I, one of the sub-editors, am keeping this diary, as a brief record of events during the present dreadful times.

"After the terrific struggle in Marylebone three days ago, Von Kronhelm saw plainly that if London were to rise *en masse* she would at once assume the upper hand. The German Commander-in-Chief had far too many points to guard. On the west of London he was threatened by Lord Byfield and hosts of auxiliaries, mostly sworn members of the National League of Defenders; on the south, across the river, Southwark, Lambeth, and Battersea formed an impregnable fortress, containing over a million eager patriots ready to burst forth and sweep away the vain, victorious army; while within central London itself the spirit of revolt was rife, and the people were ready to rise at any moment. The train is laid. Only the spark is required to cause an explosion.

"Reports reaching us to-day from Lord Byfield's headquarters at Windsor are numerous, but conflicting. As far as can be gathered, the authentic facts are as follows: Great bodies of the Defenders, including many women, all armed, are massing at Reading, Sonning, Wokingham, and Maidenhead. Thousands have arrived, and are hourly arriving by train, from Portsmouth, Plymouth, Exeter, Bristol, Gloucester, and, in fact, all the chief centres of the West of England, where Gerald Graham's campaign has been so marvellously successful. Sturdy Welsh colliers are marching shoulder to shoulder with agricultural labourers from Dorset and Devon, and clerks and citizens from the towns of Somerset, Cornwall, Gloucestershire, and Oxfordshire are taking arms beside the riff-raff of their own neighbourhoods. Peer and peasant, professional man and pauper, all are now united with one common object—to drive back the invader, and to save our dear old England.

"Oxford has, it seems, been one of the chief points of concentration, and the undergraduates who re-assembled there to defend their colleges now form an advance-guard of a huge body of Defenders on the march, by way of Henley and Maidenhead, to follow in the rear of Lord Byfield.

The latter holds Eton and the country across to High Wycombe, while the Saxon headquarters are still at Staines. Frölich's Cavalry Division are holding the country across from Pinner through Stanmore and Chipping Barnet to the prison camp at Enfield Chase. These are the only German troops outside west London, the Saxons being now barred from entering by the huge barricades which the populace of West London have during the past few days been constructing. Every road leading into London from West Middlesex is now either strongly barricaded or entirely blocked up. Kew, Richmond, and Kingston Bridges have been destroyed, and Lord Byfield, with General Bamford at the Crystal Palace, remains practically in possession of the whole of the south of the Thames.

"The conflict which is now about to begin will be one to the death. While, on the one hand, the Germans are bottled up among us, the fact must not be overlooked that their arms are superior, and that they are trained soldiers. Yet the two or three local risings of yesterday and the day previous have given us courage, for they show that the enemy cannot manœuvre in the narrow streets, and soon become demoralised. In London we fail because we have so few riflemen. If every man who now carries a gun could shoot we could compel the Germans to fly a flag of truce within twenty-four hours. Indeed, if Lord Roberts's scheme of universal training in 1906 had been adopted, the enemy would certainly never have been suffered to approach our capital.

"Alas! apathy has resulted in this terrible and crushing disaster, and we have only now to bear our part, each one of us, in the blow to avenge this desecration of our homes and the massacre of our loved ones.

"To-day I have seen the white banners with the red cross—the ensign of the Defenders—everywhere. Till yesterday it was not openly displayed, but to-day it is actually hung from windows or flown defiantly from flagstaffs in full view of the Germans.

"In Kilburn, or, to be more exact, in the district lying between the Harrow Road and the High Road, Kilburn, there was another conflict this morning between some of the German Garde Corps and the populace. The outbreak commenced by the arrest of some men who were found practising with rifles in Paddington Recreation Ground. One man who resisted was shot on the spot, whereupon the crowd who assembled attacked the German picket, and eventually killed them to a man. This was the signal for a general outbreak in the neighbourhood, and half an hour later, when a force was sent to quell the revolt, fierce fighting became general all through the narrow streets of Kensal Green, especially at the big barricade that blocks the Harrow Road where it is joined by Admiral Road. Here the bridges over the Grand Junction Canal have already been destroyed, for the barricades and defences have been scientifically constructed under the instruction of military engineers.

"One of our reporters despatched to the scene has just given me a thrilling account of the desperate struggle, in which no quarter was given on either side. So overwhelming were the number of the populace, that after an hour's hard fighting the Germans were driven back across Maida Vale into St. John's Wood, where, I believe, they were held at bay for several hours.

"From an early hour to-day it has been apparent that all these risings were purposely ordered by the League of Defenders to cause Von Kronhelm confusion. Indeed, while the outbreak at Kensal Green was in progress, we had another reported from Dalston, a third from Limehouse, and a fourth from Homerton. Therefore, it is quite certain that the various centres of the League are acting in unison upon secret orders from headquarters.

"Indeed, South London also took part in the fray this morning, for the Defenders at the barricade at London Bridge have now mounted several field-guns, and have started shelling Von Wilberg's position in the City. It is said that the Mansion House, where the General had usurped the apartments of the deported Lord Mayor, has already been half reduced to ruins. This action is, no doubt, only to harass the enemy, for surely General Bamford has no desire to destroy the City proper any more than it has already been destroyed. Lower Thames Street, King William Street, Gracechurch Street, and Cannon Street have, at any rate, been found untenable by the enemy, upon whom some losses have been inflicted.

"South London is every moment anxious to know the truth. Two days after the bombardment we succeeded at night in sinking a light telegraph cable in the river across from the Embankment at the bottom of Temple Avenue, and are in communication with our temporary office in Southwark Street. Over this we report the chief incidents which occur, and they are printed for the benefit of the beleaguered population over the water. The existence of the cable is, however, kept a strict secret from our pair of gold-spectacled censors.

"The whole day has been one of tension and excitement. The atmosphere outside is breathless, the evening overcast and oppressive,

> ### LEAGUE OF DEFENDERS.
>
> ### CITIZENS OF LONDON AND LOYAL PATRIOTS.
>
> The hour has come to show your strength, and to wreak your vengeance.
>
> TO-NIGHT, OCT. 4, AT 10 P.M., rise, and strike your blow for freedom.
>
> A MILLION MEN are with Lord Byfield, already within striking distance of London; a million follow them, and yet another million are ready in South London.
>
> RISE, FEARLESS AND STERN. Let "England for Englishmen" be your battle-cry, and avenge the blood of your wives and your children.
>
> ### AVENGE THIS INSULT TO YOUR NATION.
>
> ### REMEMBER: TEN O'CLOCK TO-NIGHT!

precursory to a storm. An hour ago there came, through secret sources, information of another naval victory to our credit, several German warships being sunk and captured. Here, we dare not print it, so I have just wired it across to the other side, where they are issuing a special edition.

"Almost simultaneously with the report of the British victory, namely, at five o'clock, the truth—the great and all-important truth—became revealed. The mandate has gone forth from the headquarters of the League of Defenders that London is to rise in her might at ten o'clock to-night, and that a million men are ready to assist us. Placards and bills on red paper are everywhere. As if by magic, London has been flooded with the defiant proclamation of which the copy here reproduced has just been brought in to me.

"Frantic efforts are being made by the Germans all over London to suppress both posters and handbills, but without avail. The streets are littered with them, and upon every corner they are being posted, even though more than one patriot has paid for the act with his life.

"It is now six o'clock. In four hours it is believed that London will be one huge seething conflict. Night has been chosen, I suppose, in order to give the populace the advantage. The by-streets are for the most part still unlit, save for oil-lamps, for neither gas nor electric light are yet in proper working order after the terrible dislocation of everything. The scheme of the Defenders is, as already proved, to lure the Germans into the narrower thoroughfares, and then exterminate them. Surely in the history of the world there has never been such a bitter vengeance as that which is now inevitable. London, the greatest city ever known, is about to rise!

"Midnight.

"London has risen! How can I describe the awful scenes of panic, bloodshed, patriotism, brutality, and vengeance that are at this moment in progress? As I write, through the open window I can hear the roar of voices, the continual crackling of rifles, and the heavy booming of guns. I walked along Fleet Street at nine o'clock, and I found, utterly disregarding the order that no unauthorised persons are to be abroad after nightfall, hundreds upon hundreds of all classes, all wearing their little silk Union Jack badges pinned to their coats, on their way to join in their particular districts. Some carried rifles, others revolvers, while others were unarmed. Yet not a German did I see in the streets. It seemed as though, for the moment, the enemy had vanished. There was only the strong cordon across the bottom of Ludgate Hill, men who looked on in wonder, but without bestirring themselves.

"Is it possible that Von Kronhelm's strategy is to remain inactive, and refuse to fight?

"The first shot I heard fired, just after ten o'clock, was at the Strand end of Fleet Street, at the corner of Chancery Lane. There, I afterwards discovered, a party of forty German infantrymen had been attacked, and all of them killed. Quickly following this, I heard the distant booming of artillery, and then the rattle of musketry and pom-poms became general, but not in the neighbourhood where I was. For nearly half an hour I remained at the corner of Aldwych; then, on going farther along the Strand, I found that the defenders from the Waterloo Road had made a wild sortie into the Strand, but could find no Germans there.

"The men who had for a fortnight held that barricade at the bridge were more like demons than human beings; therefore I retired, and in the crush made my way back to the office to await reports.

"They were not long in arriving. I can only give a very brief résumé at the moment, for they are so numerous as to be bewildering.

"Speaking generally, the whole of London has obeyed the mandate of the League, and, rising, are attacking the Germans at every point. In the majority of cases, however, the enemy hold strong positions, and are defending themselves, inflicting terrible losses upon the unorganised populace. Every Londoner is fighting for himself, without regard for orders or consequences. In Bethnal Green the Germans, lured into the maze of by-streets, have suffered great losses, and again in Clerkenwell, St. Luke's, Kingsland, Hackney, and Old Ford. Whitechapel, too, devoid of its alien population, who have escaped into Essex, has held its own, and the enemy have had some great losses in the streets off Cable and Leman Streets.

"With the exception of the sortie across Waterloo Bridge, South London is, as yet, remaining in patience, acting under the orders of General Bamford.

"News has come in ten minutes ago of a fierce and sudden night attack upon the Saxons by Lord Byfield from Windsor, but there are, as yet, no details.

"From the office across the river I am being constantly asked for details of the fight, and how it is progressing. In Southwark the excitement is evidently most intense, and it requires all the energy of the local commanders of the Defenders to repress another sortie across that bridge.

"There has just occurred an explosion so terrific that the whole of this building has been shaken as though by an earthquake. We are wondering what has occurred.

"Whatever it is, one fact is only too plain. Both British and Germans are now engaged in a death-struggle.

"London has struck her first blow of revenge. What will be its sequel?"

WILLIAM LE QUEUX

II

Scenes at Waterloo Bridge

The following is the personal narrative of a young chauffeur named John Burgess, who assisted in the defence of the barricade at Waterloo Bridge.

The statement was made to a reporter at noon on October 5, while he was lying on a mattress in the Church of St. Martin's-in-the-Fields, so badly wounded in the chest that the surgeons had given him up.

Around him were hundreds of wounded who, like himself, had taken part in the sudden rising of the Defenders, and who had fallen beneath the hail of the German Maxims. He related his story with difficulty, in the form of a farewell letter to his sister, who was a telegraph clerk at the Shrewsbury Post Office. The reporter chanced to be passing by the poor fellow, and, overhearing him asking for someone to write for him, volunteered to do so.

"We all did our best," he said, "every one of us. Myself, I was at the barricade for thirteen days—thirteen days of semi-starvation, sleeplessness, and constant tension, for we knew not, from one moment to another, when a sudden attack might be made upon us. At first our obstruction was a mere ill-built pile of miscellaneous articles, half of which would not stop bullets; but on the third day our men, superintended by several non-commissioned officers in uniform, began to put the position in a proper state of defence, to mount Maxims in the neighbouring houses, and to place explosives in the crown of two of the arches of the bridge, so that we could instantly demolish it if necessity arose.

"Fully a thousand men were holding the position, but unfortunately few of them had ever handled a rifle. As regards myself, I had learned to shoot rooks when a boy in Shropshire, and now that I had obtained a gun I was anxious to try my skill. When the League of Defenders was started, and a local secretary came to us, we all eagerly joined, each receiving, after he had taken his oath and signed his name, a small silk Union Jack, the badge of the League, not to be worn till the word went forth to rise.

"Then came a period—long, dreary, shadeless days of waiting—when the sun beat down upon us mercilessly and our vigilance was required to be constant both night and day. So uncertain were the movements of the enemy opposite us that we scarcely dared to leave our positions for a moment. Night after night I spent sleeping in a neighbouring doorway, with an occasional stretch upon somebody's bed in some house in the vicinity. Now and then, whenever we saw Germans moving in Wellington Street, we sent a volley into them, in return receiving a sharp reply from their pom-poms. Constantly our sentries were on the alert along the wharves and in the river-side warehouses, watching for the approach of the enemy's spies in boats. Almost nightly some adventurous spirits among the Germans would try and cross. On one occasion, while doing sentry duty in a warehouse backing on Commercial Road, I was sitting with a comrade at a window overlooking the river. The moon was shining, for the night was a balmy and beautiful one, and all was quiet. It was about two o'clock in the morning, and as we sat smoking our pipes, with our eyes fixed upon the glittering water, we suddenly saw a small boat containing three men stealing slowly along in the shadow cast by the great warehouse in which we were.

"For a moment the rowers rested upon their oars, as if undecided, then pulled forward again in search of a landing-place. As they passed below our window I shouted a challenge. At first there was no response. Again I repeated it, when I heard a muttered imprecation in German.

"'Spies!' I cried to my comrade, and with one accord we raised our rifles and fired. Ere the echo of the first shot had died away I saw one man fall into the water, while at the next shot a second man half rose from his seat, threw up his hands, and staggered back wounded.

"The firing gave the alarm at the barricade, and ere the boat could approach the bridge, though the survivor pulled for dear life, a Maxim spat forth its red fire, and both boat and oarsman were literally riddled.

"Almost every night similar incidents were reported. The enemy were doing all in their power to learn the exact strength of our defences, but I do not think their efforts were very successful. The surface of the river, every inch of it, was under the careful scrutiny of a thousand watchful eyes.

"Day after day passed, often uneventfully. We practically knew nothing of what was happening across the river, though we could see the German standard flying upon the public buildings. The ruins of London were smoking for days after the bombardment, and smouldering fires broke out again in many instances.

"Each day the *Bulletin* of our national association brought us tidings of what was happening beyond the barricades. We had regained command of the sea, which was said to be a good deal, though it did not seem to bring us much nearer to victory.

"At last, however, the welcome word came to us, on the morning of October 4th, that at ten that night we were to make a concerted attack upon the Germans. A scarlet bill was thrust into my hand, and as soon as the report was known we were all highly excited, and through the day prepared ourselves for the struggle. I regret to say that some of my comrades, prone to drink, primed themselves with spirits obtained from the neighbouring public-houses in York Road and Waterloo Road. Not that drunkenness had been the rule. On the contrary, the extreme tension of those long, hot days had had a sobering effect, and even men used to drink refrained from taking any. Ah! I have of late seen some splendid examples of self-denial, British patriotism, and fearless valour. Only Englishmen could have conducted themselves as my brave comrades have done. Only Englishmen could have died as they have done.

"Through all yesterday we waited, watching every movement of the enemy in our line of fire. Now and then we, as usual, sent him greetings in the form of a shell or two, or else a splutter from a Maxim, and in reply there came the sweeping hail of bullets, which flattened themselves upon our wall of paving-stones. The sunset was a red, dusky one, and over London westward there spread a blood-red light, as though precursory to the awful catastrophe that was about to fall. With the after-glow came the dark oppression of a thunderstorm—a fevered electrical quiet that could be felt. I stood upon the barricade gazing over the river, and wondering what would happen ere the dawn. At ten o'clock London, the great, mysterious, unknown city, was to rise and cast off the German yoke. How many who rebelled would live to see the sunrise?

"I had watched the first flash of the after-glow beyond Blackfriars Bridge every morning for the past ten days. I had breathed the fresh air, unsullied by smoke, and had admired the beauty of the outlines of riverside London in those early hours. I had sat and watched the faint rose turn to purple, to grey, and then to the glorious yellow sunrise. Yes. I had seen some of the most glorious sunrises on the river that I have ever witnessed. But should I ever see another?

"Dusk crept on, and deepened into night—the most momentous night in all the history of our giant city. The fate of London—nay, the fate of the greatest Empire the world has ever seen, was to be decided!

And about me in groups waited my comrades with fierce, determined faces, looking to their weapons and gossiping the while. Each of us had brought out our precious little badge and pinned it to our breasts. With the Union Jack upon us we were to fight for country and for King.

"Away, across, upon a ruined wall of Somerset House the German standard floated defiantly; but one and all of us swore that ere the night was past it should be pulled down, and our flag—the flag of St. George of England, which flapped lazily above our barricades—should replace it.

"Night fell—a hot, fevered night, breathless and ominous of the storm to come. Before us, across the Thames, lay London, wrecked, broken, but not yet conquered. In an hour its streets would become, we knew, a perfect hell of shot and shell. The oil lamps in Wellington Street, opposite Somerset House, threw a weird light upon the enemy's counter-barricade, and we could distinctly see Germans moving, preparing for a defence of their position, should we dare to cross the bridge. While we waited three of our gallant fellows, taking their lives in their hands, put off in a boat and were now examining the bridge beneath to ascertain whether the enemy had imitated our action in placing mines. They might have attached them where the scaffold was erected on the Middlesex side, that spot which had been attacked by German spies on the night of the bombardment. We were in a position to blow up the bridge at any moment; but we wanted to ascertain if the enemy were prepared to do likewise.

"Minutes seemed like hours as we waited impatiently for the appointed moment. It was evident that Von Kronhelm feared to make further arrests, now that London was flooded by those red handbills. He would, no doubt, require all his troops to keep us in check. On entering London the enemy had believed the war to be over, but the real struggle is only now commencing.

"At last the low boom of a gun sounded from the direction of Westminster. We looked at our watches, and found that it was just ten o'clock. Next moment our bugle sounded, and we sprang to our positions, as we had done dozens, nay, hundreds, of times before. I felt faint, for I had only had half a pint of weak soup all day, for the bread did not go round. Nevertheless the knowledge that we were about to strike the blow inspired me with fresh life and strength. Our officer shouted a brief word of command, and next moment we opened a withering fire upon the enemy's barricade in Wellington Street.

"In a moment a hundred rifles and several Maxims spat their red fire at us, but as usual the bullets flattened themselves harmlessly before us. Then the battery of artillery which Sir Francis Bamford had sent us three days before, got into position, and in a few moments began hurling great shells upon the German defences. We watched, and cheered loudly as the effect of our fire became apparent.

"Behind us was a great armed multitude ready and eager to get at the foe, a huge, unorganised body of fierce, irate Londoners, determined upon having blood for blood. From over the river the sound of battle was rising, a great roaring like the sound of a distant sea, with ever and anon the crackling of rifles and the boom of guns, while above the night sky grew a dark blood-red with the glare of a distant conflagration.

"For half an hour we pounded away at the barricade in Wellington Street with our siege guns, Maxims, and rifles, until a well-directed shell exploded beneath the centre of the obstruction, blowing open a great gap and sending fragments high into the air. Then it seemed that all resistance suddenly ceased. At first we were surprised at this; but on further scrutiny we found that it was not our fire that had routed the enemy, but that they were being attacked in their rear by hosts of armed citizens surging down from Kingsway and the Strand.

"We could plainly discern that the Germans were fighting for their lives. Into the midst of them we sent one or two shells; but fearing to cause casualties among our own comrades, we were compelled to cease firing.

"The armed crowd behind us, finding that we were again inactive, at once demanded that our barricade should be opened, so that they might cross the bridge and assist their comrades by taking the Germans in their rear. For ten minutes our officer in charge refused, for the order of General Greatorex, Commander-in-Chief of the League, was that no sortie was to be made at present.

"At last, however, the South Londoners became so infuriated that our commander was absolutely forced to give way, though he knew not into what trap we might fall, as he had no idea of the strength of the enemy in the neighbourhood of the Strand. A way was quickly opened in the obstruction, and two minutes later we were pouring across Waterloo Bridge in thousands, shouting and yelling in triumph as we passed the ruins of the enemy's barricade, and fell upon him with merciless revenge. With us were many women, who were, perhaps, fiercer and more unrelenting than the men. Indeed, many a woman that night killed a German with her own hands, firing revolvers in their faces, striking with knives, or even blinding them with vitriol and allowing them to be despatched by others.

"The scene was both exciting and ghastly. At the spot where I first fought—on the pavement outside the Savoy—we simply slaughtered the Germans in cold blood. Men cried for mercy, but we gave them no quarter. London had risen in its might, and as our comrades fought all along the Strand and around Aldwych, we gradually exterminated every man in German uniform. Soon the roadways of the Strand, Wellington Street, Aldwych, Burleigh Street, Southampton Street, Bedford Street, and right along to Trafalgar Square, were covered with dead and dying. The wounded of both nationalities were trodden underfoot and killed by the swaying, struggling thousands. The enemy's loss must have been severe in our particular quarter, for of the great body of men from Hamburg and Lübeck holding their end of Waterloo Bridge I do not believe a single one was spared, even though they fought for their lives like veritable devils.

"Our success intoxicated us, I think. That we were victorious at that point cannot be doubted, but with foolish disregard for our own safety we pressed forward into Trafalgar Square, in the belief that our comrades were similarly making an attack upon the enemy there. The error was, alas! a fatal one for many of us. To fight an organised force in narrow streets is one thing, but to meet him in a large open space with many inlets, like Trafalgar Square, is another.

"The enemy were no doubt awaiting us, for as we poured out from the Strand at Charing Cross we were met with a devastating fire from German Maxims on the opposite side of the square. They were holding Whitehall—to protect Von Kronhelm's headquarters—the entrances to Spring Gardens, Cockspur Street, and Pall Mall East, and their fire was converged upon the great armed multitude which, being pressed on from behind, came out into the open square only to fall in heaps beneath the sweeping hail of German lead.

"The error was one that could not be rectified. We all saw it when too late. There was no turning back now. I struggled to get into the small side-street that runs down by the bar of the Grand Hotel, but it was blocked with people already in refuge there.

"Another instant and I was lifted from my legs by the great throng going to their doom, and carried right in the forefront to the square. Women screamed when they found themselves facing the enemy's fire.

"The scene was awful—a massacre, nothing more or less. For every German's life we had taken, a dozen of our own were now being sacrificed.

"A woman was pushed close to me, her grey hair streaming down her back, her eyes starting wildly from her head, her bony hands smeared with blood. Suddenly she realised that right before her red fire was spitting from the German guns.

"Screaming in wild despair, she clung frantically to me.

"I felt next second a sharp burning pain in my chest. . . We fell forward together upon the bodies of our comrades. . . When I came to myself I found myself here, in this church, close to where I fell.

"What has happened, I wonder? Is our barricade at the bridge still held, and still defiant? Can you tell me?"

ON THAT SAME NIGHT DESPERATE sorties were made from the London, Southwark, and Blackfriars Bridges, and terrible havoc was committed by the Defenders.

The German losses were enormous, for the South Londoners fought like demons and gave no quarter. South London had, at last, broken its bounds.

III

Great British Victory

The following despatch from the war correspondent of the *Times* with Lord Byfield was received on the morning of the 5th October, but was not published in that journal till some days later, owing to the German censorship, which necessitated its being kept secret:—

WILLESDEN, *4th October* (Evening).

"After a bloody but successful combat, lasting from early dawn till late in the afternoon, the country to the immediate west of the metropolis has been swept clear of the hated invaders, and the masses of the 'League of Defenders' can be poured into the West of London without let or hindrance. In the desperate street-fighting which is now going on they will be much more formidable than they were ever likely to be in the open field, where they were absolutely incapable of manœuvring. As for the Saxons—what is left of them—and Frölich's Cavalry Division, with whom we have been engaged all day, they have now fallen back on Harrow and Hendon, it is said; but it is currently reported that a constant movement towards the high ground near Hampstead is going on. These rumours come by way of London, since the enemy's enormous force of cavalry is still strong enough to prevent us getting any first-hand intelligence of his movements.

"As has been previously reported, the XIIth Saxon Corps, under the command of Prince Henry of Würtemberg, had taken up a position intended to cover the metropolis from the hordes of Defenders which, supported by a small leaven of Regulars, with a proportion of cavalry and guns, were known to be slowly rolling up from the west and south. Their front facing west, extended from Staines on the south, to Pinner on the north, passing through Stanwell, West Drayton, and Uxbridge. In addition they had a strong reserve in the neighbourhood of Hounslow, whose business it was to cover their left flank by keeping watch along the line of the Thames.

They had destroyed all bridges over the river between Staines and Hammersmith. Putney Bridge, however, was still intact, as all attacks on it had been repulsed by the British holding it on the south side. Such was the general state of affairs when Lord Byfield, who had established his headquarters at Windsor, formed his plan of attack.

"As far as I have been able to ascertain, its general idea was to hold the Saxons to their position by the threat of the 300,000 Defenders that were assembled and were continually increasing along a roughly parallel line to that occupied by the enemy at about ten miles' distance from it, while he attacked their left flank with what Regular and Militia regiments he could rapidly get together near Esher and Kingston. By this time the southern lines in the neighbourhood of London were all in working order, the damage that had been done here and there by small parties of the enemy who had made raids across the river having been repaired. It was, therefore, not a very difficult matter to assemble troops from Windsor and various points on the South of London at very short notice.

"General Bamford, to whom had been entrusted the defence of South London, and who had established his headquarters at the Crystal Palace, also contributed every man he could spare from the remnant of the Regular troops under his command who were in that part of the metropolis and its immediate neighbourhood that was still held by the British.

"It was considered quite safe now that the Germans in the City were so hardly pressed to leave the defence of the Thames bridges to the masses of irregulars who had all along formed the bulk of their defenders. The risk that Prince Henry of Würtemberg would take the bull by the horns, and by a sudden forward move attack and scatter the inert and invertebrate mass of 'Defenders' who were in his immediate front had, of course, to be taken; but it was considered that in the present state of affairs in London he would hardly dare to increase the distance between the Saxon Corps and the rest of the German Army. Events proved the correctness of this surmise; but owing to unforeseen circumstances, the course of the battle was somewhat different from that which had been anticipated.

"Despite the vigilance of the German spies our plans were kept secret till the very end, and it is believed that the great convergence of Regular troops that began as soon as it was dark from Windsor and from along the line occupied by the Army of the League on the west, right round to Greenwich on the east, went on without any news of the movement being carried to the enemy.

"Before dawn this morning every unit was in the position to which it had been previously detailed, and everything being in readiness, the Royal Engineers began to throw a pontoon bridge over the Thames at the point where it makes a bend to the south just above the site of Walton Bridge. The enemy's patrols and pickets in the immediate neighbourhood at once opened a heavy fire on the workers, but it was beaten down by that which was poured upon them from the houses in Walton-on-Thames, which had been quietly occupied during the night. The enemy in vain tried to reinforce them, but in order to do this their troops had to advance into a narrow peninsula which was swept by a cross-fire of shells from batteries which had been placed in position on the south side of the river for this very purpose.

"By seven o'clock the bridge was completed, and the troops were beginning to cross over covered by the fire of the artillery and by an advance guard which had been pushed over in boats. Simultaneously very much the same thing had been going on at Long Ditton, and fierce fighting was going on in the avenues and gardens round Hampton Court. Success here, too, attended the British arms. As a matter of fact, a determined attempt to cross the river in force had not at all been anticipated by the Germans. They had not credited their opponents with the power of so rapidly assembling an army and assuming an effective and vigorous offensive so soon after their terrible series of disasters.

"What they had probably looked for was an attempt to overwhelm them by sheer force of numbers. They doubtless calculated that Lord Byfield would stiffen his flabby masses of defenders with what trained troops he could muster, and

WILLIAM LE QUEUX

endeavour to attack their lines simultaneously along their whole length, overlapping them on either flank.

"They realised that to do this he would have to sacrifice his men in thousands upon thousands, but they knew that to do so would be his only possible chance of success in this eventuality, since the bulk of his men could neither manœuvre nor deploy. Still they reckoned that in the desperate situation of the British he would make up his mind to do this.

"On their part, although they fully realised the possibility of being overwhelmed by such tactics, they felt pretty confident that, posted as they were behind a perfect network of small rivers and streams which ran down to join the Thames, they would at least succeed in beating off the attack with heavy loss, and stood no bad chance of turning the repulse into a rout by skilful use of Frölich's Cavalry Division, which would be irresistible when attacking totally untrained troops after they had been shattered and disorganised by artillery fire. This, at least, is the view of those experts with whom I have spoken.

"What, perhaps, tended rather to confirm them in their theories as to the action of the British was the rifle firing that went on along the whole of their front all night through. The officers in charge of the various units which conglomerated together formed the forces facing the Saxons, had picked out the few men under their command who really had some little idea of using a rifle, and, supplied with plenty of ammunition, had sent them forward in numerous small parties with general orders to approach as near the enemy's picket line as possible, and as soon as fired on to lie down and open fire in return. So a species of sniping engagement went on from dark to dawn. Several parties got captured or cut up by the German outlying troops, and many others got shot by neighbouring parties of snipers. But, although they did not in all probability do the enemy much damage, yet they kept them on the alert all night, and led them to expect an attack in the morning. One way and another luck was entirely on the side of the patriots that morning.

"When daylight came the British massed to the westward of Staines had such a threatening appearance from their immense numbers, and the fire from their batteries of heavy guns and howitzers on the south side of the river, which took the German left flank in, was so heavy that Prince Henry, who was there in person, judged an attack to be imminent, and would not spare a man to reinforce his troops at Shepperton and Halliford, who were numerically totally inadequate to resist the advance of the British once they got across the river.

"He turned a deaf ear to the most imploring requests for assistance, but ordered the officer in command at Hounslow to move down at once and drive the British into the river. So it has been reported by our prisoners. Unluckily for him, this officer had his hands quite full enough at this time; for the British, who had crossed at Long Ditton, had now made themselves masters of everything east of the Thames Valley branch of the London and South-Western Railway, were being continually reinforced, and were fast pushing their right along the western bank of the river.

"Their left was reported to be at Kempton Park, where they joined hands with those who had effected a crossing near Walton-on-Thames. More bridges were being built at Piatt's Eyot, Tagg's Eyot, and Sunbury Lock, while boats and wherries in shoals appeared from all creeks and backwaters and hiding-places as soon as both banks were in the hands of the British.

"Regulars, Militia, and, lastly, Volunteers, were now pouring across in thousands. Forward was still the word. About noon a strong force of Saxons was reported to be retreating along the road from Staines to Brentford. They had guns with them, which engaged the field batteries which were at once pushed forward by the British to attack them. These troops, eventually joining hands with those at Hounslow, opposed a more determined resistance to our advance than we had hitherto encountered.

"According to what we learned subsequently from prisoners and others, they were commanded by Prince Henry of Würtemberg in person. He had quitted his position at Staines, leaving only a single battalion and a few guns as a rearguard to oppose the masses of the Defenders who threatened him in that direction, and had placed his troops in the best position he could to cover the retreat of the rest of his corps from the line they had been occupying. He had, it would appear, soon after the fighting began, received the most urgent orders from Von Kronhelm to fall back on London and assist him in the street fighting that had now been going on without intermission for the best part of two days. Von Kronhelm probably thought that he would be able to draw off some of his numerous foes to the westward. But the message was received too late. Prince Henry did his best to obey it, but by this time the very existence of the XIIth Corps was at stake on account of the totally unexpected attack on his left rear by the British regular troops.

"He opposed such a stout resistance with the troops under his immediate command that he brought the British advance to a temporary standstill, while in his rear every road leading Londonward was crowded with the rest of his army as they fell back from West Drayton, Uxbridge, Ruislip, and Pinner. Had they been facing trained soldiers they would have found it most difficult, if not impossible, to do this; but as it was the undisciplined and untrained masses of the League of Defenders lost a long time in advancing, and still longer in getting over the series of streams and dykes that lay between them and the abandoned Saxon position.

"They lost heavily, too, from the fire of the small rearguards that had been left at the most likely crossing-places. The Saxons were therefore able to get quite well away from them, and when some attempt was being made to form up the thousands of men who presently found themselves congregated on the heath east of Uxbridge, before advancing farther, a whole brigade of Frölich's heavy cavalry suddenly swept down upon them from behind Ickenham village. The *débâcle* that followed was frightful. The unwieldy mass of Leaguers swayed this way and that for a moment in the panic occasioned by the sudden apparition of the serried masses of charging cavalry that were rushing down on them with a thunder of hoofs that shook the earth. A few scattered shots were fired without any perceptible effect, and before they could either form up or fly the German Reiters were upon them. It was a perfect massacre. The Leaguers could oppose no resistance whatever. They were ridden down and slaughtered with no more difficulty than if they had been a flock of sheep. Swinging their long, straight swords, the cavalry-men cut them down in hundreds, and drove thousands into the river. The 'Defenders' were absolutely pulverised, and fled westwards in a huge scattered crowd. But if the Germans had the satisfaction of scoring a local victory in this quarter, things were by no means rosy for them elsewhere. Prince Henry, by desperate efforts, contrived to hold on long enough in his covering position to enable the Saxons from the central portion of his abandoned line to pass through Hounslow, and move along the London road, through Brentford.

"Here disaster befell them. A battery of 4.7 guns was suddenly unmasked on Richmond Hill, and, firing at a range of 5000 yards, played havoc with the marching column. The head of it also suffered severe loss from riflemen concealed in Kew Gardens, and the whole force had to extend and fall back for some distance in a northerly direction. Near Ealing they met the Uxbridge brigade, and a certain delay and confusion occurred. However, trained soldiers such as these are not difficult to reorganise, and while the latter continued its march along the main road the remainder moved in several small parallel columns through Acton and Turnham Green. Before another half-hour had elapsed there came a sound of firing from the advanced guard. Orders to halt followed, then orders to send forward reinforcements.

"During all this time the rattle of rifle fire waxed heavier and heavier. It soon became apparent that every road and street leading into London was barricaded and that the houses on either side were crammed with riflemen. Before any set plan of action could be determined on, the retiring Saxons found themselves committed to a very nasty bout of street fighting. Their guns were almost useless, since they could not be placed in positions from which they could fire on the barricades except so close as to be under effective rifle fire. They made several desperate assaults, most of which were repulsed. In Goldhawk Road a Jäeger battalion contrived to rush the big rampart of paving-stones which had been improvised by the British; but once over, they were decimated by the fire from the houses on either side of the street. Big high explosive shells from Richmond Hill, too, began to drop among the Saxons. Though the range was long, the gunners were evidently well informed of the whereabouts of the Saxon troops, and made wonderfully lucky shooting.

"For some time the distant rumble of the firing to the south-west had been growing more distinct in their ears, and about four o'clock it suddenly broke out comparatively near by. Then came an order from Prince Henry to fall back on Ealing at once. What had happened? It will not take long to relate this. Prince Henry's covering position had lain roughly between East Bedfont and Hounslow, facing south-east. He had contrived to hold on to the latter place long enough to allow his right to pivot on it and fall back to Cranford Bridge. Here they were, to a certain extent, relieved from the close pressure they had been subjected to by the constantly advancing British troops, by the able and determined action of a portion of Frölich's Cavalry Brigade.

"But in the meantime his enemies on the left, constantly reinforced from across the river—while never desisting from their so far unsuccessful attack on Hounslow—worked round through Twickenham and Isleworth till they began to menace his rear. He must abandon Hounslow, or be cut off. With consummate generalship he withdrew his left along the line of the Metropolitan and District Railway, and sent word to the troops on his right to retire and take up a second position at Southall Green. Unluckily for him, there was a delay in transmission, resulting in a considerable number of these troops being cut off and captured. Frölich's cavalry were unable to aid them at this juncture, having their attention drawn away by the masses of Leaguers who had managed to get over the Colne and were congregating near Harmondsworth.

"They cut these up and dispersed them, but afterwards found that they were separated from the Saxons by a strong force of British regular troops who occupied Harlington and opened a fire on the Reiters that emptied numerous saddles. They, therefore, made off to the northward. From this forward nothing could check the steady advance of the English, though fierce fighting went on till dark all through Hanwell, Ealing, Perivale, and Wembley, the Saxons struggling gamely to the last, but getting more and more disorganised. Had it not been for Frölich's division on their right they would have been surrounded. As it was, they must have lost half their strength in casualties and prisoners.

"At dark, however, Lord Byfield ordered a general halt of his tired though triumphant troops, and bivouacked and billeted them along a line reaching from Willesden on the right through Wembley to Greenford. He himself established his headquarters at Wembley.

"I have heard some critics say that he ought to have pushed on his freshest troops towards Hendon to prevent the remnant of our opponents from re-entering London; but others, with reason, urge that he is right to let them into the metropolis, which they will now find to be merely a trap."

EXTRACTS FROM THE DIARY OF General Von Kleppen, Commander of the IVth German Army Corps, occupying London:—

DORCHESTER HOUSE, PARK LANE, *Oct. 6.*
"We are completely deceived. Our position, much as we are attempting to conceal it, is a very grave one. We believed that if we reached London the British spirit would be broken. Yet the more drastic our rule, the fiercer becomes the opposition. How it will end I fear to contemplate. The British are dull and apathetic, but once aroused, they fight like fiends.

"Last night we had an example of it. This League of Defenders, which Von Kronhelm has always treated with ridicule, is, we have discovered too late, practically the whole of England. Von Bistram, commanding the VIIth Corps, and Von Haeslen, of the VIIIth Corps, have constantly been reporting its spread through Manchester, Leeds, Bradford, Sheffield, Birmingham, and the other great towns we now occupy; but our Commander-in-Chief has treated the matter lightly, declaring it to be a kind of offshoot of some organisation they have here in England, called the Primrose League. . .

"Yesterday, at the Council of War, however, he was compelled to acknowledge his error when I handed him a scarlet handbill calling upon the British to make a concerted attack upon us at ten o'clock. Fortunately, we were prepared for the assault, otherwise I verily believe that the honours would have rested with the populace in London. As it is, we suffered considerable reverses in various districts, where our men were lured into the narrow side streets and cut up. I confess I am greatly surprised at the valiant stand made everywhere by the Londoners. Last night they fought to the very end. A disaster to our arms in the Strand was followed by a victory in Trafalgar Square, where Von Wilberg had established defences for the purpose of preventing the joining of the people of the East End with those of the West. . ."

IV

Massacre of Germans in London

'Daily Mail' Office, *Oct. 12*, 6 p.m.
"Through the whole of last week the Germans occupying London suffered great losses. They are now hemmed in on every side.

"At three o'clock this morning, Von Kronhelm having withdrawn the greater part of the troops from the defence of the bridges, in an attempt to occupy defensive positions in North London, the South Londoners, impatient with long waiting, broke forth and came across the river in enormous multitudes, every man bent upon killing a German wherever seen.

"The night air was rent everywhere by the hoarse, exultant shouts as London—the giant, all-powerful city—fell upon the audacious invader. Through our windows in Carmelite Street came the dull roar of London's millions swelled by the Defenders from the west and south of England, and by the gallant men from Canada, India, the Cape, and other British colonies who had come forward to fight for the Mother country as soon as her position was known to be critical.

"In the streets are seen Colonial uniforms side by side with the costermonger from Whitechapel or Walworth, and dark-faced Indians in turbans are fighting out in Fleet Street and the Strand. In the great struggle now taking place many of our reporters and correspondents have unfortunately been wounded, and, alas! four of them killed.

"In these terrible days a man's life is not safe from one moment to another. Both sides seem to have now lost their heads completely. Among the Germans all semblance of order has apparently been thrown to the winds. It is known that London has risen to a man, and the enemy are therefore fully aware of their imminent peril. Already they are beaten. True, Von Kronhelm still sits in the War Office directing operations—operations which he knows too well are foredoomed to failure.

"The Germans have, it must be admitted, carried on the war in a chivalrous spirit until those drastic executions exasperated the people. Then neither side gave quarter, and now to-day all through Islington, Hoxton, Kingsland, and Dalston, right out eastward to Homerton, a perfect massacre of Germans is in progress.

"Lord Byfield has issued two urgent proclamations, threatening the people of London with all sorts of penalties if they kill instead of taking an enemy prisoner, but they seem to have no effect. London is starved and angered to such a pitch that her hatred knows no bounds, and only blood will atone for the wholesale slaughter of the innocent since the bombardment of the metropolis began.

"The Kaiser has, we hear, left the 'Belvedere' at Scarborough, where he has been living incognito. A confidential report, apparently well founded, has reached us that he embarked upon the steam-trawler *Morning Star* at Scarborough yesterday, and set out across the Dogger, with Germany, of course, as his destination. Surely he must now regret his ill-advised policy of making an attack upon England. He had gauged our military weakness very accurately, but he had not counted upon the patriotic spirit of our Empire. It may be that he has already given orders to Von Kronhelm, but it is nevertheless a very significant fact that the German wireless telegraph apparatus on the summit of Big Ben is in constant use by the German Commander-in-Chief. He is probably in hourly communication with Bremen, or with the Emperor himself upon the trawler *Morning Star*.

"Near Highbury Fields about noon to-day some British cavalry surprised a party of Germans, and attempted to take them prisoners. The latter showed fight, whereupon they were shot down to a man. The British held as prisoners by the Germans near Enfield have now been released, and are rejoining their comrades along the northern heights. Many believe that another and final battle will be fought north of London, but military men declare that the German power is already broken. Whether Von Kronhelm will still continue to lose his men at the rate he is now doing, or whether he will sue for peace, is an open question. Personally, he was against the bombardment of London from the very first, yet he was compelled to carry out the orders of his Imperial master. The invasion, the landing, and the successes in the North were, in his opinion, quite sufficient to have paralysed British trade and caused such panic that an indemnity would have been paid. To attack London was, in his opinion, a proceeding far too dangerous, and his estimate is now proved to have been the correct one. Now that they have lost command of the sea and are cut off from their bases in Essex, the enemy's situation is hopeless. They may struggle on, but assuredly the end can only be an ignominious one.

"Yet the German Eagle still flies proudly over the War Office, over St. Stephen's, and upon many other public buildings, while upon others

British Royal Standards and Union Jacks are commencing to appear, each one being cheered by the excited Londoners, whose hearts are now full of hope. Germany shall be made to bite the dust. That is the war-cry everywhere. Many a proud Uhlan and Cuirassier has to-day ridden to his death amid the dense mobs, mad with the lust of blood. Some of the more unfortunate of the enemy have been lynched, and torn limb from limb, while others have died deaths too horrible to here describe in detail.

"Each hour brings to us further news showing how, by slow degrees, the German army of occupation is being wiped out. People are jeering at the audacious claim for indemnity presented to the British Government when the enemy entered London, and are asking whether we will not now present a claim to Germany. Von Kronhelm is not blamed so much as his Emperor. He has been the catspaw, and has burned his fingers in endeavouring to snatch the chestnuts from the fire.

"As a commander, he has acted justly, fully observing the international laws concerning war. It was only when faced by the problem of a national uprising that he countenanced anything bordering upon capital punishment. An hour ago our censors were withdrawn. They came and shook hands with many members of the staff, and retired. This surely is a significant fact that Von Kronhelm hopes to regain the confidence of London by appearing to treat her with a fatherly solicitude. Or is it that he intends to sue for peace at any price?

"An hour ago another desperate attempt was made on the part of the men of South London, aided by a large body of British regulars, to regain possession of the War Office. Whitehall was once more the scene of a bloody fight, but so strongly does Von Kronhelm hold the place and all the adjacent thoroughfares—he apparently regarding it as his own fortress—that the attack was repulsed with heavy loss on our side.

"All the bridges are now open, the barricades are in most cases being blown up, and people are passing and repassing freely for the first time since the day following the memorable bombardment. London streets are, however, in a most deplorable condition. On every hand is ruin and devastation. Whole streets of houses rendered gaunt and windowless by the now spent fires meet the eye everywhere. In certain places the ruins were still smouldering, and in one or two districts the conflagrations spread over an enormous area. Even if peace be declared, can London ever recover from this present wreck? Paris recovered, and quickly too.

Therefore we place our faith in British wealth, British industry, and British patriotism.

"Yes. The tide has turned. The great Revenge now in progress is truly a mad and bloody one. In Kilburn this afternoon there was a wholesale killing of a company of German infantry, who, while marching along the High Road, were set upon by the armed mob, and practically exterminated. The smaller thoroughfares, Brondesbury Road, Victoria Road, Glendall Road, and Priory Park Road, across to Paddington Cemetery, were the scene of a frightful slaughter. The Germans died hard, but in the end were completely wiped out. German-baiting is now, indeed, the Londoner's pastime, and on this dark and rainy afternoon hundreds of men of the Fatherland have fallen and died upon the wet roads.

"Sitting here, in a newspaper office, as we do, and having fresh reports constantly before us, we are able to review the whole situation impartially. Every moment, through the various news-agencies and our own correspondents and contributors, we are receiving fresh facts— facts which all combine to show that Von Kronhelm cannot hold out much longer. Surely the Commander-in-Chief of a civilised army will not allow his men to be massacred as they are now being! The enemy's troops, mixed up in the maze of London streets as they are, are utterly unable to cope with the oncoming multitudes, some armed with rifles and others with anything they can lay their hands upon.

"Women—wild, infuriated women—have now made their reappearance north of the Thames. In more than one instance where German soldiers have attempted to take refuge in houses these women have obtained petrol, and, with screams of fiendish delight, set the houses in question on fire. Awful dramas are being enacted in every part of the metropolis. The history of to-day is written in German blood.

"Lord Byfield has established temporary headquarters at Jack Straw's Castle, where Von Kronhelm was during the bombardment, and last night we could see the signals exchanged between Hampstead and Sydenham Hill, from whence General Bamford has not yet moved. Our cavalry in Essex are, it is said, doing excellent work. Lord Byfield has also sent a body of troops across from Gravesend to Tilbury, and these have regained Maldon and Southminster after some hard fighting. Advices from Gravesend state that further reinforcements are being sent across the river to operate against the East of London and hem in the Germans on that side.

"So confident is London of success that several of the railways are commencing to reorganise their traffic. A train left Willesden this afternoon for Birmingham—the first since the bombardment—while another has left Finsbury Park for Peterborough, to continue to York if possible. So wrecked are the London termini, however, that it must be some weeks before trains can arrive or be despatched from either Euston, King's Cross, Paddington, Marylebone, or St. Pancras. In many instances the line just north of the terminus is interrupted by a blown-up tunnel or a fallen bridge, therefore the termination of traffic must, for the present, be at some distance north on the outskirts of London.

"Shops are also opening in South London, though they have but little to sell. Nevertheless, this may be regarded as a sign of renewed confidence. Besides, supplies of provisions are now arriving, and the London County Council and Salvation Army are distributing free soup and food in the lower-class districts. Private charity, everywhere abundant during the trying days of dark despair, is doing inestimable good among every class. The hard, grasping employer, and the smug financier, who hitherto kept scrupulous accounts, and have been noteworthy on account of their uncharitableness, have now, in the hour of need, come forward and subscribed liberally to the great Mansion House Fund, opened yesterday by the Deputy Lord Mayor of London. The subscription list occupies six columns of the issue of to-morrow's paper, and this, in itself, speaks well for the open-heartedness of the moneyed classes of Great Britain.

"No movement has yet been made in the financial world. Bankers still remain with closed doors. The bullion seized at Southminster and other places is now under strong British guard, and will, it is supposed, be returned to the Bank immediately. Only a comparatively small sum has been sent across to Germany. Therefore all Von Kronhelm's strategy has utterly failed. By the invasion Germany has, up to the present moment, gained nothing. She has made huge demands, at which we can afford to jeer. True, she has wrecked London, but have we not sent the greater part of her fleet to the bottom of the North Sea, and have we not created havoc in German ports?

"The leave-taking of our two gold-spectacled censors was almost pathetic. We had come to regard them as necessities to puzzle and to play practical jokes of language upon. To-day, for the first time, we have received none of those official notices in German, with English translations, which of late have appeared so prominently in our columns.

WILLIAM LE QUEUX

The German Eagle is gradually disentangling his talons from London, and means to escape us—if he can."

"10.30 P.M.

"Private information has just reached us from a most reliable source that a conference has been arranged between Von Kronhelm and Lord Byfield. This evening the German Field-Marshal sent a messenger to the British headquarters at Hampstead under a flag of truce. He bore a despatch from the German Commander asking that hostilities should be suspended for twenty-four hours, and that they should make an appointment for a meeting during that period.

"Von Kronhelm has left the time and place of meeting to Lord Byfield, and has informed the British Commander that he has sent telegraphic instructions to the German military governors of Birmingham, Sheffield, Manchester, Bradford, Leeds, Northampton, Stafford, Oldham, Wigan, Bolton, and other places, giving notice of his suggestion to the British, and ordering that for the present hostilities on the part of the Germans shall be suspended.

"It seems more than likely that the German Field-Marshal has received these very definite instructions by wireless telegraph from the Emperor at Bremen or Potsdam.

"We understand that Lord Byfield, after a brief consultation by telegraph with the Government at Bristol, has sent a reply. Of its nature, however, nothing is known, and at the moment of writing hostilities are still in progress.

"In an hour's time we shall probably know whether the war is to continue, or a truce is to be proclaimed."

"Midnight.

"Lord Byfield has granted a truce, and hostilities have now been suspended.

"London has gone mad with delight, for the German yoke is cast off. Further information which has just reached us from private sources states that thousands of prisoners have been taken by Lord Byfield to-day, and that Von Kronhelm has acknowledged his position to be absolutely hopeless.

"The great German Army has been defeated by our British patriots, who have fought so valiantly and so well. It is not likely that the war will be resumed. Von Kronhelm received a number of British officers at the War Office half an hour ago, and it is said that he is already making preparations to vacate the post he has usurped.

"Lord Byfield has issued a reassuring message to London, which we have just received with instructions to print. It declares that although for the moment only a truce is proclaimed, yet this means the absolute cessation of all hostilities.

"The naval news of the past few days may be briefly summarised. The British main fleet entered the North Sea, and our submarines did most excellent work in the neighbourhood of the Maas Lightship. Prince Stahlberger had concentrated practically the whole of his naval force off Lowestoft, but a desperate battle was fought about seventy miles from the Texel, full details of which are not yet to hand. All that is known is that, having now regained command of the sea, we were enabled to inflict a crushing defeat upon the Germans, in which the German flagship was sunk. In the end sixty-one British ships were concentrated against seventeen German, with the result that the German Fleet has practically been wiped out, there being 19,000 of the enemy's officers and men on the casualty list, the greatest recorded in any naval battle.

"Whatever may be the demands for indemnity on either side, one thing is absolutely certain, namely, that the invincible German Army and Navy are completely vanquished.

"The Eagle's wings are trailing in the dust."

V

How the War Ended

D ays passed—weary, waiting, anxious days. A whole month went by. After the truce, London very gradually began to resume her normal life, though the gaunt state of the streets was indescribably weird.

Shops began to open, and as each day passed, food became more plentiful, and consequently less dear. The truce meant the end of the war, therefore thanksgiving services were held in every town and village throughout the country.

There were great prison-camps of Germans at Hounslow, Brentwood, and Barnet, while Von Kronhelm and his chief officers were also held as prisoners until some decision through diplomatic channels could be arrived at. Meanwhile a little business began to be done; thousands began to resume their employment, bankers re-opened their doors, and within a week the distress and suffering of the poor became perceptibly alleviated. The task of burying the dead after the terrible massacre of the Germans in the London streets had been a stupendous one, but so quickly had it been accomplished that an epidemic was happily averted.

Confidence, however, was not completely restored, even though each day the papers assured us that a settlement had been arrived at between Berlin and London.

Parliament moved back to Westminster, and daily meetings of the Cabinet were being held in Downing Street. These resulted in the resignation of the Ministry, and with a fresh Cabinet, in which Mr. Gerald Graham, the organiser of the Defenders, was given a seat, a settlement was at last arrived at.

To further describe the chaotic state of England occasioned by the terrible and bloody war would serve no purpose. The loss and suffering which it had caused the country had been incalculable; statisticians estimated that in one month of hostilities it had amounted to £500,000,000, a part of which represented money transferred from British pockets to German, as the enemy had carried off some of the securities upon which the German troops had laid their hands in London.

Let us for a moment take a retrospective glance. Consols were at 50; bread was still 1s. 6d. per loaf; and the ravages of the German commerce-destroyers had sent up the cost of insurance on British shipping sky-high. Money was almost unprocurable; except for the manufacture of war material, there was no industry; and the suffering and distress among the poor could not be exaggerated. In all directions men, women, and children had been starving.

The mercantile community were loud in their outcry for "peace at any price," and the pro-German and Stop-the-War Party were equally vehement in demanding a cessation of the war. They found excuses for the enemy, and forgot the frightful devastation and loss which the invasion had caused to the country. They protested against continuing the struggle in the interests of the "capitalists," who, they alleged, were really responsible for the war.

They insisted that the working class gained nothing, even though the British Fleet was closely blockading the German coast, and their outcry was strengthened when a few days after the blockade of the Elbe had begun two British battleships were so unfortunate as to strike German mines, and sink with a large part of their crews. The difficulty of borrowing money for the prosecution of the war was a grave obstacle in the way of the party of action, and preyed upon the mind of the British Government.

The whole character of the nation and the Government had changed since the great days when, in the face of famine and immense peril, the country had fought Napoleon to the last and overthrown him. The strong aristocratic Government had been replaced by a weak Administration, swayed by every breath of popular impulse. The peasantry who were the backbone of the nation had vanished, and been replaced by the weak, excitable population of the towns.

Socialism, with its creed of "Thou shalt have no other god but Thyself," and its doctrine, "Let us eat and drink, for to-morrow we die," had replaced the religious beliefs of a generation of Englishmen taught to suffer and to die sooner than surrender to wrong. In the hour of trial, amidst smoking ruins, among the holocausts of dead which marked the prolonged, bloody, and terrible battles on land and at sea, the spirit of the nation quailed, and there was really no great leader to recall it to ways of honour and duty.

Seven large German commerce-destroyers were still at sea in the Northern Atlantic. One of them was the splendid ex-Cunarder *Lusitania*, of 25 knots, which had been sold to a German firm a year before the war, when the British Government declined to continue its subsidy of £150,000 per annum to the Cunard Company under the agreement of 1902. The reason for withdrawing this subsidy was the need for economy, as money had to be obtained to pay members of Parliament. The Cunard Company, unable to bear the enormous cost of running both its huge 25-knot steamers, was compelled to sell the *Lusitania*, but with patriotic enterprise it retained the *Mauretania*, even though she was only worked at a dead loss.

The *Mauretania*, almost immediately after the outbreak of war, had been commissioned as a British cruiser, with orders specially to hunt for the *Lusitania*, which had now been renamed the *Preussen*. But it was easier to look for the great commerce-destroyer than to find her, and for weeks the one ship hunted over the wide waters of the North Atlantic for the other.

The German procedure had been as follows:—All their commerce-destroyers had received orders to sink the British ships which they captured when these were laden with food. The crews of the ships destroyed were collected on board the various commerce-destroyers, and were from time to time placed on board neutral vessels, which were stopped at sea and compelled to find them accommodation. For coal the German cruisers relied at the outset upon British colliers, of which they captured several, and subsequently upon the supplies of fuel which were brought to them by neutral vessels. They put into unfrequented harbours, and there filled their bunkers, and were gone before protests could be made.

The wholesale destruction of food, and particularly of wheat and meat, removed from the world's market a large part of its supplies, and had immediately sent up the cost of food everywhere, outside the United Kingdom as well as in it. At the same time, the attacks upon shipping laden with food increased the cost of insurance to prohibitive prices upon vessels freighted for the United Kingdom. The underwriters after the first few captures by the enemy would not insure at all except for fabulous rates.

The withdrawal of all the larger British cruisers for the purpose of defeating the main German fleets in the North Sea left the commerce-destroyers a free hand, and there was no force to meet them. The British liners commissioned as commerce-protectors were too few and too slow, with the single exception of the *Mauretania*, to be able to hold their adversaries in check.

Neutral shipping was molested by the German cruisers. The German Government had proclaimed food of all kinds and raw cotton contraband of war, and when objection was offered by various neutral Governments, it replied that Russia in the war with Japan had treated cotton and food as contraband, and that no effective resistance had been offered by the neutral Powers to this action. Great Britain, the German authorities urged, had virtually acquiesced in the Russian proceedings against her shipping, and had thus established a precedent which became law for the world.

Whenever raw cotton or food of any kind was discovered upon a neutral vessel bound for British ports, the vessel was seized and sent into one or other of the German harbours on the West Coast of Africa. St. Helena, after its garrison had been so foolishly withdrawn by the British Government in 1906, remained defenceless, and it had been seized by a small German expedition at the very outset. Numerous guns were landed, and it became a most useful base for the attacks of the German commerce-destroyers.

Its natural strength rendered its recapture difficult, and the British Government had not a man to spare for the work of retaking it, so that it continued in German hands up to the last week of the struggle, when at last it was stormed after a vigorous bombardment by a small force despatched from India.

The absurd theory that commerce could be left to take care of itself was exploded by the naval operations of the war. The North Atlantic had continued so dangerous all through September that British shipping practically disappeared from it, and neutral shipping was greatly hampered. All the Atlantic ports of the United States and the South American seaboard were full of British steamers, mainly of the tramp class, that had been laid up because it was too dangerous to send them to sea. The movement of supplies to England was carried on by only the very fastest vessels, and these, as they ran the blockade-runners' risks, demanded the blockade-runners' compensating profits.

In yet another way the German Government enhanced the difficulty of maintaining the British food supply. When war broke out, it was discovered that German agents had secured practically all the "spot wheat" available in the United States, and had done the same in Russia. Germany had cornered the world's available supply by the outlay of a modest number of millions, and its agents were instructed not to part with their supplies except at an enormous price. In this way Germany recouped her outlay, made a large profit, and caused terrific distress in England, where the dependence of the country upon foreign supplies of food had been growing steadily all through the early years of the twentieth century.

The United Kingdom, indeed, might have been reduced to absolute starvation, had it not been for the fact that the Canadian Government interfered in Canada to prevent similar German tactics from succeeding, and held the German contracts for the cornering of Canadian wheat, contrary to public policy.

The want of food, the high price of bread and meat in England, and the greatly increased cost of the supplies of raw material sent up the expenditure upon poor relief to enormous figures. Millions of men were out of employment, and in need of assistance. Mills and factories in all directions had closed down, either because of the military danger from the operations of the German armies, or because of the want of orders, or, again, because raw materials were not procurable. The British workers had no such accumulated resources as the French peasant possessed in 1870 from which to meet distress. They had assumed that prosperity would continue for all time, and that, if it did not, the rich might be called upon to support them and their families.

Unfortunately, when the invasion began, many rich foreigners who had lived in England collected what portable property they possessed and retired abroad to Switzerland, Italy, and the United States. Their example was followed by large numbers of British subjects who had invested abroad, and now, in the hour of distress, were able to place their securities in a handbag and withdraw them to happier countries.

They may justly be blamed for this want of patriotism, but their reply was that they had been unjustly and mercilessly taxed by men who derided patriotism, misused power, and neglected the real interests of the nation in the desire to pander to the mob. Moreover, with the income-tax at 3s. 6d. in the pound, and with the cost of living enormously enhanced, they declared that it was a positive impossibility to live in England, while into the bargain their lives were exposed to danger from the enemy.

As a result of this wholesale emigration, in London and the country the number of empty houses inordinately increased, and there were few well-to-do people left to pay the rates and taxes. The fearful burden of the extravagant debts which the British municipalities had heaped up was cruelly felt, since the nation had to repudiate the responsibility which it had incurred for the payment of interest on the local debts.

The Socialist dream, in fact, might almost be said to have been realised. There were few rich left, but the consequences to the poor, instead of being beneficial, were utterly disastrous.

Under the pressure of public opinion, constrained by hunger and financial necessities, and with thousands of German prisoners in their hands, the British Government acceded to the suggested conference to secure peace. Von Kronhelm had asked for a truce, his proposals being veiled under a humanitarian form. The British Government, too, did not wish to keep the German prisoners who had fought with such gallantry longer from their hearths and homes. Nothing, it added, was to be gained by prolonging the war and increasing the tale of bloodshed and calamity. A just and honourable peace might allay the animosity between two great nations of the same stock, if both would let bygones be bygones.

The response of the German Government was chilling and discouraging. Germany, it practically said, had no use for men who had surrendered. Their hearths and homes could well spare them a little longer. The destruction of the German Navy mattered nothing to Germany, who could build another fleet with her flourishing finances. Her army was in possession of Holland and the mainland of Denmark, and would remain so until the British Army—if there were any—arrived to turn it out. The British Government must state what indemnity it was prepared to pay to be rid of the war, or what surrender of territory it would make to obtain peace.

At the same time the German Press, in a long series of inspired articles, contended that, notwithstanding the ultimate British successes, England had been the real sufferer by the war. The struggle had been fought on British soil, British trade had been ruined, British finances thrown into utter disorder, and a great stretch of territory added to the German Empire. Holland and Denmark were ample recompense for the reverses at sea.

The British blockade of the German coast was derided as ineffective, and the British losses due to German mines were regarded as a sign of what the British Navy had to expect if it continued the war. Then a picture was painted of Germany, strong, united, triumphant, confident, firm in her national spirit, efficient in every detail of administration, while in England corruption, inefficiency, and incompetence were alleged to be supreme.

But these Press philippics and the haughty attitude of the German Government were, in reality, only attempts to impose upon the British people and the British Government. Subsequent information has shown that German interests had suffered in every possible way, and that there was grave danger of foreign complications. Unfortunately, the behaviour of the German Press had the expected effect upon England. The clamour for peace grew, and the pro-Germans openly asserted that a cessation of hostilities must be purchased at any price.

At the mediation of the French Government negotiations between the British and German Governments were resumed in the first days of November. But the Germans still adhered inflexibly to their demand for the *status quo*. Germany must retain Holland and Denmark, which were to become States of the German Empire, under their existing dynasties. Turkey must retain Egypt, whither the Turkish troops had penetrated during the chaos caused by the invasion of England. The Dutch East Indies must become a part of the German Empire.

Certain foreign Powers, however, which had been friendly to England now avowed their readiness to support her in resisting these outrageous demands. But the outcry for peace in England was growing continually, and the British Ministry was helpless before it. The Germans must have got wind of the foreign support which was secretly being given to this country, since at the eleventh hour they waived their demands as regards Egypt and the Dutch East Indies.

The lot of these two territories was to be settled by an International Congress. But they finally secured the consent of the British Government to the conclusion of a peace on the basis that each Power should retain what it possessed at the opening of October. Thus Germany was to be confirmed in her possession of Holland and Denmark, while England gained nothing by the peace. The British surrender on this all-important head tied the hands of the foreign Powers which were prepared to resist vehemently such an aggrandisement of Germany.

As for the Congress to deal with Egypt and the East Indies, this does not fall within the sphere of our history.

PEACE WAS FINALLY SIGNED ON 13th January 1911. The British Empire emerged from the conflict outwardly intact, but internally so weakened that only the most resolute reforms accomplished by the ablest and boldest statesmen could have restored it to its old position.

Germany, on the other hand, emerged with an additional 21,000 miles of European territory, with an extended seaboard on the North Sea, fronting the United Kingdom at Rotterdam and the Texel, and, it was calculated, with a slight pecuniary advantage. Practically the entire cost of the war had been borne by England.

Looking back upon this sad page of history—sad for Englishmen—some future Thucydides will pronounce that the decree of Providence was not undeserved. The British nation had been warned against the danger; it disregarded the warning. In the two great struggles of the early twentieth century, in South Africa and the Far East, it had before its eyes examples of the peril which comes from unpreparedness and from haphazard government. It shut its eyes to the lessons. Its soldiers had called upon it in vain to submit to the discipline of military service; it rebelled against the sacrifice which the Swiss, the Swede, the German, the Frenchman, and the Japanese made not unwillingly for his country.

In the teeth of all entreaties it reduced in 1906 the outlay upon its army and its fleet, to expend the money thus saved upon its own comfort. The battalions, batteries, and battleships sacrificed might well have averted invasion, indeed, have prevented war. But to gain a few millions, risks were incurred which ended ultimately in the loss of hundreds of millions of money and thousands of lives, and in starvation for myriads of men, women, and children.

As is always the case, the poor suffered most. The Socialists, who had declaimed against armaments, were faithless friends of those whom they professed to champion. Their dream of a golden age proved utterly delusive. But the true authors of England's misfortunes escaped blame for the moment, and the Army and Navy were made the scapegoats of the great catastrophe.

That the Army Council and the Admiralty had been criminally weak could not be denied. Their weakness merely reflected the moral tone of the nation, which took no interest in naval or military affairs, and then was enraged to find that, in the hour of trial, everything for a time went wrong. When success did come, it came too late, and could not be utilised without a great British Army capable of carrying the war into the enemy's country, and thus compelling a satisfactory peace.

THE END

A Note About the Author

William Le Queux (1864–1927) was an Anglo-French journalist, novelist, and radio broadcaster. Born in London to a French father and English mother, Le Queux studied art in Paris and embarked on a walking tour of Europe before finding work as a reporter for various French newspapers. Towards the end of the 1880s, he returned to London where he edited *Gossip* and *Piccadilly* before being hired as a reporter for *The Globe* in 1891. After several unhappy years, he left journalism to pursue his creative interests. Le Queux made a name for himself as a leading writer of popular fiction with such espionage thrillers as *The Great War in England in 1897* (1894) and *The Invasion of 1910* (1906). In addition to his writing, Le Queux was a notable pioneer of early aviation and radio communication, interests he maintained while publishing around 150 novels over his decades long career.

A Note from the Publisher

Spanning many genres, from non-fiction essays to literature classics to children's books and lyric poetry, Mint Edition books showcase the master works of our time in a modern new package. The text is freshly typeset, is clean and easy to read, and features a new note about the author in each volume. Many books also include exclusive new introductory material. Every book boasts a striking new cover, which makes it as appropriate for collecting as it is for gift giving. Mint Edition books are only printed when a reader orders them, so natural resources are not wasted. We're proud that our books are never manufactured in excess and exist only in the exact quantity they need to be read and enjoyed.

bookfinity™

Discover more of your favorite classics with Bookfinity™.

- Track your reading with custom book lists.
- Get great book recommendations for your personalized Reader Type.
- Add reviews for your favorite books.
- AND MUCH MORE!

Visit **bookfinity.com** and take the fun Reader Type quiz to get started.

Enjoy our classic and modern companion pairings!

Classic & Modern

Printed in the USA
CPSIA information can be obtained
at www.ICGtesting.com
JSHW022203140824
68134JS00018B/836